# THE DEVIL WON'T KEEP US APART

## SHANE T. CLARK

MINDSTIR MEDIA

Published by Mindstir Media, LLC
45 Lafayette Rd | Suite 181| North Hampton, NH 03862 | USA
1.800.767.0531 | www.mindstirmedia.com

Printed in the United States of America
ISBN-13: 978-1-960142-71-9

*To my Dad—You were here when I started this project and I looked forward to sharing each page with you. I know you would be proud of the finished product. I love you and miss you tremendously.*

Thank you,

First, to my wife, Bethany Clark. You listened countless nights of me complaining about how bad this manuscript was: "This book is awful." And the next night, "This book is pretty damn good." You stayed steady with my yo-yo emotions and never stopped encouraging me. When I decided to go with Mindstir Media for self-publishing, you never doubted the process and stood by my side and let me chase my dream. I'll forever be grateful for that love.

To my kids, only thing I'm more proud of than this book is the growth of all of you. The four of you are growing into incredible, unique people and I'm proud to call you my children.

To my friends, who read the first draft, I appreciate all of you taking valuable time to read a manuscript written by a prison worker. I would have never finished this without your support and feedback.

To William Dunn and Anthony Spaniol, you two rode me like Seabiscuit to get this thing published. I know I would have jumped off the horse without your words of encouragement.

To Linda Harold, you worked outside my office for over two years and offered me encouragement to get published numerous times. I appreciate your kind words. You have impacted this journey as much as any person.

To Rick Parnell, you were with me every step of the way and hearing your opinion impacted my writing.

I had a ton of self-doubt over this six year journey and still can't believe the finished product is here. I send this to the world knowing I put my heart and soul into this manuscript. I love these characters, these people who live in my mind. Finally, I can say today and each day moving forward, I'm a published author and say the words, "this is pretty damn good."

# CHAPTER 1

# Present Day

Blood oozes out from under the prison cell door slowly, methodically, and purposefully, like it had a predetermined destination in mind. Below, on the first tier, two correctional officers lounge, oblivious to the actions above. The first officer is at the computer screen, using the light to study notecards. Today, he brought thirty-one. He is in his second semester of nursing school and is working third shift. Seven hours into his shift, he has memorized twenty-nine. Six months removed from the academy, he has grown quite proficient at studying while listening to inmates sleep, pass gas, and snore. The second officer reclines in a chair with one boot over the other. He is forty minutes into a deep sleep, dreaming of lotto numbers, mansions, and Swedish maids, Babette and Inga. He is the senior officer.

The first officer reads over his thirtieth card and notices the time. He fists the thigh of his partner. "It's four forty-eight." He hears him stir, adds, "It's count time."

Sleepy croaks back, "I got it," moans, and stretches his arms. He comes down hard on both feet and lets out a whine and stands up. He yawns and sticks out a hand. "Keys?"

The first officer unclips the keys, extends them, and returns to his cards. Sleepy flips the flashlight on and starts his round on the right-hand side of the range. He draws close to the door and squints through the window. When he sees two bodies breathing, he pushes on, continues, and crosses over to the

1

other side. When he reaches the desk, he says, "All good," and heads toward the stairs. Swipes away a bead of sleep from an eye and lumbers upstairs.

Hears his partner call out, "Are you counting?"

He squints down and says, "Huh?" When he receives an annoyed grin, he says, "What time is it?"

"Told you it was almost five."

"Oh," he says and continues on. His eyes seesaw between cells as he counts the condemned. He gets to the end of the range with a count of sixteen and crosses to the other side. *Eighteen . . . twenty . . . twenty-two . . . twen- . . .* "Oh, shit!" he yells as his feet slip and he lands on his back. He fishes for the light with his right hand. His left goes to the back of his head.

He hears the steps below, and a voice calls out, "You okay?"

"Yeah," he says as he struggles to pull his head off the concrete. He gathers the flashlight and notices blood on his palm. Light on his hand. He follows the blood under the cell door and stands up, and peers over the rail. "Call help!"

"What is it?"

"Just call," he says and gropes for his keys. *Come on. Come on.* The darkness, adrenaline, and fear of the unknown hinder his depth perception. He unclips the keys, shines the light on the door, and keys the lock.

Before he turns it, he hears, "What are you doing?"

He grits his teeth at his partner jogging toward him, airs a fist, and grinds out, "Can't you see the fucking blood?" When the rookie looks down at the pool under their feet, Sleepy adds, "We are only standing in it."

"Don't open the door," the rookie says and slows to a tiptoe. "Someone might have a weapon."

"Did you call for help?"

"No."

He leaves the keys hanging and hands the radio to the rookie. "Call for assistance and go wait by the door."

The rookie is flustered. He stomps around and stutters, "Is someone dead?" Rips at his hair, "Are you going . . . we're dead. Didn't I tell you I heard some screaming earlier?"

"Relax."

"You didn't hear the screaming?" His voice ricochets down range, fills the air.

A voice hollers out, "Shut the fuck up. People are sleeping." There are bangs against a cell door. Disjointed sounds follow. Like a man wandering into a cave and waking the bats above, they alarm the cons.

From the other end. "You shut the fuck up." Neither respond to the calls, and before the masses get riled up and flap their wings, both go silent for a moment.

The rookie speaks softly, "You haven't made rounds all night." That didn't last long. He rattles on like a fat kid who just ate a box full of sugar on Halloween night. "I have five months in, five! They told us at the academy to not forget our rounds." He points at his partner and lets out an 'I am going crazy' laugh. "You haven't made a round all night." He cackles and grabs his chin, "They told us not to listen to you old-timers. Said you would tell us to forget everything we learned at the academy." He grabs his shirt at the heart, says, "I was our graduation class president," and pulls at the pennant he received at his six-week graduation.

"Class president, huh?" Adds, "Damn, bruh, you're a smart one."

"Yes," the rookie screams, "and I'm going to get fired before my six-month probation. What am I going to do? I'm using the union money to pay for school." When he realizes how calm his partner is, he says, "Aren't you worried about losing a job you have had for years?"

"I've been here nine months."

A stare.

"Actually," he rolls his eyes toward the back of his head and mouths numbers, "nine next week."

The sugar high returns. "Nine months? You walk around here like you know everything. Told me not to worry about it. Everything will be fine." A vein pulses out of his neck every time he yells, like a child playing peekaboo. His arms shoot into the air like he's preaching to the ceiling. "All we have to do on third shift is count every two hours: eleven, one, three, and five, and make security rounds every half hour to make sure nobody is dead or hanging by the bed sheet." He gasps for air, gets louder, "We're going to get fucking fired." He begins to wheeze and twirls around and faces his partner, who is remaining way calmer than he should. He babbles on, "I just took this job to get through school. I was going to graduate and get a job at the James Cancer Center." The vein ran on the surface of his neck like a snake skimming over the top of water.

"Stop stomping around. You're splashing blood on my pants." When he did, "Take a damn chill pill or something, bruh." The rookie slows his breathing. "Murders happen every day in prisons. In prisons all over the world." A shrill. A step back. A squeal from deep in the belly.

The rookie stops quivering and shoots a blank look. His face goes sideways, says, "You're worried about me splashing blood on your pants?"

"Yeah."

A finger point leads to, "What the hell you call that all up your leg. All over your ass?" Another finger traces the outline of splatter, "You have blood on your neck." His lips curl. He snaps his mouth shut before he vomits and turns around to escape the view. Mumbles, "That is fucking gross."

"Good point."

The rookie continues, "Can't believe I've listened to your advice. I must be an idiot. Probably the first-class president to be removed while on probation. I will be the laughingstock at the academy for years to come. People will walk by and look at my picture on the wall and the instructors will laugh as they tell the story." The loudest yet, "Story of the idiot who listened to the moron with nine months in the system!"

"At least you will have a memento."

"Huh?"

"The pennant for being class president."

"Time for jokes? Now we're telling jokes as people die in their cells. Nice," He steps around the blood as it inches toward the guard rail before gravity takes over, and it tumbles over the range like rainfall. "Oh God," he cries, "you think someone was murdered?" He stands next to his partner and grabs onto his shirt like a teenage girl at a horror movie. "We . . . you didn't make a fucking round all night."

"You said that already," Sleepy says and pushes him away, "Act like a professional or at least act like a man.

"We're fired," the rookie says and rubs above the eyes. Faces Sleepy, "I'm not going down for this. This is on you. You said don't worry about making rounds. You said you had it covered."

"Go down to the door and wait for assistance to arrive."

"They have keys."

Sleepy forcefully palms a shoulder. "Just go," he says and grabs the rookie by the shoulder and shoves him away.

The rookie shuffles away, says, "What are you going to do?"

"Check to see if someone is alive."

He skids to a stop, goes stiff, cries out, "You really think they are dead?"

"Lots of blood." He watches him bolt down the stairs, panting as he calls for assistance on the radio. Keys cause a ruckus as they whip against the side of his leg. Both hear inmates mumble and groan as they wake hours too early. When his partner is out of sight, he unlocks the cell door and stands in under the frame. "Oh my God!"

# CHAPTER 2

# Two Days Later

Elmer wakes with ceaseless pain in his legs. It is overwhelming in the mornings. He grimaces as he leans up in bed. Buck, his Labrador Retriever, paces underneath. "I know, boy," he says and swings his legs over the side of the bed, struggling to get his back off the mattress. He slides off the bed like a child toeing cold water. Stands up and stretches his back. Left hand curls around to the middle. Reaches over and picks up the picture frame. Wipes dust off with a palm and kisses her picture. "I love you," he says A whiff. "I can still smell your coconut lotion in the mornings." He kissed her picture every morning since she passed away twenty-two years ago. That damn cancer. His Betsy. His wife. His soulmate.

He shuffles over to the dresser and grabs his cane hanging off the top rung of the drawer. Steps toward the door, pulls on his robe, and gingerly covers himself. He drags himself out of the bedroom with Buck panting relentlessly behind. "Okay, boy," he says and enters the kitchen, heads toward the back door, dragging his left leg behind. He unlocks the door and shivers as Buck leaps off the porch. He watches Buck relieve himself and frolic around the yard. His footsteps will be visible hours later in the frost. He goes into the kitchen and pulls out a mug. Fills it with freshly brewed coffee. Watches Buck roll and scratch his back on the frozen ground. After his morning surge, he limbers up the best he can and gets dressed. He feeds his pup and starts his four-hundred-yard journey to his morning spot, Crispie Crème.

He stops at the end of his street to catch his breath. Leans his right shoulder against the brick wall of the Plumbing Shop as his left hand holds the cane to steady himself. He can see his destination a hundred yards ahead, across Main Street. He lived in Sherman, in his house, his entire life. Through the worst of times and now in its best, his neighborhood has come a long way over the years. At the shop, he nudges the door open with a hip and enters. The shop is full of life. He waddles behind his morning crew with his tongue lolling out in anticipation for his brew.

Eric says, "Elmer, did you hear about the murder out at the pen?"

He sits, eyes Amy, signals for a coffee, and says to Eric, "How the hell should I know?" He cools his tone and mumbles, "Everybody I knew is retired or dead."

Amy interjects, "Mostly dead."

Eric, the dentist, ironic to Elmer, his teeth are etched stones, broken and split from a thousand years of tectonic movement. He lives by the notion, Do as I say, not as I do. He adds, "My boy said it was a real bad scene."

"Probably deserved," leaks out from Elmer. His body is stiff still from the walk, body throbs, he shakily fingers his mug as Amy pours. "How about someone say good morning before . . . you start firing off questions."

Eric's eyes droop, "You okay?" Sees their fourth, Ralph, enter and sends a salute. To Amy, "Someone is sensitive this morning," and looks at Elmer.

Elmer feels him looking, "Stop looking at me like I'm a Picasso painting, beautiful and priceless."

An eye roll: dramatic and swooping, Eric says, "You're definitely an antique."

Ralph butts in from the other side of Eric, "Elmer," he says and folds the paper over his lap, "you hear about the pen?"

Eric nudges Ralph. Elmer barks, "Get the shit out of your ears, Ralph."

"What?"

Eric says, "I've already asked him." He looks at Elmer, "I think Ralph was in the bathroom when I asked you."

"Yeah," Ralph says as he sits his gut on the counter, "I just sat down and read it in the paper." He retreats in his seat, "Damn." Shoulders Eric, "Someone woke up on the wrong side of the bed."

Elmer starts to apologize, sees Fred take his normal spot on the end, next to Ralph. "Morning," he says.

"Heard you're going to be a grandpa again." That was Eric.

"Yeah," Fred says less than enthusiastic, "another girl."

"Damn, what is that, four?" Ralph says.

"Five," Fred whines.

"Tell that boy of yours that when he goes down between her legs to stop eating the damn balls off those kids," Elmer abruptly says to nettle him.

Fred made it easy to get under his skin. He splashes around his coffee trying to shake the sting away. Amy steps in with an assist. She drops the pot on the counter. Loud. Mouths shut. Eyes stop on her. Elmer stops mid sip as they go quiet, glances up at Amy. They all look at Elmer as she speaks, scolds him, "This is a family establishment, Mr. Ray." She always uses "Mr." when she is upset with something inappropriate. A daily thing with Elmer. "If you run off a customer, I'll run you off." Stern and deep. "Permanently."

Something she says weekly, sometimes daily. Like a father threatening to pull over the car in the middle of traffic to spank his kids, he never does and neither did Amy. Elmer and the morning crew have come to the shop every morning for the past ten years. Elmer was too old to be politically correct.

A knock on the table from Eric.

Ralph giggles like a child.

Fred winks, says, "Thank you," as he looks at Elmer.

"Kiss ass."

"What was that, Elmer?" Fred says, leaning in his direction with a palm cupped around his ear. "I'm getting old. My hearing is going bad." He nudges Ralph, and both share a laugh. "Did you curse at me?"

Elmer sounds shy-boy innocent when he says, "Sorry," to Amy, ignoring Fred. A giggle on his left caught his attention, two customers down. He leans up, sees a tangle of blonde hair. Leans back and reaches over the stranger between them and taps her on the shoulder with his cane. They meet in front. She says, "I thought it was funny."

Elmer shoots her a lazy wave and says, "Thank you," and sends a gummed smile back.

Both hear, "Don't encourage him," as Amy slaps a menu in front of him.

"Same as always," Elmer says and hands her the menu. To the lady, "I get funnier as I age."

"Must be a damn comedian then." Now Amy has the lady laughing.

"I heard that."

"It was meant to be heard, Elmer," Amy adds as she walks by with a pot in hand.

He shifts awkwardly in his seat like a Humpty Dumpty egg to stymie one of his many aches. Twists an eye at Eric when he hears him say, "My son says they can't find a next of kin on one of the guys at the pen."

The prison talk NOS his system, his heart rate red lines, skin crimsons over, "Enough of that shit. If I wanted to talk about some asshole at the prison, I wouldn't have retired."

All go quiet and sip their coffee.

Twenty minutes later, Eric slumps in his chair after hanging up from a call with his son. He studies his coffee. A whiff. A tingle in the nose. He leans forward. "Elmer," he says and gets Ralph's attention.

Elmer chews and watches Eric lean over and whisper something to Ralph, who passes it on to Fred. Elmer looks like a pufferfish as he contemplates what the hell is going on. Eric stands, looms behind Ralph and Fred, whispering between them. Ralph spits his coffee in the cup, glances down at Elmer, then snaps his neck toward Eric.

Elmer blows out his air. Hovers his fork before he makes another stab at a pancake.

Ralph eyes Elmer. Drops his eyes as he rubs his chin. Elmer has seen enough. He drops his fork, says, "What the hell you stooges sneaking around about?"

Ralph and Fred join Eric on his feet and stand behind Elmer. One on each side, touching him on the shoulders. "Elmer," Ralph says.

"Yeah."

"The victim at the pen."

"I told you," Elmer starts to say as he swivels around, stops when he sees the looks, hesitates, "What is it?" Eric eyes Ralph, who studies Fred. Elmer considers their dispositions speculatively, begins to waver as their faces told him something has occurred, "What is it, damn it?"

Eric prompts himself with a low growl, says, "It was him."

"Him?" Elmer asks. A swallow. A cough, "You mean him?" Him can only be one person. The scratch Elmer can't itch. Lives right in the middle of his back. No matter how hard he tries, he can't get it to stop itching.

Eric drops his eyes. Ralph contorts his face as confirmation. Fred pats him on the shoulder.

Elmer stabs his food. Swallows his bite, drops his fork, as the picture from the newspaper twenty years ago flashes in his mind. Ralph says, "I know you been thinking about this day," and palms Elmer's shoulder.

Elmer shakes it off and rocks in his seat.

Everybody knows the story, the murder of one of their own. Elmer's face filled the television and newspapers as he cried all those years ago. Eric, Ralph, and Fred had yet to return to Sherman. Yet to be retired, they lived in other Midwest cities. Returned a decade ago to retire to familiar roots and family. Story reached far beyond Columbus. Elmer was one of their first calls when they returned home. They were strangers with one thing in common: Elmer Ray.

"Yeah," Elmer says. The revelation numbs Elmer. His mind works in overdrive. He hoists himself off the stool. The stranger next to him substitutes for a wall and prevents a face plant, as his body is dislodged from his mind. He ignores the pain in his legs and hustles toward the exit as a train of eyes follow.

In all his years, he has never had a panic attack; not when his beloved died or when the boy disappeared. In his thirty years at the pen, he always remained calm and collected. He needs space and air.

Ralph and Fred turn and watch him hobble toward the exit. Neither know what to say. What do you say to a man who wished this day true for so long? Kneels at his bed and clasps his hands, and begs the man above to take the person who caused him so much pain. A pain as deep as he felt when Betsy passed. They've never seen him this way. Figure Albert Clouser would have died an old man long after Elmer, after all of them passed. Sherman Rehabilitation Center is not one to be featured in a documentary. Not a violent place. Old cons, short-time offenders, criminals on their last legs, Sherman has not had a murder in over a decade. Shared its name with the local town. Violent crime and assaults on staff are reserved for Montgomery, Hamilton, and Portsmouth Centers. Sherman is a family business; Eric has a son and two nephews who work there. Ralph's brother retired from there and moved to Florida. People flock to work there. For years, other than the paper mill, it was the place to work. Even now, with the growing hospital, Kenworth truck plant, and new construction racing up US 23 toward Columbus, it is a desired career. Like thoroughbred racehorses put out to pasture to satisfy their last days on earth, Sherman is the nursing home the old go to tell stories of their past lives. Coined Camp Honey Bun by the inmates, some wonder when the pool is going to be installed. A pleasure palace compared to other centers in the state. An officer once said, "If I'm going to do time, I sure hope to do it here." As they say, if a dog bites a man, that isn't a story. But, if a man bites a dog, you have a story. This wasn't just a man biting a dog. This is equivalent to a man biting a dog, boiling his skin off, and eating him for breakfast, lunch, and dinner.

Eric stands. "Elmer," he says, when Elmer stops at the door, he adds, "if you need anything." Figures that will be enough. Hopes. Eric is closest to Elmer. He learned to be a good listener over the years. He heard all about Adrian and the girl. How Adrian impacted his life after Betsy died. The son he never had is what he always tells Eric. Elmer always speaks about Albert Clouser through gritted teeth. When Eric's son got hired at the pen, Elmer called weekly and checked on him. After a few years, it became monthly. Ironic really, Elmer has not mentioned the name Albert Clouser for over six months. Eric didn't mention Albert Clouser's transfer to Sherman Rehabilitation Center when his son told him months ago. Time heals all wounds is what keeps entering his mind. Twenty years of healing, at least he hopes. Eric wonders if he has finally learned to live with it or if Elmer knows his days are numbered. Albert Clouser was going to outlive him. Elmer always said he is going to see that son of a bitch take a dirt nap. Eric didn't believe it then, but he does now.

Elmer lowers his head, turns, and feigns a smile. "Was it bad?" They hear the change in his cadence, the rapid breathing, the color of his skin fades.

"My boy," Eric says, "eh . . . he says it was as bad of a scene as you could imagine." He considers Elmer's demeanor, adds, "He was tortured throughout the night."

Elmer stares silently at the legs of a stool with a stoic expression. He doesn't hear Amy when she asks if he is okay. Or the sound of the broken plate after it spins off the table directly behind him. As his leg begins shaking from standing at the threshold of the door, he feels Amy looking at him, he smiles at her, says, "Amy, I'll get you tomorrow." To his three friends, "Thanks for telling me." He closes the door behind him, stops for a moment and reflects on the man he has long tried to forget. A man who impacted his life more than anybody. He imagines he would be more excited about hearing his demise. Make him feel twenty years younger, even for a minute. But now, years removed, he just feels empty, hollow, and old. For his death did not answer the questions Elmer needs answered. How did Adrian die? Figures the kid is looking down from a cloud above and smiling at today's events. He waddles home as old emotions waterfall out of his eyes. Collects himself and entertains Buck for hours with the memories of his loved ones swarming in his mind.

# CHAPTER 3

Elmer is in his recliner searching deep thoughts and faded memories. Sated and confused. Hours fly by as he wonders if he was lucky or unlucky in life. He juliennes his life like an onion, tears and all. He has been on this earth eighty-seven years, decades longer than Betsy. Lived fifty years longer than Adrian. He has aches and pains from old age and a bum hip, but overall, he has been lucky. Why was he spared and the two best people he had ever known taken long before him? Her death hardened him. His? Turned his blood into mercury, stormed through his veins heavy and cold. Hardened the hard. The questions fester and irritate like an old wound. You can put medicine on it and band-aids, but it returns and grows with bigger bones and teeth. Hardening the hard. He is broken, hanging on the precipice, waiting for someone or something to push him off the cliff. The light in his soul is flickering. If he had a fire extinguisher, he would put the light out. Eighty-seven years is enough for any man. Enough for a man who lost everyone.

He hears a thud on the porch, followed by another. A knock. "Who is it?" he hollers.

"I have a package for a Mr. Elmer Ray."

*What the hell?* Elmer struggles to get out of the chair, mumbles to himself, and pulls the door open as the man is eyeing his paperwork. "Can I help?" he asks suspiciously.

A smile greets him. "Package for you, sir. Sign here, please."

Elmer squints, looks up to find the delivery guy waving a clipboard in his face, "I didn't order anything."

"Sir, are you Mr. Ray?"

"For the past eighty-seven years."

"Someone is thinking of you," he says and nudges the board at him.

Elmer signs and hands the board back. The delivery guy tears a copy off and gives it to Elmer, saying, "Can I help you with these boxes?" Elmer taps one with his cane, "They are heavy," he hears.

"Ay-huh," sneaks out, as his mind is preoccupied thinking who would send him anything. For the past twenty years, he has grown to be a recluse. Alone with his memories of his past. An extended time in solitude with his dog. Only venturing out in the mornings for his exercise and social interaction with his friends. The delivery man places three boxes on the kitchen table and walks out, "Thank you," Elmer says and shuts the door.

Elmer sits at the kitchen chair and opens the box labeled number one. "Going to assume they want us to open this one here," he says to Buck and tosses a toy. In the box, a business envelope has large black lettering: OPEN ME FIRST, OLD MAN. Elmer mumbles, "What the hell kind of shit is this?" He opens and finds a letter and begins to read. He reads and lets it slip out of his fingers. "Adrian," he says.

He sulks for the boy as much as his beloved Betsy. More as the years pass and the silt collects on her frame. The small muscle in his chest causes the greatest of aches. Pain which makes his hip and knee bearable and sometimes pleasurable. He aches for only a dull pain in his body. In an instant, in a few lines read in a letter, the lies of yesterday succumb to the truths of today. The things he believes in the world, of Adrian's fate, launched to fable lands of fairy tales and myths after reading one sentence. No more or less of the unicorn standing gracefully and majestically in the gaze of a nonbeliever. Like a sudden blaze of fire, his memories of Adrian are charred to ash and blown away in a ferocious wind.

Elmer finishes the letter from Adrian and numbly stands up and reaches for his cane. He goes to the front door and peers out. "Hellfire," he yells when he sees the white lettering of the Law Offices of Overmeyer and Stanley on the building across the street. "Buck," he says and slams the door, "He's been here already." He takes two steps and collapses into the couch. He drifts into a fog. In the deep of the ocean, dog-paddling tired with no land in sight. Buck jumps on the couch and sidles up next to him. Wedges his nose between the cushion and a hand. Spoiled eyes searching for a rub. Questions niggle Elmer's mind like a slow drip from a faucet. The written words obfuscate his feelings for his lost boy. His mind reaches back into the past as he strokes the closest living creature to him since Adrian.

*Where has he been all these years? Why didn't he get in touch with me sooner? Did I search enough? Long enough?*

His vision goes cloudy. Heart plunges into a well of the unknown. The acceleration pulls him back to dark memories. Buck interrupts the descent with a bark. Elmer snaps out of it. "It's okay, boy," he says and gives a reassuring pat. A lie. Elmer hasn't been okay for decades. He has learned to deal with the loss of Adrian, but now he is confused and hurt. His throat tightens as he struggles to swallow this new truth. He flicks the falsehood away like ash from a cigar and stomps it with the heel of a boot and picks up the letter and reads it a second time.

It takes him hours to read the notebooks in the first parcel. He finishes and feeds Buck and peers out the window at the law offices. Imagines Adrian walking up the steps, stopping and staring back at him as he rocks in his porch chair with a cigar hanging out of his mouth. He shakes the image loose and goes back to the table and opens the next box.

He wakes the next day and skips out on the guys in favor of a visit to the public library. After a few hours, he returns home and reads over the parcels again. Friday, he visits the law offices and spends the day on the phone with authorities in Nevada, California, and Cleveland. Uses old contacts and speaks with the administration at Sherman, Montgomery, and Hamilton County.

Saturday, he dials, "Eric?"

"Elmer?" Eric says, "Where have you been? The guys, Amy, everybody is worried about you. Ralph and I stopped by yesterday and you were gone."

Elmer lies, "I'm fine." Clears his throat, "I need to speak with your son about the incident."

"Oh." He pauses, "Is this about . . . ?"

"I'll explain later. Just have him call, please."

He meets with the son and spends the week reading, memorizing the story, and collecting information. He has slept little since the boxes arrived.

# CHAPTER 4

Elmer pulls into the parking lot seven days after the package arrives, after he couples the stories of the two men and languidly shuffles in the local Ohio Highway Patrol station. He stops and rehearses his story in his mind and shoulders his way in. He enters and walks up to the glass. Empty, he knocks and rings the buzzer. He steps back and scans around. *What the . . .* He swivels around at the sound of the door. "Hello?" the officer says.

Elmer stares for a moment. Knocks the folded papers against his thigh.

The officer approaches, "Sir," he says, "can I help you with something?"

Elmer scans the room. Another knock on the thigh, "I'd like to speak with the person in charge."

"Can I tell Post Commander Murphy what this is in regard to?"

He releases a rumble from his throat, "I," he shakes his head, "I have information about the murder out at Sherman."

A long pause.

"Well?"

The officer points, "Take a seat."

Elmer sits and waits. Watches the officer enter the office down the hall and reappear. He walks back to Elmer, "He will be with you in a moment."

He waits, grows agitated, and almost gets up and goes home. Adrian appears in his mind. He picks at memories like pieces of a jigsaw puzzle as he constructs a picture of his boy. Adrian, young and troubled, frolicking around with the dog in a bed of leaves as they wait for the football game. Rare moments of calm. Elmer driving out to his wife's grave on a birthday and stumbling on Adrian cleaning her stone and laying flowers. The first time Elmer cried in the presence of his boy. *Just get this over with.*

"Post Commander Murphy," the voice says to his side and extends a hand.

Elmer rises and offers his, "Elmer Ray." He releases the hand and walks by Murphy toward the hall, stops, and turns his head, "Your office this way?"

"Yep."

Elmer walks down the hall until he sees Murphy's name on the door. He enters and sits in a chair. Murphy enters, closes the door, and sits behind the desk. Elmer eyes jaunt around the room. The office is in pristine condition. Clean and professional. An undergraduate degree from The Ohio State University hangs next to a master's degree from Ohio University. Pressed shirt. High and tight cut. Elmer knows he has his work cut out. He figures Murphy is indoctrinated in the new school of law enforcement, data and graphs and theories. He inhales deeply, filling his lungs with the stale air as he prepares to tangle with a sophisticated man. Out of his element indeed. He starts out easy, "Ohio State, huh?"

"What is this about, sir?"

Oh well, Elmer tried. Murphy has a snobby, cold tone. "I hear you had a real bad murder out at the pen."

"Sherman?"

"Is there another prison near?"

"Are there any other murders except real bad ones?"

"Guess I deserved that."

"Yes, you did."

They sit in awkward silence for a moment. Felt longer, Elmer checks his watch, gasps when he realizes he left it at home. He flips his off hand over his wrist and pretends to examine the two paintings on the wall. Figures he would try again, "Nice paintings."

"Excuse me?"

"The paintings." Murphy looks over expressionless. "They . . . are . . . nice," Elmer says slowly. Twice he pulls some snarky shit. It is hard for him. Before today, his crew was the only people he associated with. A fish out of water.

"Oh," Murphy says and flips his hand at the wall and slides his glasses on his nose, "They were left by the former Post Commander."

Elmer remains silent.

"Mr . . ."

"Elmer Ray."

"Mr. Ray," Murphy says and tosses the glasses and rubs his eyes, "why are you asking about the incident out at the center?" Elmer gulps and grabs a cigar out of his pocket, and before he can start his spiel, Murphy pulls his issued ten-gallon hat toward him, fidgets with the tassel. "Yes, Sherman had," he pauses, "an unusual incident. Our office is working with officials to figure out what happened."

Elmer bites at the end of the cigar, spits it in the basket. Murphy eyes the discarded end. He turns toward Elmer when he hears, "I have all the information you need about the murder." Murphy scoots his chest up toward the desk, places both elbows on the desk, head in hands, a skeptical posture. Elmer notices, "Seems you don't believe an old man."

"Mr. Ray," Murphy says, "we have—" Adds, as he sees Elmer pull out a lighter, "this is a non-smoking facility."

"I have a story to tell," Elmer says earnestly as he pitches the lighter and cigar in the can. The mental strain of the past week shows itself physically and verbally.

"Like I was saying . . ." Murphy clears his throat, "Mr. Ray, I don't mean to be disrespectful but . . ." He reaches for his pen, twisting his watch toward him to check the time. He quickly dismisses the idea that this man has any information to contribute to his investigation and wants him gone. He appraises him quickly, old, short, and heavy, cane in hand, faded blue bibbed overalls, and a heavy smell of cigar smoke. Only smell missing is liquor. Not the appearance of a police officer or private detective. Senile jumps to the front of the mind.

"Do- you- want- to- know- why- he- did- it?"

Elmer knows he does. It hit the Columbus papers after Albert Clouser's mother, the victim's mother, that is, stood in front of the news camera and cried like a ten-year-old girl who got her bicycle stolen. While the father stood properly behind her in his suit. Her poor boy, she said. Should have said show me the money. Elmer had followed Clouser's trial; did not miss one day, heard every word. Listened to every testimony like he was the court reporter. He knew Clouser better than his parents. They were never there. He knows it. Never visited him. The perks of being lifelong prison workers. Elmer knows how this works; a family played this tune on him before.

He was sitting in his office, feet on the desk and coffee in his hand, gossiping with a colleague on a Sunday morning. They were ten minutes from transporting a death row inmate to Portsmouth prison to await his execution on the following Tuesday. When the man down alarm went off, he knew exactly what was going on. Jack Banks hung himself. Two days before the state of Ohio was going to put him in the gas chamber. His family cried. Poor bastards hadn't visited or called Jack for over thirty years. Show – me – the – money. Now, after the *Dispatch* picked it up, Columbus's Channel 10 TV News blasted the airways with the face of Sandy Clouser. Sherman, located forty-five miles south of the capital city, was part of Columbus, Ohio's, viewing audience. CNN and others picked it up. The Ohio Rehabilitation System let her boy get tortured as he lay in his bed. Nothing sells like government causing a grieving mother to mentally breakdown on national television. Someone needs to pay. The director was on the warden like a tick on a dog. The governor climbed in the director's ass and built a campsite; smoke would be coming out of her ass for weeks. Shit rolls downhill, and someone needs to be held accountable. Flies are circling above and need someone to point to the pile. Need a motive first, and officials and the good ole Ohio State Patrol can't provide one. Now, an old man is sitting across from the lead investigator and asking about a motive. Murphy's job is safe. But he's only human. Has never seen anything like what hit his eyes when he entered that cell and saw the remains on the cold concrete. He knows what Clouser did to get his life sentence, and he knows no man deserves what he got. He wants to know the reason for the carnage. Needs to know. He is only human, after all.

Elmer adds, "I know why he did it."

This catches Murphy by surprise. He figures he read about the story in the *Columbus Dispatch* and stumbled into his office, mindless and bored.

His days and nights have gotten mixed during the investigation, on the phone, reading reports, talking to authorities in three time zones. Two weeks later, nobody knows anything about Conner Wallace. Now an eighty-seven-year-old man is sitting across his desk claiming he is Sherlock Holmes.

"I know everything."

"Interesting." Murphy massages a temple as his eyes skim across his desk. He stops before he says another word about the case. Maybe if he humors the old man, it will bring him the pot of gold at the end of the rainbow. What harm could come of it if he showers the old-timer with the gift of gab? He has seen cases get cleared by stranger means. He pulls open the drawer and opens a bottle, eyes on Elmer, slips two pills under his tongue, and sucks as he thinks about his move. Swallows, "You know everything?" He looks across and straightens a folder on the desk and taps it against the oak, drops it and stands up, and goes to the window. Peers out the window and watches traffic scoot by, speaks in a light monotone, "A number of," glances back at Elmer, "the best law enforcement agencies in the country have looked into the past of Mr. Wallace and—'

"And you can't find any information about him prior to 2004?"

Murphy hesitates, then turns to the window, "Not exactly."

"What do you have?" Elmer says. Murphy glances at his watch again. He adds, "It's three minutes later than before." After a fleeting moment, he mumbles to himself, "They don't have shit." Murphy rocks on his heels as he stares out the window like a ghost stuck in the house. Elmer needles him, "Mrs. Clouser probably home making her Christmas list as we speak. Governor Brown, in the office, talking about whose taxes to raise because of this fiasco." Hyperbole and far-reaching even for Elmer. But he is getting desperate in his old age; time was not on his side. "How many times a day does the warden call you? I bet he is shitting bricks. Career up in flames. People roasting marsh—"

Murphy cuts him off, pointedly says, "Enough." He tucks his hand in his pocket and sits on the edge of the desk. Feels a trifle of empathy in the back of his skull for some odd reason. A boatload of apprehension about what information an old man has about the murder. Elmer is right. Warden Robinson has Murphy on speed dial, calls more than his ex-wife, and she calls a lot. He surrenders, the headache has punched holes in his head for the past week, and shows his hands, "Go ahead and tell your story." Retreats to his seat and lets out a long sigh. "Can we make it quick?"

Elmer's emotions are plagued by the long week. Today is harder than the rest. The mornings are the hardest, alone with memories birthed in his nightly dreams. Faces bright and alive. Glimpses of a past yearn to remember and forget. By afternoon, just pixels on an Etch-a-Sketch slowly being shaken away. He cries every day. Last night he did not dream. He opens his roll, unfolds a letter with shaky hands, and begins. Tears up as he reads the letter.

*Dear Elmer,*

*I don't take solace in writing you this letter. I've thought about the words to say to you after all these years with your belief I perished. After the death, I just couldn't deal with it. I tried. I really did. Just think it was my fate since birth for it to end this way. By the time you read this letter, I will be gone. I hope I'm in heaven, I believe in it, but do I deserve to be there? Well, that isn't my decision to make.*

He loses his spot, words tumble in his throat, his stomach knots, his hands tremble, hundreds of memories float in his mind like confetti dropped at a party. His heart speeds up, wailing as it pumps blood. He remembers the last time he cried. Last time he felt this way. He forces the tears back and fights against his hands. The confetti blows away like leaves in a storm. Adrian flashes. Was this his attempt to repent for his sins? If this is the last thing Adrian wants him to do, then he is going to push on.

*Over the last twenty years, I've thought about you and Rocky a lot. Our talks on the porch, your advice and lectures. You tell me you're drinking Coke, conveniently leaving out the Jack part. In all my years, you're the best friend. Elmer, you were my mom, my dad, my brother, and the one who showed me what a man should be. The wisdom you shared was never forgotten. I know I must have been a big disappointment to you, and I'm so sorry I let you down. Hopefully, you will find the answers you seek in the packages I sent to you.*

Murphy sees the struggle on his face, anger spawned by confusion and loss. He interrupts with an overexaggerated growl from the throat. When Elmer stops, he says, "Sir, why are you telling me this? What is this letter about?"

"You need to hear about Adrian Franklin and Conner Wallace." Murphy sends a glare across the desk. Clears his throat in embarrassment. Elmer catches on: "Commander?"

A hand up. He scratches at his face, says, "Mr. Ray, I'm sorry but you must be confused . . . Uhm . . . Um . . . we don't know anything about an Andy Fra—"

"Adrian Franklin."

"We don't know an Adrian Franklin."

"I'm trying to tell you everything you need to know," Elmer says and waves the roll in between them and drops it. "Oh, sorry," he bends down and picks it up, and lays it on his lap, "I can help you." A pause. They stare. "I'm not a crazy old man."

*Yes, you are. And I'm crazy for thinking about entertaining you.* Murphy glances at his watch a third time.

"The story needs to be told," Elmer says and slaps the roll hard against his leg.

Murphy shakes a finger at Elmer, slowly. Makes a fist, opens it, and gently slaps the desktop. "Okay," he says trying to appease the old man. Murphy is a big believer in good deeds. Maybe doing a favor for one lonely old man will bring him karma. Soon.

Elmer smiles.

"Don't get too excited yet."

Elmer covers his mouth with a hand like a child.

"If . . ." He points again, "Mr. Ray, if I think this information is . . . let me be clear, if I think this is some type of b—"

"It's not."

"If I think this is going nowhere, you're out of here." Looks at his watch a fourth time. "How long is this going to take?"

Elmer doesn't answer. He offers up his own question. "Do you have any coffee?"

Murphy returns his hat to the corner and spouts out, "Only in the mornings."

"It's morning somewhere. Plus, wait till you're older. You will drink more."

Murphy catches the hint, "How do you take it?"

"Black."

Minutes later, Murphy returns and hands Elmer a cup. "Go ahead," he says and sits behind the desk. He pauses and pulls out a notepad, "Mr. Ray, Albert Clouser was a local kid?'

"Yep," Elmer says, knows Murphy already knows that one.

"Did you know him or his family? The town seems like it was a much smaller town back in those days."

Elmer breathes heavy through his nose and holds it. Releases the air slowly. Sends a vicious eye to Murphy; not to him, through him, seeing Albert Clouser. Imagining blood spewing from his pores. Before, he didn't know how to feel about his death. He traps a smile from stretching across his face and says, "I didn't know him. I know what he did . . . I . . . can I just tell their story?"

"Yeah, yeah, just trying to connect Clouser and Wallace and now . . ." He taps his pen. "You mention a guy nobody has heard before."

Elmer sips and swallows. "I've been to three rodeos, two county fairs, and a Georgia goat-roping contest, but I've never . . ." He lets it dangle between them. " . . . never seen any shit quite like this."

"Wallace?"

"Where to begin?" Elmer points at him. "To understand why it happened, you need to understand both of these men."

"And you know Conner Wallace and Albert Clouser?" Murphy says in a snide tone.

Elmer looks at him cross-eyed and sternly says, "Wallace and Adrian Franklin."

Murphy taps his index finger on the desktop three times as he stares at Elmer, "Go ahead."

Elmer salutes him with his cup, "I know them better than anybody." Points at his head, "I have personal knowledge, right up here of those two boys. Plus," he wiggles the paperwork, "I've done the proper investigative work, have the material sent by both. By the end of the day, you will know why Albert Clouser was murdered in his cell."

Murphy's eye tracked the papers as they move in front of Elmer. Massages above the eyes and pulls at a lobe.

"It's going to be a long day," Elmer says, almost beaming. "You better get comfortable."

Murphy crosses his arms over his chest and leans back, "I thought I said make it quick."

"Sherman wasn't the town you see today. I assure you that. Back in the eighties, after all the jobs moved away, people fled the area like it was on fire. The new became the old. Businesses, people moved out. Our neighborhood was left with the never-haves and never-wills. Never seen anything like it. New communities built ten, fifteen miles away felt like another world. Only time anybody came to our community was to buy drugs. The people who stayed, well, they drowned themselves in booze and drugs to numb themselves of the pain. Commander, can you imagine not knowing how you would pay for the electric bill?"

Murphy stroked his chin.

Elmer speaks with a cheeriness in his voice. In all the years since Adrian, he hasn't spoken in detail about him and their relationship with many people.

He feels at ease, alive, a cathartic moment. "Well, that was the type of neighborhood we lived in four decades ago. Adrian Franklin was raised in death and destruction. He moved next door to me in 1985, and my life would never be the same."

"1985", Murphy throws up a stop signal with his hand. "1985," he repeats. Elmer steeples in his seat with his mouth ajar. "Mr. Ray . . . Uhm . . . I'm sorry but I don't have time to sit here and go over a history lesson."

"But—"

Murphy says, "No, no," with his hand still up, "I thought, I hoped, this would take an hour or so." He sits and fumbles in a desk drawer, pulls out a card, and extends it toward Elmer. Shakes it, "Give this to the officer," he gestures with his head, "you can write a report, and we'll look into it." The heck with karma.

Elmer changes his tune: "Post Commander Murphy," he says. Hesitates and holds a forlorn look. "I'm eighty-seven years old. Haven't done much of significance in a long time. I came in here today, and we got off to a bad start. I don't blame you. But," he shifts his hips, "I don't have much interaction with people." Murphy listens, starts to fidget with his hands under his desk. Pushes his cuticles with his thumb. He starts with his right. After he gets through all his fingers, he's going to end this conversation. Index finger.

Elmer continues to try and make amends: "It's just me and my dog, Buck. Before him, Brutus. Before Brutus, Rocky. I don't have much time to live." Those words hang between them. "Maybe days, maybe months." Chuckles, "Heck, I hope I don't have years left." Murphy grunts. Middle finger. "You're right. This story, the story I need to tell you, it will take most of this day and maybe more."

Ring finger. "Mr. Ray."

"But," Elmer is working the roll, "I wouldn't be here today if I did not believe this would give our community, the people of our town closure. Employees of Sherman Rehabilitation Center closure. Give you closure."

Little finger. Murphy sniffs, "You say you received a package?"

"Yes . . . three."

"Then you can just give me the material . . . uhm . . . You don't need to sit here all day and tell the story. I'm sure there are other places you would rather be," Murphy says with a querying look on his face.

Elmer scoots to the edge of the seat, leans in. "I guess I need to do this for *my* closure."

"Aw . . ." Murphy says. Pulls at his nose for a second, adds, "I see."

Elmer offers a sneak peek: "I never got the privilege to meet Mr. Wallace."

Murphy pushes in the cuticle of his left index and mumbles, "Not so sure it would have been a pleasure."

Elmer ignores him. Offers up additional information: "Wallace shows up in Nevada and goes to California and then here in Ohio."

Middle finger. "And Adrian Franklin?"

Elmer says, "If you get on your computer there, I believe the kids call it YouTube." Murphy's eyes hold Elmer's. He gets behind the keyboard when Elmer says, "Wallace has an interesting video on there from over a decade ago." He leans back and watches. Pushes in at the ring finger and ends at the little finger.

Elmer waits and perches at the edge of the seat.

Murphy strokes his jaw.

Elmer wasn't done: He pulls a picture from his pocket and places it on the edge of the desk. "This is a picture of Conner Wallace taken over ten years ago in California."

Murphy scratches his nose with the end of his pen as he looks at the picture. Pushes it away with his off hand. He locks one of those drug-induced grins; first known picture of Conner Wallace in the wild. No mother, father, distant uncle, or cousin has been found. This wasn't a found Bigfoot moment, but it was a moment.

Elmer tries to close the deal. "I'm not crazy, senile, or bored with life, Mr. Murphy. I retired from Sherman over thirty years ago as an Assistant Warden. Back in the law and order days. Back when the prison system was about retribution and deterrence. As you know, our system used to be called Ohio Prison Systems." Elmer wants Murphy to know he is in his right frame of mind. Adds, "The department's name was only changed to Ohio Rehabilitation Systems about ten years ago. The facilities names were changed from prisons to centers." He waggles his finger out the window, "Sherman Rehabilitation Center was called Sherman Correctional Institution when I walked those halls." He interlocks his fingers and holds Murphy's eyes, "Got to say," he says, "prouder of the system now than before." He nods, "We are supposed to help people get better. Help people feel whole again. Be whole. Get jobs. Reunite with loved ones." Raises his voice, "Become productive members of our society. And we do. Now," he perks up, "a man with a felony conviction, a man who did time in one of our centers, can do his time, go home and come back and get a job in the place where he was an incarcerated adult." Elmer eats his lip, smiles, says, "I'd call that progress. Turning a negative into a positive." He chuckles, "Funny, all old-timers and most of the young people still call them prisons. Use the derogatory terms for those individuals locked up: prisoners, inmates, convicts, the condemned. Takes an awful long time to get people to use more enduring terms such as incarcerated males. Old habits die hard, I guess." He finishes with, "This might be the last real thing I ever get to do. I'm only here to help. Not here to cause you trouble or grief. Only want what is best for the town." He points again, "only what is best for the place out there, the place that provided me and hundreds of good people a weekly paycheck. Closure for everybody involved." Elmer's vision tracks toward the ceiling. He blinks twice, says, "And to be honest . . . the closure I have been seeking for a very long time now."

Murphy holds his water and grabs a piece of paper, speaks to Elmer as he writes, "You better not be wasting my time." Takes the receiver off the phone, says, "Clear my schedule for the day."

# CHAPTER 5

# Adrian Franklin
# 1985

drian and the window were one as they drove into Sherman, Ohio. Long drive. Bad car. His first time in Ohio. Illinois was flat as a pancake. Southern Ohio had mountains; at least they looked like mountains to him. Mother Nature in Ohio had a bad sense of humor. On a Monday, the car needed to be preheated to break up the night ice on the windshield. Tuesday, the sun sat in the sky like a sunflower and released summer heat three months too soon. Elmer Ray always said, "If you're waiting for the weather to change, wait five minutes." April was brutally warm. Mosquitoes grew big enough to stand flat-footed to have sex with a turkey.

Elmer leaned up in his chair after hearing a commotion. "What the hell is all the yelling about?" he said to Rocky. The house next door had been emptied months ago; an eviction led to the former tenants leaving the structure in an uninhabitable state. Elmer had mixed feelings; he enjoyed the quietness of his little part of the neighborhood. Some days he missed being human and interacting with someone other than his dog. Heard the car door first. Open and close. Footsteps up the stairs. When he looked out the window, he didn't see anybody. He heard the car door open and slam shut a second time, then, "Mom . . . Mom . . . this box isn't labeled."

The young boy continued to call out from the front porch, "Mom!" he screamed and kicked the door with his foot. "Mom, where does this box go?"

"Bedroom."

"Open the door."

Elmer was pleasantly surprised by the voice. He opened the front door and stepped toward the porch rail near the empty house and saw a young boy cradling a box in his arms and screaming at the front door, "Open the door, Mom."

Elmer moved over to the rail and leaned over. "Who's moving in?"

"Me and my mom."

"You mean your mom and you."

The boy dropped the box and defiantly stood and glared over at him. "You an English teacher or something?"

Elmer sucked on his bottom gum, itched his chin, "What's your name, kid? Hope nothing broke in there," as he used his cane as a pointer.

"Bam," he said. Kicked the box, "We don't own anything but junk."

"Bam?" Elmer smirked back.

Two stomps toward his rail. Firmly, he said, "That is what I said, mister."

Elmer mocked the boy with a head rattle and cartoon face. Sent over a Daffy Duck tongue punch, wet rattle.

Bam stepped back toward the front door, "Mom!" he screamed. "There is a weirdo out here."

Elmer flattened his hand out and gestured for the boy not to scream. "Relax, I'm playing with you."

"Mom."

"I know no parent in his or her right mind would name their kid Bam." He nodded at the boy with his nose. "What's your real name?"

He pocketed his hands, leaned away in a defensive stance. "My name is Bam." Elmer looked over the boy, figured he was fourteen or older. The boy cocked his head to the side. "What are you looking at?"

This was the most fun Elmer had had since he could remember. He grinned and continued to needle the boy. "Name?"

Both eyed the door when Cindy came out. Bam backed away and stood with his hands on his hips. She saw his agitation. "What?" When she noticed Elmer on his porch, she smiled. "Hello," she said and threw him a wave.

"Howdy, neighbor," Elmer said and sent a wink and a smile. "I've been out here talking to this young man. He must be your son."

"Adrian," she wrapped her arm around him and pulled him tight against her side. His head was above her shoulder. "Mister?"

"Elmer Ray."

"Mr. Ray," she said and squeezed her son against her. He rolled his eyes and gasped. Elmer choked down a laugh. She continued, "I'm Cindy and this," another squeeze, a kiss on the head, "this is Adrian."

Adrian interrupted, "Bam," he continued to pout. "Mom, you call me Bam. You never call me Adrian."

Bam, the nickname Adrian was called since his birth in seventy-three, started as Bam-Bam. It was either because he was violent or because the little towhead looked like the character from *The Flintstones*. Sometime around ten, it shortened to Bam; it sounded more mature and appropriate for a growing boy.

She ran her hand over his hair. "Yes, Bam," she corrected herself and laughed. Looked at Elmer, "Everybody calls him Bam. Been his name since I can remember. When people ask about Adrian, I sometimes catch myself. Who is Adrian?" That laugh returned. She shook him by the shoulders. "His grandkids will probably have to put Bam on his tombstone." Bam continued staring. She kissed him on the cheek and said, "He will always be Adrian to me."

"I heard," Elmer said. "Adrian is a very nice name." Bam blew a tire out the side of his lip. "It is a proper boy's name. Are you local?"

"No, sir. Bam and I moved here from Illinois. Small town south of Chicago. Moved over here to be near my sister. She lives in Columbus."

"I see."

"Yeah," she said and squeezed Bam tight, "just me and my little boy."

"Good to finally have neighbors."

She released him. "After we get settled, we will have to have you over for dinner."

Elmer slapped his belly, "If it isn't obvious, I like to eat."

A giggle. A pause. She shook Bam's head like it was a mop. "I'll start unpacking." She caught Elmer's attention. "Leave you two out here to get to know each other."

"Ma'am." After she entered the house, "Adrian, huh?"

A death stare. A stomp toward the rail. He gripped the top with both hands, "My-name-is-Bam."

"Adrian is a good name," Elmer said, unrelenting, and retreated to the porch chair. He glanced back toward Adrian, who was still in his defiant position, two brows curled into one. Elmer flatly said, "Bam is a cartoon name."

Rocked and pulled a cigar, spoke to Adrian, "Think we are both too old to be watching cartoons."

Adrian released his grip, crossed his arms over his chest, stared at Elmer, and smiled. "I'm going to call you Mr. Fudd." He dropped his head and stomped off into the house.

A shake of the head. A sly smile. A quick look at the house. "Damn kids these days," he said and lit.

# CHAPTER 6

After a few days of unwinding and unpacking, Adrian figured he would check out the neighborhood. His mom lied; this place was just as bad or worse than the place in Illinois. *New beginnings, my ass.* The dog brought a smile when he saw him, he said, "Hey, pup, who do you belong to?" He bent to a knee and rubbed the head of the dog.

Heard, "I see you found a friend."

Bam eyed him as he rubbed, stood up and frowned. "Oh, it's you."

Elmer released the lock on the gate and walked out from the side of the house, said, "Haven't you ever heard the term, 'turn that frown upside down.'"

Bam darted his eyes at him, bent down and continued to rub the dog. "Yeah," he said, "it's stupid. What is his name?"

Elmer walked over and stood next to him, nudged the dog with his cane. "This is Rocky. Rocky meet Adrian." Adrian cradled the dog with his hands, nose to nose. Elmer said, "I think you two will be fast friends." Then as he watched them, "Still a pup, got him a few months ago."

"You're shitting me."

"Watch your language."

"Your dog is named Rocky?"

"Yeah, why?"

Bam massaged his forehead, "Haven't you seen the movie? Get it?" A long look. Silence. "Rocky and Adrian?" After Elmer didn't respond. He sighed, "From the movie. Boxer. Husband and wife."

Elmer sucked in his lips and swallowed.

"Guy with the big nose. Talked funny. Weirdo like you."

Elmer waved him off, "I know what the hell you are talking about. I was just pulling your leg. Weirdo like me?"

"Yeah, that is what I said."

Elmer mumbled, "Just because I don't like some stupid nickname."

«Adrian is a girl's name."

Elmer handed a shoulder. "Kid, trust me." He gently pushed him away. "You will learn to love it, and it is better than that damn cartoon name."

He sniffled. Eyed the dog. Inhaled and looked at Elmer, "Watch your language, Mr. Fudd. I'm only twelve."

"Mr. Fudd," he said and laughed, "That was a snappy come-back." "Twelve?"

A twisted smile led to, "That is what I said."

"Damn," Elmer said, "kids grow big these days." He stepped away and called for Rocky. He closed the gate behind them and hollered, "Adrian," he wailed, "I did it!" He lifted his right arm in the air and cringed his face.

Adrian did a few jabs in the air and laughed. "Mr. Fudd," he said, "you're a goofball."

"See you later, kid," Elmer said and waved as he walked off.

"Not if I see you first," Adrian hollered.

# CHAPTER 7

# Adrian Franklin
# Months Later

A drian grew on the old man. He was the only friend Adrian had, and if you had pressed the issue, Elmer would tell you Adrian was his only friend. They were stuck with each other, and that was alright by Elmer. "Mr. Fudd," Adrian yelled from the sidewalk. "Mr. Fudd, are you home?"

Elmer opened the screen door with his cane and walked onto the porch. "Hellfire," he barked back, "what the hell is all the yelling about?" He gazed over the street. "You're going to scare the damn neighborhood."

Adrian followed Elmer's eyes, "Mr. Ray," he put his hand under his chin, "we live in a shithole. Nobody gives a shit about me out here yelling at ya."

Elmer snickered, pulled a cigar, and put it in his mouth, waved Adrian onto the porch. "Good point, kid," he said and turned to open the screen door, "but watch your damn mouth," he held the screen door open, "Well, are you going to stand out here and kill grass, or are you going to get your boney ass in the house?"

Adrian walked up the steps, "Mr. Ray, you tell me to watch my language but then you cuss me."

Elmer said, "I'm old, and I'm allowed to say shit like that. You're not. Too old to change, kid. Not enough hours in the day." Adrian dropped his head. Elmer put his hand on Adrian's back. "Get in the house. I know you want to see the dog."

Adrian smiled. "Thanks, Mr. Ray," and pushed by. "Rocky," he said and crouched down and rubbed the canine.

Elmer closed the door behind him and headed to his recliner. "You can come over anytime you want."

Adrian continued to rub and spoke to Elmer, "Okay," he said, "you might regret saying that."

Elmer grabbed his lighter off the stand and pointed it at Adrian. "It doesn't mean come over all hours of the night," he gestured toward the kitchen, "and get in the fridge and eat all the damn food," he grumbled and feigned a scowl.

Adrian frowned and stopped rubbing, "I can't get anything to eat?"

"Well," Elmer said and turned his head toward the television and lit a cigar, "guess you can get a sandwich or something." Adrian shot toward the kitchen, heard Elmer say, "leave me a breadcrumb or two."

"Okay, Mr. Ray."

"And stop calling me Mr. Ray or that damn Mr. Fudd."

Adrian peeked his head out from the refrigerator. "What do you want me to call you?"

"Elmer."

Adrian grabbed a pack of bologna and closed the fridge. Laid the bologna on the kitchen table. "Only if you call me Bam."

Elmer said, "I'm not calling you Bam."

Adrian stomped his foot. "Why not?"

Elmer remained calm. "We have talked about this." Then, "The bread is in the cabinet to the left of the sink."

"Fine," Adrian said and took a step, hesitated. "Thanks, Elmer," he said and hid his eyes.

A sly smile. "No problem, Adrian."

Adrian made his sandwich. "Clean up the mess," Elmer said.

"You don't want one?"

"Nah," Elmer said and puffed, "I ate an hour ago." He waved the smoke from his face.

Adrian straightened up the kitchen, flopped on the couch with his sandwich, and stared at Elmer.

"What?"

Adrian chewed and swallowed. "You shouldn't smoke in here," he said and waved his hand in front of his nose. "Smoke will give you and me cancer."

"Ay-huh."

"Rocky could get cancer and die." Chewed and gestured for Rocky to join him. Rocky plopped on the couch and put his head on Adrian's knee. Adrian put his hand on the canine's neck and peered down at him. "Sure would be sad if our dog died because of your nasty habit."

"Our dog?" Elmer said and stubbed the end of the cigar and put it on the stand. "There," he whined, "you happy now?"

Adrian bit and chewed, stopped with a mouth full. Swallowed, "Yep," he said, "our dog."

Elmer got up from his chair. "Damn, kid," he mumbled through his teeth. He walked into the kitchen. "Leave me any?"

"Thought you didn't want one."

"Well, I can't smoke, so I figured I'd eat."

"Can I take Rocky for a walk?"

Elmer looked at his watch. "It's seven thirty at night."

"So."

"It's Sunday."

"And?"

"You have school tomorrow."

"I'm not a baby, Elmer. My mom lets me stay up late all the time . . . when she is home."

Elmer looked at his young friend, who had on black shorts and a banana yellow t-shirt picked up at a yard sale. He picked up his cane, pointed it at Adrian's feet and narrowed his eyes, and wrinkled his nose. "Go get some damn shoes on," he said and got up from the chair and grabbed the leash off the chair in the kitchen. Adrian remained still. "Go get some damn shoes on," Elmer repeated. "You look like welfare." Then, "Hurry up. It will get dark soon."

Adrian jumped from the couch. "Thanks, Elmer," and he ran out the door and jumped off the porch.

Elmer leashed Rocky and met Adrian at the door. "Be home before dark and stay near the house."

"I will." Adrian pulled Rocky away, "what way, boy?"

Elmer looked out the window and watched Adrian and Rocky walk off and lit a cigar, "Kid is going to be the end of me."

The fifty-pound black Labrador Retriever escorted Adrian south on Ewing Street. They evaded glass and litter trapped under the dislodged concrete sidewalk and maneuvered over tree branches swept in the yards from the dying trees. Passing Buckeye Street, they turned left onto Ohio Street. Adrian saw similarities flash—dilapidated, subpar housing, a faded collage of greens, blacks, white, and blue paint splattered, cracked windows covered with dirt and blankets. Overgrown trees and dying leaves seeded by corrupted trees rained over the sidewalks. The neighborhood raised desperate children in desperate times and cheered the violence it bred. They turned left on Buckeye and headed home to end their short roam. Adrian reminded himself to be home before dark as the sun lay lazily over the neighborhood. Soon the night and the moon, the darkness, and the yellow eyes would climb high and wide. The sun was slowly creeping below the trees, and the sounds of flapping wings prevailed over the sonnet of leaves moaning in the wind.

"Yelp, yelp."

Adrian pulled on the leash and stopped. He heard the release of pain. He scanned left and heard the cries again. It was a wretched noise, a dying cry. He took a couple of steps into the yard, walking through three-week-old growth, and heard the cry again. "Where are you, boy?" he called out.

Adrian wrapped the leash around the base of a tree. "Stay here, Rocky." He kept his eyes on the olive-green house as he tiptoed through the yard. Black shingled roof spotted with patches of gray rot, tired and dirty white columns drained weary, Christmas lights eight months past due hung off them. He stopped at the wood fence, braced his foot, and peered over the fence. The dog lay between two trees. As far as Adrian could see, the dog was alone, scared, hurt, or both, hungry. His mouth hung wide open.

Adrian dropped off the fence, inhaled deeply, scurried back and untied Rocky, and ran back to Elmer's.

He barged in and unhooked Rocky. "I'm back," he said and stuck out the leash.

"Put it on the chair."

Adrian tossed it. "Got to go," he said and opened the door.

"Is your mom home yet?"

Adrian stepped outside and looked at his house. "No," he said, "all the lights are off." He shut the screen door and faced Elmer, "She gets home around dark time."

"Get your butt in here."

Adrian stood silent for a moment, "Elmer, I have homework," he gestured with his head, "I probably should get home and get it done."

Elmer rose. "You had homework all weekend, and now you're talking about getting it done." Adrian looked away. Elmer approached and put his hand on his shoulder, "Go get the damn homework and come back. You should have done it yesterday."

Adrian hesitated, "Okay . . . I'll take a quick shower and come back."

"Hurry up," Elmer said and pushed Adrian away. "I'll make you a sandwich." He turned toward the kitchen, "What do—"

He heard the screen door slam, "I'll be back soon, Elmer."

"Hellfire."

Adrian jumped off the porch and ran toward his house. He stopped outside, below his porch, and hunkered down. When it was clear, he crept by Elmer's and headed for the dog. He ran and slowed his walk as he approached the house. Ghouls of eyes stirred high; the wind howled a lullaby as Adrian kept walking. He reached the olive house and crept toward the fence, and saw the Confederate flag hanging in the window. *At least they like The Dukes of Hazzard too.* Shrubbery masked the front. He reached the fence, steadied himself, and climbed. Two maple trees sheltered the dog. The moon was climbing high, and smoke-filled haze from the paper mill contributed to the darkness. Trees roared. Adrian heard movement in the trees and slowly walked toward them. Between two trees lying in the dirt sod, a large Saint Bernard was glued to the ground. Stretched across the earth like he had given up to an illness. Flies masked his appearance. He gazed up at the boy, too scared to fight. Adrian ignored the stench, the blood-soaked and wet coat, and released the animal from the chain. He whispered, "Come on, boy. You're free now. I'm going to take you home." He pulled on his collar. The dog gingerly got up like an old man, his bottom half covered in dirt, top half matted in blood, mosquitoes feasting. Adrian heard the crackle of the door. "Run, boy, run," he yelled and sprinted to the fence.

"Who's out here?" The man stomped down the steps, "What are you doing with Jack," he questioned when he saw the silhouette run by the light with the dog in hand.

The man hurried toward the fence and grabbed Adrian by the back of his shoulder as he climbed, "Got you!" he said and pulled him off. Adrian fell on his butt and shot up, and ran through the yard. The man scanned the yard, There is no place to go."

Adrian's heart sped up. He ran to the other end of the yard and stopped at the fence. He shuffled to his right, pounding on the fence with both hands. He ignored the pain when the splinter embedded in his palm. He stopped, turned around, and faced the yard. The man was nowhere in sight; the yard seemed darker than before, and brush hung over the fence, canopying the yard. He heard the man growl, "Where are you, you little piss ant?" His eyes danced around the fence and ran down the left side, ending at the backside of the garage and directly behind the maple trees, the natural cage of the animal. Down his right, the fence ran to the house. He was trapped in the abyss. In the overactive imagination of a thirteen-year-old, Adrian began imagining his fate. He was going to be caught, dragged into the basement, and fed to some alien creature chained to a wall. He hyperventilated, sprinted toward the maples, and dove into the habitat. He was swaddled in the trees. He sprawled on the earth, body flat and head down.

"There is no place to hide," the voice grew closer as the giant silhouette stalked the ground. His hand swept left, and he felt an object against the back of his hand. Adrian picked it up and peered out between the maples. The man was standing in the middle of the yard, facing the other way. Adrian crept up to his feet. He sprinted from the trees to the fence. His right foot hit the fence, "I got you," he heard. He used his right foot to push off and fell on top of the man and rolled off. He stood up and swung the limb at his face. Dropped the limb and climbed over the fence and ran home.

"I'll get you, kid," the man yelled. "I know what you look like."

Adrian stopped at his door, went in, grabbed his bookbag, and went off to Elmer's. "Why are you sweating?" Elmer said.

"I," Adrian started to tell Elmer, but instead said, "You know kids," he feigned a smile. "I started to play a game."

Elmer ran his hand over wet hair. "Get in the kitchen and get the homework out," he said and shut the door. Adrian sat at the table and pulled out his homework. "I'll make you something to eat."

# CHAPTER 8

The next evening, Adrian was in the yard teaching Rocky tricks. "Stay," he said and showed Rocky the ball. "Stay." He threw the ball. "Go get," he said and watched Rocky pant and stay seated, looking up at him.

Adrian looked at Elmer inquisitively, "Why won't he get the ball?"

Elmer sipped at his iced tea, rocked in the chair, and chuckled. "You just have to keep working with him." Adrian sighed. "He listens about as well as you," Elmer said.

"Funny," Adrian said and kicked at a rock.

The 1979 Ford pickup with a dark blue cab, dirty black bed, and jacked up with oversized tires stormed down the street without fanfare. When it passed Adrian, it slammed on the brakes and stopped on the other side of Elmer's house. The man jumped out and walked toward Adrian. He waggled his finger, "I told you I'd see you one day, you little piss ant."

Adrian turned and jumped in his skin. He climbed up the steps and hugged up against Elmer. Elmer dropped his glass and approached the rail. "What seems to be the problem, mister?"

The man stopped at the sidewalk; Leo Castellaw demonstratively waved his finger at Adrian. "That little punk tried to steal my dog." He reached to the back of his head. "Then he hit me with a damn stick and ran off."

Adrian gripped Elmer's shirt, sputtered out, "Elmer, the dog was crying."

"It's my dog," Leo said and sent two birds at a car as the driver drove by, hanging out the window watching the commotion. He added, "Come on back, and I'll show you something." Spread his legs and cupped his family jewels, and shook them a little too long.

"I was just trying to help the dog, Elmer." Elmer and Adrian looked down at Leo. Adrian yelled, "You don't deserve a dog." He took a baby step, "You're a mean owner."

"Adrian," Elmer said and wrapped his right arm around his back and pulled him back.

"You were being mean to him!"

Leo laughed out his mangled face. He was short, bowling-pin-shaped, with birthing hips, and hanger-ready, thin shoulders. He lived in Sherman, dressed Appalachian, in dingy, faded overalls and camouflage hunting boots. The only thing missing was a straw hat. He wheezed when he spoke, sweated as he walked, and his belly swelled like a biscuit baking in an oven. He stopped laughing and hung his clenched fists at his sides. "That's my dog, boy." He stepped closer.

"Stay where you are, mister."

Leo stopped. "I can do whatever I want with my dog." He stared hate at the boy, "Do you hear me?" He punched a fist into the other hand. "I'm going to give you a beating your daddy should have given you years ago." Leo reached down and started to undo his belt.

Elmer moved his right arm in front of Adrian, pushed him back against the wall, and stood in front of him, spoke to Leo, "We don't want any trouble."

Leo undid his belt and slapped it against a hand. "Give the boy up." Smacked hard. Adrian's head snapped back. "The boy!"

Elmer kept his eyes on Leo and spoke to Adrian, "Go in my bedroom." He stopped when Leo shifted his weight. He continued, "Get in the nightstand and bring me the object in the top drawer." He pushed Adrian toward the door, "Hurry." He turned his attention to Leo, "Go on home." Yelled back at Adrian, "And be careful."

Leo watched Adrian go into the house and growled at Elmer, "Give him up, old man." He shifted his head to see where Adrian went, "This is none of your business." When Adrian was out of sight, he moved up to the bottom step, "You don't know who you are messing with."

"Yes, I do," Elmer said, "You're Leo Castellaw. You been slinging drugs in this neighborhood for years."

Leo showed teeth. "This is my neighborhood." A hard thumb at his chest, "All mine."

Elmer glared and spoke calmly, "The kid hasn't even reached puberty. Whatever he did, he will apologize for, and you can be on your way."

"I said give him up, old man."

"I'll discipline the boy," Elmer snapped back and waved his left hand. "Go on, get in your truck, and go home. There is nothing here for you but trouble."

"Trouble?" Leo chuckled. "That kid must be unlucky or something." He put his right foot on the first step and leaned on his leg with an arm. "You're going to give me the boy." He shook his head. "I'm not leaving until you do." He extended his arms out at his sides. "I told you; this is my neighborhood, old man." He revved his voice, "I can do whatever I want with the both of you," he split his fingers at Elmer. Dialed it up, "Nobody . . . nobody is going to do anything about it. Don't be stupid, old man. Step aside." He laid his belt around his neck like a necklace and ran his thumbs up the inside of his suspenders, "Don't make me hurt you."

Adrian emerged from the house and stood behind Elmer. Elmer reached his right hand behind his back and snapped his fingers. Adrian put the gun in his hand and scooted to the other side of Elmer.

Elmer put the gun in his front pocket after showing it to Leo. He took out a cigar and lit it, puffed, and said, "I wouldn't take any more steps if I was you." Again, he tried to wave Leo away in a sign of strength, "Go on home now."

Adrian shivered next to Elmer and glued himself to his side.

Leo blustered, "No gun scares me." He spit tobacco juice on the bottom step, cleared a speck off a whisker with his finger, licked it, and spurted out, "I'm coming to get the boy." He moved a playing card away from the second step. He smelled like he bathed in the vomit of his customers and looked worse.

His toes hit the second step. Elmer said, "Don't get any closer," and raised the gun in front with both hands.

Leo stood on his tips, and looked at the end of the barrel, deep and black, smirked, "You going to shoot, old timer?" His right foot, left toes on the second step, teasing to reach the third and last step to join Elmer and Adrian.

Adrian grasped Elmer's shirt and squeezed tight.

Elmer reached down with his left hand and pulled Adrian behind him, and two-handed the gun.

"I'm coming," Leo teased and leaned forward. Leo was a blunt on life even in this neighborhood. Got rich on the suffering of others. Marred the hapless souls of the walking dead and had a bullseye on Adrian. Aiming to mete out his form of retribution for stealing his dog, spilling his own blood in his kingdom.

Elmer didn't want to shoot Leo and tried to appease him. "Go on home. I'll come down shortly and settle what the boy did to you."

Leo moved up to the third step. Elmer shuffled back, pushed Adrian against the wall and firmed his grip on the gun. "Stop," he said, a tingling ran up his spine.

Leo hesitated and slinked back down the steps, eyes on Adrian, spoke to Elmer, "You're making a big mistake."

"Not as big as the one you're about to make."

Leo tensed, grunted, and swallowed a mouthful of spit. Eyes on fire, he sneered, "The boy." He thudded the flesh of his palm against his forehead until it turned red and stepped back to the sidewalk. Venom dripped from the edges of his lips. "Now."

Elmer stayed even and calm, repeated, "Go home," barrel high and angled center mass on Leo. Loaded and ready to fire.

The calm wiggled into the mind of Leo. He slid back to the edge of the road.

Elmer relaxed and lowered his gun to a forty-five-degree angle, told Adrian, "Go in the house."

Leo watched with unsteady eyes and agitated feet. He spat and slobbered out, "This isn't over, kid," and backed away into the road.

Adrian stopped at the door and looked back. "In the house . . . now," Elmer said.

Elmer sighed. He believed Leo and shelved any words he had yet to speak and stood tall with the gun at his side and watched Leo lurk back, turn around and stomp off. Elmer released a long sigh of stress.

Leo pushed himself up into the truck and slammed his door, let the engine roar loud and angry, spun off as he honked. Didn't swerve to miss a cat. Elmer would clean that up the next day.

Elmer walked in the house, put the gun on the kitchen table, and looked at Adrian. Adrian was nestled up with Rocky on the couch, crying and hugging the dog like he was a child's tattered blanket. Rocky rubbed his jaw on Adrian's arm. Sternly Elmer said, "Stop your crying."

Adrian sputtered out, "I only wanted to help the dog," and caterwauled in the chest of Rocky.

Adrian's reasoning made Elmer happy, considering the situation. He had grown concerned with the hardening of the boy. He gently rubbed Adrian's head and peered out the window. "It's going to be okay." He glanced down at Adrian and saw a glint of perfection. Elmer would never admit it, but that is when he called Adrian his own. The son he never had. "Tell me what happened." Before Adrian could speak, Elmer flipped off the boy's shoes and socks and rubbed his feet until he calmed. Gently, he said, "Tell me, son."

Adrian wheezed and slobbered. Bubbles came out of his nose. He wiped it with a sleeve and spoke with ferocity. "I- let- the- dog- off the chain and . . . and . . . was going to bring him home. When I got up the fence, he threw me down to the ground." He raised his elbow and showed Elmer the scrape. "You see it, Elmer?"

"I see it."

"I tried to find another way out. He was going to kill me, Elmer." He covered his face with both hands and sobbed. Elmer stood up when he heard the squealing of tires.

He peeked out the drapes as he spoke, "Adrian, uncover your face. I can't understand what you are trying to say." He exhaled when the car screamed by the house and headed toward Main Street.

"He's going to come back and kill me," he wailed.

"Calm down. He isn't going to kill anybody. Relax," he said and walked in the kitchen, "I'll get you a drink."

# CHAPTER 9

Adrian had peace the first few days of the week. Thursday morning, Elmer sipped coffee and watched the news. Contemplated what to do about the situation and questioned himself. Why did he let Adrian walk the dog alone at night, especially in this neighborhood? Guilt settled in his stomach like concrete. He feared this was the episode that would mentally and spiritually break the boy. He knew Leo's type, had seen his type of behavior for over thirty years. Elmer rehearsed the night in his mind. *Was I too calm? Did the gun spook him or incense him more?* He knew the answer before he finished the thought; Leo was no stranger to gunplay.

Elmer picked up the phone and dialed. After she answered, he said, "Jane Mitchell, please."

"This is Jane."

"Jane, Elmer Ray, I was hoping you would remember me."

"Oh," she said, "of course, I remember you, Mr. Ray. How can I help you?"

Elmer got right to the point. "Jane, I'm in need of some professional advice, and you're the only social worker I know."

"Okay . . . I guess I might be able to help."

Elmer explained the relationship between Adrian and himself. "I'm really worried about the little guy."

"Did you and Bessie ever have children?"

They wanted children, tried without success, but she ended up getting the death in her chest and succumbed too early in life. "No," he said, "wasn't in the cards for us."

"Oh," she said. After seconds of silence, "Elmer, children need to be nurtured." She laughed as thoughts of her own children entered her mind. "I remember when my own were little, my husband and I would have to chase them around the house and hold them down to brush their teeth."

Elmer questioned why he made the call. He sat and held the phone out from his ear and gasped. *Oh boy.*

She continued, "We would brush for them, call for them to spit and continue the same routine day and night. Some parents do it for years before their children learn to brush on their own."

"You saying to saying to teach Adrian to brush his teeth? I'm not sure but I believe he does. I haven't got a strong whiff of his breath, but . . ."

Laughter.

Elmer extended the phone once more.

She said, "No, Mr. Ray . . . what I'm trying to say is that if we don't show them how to act, then how will they know the proper conduct?"

Elmer went with her explanation. "Guess it makes sense."

"You say, Adam?"

"It's Adrian."

"Adrian likes to fight?"

"Yeah, the little shit likes to use his fists. Has a bad mouth. Says a lot of dumb shit."

"I'd say he has experienced some type of trauma or has been taught to use physical actions to communicate." She cleared her throat, "He probably hears bad words come out of the mouths of adults he is around. Maybe," she paused, "try using the word poop instead of . . . um . . . um . . . you know."

"Poop?"

"Yes, poop or crap. Whatever word best fits the context."

"Most of the time, shit seems like the best word to use. Stop the dumb poop doesn't sound the best."

"Mr. Ray, those decisions are up to you. However, just so you know, Adrian will develop based on those around him. If you curse, more than likely, he will curse."

"Interesting."

That night, after the sun slept, Adrian jumped off Elmer's porch, cleared all three steps, and bolted toward his house. Excited to see his mom for the first time all day, he wanted to get a quick bath. He hopped on the second step of his porch, right hand on the rail. Hopped again, the slick surface tossed him high, legs vertical, back flat. He landed and slid toward the house. Heels banged against the door. He gathered himself and palmed the porch with his left hand. Flipped over on his stomach in a push-up position. Pushed up, he saw a sight he would never unsee. Nose to nose. One dead eye, dried and flat black, stared back at him. He pushed back with his legs and hands, landing on his butt. His gaze took his head to the right, and he saw the rest of the dog's body. Severed from the head. He scooted back to the door. Kept his eyes on the dog and pushed his legs to get upright. Turned to run and slipped, landing face-first in the blood of the dog. He released one piercing cry before the fear shock-collared around his throat and muted his voice.

Elmer heard the cry, barged out the door, and looked over at the Franklin house. He hobbled down and swallowed at the sight—a wisp of a boy, streaks of blood from the animal clung to him. The animal Adrian tried to save. The sight stunned Elmer momentarily, and he hesitated before grasping Adrian by the shoulders. He was covered in blood, thick and sticky. Eyes absent of life, no fear, ghost eyes.

Elmer tried to shake him out of his tonic state. He froze. Hands on his face. He pinched his face and said his name. Nothing. Adrian didn't move or blink. Elmer stared at a black hole of nothingness. He said, "I'll be right back," and laid Adrian on the ground.

He stumbled as he began to run. Ignored the twinge in his hip. He blocked the pain and clambered up the steps and into his house and called for help. When he returned, Adrian was sitting up and shivering and trembling as his eyes locked on the dog like magnets. Elmer wrapped him in his arms. Adrian's eyes went vertical. The earth rotated around him, and stars swirled and spun. "Elmer?" His eyelids drooped below the whites, and his body went limp. Elmer caught him. Held him tight and rocked him until help arrived.

After Adrian was transported to the hospital, Elmer could not quell his tears any longer. He sat at the kitchen table and sobbed as he waited for Cindy. Wondered what he could have done differently. Why did he let him take Rocky for a walk? He knew Leo's type. Saw his type of behavior in the joint. He should have known Leo would do something so corrupt and evil. How did he miss it? He gripped his head and pictured Adrian, pale in the night, blood-soaked, sodden hair, whites comatose in fear and continued a lamentable cry.

Elmer brooded over the incident for hours. He lumbered around the kitchen at the pace of a dead man as he waited for Cindy.

She knocked and called out, "Mr. Ray?"

"Coming," he said. The few steps to the door were a marathon. How do you tell a mother her only child was transported to the hospital? He stepped, felt like he was carrying sandbags. Next step felt like cinderblocks were shackled to his feet. As he approached the door, the weight of the world compressed him. He opened the door with a doleful face, "Mrs. Franklin," he said softly. He stepped to the side, "Please come in and sit down."

"Is Adrian here?"

"There has been an accident."

She faced him. "Accident?"

He gestured toward the couch. "Please sit, Mrs. Franklin."

"Where is Adrian?" She twisted away, called out, "Adrian?"

"Cindy?" Hand in hand. "Please."

She sunk into the couch. Imagined the worst. Been through the worst. Not again. She sucked the air out of the room and said, "What is it?"

Elmer sat, cupped her hands in his, and calmly said, "Adrian is in the hospital."

Her head vibrated from side to side. She began crying.

"He is okay."

She calmed, gasped air, and asked, "What happened?"

Elmer explained the situation without mentioning Leo or the incident from the other day. She stood. Elmer joined her. She hugged him and whispered, "Thank you for everything you do for him." At the door, she said, "I'll call you in the morning."

"Please do."

The next three days moved at a snail's pace. Adrian was released from the hospital and carried on like nothing had happened. The incident occupied Elmer's mind all day and night. Leo wasn't charged with a crime, not even a jaywalking ticket.

On the fourth day, Elmer went for a walk to Leo's house. Limped down the road with a purpose and knocked on the door.

Leo smirked when he saw Elmer at the bottom of his steps and stepped out, "What are you doing here, old man.?" "You must have a damn death wish or something."

"Or something."

Leo coiled back when Elmer reached in his pocket. Elmer pulled the card and stuck it out. "What's that?"

"Take it."

Leo kept his eyes on Elmer as he reached for the card. That smirk again, "1-222-555-9999. Whose number is this? Your wife's?" A laugh. A flip of the card at Elmer, "Go away, old-timer, before you regret it."

As Leo turned around, Elmer called out, "Mr. Gallo would like to talk to you."

Leo stopped midstride and lowered his face. As he turned to face him, he spoke lightly, "Angelo Gallo?"

Elmer shot a smirk back, spoke with confidence, "Oh, forgot to tell you the other night. The night when you chose to prey on a young boy over a dog. The night you—"

"I know what night you are talking about," Leo fidgeted as fear dropped from the sky and smacked him in his face.

"Angelo and I were friends when you were sucking Mountain Dew out of a baby bottle down in Kentucky." Elmer was sure Leo and Angelo Gallo were not on a first-name basis. He was enjoying this moment more than he could have imagined. He rehearsed these words in his mind over the past few days. Words he wanted to say to Leo. Now, listening to the words flow out of his lips made him feel a decade younger. Old pains subsided momentarily.

Leo's lips quivered. He reluctantly grabbed the card from Elmer when he stuck it out once again.

"I'd call if I was you, Leo."

Leo winced as he thought about the call. Elmer recoiled at his facial expression. "Go on," he said to Leo. "I got dinner on the stove, and Adrian is waiting for me." Leo shivered. Elmer saw the fear, and he continued, "You brought this on yourself, Leo." Now more forceful, "Hurry up and call Mr. Gallo." Leo didn't respond. "Care if I sit on your steps?" He grabbed his knee. "I ache at my old age." No response. "I'll just wait right here while you call." Elmer heard the door close and peered back to see Leo take the phone off the wall and dial. He stood up when he heard the door open. With a flat expression, he cleared his throat and said, "You won't be coming back." Looked at the time on his watch, "You have three minutes to gather what you can."

Slumped shoulders, a tiny voice, "Three?"

"Two and half now."

Leo turned quickly into the house. Elmer heard some banging and shuffling feet. He turned toward the street when the limo arrived. Spoke to Leo when he felt him from behind, "It's time." He pulled a cigar from his shirt and lit it. Smoke dribbled out of the corner of his mouth. A boss move. It couldn't have been more perfect if he practiced it in front of a mirror as he watched a gangster flick. He turned and blew smoke at Leo. "He wanted to kill you, Leo."

"Is he?"

"I wanted to kill you. You terrorized a young boy because he trespassed in your yard. How does that make you feel?"

Leo slumped.

"Not so tough now." Elmer nudged his cane toward the car, "Get in the car."

Leo took a step and spoke, "Where am I going?"

"The driver has been instructed to drop you off at the state line." He inched closer. "You're going home, Leo."

"Kentucky?"

"You're not to come back . . . ever." Elmer shooed him like a mangled mutt begging for scraps. "Go on," he said and gestured with the back of his hand. Leo glanced back momentarily, then put his head down and walked toward the limo. The driver got out, dressed to the hilt, even at this time of night, saluted Elmer, walked behind the limo, and opened the door for Leo. He got in reluctantly. Elmer leaned his head in, snapped his gums, and lit another cigar. Slowly, his lips puffed the cigar. Leo held a suffering gaze and imagined what sinister plan was in play. As Elmer jostled the cigar between his lips, it reminded Leo of the madman Gallo without the suit. Frightened him no less. Elmer flicked ash in Leo's lap like a boss. Leo's eyes were repelled by the ash, and he gulped his saliva. "Leo," Elmer boasted and sent a jaundiced eye, "if you ever come back . . ." Leo gulped again as he waited for him to finish. Elmer wagged a thick, night-crawler finger at him, finished with, "I'll have you killed," and slammed the door shut. He stepped away from the curb, offered his appreciation to the driver, and watched the wheels roll away.

# CHAPTER 10

# The Day Before

Elmer sat in his chair under the light of the streetlamp in the darkness, smelling the aroma of his morning drink, feeling the warmth of the ceramic cup as he anguished over making the call years in the making. He never expected to make the call. If he did, never over dire circumstances. He picked up the receiver and dialed. "Angelo Gallo, please."

"Hello?"

Louder, "Mr. Gallo?"

She spoke in a matter-of-fact tone. "What is this regarding?"

"Tell him Elmer Ray is calling. I . . ." The sentence stuck in his throat. Asking him, of all people, for help was not in the cards.

"One moment." Minutes later, she spoke in an apologetic tone, "I'm sorry, sir. Mr. Gallo is in a meeting."

"Oh . . . um, can I leave a message?"

"Yes, sir."

"Hell, he probably won't even remember me, but can you tell him Elmer Ray called?" He gulped as his pride hit his stomach.

"Does Mr. Gallo have your—"

Elmer hung up without letting her finish. If Angelo remembered him, he had the resources to find his number, any number. Hours later, the phone rang. "Hello."

"My old friend."

"Angelo."

"Mr. Ray, it has been way too long," the strong voice said. Type you hear in an Old Spice commercial.

"Ten years or so."

"Or so."

"Yeah."

"Mr. Ray, is this business or pleasure?"

It was the second time he called him Mr. Ray. It wasn't lost on Elmer. Angelo Gallo was the guy who slept with the prom queen. All of them. Every man was afraid of him, and every girl wanted him. Even inside the pen, Angelo didn't meander around; each step, decision, and word had a purpose. It was satisfying to Elmer that he still had the respect of his old clerk in prison all these years after he was released.

Angelo told him to call him if he needed anything. He never did. They interacted twice previously after Angelo's release from prison. First, when Angelo's daughter, Nicole, was murdered. It sent Columbus into a frenzy. Those things happen when the daughter of the head of the Gallo Clan, Drug Lords of the Midwest, dies under suspicious circumstances. The CPD and the Feds assumed it was a hit. It was a run-of-the-mill murder. Abusive husband finally went too far. Poor bastard didn't last a weekend in county.

Elmer went to the funeral. Stood out like a sore thumb. Thousand-dollar suits, cars more expensive than his house, and one old man on a cane with suspenders to hold up his pants. He stuck out like a pimple on a Victoria's Secret supermodel. Angelo spotted him. They shared a nod. Respect and admiration were cemented with the gesture from Elmer.

"I'm afraid this is a business call."

"One second, Mr. Ray." Elmer heard Angelo tell his secretary to cancel his next meeting. Then, "Let's meet."

"Well . . ."

"Mr. Ray, I'll have a car pick you up in a half hour."

Heavy breathing.

"Elmer?"

"Sure. Yeah. Sounds good, Angelo."

"Elmer?"

"Yeah."

"You still on Ewing?"

"Ay huh . . ."

Elmer sounded surprised Angelo knew his address. Since the first day the new inmate be-bopped into his office like John Travolta with a swagger and confidence no other inmate had, they had a strange and instant connection. Deputy Warden Ray heard the rumors about his new clerk. Powerful, influential, the most corrupt individual member of the clan. Angelo should have been doing decades in prison, but witnesses were either too afraid to testify or ended up disappearing without a trace. He got fifteen years. Did his last seven as a clerk for the deputy warden. Elmer figured that assignment was rigged. No way in hell a person with his reputation would normally get a primo inmate job.

No matter. Elmer was not one to judge. They spent hours together talking about football, kids, and world events. No topic was off-limits. Elmer never brought up Angelo's appetite for the criminal life or his pheromones for attracting trouble. An unexpected friendship, two friends talking about life. Angelo always respected Elmer for treating him with respect, as an equal. Elmer fetched him coffee as much as Angelo did for him. As an inmate trustee (secretary), Angelo made copies of reports, answered his phone, boring remedial duties. Elmer always greeted him with a please and thank you. Asked and not ordered. Neither man asked the other to cross the ethical line in their relationship, to bring in drugs or other contraband. And both knew a boatload of money was to be made if they did.

The day of Angelo's release, the men embraced, and Angelo looked at his friend and said, "If you ever need anything, you make sure you call me." He spoke with a sincerity that could not be mistaken.

Elmer said, "Live long and prosper."

Angelo got the last word, "I'll never forget how decent you have been to me."

Elmer stared.

"I'll always consider you a dear friend, Mr. Ray."

The car picked Elmer up at nine thirty sharp and drove him to a local diner. A spot Angelo Gallo had never frequented. A place he figured Elmer would be comfortable.

After a few minutes of pleasantries, Angelo broke the ice, "What is this about, Mr. Ray?"

Elmer explained the situation with Adrian, down to the last drop of blood on the porch. He even told him about their background, the day they met.

Angelo saw the affection for the boy in the tone and his facial expressions, "It's obvious the kid is important to you."

"If he wasn't, I wouldn't have called you."

"When do you want this done?"

"Tomorrow."

Angelo signaled for the driver, who quickly walked over. Angelo spoke in his ear, and when he walked away, he pulled a card out of his pocket and slid it across the table. "Tom," he gestured with his head to the door, "he'll be there at eight."

Elmer examined the card.

"Have Leo call that number. We.........you and I will make sure Leo never bothers anybody in your neighborhood again."

"Thanks, Angelo."

Angelo stood up and shook Elmer's hand, "Don't be a stranger."

"Everybody is a stranger these days."

"Oh," Angelo said, "you sure did look handsome at Bessie's funeral."

# CHAPTER 11

# Conner Wallace
# 2004

onner rode the rat bike across the Nevada sands like a Frankenstein monster in an apocalypse. He pulled into the Sand Pie Bar off I-80, outside of Reno, and cooled the engine. He rolled off the bike horse-saddle sore in his crotch and stiff-legged. Put his eyes toward the sun and let out a howl to wake his limbs. He waddled toward the door and entered the bar with the sands of the desert nibbling at his feet. A man stood behind the bar. Four men and a little lady hovered around a pool table on his right. He beat a crick out of his neck and stretched his legs in the doorway, and surveyed his surroundings. Nicotine stains coated the ceiling yellow. Smoke lingered. The Sand Pie had four windows. Three were shaded, strings of sunlight bent around thick dust motes. Neon beer lights provided most of the light. *My kind of place.* He walked with a swagger toward the bar and took a seat at a high boy.

"Canna get a drink?" the stranger said, coughed a plume of dust, and blew sand out deep from his lungs. His throat felt like he had bathed in it. The bartender considered the man in front of him a foreigner, he guessed, big and bold. The heat and the sand rutted wrinkles deep in his face like wet grass earthed over by an eighteen-wheeler. His skin was leathered, and sand clung to his clothes. The tender remained silent; he slid a cold one over the counter. "See is hot out thus," the man said and gulped half.

The bartender grabbed a towel from behind, tossed it at his patron, and said, "Ayuh, summer in Nevada, summer in the desert." As the man wiped his forehead, he added, "You're not from around here? Headed to Vegas?"

"Nah sir, am from over de pond, der pawl," the stranger said and guzzled down the second half. He slammed the bottle and said, "Ay thought I'd come over and check out yours Yanks." He tapped the bar with a knuckle and motioned with a finger for another, "Ay came over a few years back, and na left." The bartender slid another over, and the stranger lifted the bottle and stopped at a lip. "Ay 'uv date wi' a friend down de road," he said and gulped his second. He wiped his neck and arms with the towel and tossed it at the bartender.

"I've never been to England," the tender said and caught the towel, "Heck, I've never been any place."

Both heard the banging and yelling over the stranger's right shoulder. A hard smack of flesh on flesh, then, "Bitch, I told you to go get me another beer." The commotion took their eyes. A man had a woman in his grasp. Three others cackled behind a table a foot away. "Ah," he continued and pulled her long dark mane close to him.

The four men dressed the same: faded jeans, black vest over a white t-shirt. The girl wore a skintight blouse, a short skirt, and knee-high boots, her long black hair in a ponytail.

She whined, "Colt, I didn't hear you." Gargled and tried again, "Colt, please let me go . . . let me get you another beer."

"Fucking tired of you not listening," he moaned and pulled and spun her around and slapped her again.

She gasped and pleaded, "Babe, I'm sorry. I'll go get you another right now."

"Damn local idiots," the bartender said. He was flustered by the constant conflict created by the local biker gang. He slid a third over to his customer and poured a shot, and downed it.

The stranger pounded down the third and fisted it on the table. Three was enough to sate his thirst momentarily. He thumbed a cap until he drew blood. He eyed the boyfriend as he pulled her hair again to show off for his buddies, and the four shared a laugh at her expense. "Whuz is de bathrewn?" he asked as he stood and tightened his belt, and shook out his hands. He sucked the end of his thumb and started a slow walk. Eyes on the table.

The bartender gestured with his head to his left, the stranger's right. Lifted his head and studied the stranger. The foreigner seemed a little giddy. Thinking there was an inscrutable allure about him as he walked toward the bathroom, he stroked his jowl and hollered, "Leave it alone." The bartender grew uneasy. He sensed something bad turning worse. He rooted around under the bar and grabbed his aluminum bat, laid it on the counter, and massaged it like a woman. He drummed his knuckles on the bat and wondered if he had been cursed by some witch doctor in a previous life.

The stranger ambled toward the pool table. Colt had his right hand wrapped around the neck of his lady. A table full of empties separated Colt from his three friends. "Ay yous an Indian?"

Colt pivoted around when he heard the voice. He faced the stranger. Eyed his girl, she had a clown's mouth as he held her firm. Looked over at his friends, laughed, he said, "Who the hell is this guy?" Words soaked in whiskey.

Two shrugged their shoulders. The third said, "Beats the hell out of me," and nudged one on his left.

He said, "No, Colt, never seen him."

"Nicole," Colt said, "a friend of yours?" He pulled her around so she could see his face.

"No, babe," she winced when he pulled on hair again, "I've never seen him before."

"Yous keep pullin', she wul be ugly as yous."

"Excuse me?" Colt said and when the stranger didn't answer, his voice surged at the third guy, "You?"

He piped up, "Doesn't look familiar."

"Who the fuck you think you are?" That was Colt.

The stranger took three steps forward, stood next to the side pocket and leaned his left hip against the rail, "W's yer Indian name?" he asked, relaxed and confident.

Colt pushed his girl away by the throat and tensed up, asked again, "Who the fuck are you?" He fisted a stick and slammed it against the table. After the third time, it snapped in half.

The stranger didn't answer the question but did offer up, "Ler me guess yous Indian name." He put both hands on the rail, stretched his left calf, then his right. "Ay 'eard dee name babies," he said and stared at Colt, paused, cracked the knuckles in both hands, "Afti wa'is appen doin their birth." Another step, Colt and stranger stood an arm's length away. Colt put his right hand behind his back, a blade or pistol assumed the stranger, a blade or bullet meant for him. His left hand held the stick. Sounds of bottles bouncing off the table caught their attention, three now stood. "So," the stranger said and glanced at the table and leaned in low and looked up at Colt, giving him the sense of strength. "Am go'n ter say yous name is two fags fuckin."

"You—"

Before Colt finished his sentence, the stranger stepped with his right foot and right hand and grabbed him by the throat. He pivoted with the rhythm of a ballet dancer and held Colt between himself and the friends. Sized them up and slammed Colt's head into the pool table. The stick bounced. The stranger blocked it with his right foot and kicked it under the pool table. Two pulled their weapons. The stranger pulled a .45 out of his waistband and sized up the middle guy as he held the neck of Colt. "Am not I'd move if any wuz yous three." The words might have been foreign, but the barrel spoke a universal language. He heard the girl mewl to his right. He caught her out of the corner of his eye. She was cowered under the window. He gestured for the two to lay their weapons on the table, and when they did, he spoke to the girl, "W's name, love?"

Jaws as tight as a bear trap. The stranger huffed and grinded molars. Felt the girl drift toward him from the window. "Mister," she said, "what is your name?"

He turned, smiled with his mouth wide, and spoke in a genteel tone, "I'm Conner Wallace, ma'am," he said and lowered his head. "It's nice to meet yous."

"I'm Nicole," she said and flipped tendrils of black hair from her face. "Conner, sir," she fumbled her words, "Honestly, Colt didn't mean anything by it," she pleaded, almost cooing to Conner as if they were together. He was jealous of her act. He missed the touch of his girl, her encouragement, the stand-by-your-man type of girl.

His facial expression softened as he spoke to her, "Ay," he started to say when Colt said, "I'm going to kill you, foreigner."

Conner squeezed the throat until he heard a gurgle, "Ah ye nah." He lifted Colt off the table, reached behind his back with his left, took the piece and secured it in his waistline, then spoke to the four of them, "Ay juss came e'yer ter get refreshed and ay see yous be'n disrespectful ter yous woman." He leaned his backside against the table with Colt in his lap. Gestured for the three to sit. After they did, "Didn't yer mom ever teach yous manners?"

Colt strained to say, "You don't know who you are messing with." Colt and his friends were part of a Reno motorcycle gang, the Desert Rats, a mush fake gang that thought more highly of themselves than others did. In the mind of others, they were more like the Apple Dumpling or the Dirty Underwear Gang. Outlaws would allow, use them to distribute small quantities of drugs throughout northwest Nevada to the outskirts of California. They provided the kiddie gang protection and lined their wallets with a little money; enough to allow them to escape real jobs and lay around in bars and terrorize the locals. They were destined to be no more than rapscallions owned by the one percenter.

He gripped Colt's hair tight around his hand, "Ay huh," he said. "Ow do yous like it?" and stared at the three. He kicked the tabletop toward them, "Yous tree like ter deck womun ter?"

The table creaked as it slid. One guy overflowed and collapsed the seat into pieces and hit the floor. A hell of a moment in his first siege, a time to show his worth to his brothers in arms. A looby sack of shit. Bulbous body. His mother first, then his ex-wife, and now his crew had preached to him he needed to lose weight. He hustled up on his feet when he heard, "Get up," and adjusted his pants.

One said, "You okay."

Another, "Oh shit."

"Yup," the fat boy stammered and stood.

Conner watched them with amusement. He quipped, "Yer mommas would 'uv gottun better use outi yous if she swallowed." He picked up the only drink left on the table and splashed it down his throat, "Damn millennials." He continued, "10,000,000 sperm and yew were the fastest?" Then to the bartender, "Oo de fuck puts frewt in alcohol?" He faced the three again, "Yous tree like ter deck womun ter," he repeated. He jutted his forehead out and searched for the answers out of the top of his eyes. Conner had learned over the past few years, when confronted with strength and anger, most men squirmed for a way out of conflict. They were no different, dams broke in their mouths, words flooded the room, "No, my momma always taught me to respect the female gender," one said.

Another said, "I'm just here to enjoy the day . . . like you, Mister."

Slavish followers.

Colt said, "You're a dead man."

A squeeze led to Nicole to say, "Shut up, Colt."

The tender limped over and grasped the table with a hand. Cleared his throat to knock the gravelly tone out, "Mister," he called out and gasped heavily. When he caught the stranger's attention, he spoke with his bat, "Don't mind him." He waved the bat over his shoulder toward the bar, "Come on back. I'll buy you a drink."

Conner grimaced and squeezed the apple once more, a prehensile tool attached to his arm, gave a curt nod and dismissed him quickly, "I'll buy me bill bevvy, ta." Nodded vigorously. As Colt tried to slink away to his left, Conner said, "I'll break yer arm if yous move again."

Conner looked at the bartender, who was now standing at the other end of the pool table. The light from the neon above spotlighted the aluminum in his hand. "His multitalented, sure," he said to the bartender, "He can talk and piss me off at the same time." He glared at Colt, his partners, who had their chairs pushed back from the table. Conner shimmered in his arousal.

The bartender said, "Oh, Colt isn't worth it. Let him go." When Conner only responded with a bulldog stare, he tried again, "Come over to the bar," he gestured with his head, "Drinks are on me." Conner wrapped Colt's tiny apple in the palm of his hand. Looked like a banana in the palm of a gorilla. Colt opened wide; three crowns glistened in the lights. The tender's balls sucked up his scrotum. He stepped and stumbled forward and knocked the six ball in the corner pocket with his hand. He pivoted around and crabbed back toward the bar with a withered look.

"Nice shot," Conner said. Shifted around to face the three friends, "Yous tres better 'ed get outi e'yer before yous got shot." They remained seated. Conner chambered one and dead-eyed it at the one in the middle, "Go!"

The tender poured himself a drink. Flipped the bat to the ground and pouted as he slung down two. Spoke loud and angry, "You're going to cause me a lot of trouble." He belched and hammered his head into the table. He picked up the bat, canoodled it like a silk blanky. He called for Conner again, "Come on," this time small and whiny.

Conner gave him a dubious glare and threw a wink. The tender groaned with an enfeebled face. Conner firmed his grip and jabbed the gun toward the three, "Go!" After they scurried out of the front door, Conner thought to himself, *Americans were supposed to be tougher than this.* He combed his teeth with his scratchy tongue, ached to return to his drink, pissed the yellow belly's split, and he still had to deal with the one who brought him off his stool. He mounted his gun at the waist, wrapped Colt's hair with the left, held the apple with his right and got mouth to mouth with Colt and barked in his face like a dog. He scrunched up his nose and showed a point of a tooth. He felt Colt's paunchy midsection against his, thumped against him quick and sudden. Full of piss and vinegar before, now frightened to the core.

Colt thought he was going to die. Conner's eyes told him so. Pupils swelled angry and burst like exploding stars. And his smile, that glorious smile, only shown in people in the happiest moments. The smile scared Colt the most. As he watched from afar, the tender noticed Conner was more boisterous with each word. He knew he needed another drink. He pulled a full fifth from below and slammed a mug on the counter and poured. Drank as he watched the destruction.

A nimbus followed Conner, haloed over him, a contempt for the world. Hate slowly ate him like rust on a car. Brawling and breaking bones felt as natural to him as a family opening presents on Christmas morning. Colt's blistering tone replaced by a small mouth and mice words, he spoke like he was pleading for another day, "M-S-T-E." Conner released his grip, the bruised apple had a moment to heal, words sprung from the gut, "I didn't mean any harm." He swallowed, "I'll be better to her." Conner tightened his grip on the pipe. Colt wheezed.

Conner saw a flicker of movement out of the corner as the girl squirmed at his side. She stared at Conner like he was a phantom in the night, coming to steal her soul, not the knight in shining armor that just saved her ass and a chunk of hair. Rummaged in her purse and pulled a gloss. Vain. Woeful eyes. Blood trickled out the corner of her mouth. She lizard licked it and swallowed. Brought a beckoning smile. Conner was keenly aware of her game. To him, she looked like a possessed victim in a horror movie. Tone changed like the wind in a storm as she approached from over his shoulder with ominous ambition. "Let my ole man go, you son of a bitch," she hollered and palmed him on the back of the shoulder. Not the pleading face or the beggar's tone from before. She was close enough to taste her scent.

His eyes glazed over the top of her head. Blotched hair. Told him something about Colt: this wasn't the first time. She'd pull remnants of hair for days. An emanated ignorance. In Nicole, he saw a familiar face. Smile faded. He had a thought: *Self-hate.*

His heart swelled with pity for her and her pending future with Colt. For tomorrow, he knew she would be at his side like a good puppy fetching drinks and taking shots. But today, he held Colt's future in his hands. But no matter what rancid imagination he thought Colt would do to her in the future could lead him down the path of killing him. He didn't have time to deal with bullshit. She tapped her heel on the wood floor; sounded like a damn woodpecker. He began bobbing his head with the sound of her foot. His eyes cut through her like glass, he hoarsed out, "Stupid bitch." He didn't expect her to squabble and villainize him. She sent Medusa eyes back and wagged her tongue out. He blinked, refocused, and telescoped an eye at her, hissed and said, "Yous get wa' yous deserve." His words lashed her heart like a thousand paper cuts. She coiled back and looked at Conner with a scornful face. He pulled his gun with his right hand, waved it at the girl until she walked away. When she did, he faced Colt and tapped the gun on his forehead to make sure Colt was as focused as him and eased the pressure on the pipe. "Yous a wanna die?" He held him tight, pressed down in the mouth like he was aiming to collect a precious jewel lost in his throat. Face broke out into a horror movie leer. Venomous teeth hung like chimes in a window.

"No, no, I—" Conner put his finger to the lips and shushed him.

He extended his left arm with Colt hanging at the end, raised his head to the ceiling and struck himself in the head with the handle of the gun, and cackled like a villainous cartoon character. The bartender and Nicole ran for the door when they heard sirens. Conner brought Colt close, intimately close and said, "Can we be friends?"

His lips quivered, parted slowly as he considered the right words, voiced hitched, "Yes, yes, we are friends."

The gun went to the waistband, hands on the front of Colts shirt, eyes bulged, Conner stepped back said, "Ay dun need any friends." Colt felt the jolt of the words like he was on a thoroughbred. "I'm go'n ter stop yous from be'n saddy," Conner said and cocked the hammer of his head back and slammed it into the nose of Colt. He shifted his hips, threw Colt out of the window, walked back to the bar, and waited to order another drink. He heard the whipping sound of the sirens and spun around in the chair. Nicole and the others stood outside the door. Conner got to his knees and interlocked his fingers behind his head a stared at the door. When Nicole peered in through the window, he said, "You're a blaggin anytime, Annie."

Police arrived. Nicole, the friends, and the bartender denied Colt started any confrontation and all went on about the foreigner who went mad. Conner stood in front of the county magistrate and pleaded guilty to assault with a deadly weapon. He was sentenced to five years in the Nevada State Prison System.

# CHAPTER 12

# Adrian Franklin
# 1991

B am woke from a four-day hangover and stared at the ceiling fan as the banging continued at the front door. Then, the strangest thing crossed his mind. *Why do they have a ceiling fan in this rat trap?* He blinked with each bang. Felt like a nail was being hammered between his eyes. "Stop!" he yelled and rolled off from the center of his bed. His face hit first. He wobbled down the steps, one foot then the other like an old man with a back problem and lack of bladder control.

Another bang.

"I'm coming!" he screamed. To Russ, who had his head cocooned under the couch pillow, "You don't hear that?"

A mumble and a roll.

"Figured as much." He kicked an empty pizza box from in front of the door and tried to pull the door off its hinges as he opened it. He rasped out, "What?" His hands went to his eyes, calmer, "What do you want?"

"Good morning, sir."

Bam blinked a few times in the light. The blue-collar shirt with BIG AL's lettered in a bold white caught his attention first, "Can I help you with something?" he said, a stench of vomit chasing each word. His eyes cut away to the twenty-four-foot truck behind the two guys at the door. He turned and shook his head and kicked the couch. "Get up," he said and sat at the feet of Russ. "Come on. Get moving."

Russ stirred, raised his head, "What is it?"

"Just get up," Bam said and hollered at the door. "You guys can come on in." The men stood on the threshold. After they entered, he said, "Don't mind the mess."

"We drank too much." That was Russ.

Bam picked up the pizza box, and frisbee swung it at him, "Just get up."

Russ caught it, flipped the lid, and mumbled, "Sure I left one piece," and flung it over his head into the kitchen.

"You taking the fridge?"

Russ piped up, "Why they taking the fridge?"

"It wasn't a statement; it was a question," Bam said as the guy flipped through Cindy's purchase sheet. He flipped and flipped. "Get up. I'm positive they need the couch."

"Damn," Russ said, "your mom sure rents a lot of shit." He had seen this picture before, a rent-to-own company showing unannounced to repo furniture after Cindy failed to pay the weekly bill. He got to his feet and touched shoulder-to-shoulder with Bam. "Why you positive about the couch? It's my bed."

"It's the newest thing in here."

Both turned when the guy said, "Fridge is paid up til next week."

"You can get it then," Russ said, chuckled, ate his lip when Bam glared.

The guy looked beyond the boys into the kitchen and glanced around the room at his inventory, and motioned for the movers. A heaping pile of bottles and cans flowed over the side of the trash can, looking like ten pounds of sugar in a five-pound bag. First, it was Bam's breath, now the smell of a party house wafted toward them. A god-awful smell built into the bones of the house. One mover wanted to ask if he could come to the next party—it was that night—as he drifted toward the rail, wrapped his hand around a spindle, and looked up the stairs. The other was half-tempted to let the furniture die with the house.

Russ gave him a sideways glare and whispered to Bam, "They taking your fucking bed, dude?"

Bam pushed him, "You've seen my bed." Then, after Russ landed on his ass, "Get up and help me clean this place up." To the guys, "We would help, but . . ." His arms flailed at the room.

The partner picked up on it. "Been there before . . . we got it."

The other guy interrupted, spoke to his partner, "Television, couch, chair." He motioned over the boy's head, "Kitchen table—"

"Kitchen fucking table . . . your mom rents the table and chairs?"

"Shut the fuck up."

Russ mocked Bam, lolled into the kitchen, and opened the fridge, "Yeah," he eased out, "still have beer." He burped a spoonful of last night into his hand and stood there and examined it. "What?" he said as six eyes studied him like he was a dead body.

One shivered like he had the willies. The other hid his eyes and pretended to flip through the purchase order. Bam stood expressionless, flatly said, "You are the biggest idiot I know."

A cackle. Red-faced, sweat eased down his face. Russ swiped at his thigh, "Couldn't help it."

Bam ignored that, spoke to the movers, "How long you need?"

"Hour tops."

Bam went upstairs, left the movers to attend to their jobs, their product, his furniture. He flopped on his bed and chased the oar of the ceiling fan, like a cat chasing a blinking light. Round and round. Hours later, with an empty house and no money for food or beer, they did what any teenage boys would do. They threw a party.

The house was bursting from the seams with teenagers and a few adults. He almost told Russ no when he mentioned a party. Almost. Like the pied piper, teenagers worked their way toward his house like they were being pulled by gravity. It was inevitable dozens would show up at his front door regardless of an invite. Nobody else knew a parent who left every single weekend, left their only child to fend for himself. In the two previous senior yearbooks, the graduating seniors picked Bam's house as the place to be on weekends. If you asked him, he wouldn't call any of them a friend. An acquaintance, maybe. From the looks of it, he was going to be a three-time winner.

Today, unlike the others, he wasn't feeling it. Tired of the babbling. Sick of the crowding. He escaped the noise and settled on the porch. He felt lower than a snake's belly, a few shovels away from being in the ground. He studied the sky with a subdued expression and flared his nostrils as the Mead paper mill's candy cane smokestack released its tonnage of gray from its bowels. Smoke umbrellaed the neighborhood as the stacks punctured the clouds. It was the place to work, paid the best, left its waste on everything and person. Ewing was two streets away. Dirt on dirt. Waste on waste. Smell was the worst. Smell of money was the term used by locals. Bam never got used to the smell. The smoke domed over the neighborhood. Protected the world from the east end. Trapped them in the life of the lower class. Rust on rust. A neighborhood held hostage by the dealers. Any parent in their right mind wouldn't live on Ewing in the east end of Sherman, Ohio.

Voices boomed out. Bam quickly turned toward the Red Bone Bar. A cloaked figure was running with purse-snatching speed toward him, with three chasing. He squinted. His eyes shot moon-sized open when he realized it was Russ. He stood tall, and glared at Russ as he leaped up the steps and into the house. Bam slid to his left and blocked the three from ascending his porch.

Russ heaved from his chest, squawked out, "Get in here."

Bam twisted his head around and paused and winked. Face went stone-cold crazy and faced the three. A serene smile. Rugged tongue. He had a taste for blood. Liquid courage and boredom stung him, "Who's first?" he said as he skyscraped over them. He kept his eyes on the one in the middle; in his short time, he had realized the leader always stood between the minions.

The leader tittered at his comment, face turned to a sneer and said, "He grabbed my girl's ass."

Bam grinned ear to ear, held it until it hurt, and drawled out, "Woo-fucking-woo." Patron must have been in love; he stole a shot at Bam as he was turning to check on Russ. Knuckles met jaw. Bam didn't fall; he bent down and caught himself with the rail. One minion tackled him; the others kicked at his chin. When the haze cleared, he twisted and tossed one off him and into the yard. When he got to his feet, they were long gone. He went to his ass and sat on the steps to clear the remainder of the haze.

He got up from the knockout hangover and blinked the tweety birds away. He was discomfited by what just happened to him; he had lost his first battle. He looked over his right shoulder at his house, then toward the Red Bone. Cracked his neck and stepped into the middle of the road. Bloodshot red, knuckled white, looked like a bull waiting for a matador. He ratcheted up the long-sleeved shirt bunched around his shoulders, tightened around his chest. Adrenaline pushed out screams of rage and pleaded for the hoppers to return to the fight. Partygoers shot toward his house; jocks sprinted, rockers bounced, a goth couple shuffled around the side of the house masked in black. Down the road, drunks swayed and scurried in the cover of the door like alley cats. Bam was alone with ogling eyes staring out the windows. Sounds of the decaying neighborhood, dogs barking, chains rattling, and his own belligerence as his company. Belligerence was his blankie, his comforting hand, his saving grace. It sang sad songs at night to soothe him to sleep and heavy metal music during the day to keep him awake. He wore it as a halo, a badge of honor.

A wino, hunkered down across the street, yodeled, "What the fuck, man? Can't you see this is a neighborhood of tranquility," and let out a hoarse cackle and a cough. He flipped his bottle on the road. It clinked against the asphalt with a rattle, then it exploded. Lit the fuse in Bam's mind.

Adrenaline and rage sheared the neurons in his brain. Fog was blooming in his mind. He screamed like a feral animal and dropped the hammer of his chin into his chest and clogged forward. She stepped behind and tapped him on the shoulder. Bam turned, looking to crater a face, stopped and unclenched his fist. She glowed like a candle on a cold winter night. She smiled, touched his hand, "There you are." Her voice was candy sweet, a gentle touch, newborn skin smooth, dropped straight from the gates of heaven. The pulpy knot in his neck subsided and his breathing calmed. She guided him toward his steps and released his hand as he sat and walked away. He watched her go without uttering a word. He swallowed hard and grimaced with a pain in his cotton mouth. A flash of white light took his eyes, and then he was out cold on the stoop.

# CHAPTER 13

When the sun rose, Elmer popped out of the house and down his porch, stepped gingerly over broken bottles, smashed cans, two piles of puke. Someone urinated in the planters. Took a dump in the shrubbery. The revelation hit Elmer; all the plants had been dying, regardless of the amount of sunlight or water. Trash strewed across the yard into the street. He golf-smacked a twelve-ounce can and plopped down next to Adrian on the steps. He brought a frown, growled in his dissatisfaction, not of the yard, of Adrian. The yard could be cleaned, planters replaced. Adrian was dirty in spirit and mind. Elmer was beginning to wonder if there was enough soap in the world to clean him. He started off calmly, "Saw something interesting last night," he said and flicked at the earring hanging from Adrian's lobe. Added, "Thing is as dumb as that hair on top of your head."

Adrian flinched, instinctively covered his ear, "Yeah," he moaned and grabbed his head again, "got drunk again."

"Looks like a damn worm attached itself to the top of your head."

"It's the in thing, Elmer."

"Only if you're trying to get a part in Rocky . . . Clubber Lang's lost son or something."

"Yeah."

Elmer eased back, "Mom?"

"She's off doing more important things," Adrian said with a smidge of sarcasm. "Think Scott took her to Tennessee." Russ stepped between them and into the yard. "Did I say she was in Tennessee?"

"Who?"

"My mom."

"Yeah . . . yeah . . ." Russ said and bent down to pick up a can, "said she would be back in five days . . . been six."

Elmer gasped. "Well, he addressed Russ, "why are you picking up the damn cans?" Russ didn't say anything but stopped with an empty in his hand. "There will be new cans in the same place tomorrow." Now, he was being sarcastic, "Leave them. There will be friends waiting for them in the morning."

The boys laughed.

The calm was over. "You two think you're such hot shit." He turned red, "Get woke up last night to Rocky barking and carrying on . . . go to the window and see you out there playing grab-ass with three others." Adrian turned away. Russ floated toward the far end of the yard. Too late. "You," Elmer said and jabbed his cane toward Russ, "where were you?"

"I . . . I . . . thought—"

"You thought shit. You should have been out there helping him."

"Bam—" Russ couldn't get the words out fast enough.

"What I tell you about that Bam shit? He's got a damn name. He's not a fucking cartoon character." He preached, continued to bark, "You two want to sit around and drink all damn day and watch cartoons? You're not kids anymore." He eyed Russ, spoke to both, "You're seventeen years old." Now he was on a roll, "you suppose to graduate next year." To Adrian, "You quit the football team after a week to hang out with goof dick here." Russ's chin hit his chest. "What the hell do you think is going to happen after you graduate?"

"Elmer," Adrian said and tried to grab his shoulder before he had a heart attack.

He was undeterred. "I'll drive you down to the store, buy all the beer and cartoons you two want." Back to Russ, "You should have helped him."

Russ stood there like he just got caught stealing candy from the store.

Elmer screamed like the store owner who caught him, "You some type of sissy?" His brazen eyes burned through him as he waited for a response. "You didn't quit the team."

"I—"

"Oh," Elmer revved up, "I know your sissy ass didn't play." Then, "I was being sarcastic."

Russ turned away in embarrassment at the truth of the words, "I'm going into the house."

"Good," Elmer snapped back and flicked a hand, "that is where you belong."

Adrian turned around as the door closed and saw the look on Elmer's face. Lower lip swelled and quivered in anger.

"What the hell were you thinking?"

Adrian jumped up and stomped over to Elmer's and sat in a chair. He didn't want Russ to see this beatdown.

Elmer grunted and joined Adrian. "Why do you feel the need to fight all the time?"

Squinting into the sun, Adrian said, "I'm sorry," and stomped across the porch.

Elmer's eyes hard set on him," Adrian," he yelled. His voice softened when he stopped. He pulled a cigar, "Come sit."

Adrian turned and dropped, sighed like a teenager, "Yes, sir."

He lit it. Chewed on the end. Asked again, "Why?"

"I don't." Then, "Depends on what your definition of a lot means."

"You been in three fights that I know of." A moment of silence, then, "Three."

Adrian leaned forward and masked his face in his hands.

"Probably more I don't know about." Puffed. Exhaled. Leaned back and blew smoke above, "Yeah," he continued, "I can think of at least three others." Elmer sent a searching eye and reached for his hand. His voice faded as the guilt in Adrian's face showed itself and told him there were more than the three Elmer knew.

Adrian gulped, dropped his chin and mumbled, "Three sounds about right." *Five . . . no, wait, six.* "Think you are counting one too many, Elmer. Two."

Elmer didn't push, "Why?"

Calmly, Adrian raised and interlocked his fingers behind his head, "Elmer . . ."

They met eyes.

"Why?"

Adrian jerked away. "I don't know." He rolled his chin over his right shoulder toward his house and away from Elmer. Russ was peering out of the window, pointing and laughing at Adrian. Conveniently, safe from Elmer's wrath. Adrian stared back.

He sighed when he heard Elmer say, "Let me tell you a story."

"I'm all ears," he said and slid into a defiant pose with his arms across his chest, feet out. Ankle over knee. Head cocked back, watching the paper mill smoke sketch into clouds above. Just once, he wished Elmer could have an inane conversation.

A whack on the knee to get Adrian's attention and crack his pose, "I read a story about Chuck Norris once."

A turn. A gesture. A machine gun sound. "Invasion USA," Maybe today would be their first conversation with no meaning.

"Stop screwing around. I'm serious." His gravel voice turned asphalt smooth, "Let's have a serious conversation about the fighting," he said and slapped Adrian's leg one last time. Asked again, "Why the fighting?"

Adrian stared ahead in silence, listening to Elmer's lips smack against the cigar. Heard the puff, smelled the smoke. Ran through several answers in his head, picked one, and abandoned it. Before Elmer started to speak, he went with, "It's all I'm good at."

Elmer coughed, gulped and flipped the cigar toward the rail. Adrian's eyes trailed behind. Back to the gravel road. "That is some bullshit," Elmer barked again. "You been bamboozled."

A chuckle. Teeth over lips. "Bamboozled?" He picked at the corner of his eye and said, "What the hell does that mean?"

Elmer stopped, hesitated, and said, "Look it up. You're so damn smart and know everything about everything . . . tough guy, my ass."

Adrian tore his eyes away, leaped from his seat, and raised his arms. Stretched, fingertips touched the fascia.

"All this fighting . . ." He pointed north. Adrian could see the hand with his left eye. "You're going to end up out at the pen one day."

Adrian recoiled. Face deadpanned.

More soothing, "Is that what you want?"

"No," Adrian said from below.

Elmer relaxed in his seat. "Let me tell you about the book."

Adrian spun around with two palms out, "Okay, tell me about Chuck," he said and plopped down and ran his hand over his mohawk.

Elmer jumped right in. "I read this book about or written by Chuck Norris. His master or sensei or something like that—"

"Well, who was it?"

He waved him off. "Don't matter . . . just listen to the point."

"Fine."

"His sensei . . . yeah . . . it was his sensei," Elmer said and rubbed his head. "He was driving home from an event and somewhere down the line, he accidentally cut someone off."

"Like you do?"

Elmer skimmed over a tooth, spit and said, "Are you going to let me tell the story?"

"Yeah."

"I mean, if you . . ." Elmer started to say and get up.

A hand on the shoulder, "Elmer?"

"If you don't want to . . ."

Louder, "Elmer, tell the damn story."

"Okay," he said and pulled another cigar.

Adrian grabbed the lighter as Elmer pulled, "You just had one," and stuffed it in his shorts.

"Why the hell you put it in there?" Elmer said. He pointed at his crotch, "Don't want the damn thing now with all your ball juice and shit like that on it."

"Do you want to tell me the story or not?"

Elmer laid the cigar on the arm of the chair, "You're buying me a new one."

"Fine."

Elmer continued, "So the sensei gets to a stoplight and the guy he cut off jumps out of his car and runs up to the truck window."

Now Elmer had his attention. Adrian showed interest and perked up. He leaned forward and swung the chair around to face Elmer. Head out. Elbows on knees. Eyes shined through the haze of the hangover. "He kick his teeth in?" he asked in anticipation.

A dismissive hand. Finger to the lips. "Ole boy was just trying to get home from a long day and some hard ass comes up and starts banging on his window."

Now, Adrian was on the edge of his seat. "He kick his ass?"

He waved him off, smirked. "So the sensei rolls down the window," Elmer demonstrated.

"He beat him into tomorrow?"

Elmer chuckled, coughed in his hand, "Asks the guy if his car was broken down. Thumbed over his shoulder and said he had jumper cables."

A frozen grin, "No shit?"

"No shit." Elmer demonstrated with his hand and said, "Tough ass was yelling back for him to jump out the truck." Elmer gave a weak jab at the air between them, "Come out and fight, the man hollered."

"What the fuck, I—"

Elmer cut him off, "Cars were honking as they drove by."

"He get out?" Adrian huffed and rolled his eyes. Sternly said, "I would have jumped out." Adrian stood and motored his legs like an aerobics instructor and jabbed at the air between them, let out a midnight howl and said, "Man, if that was me." Elmer ignored him and remained on point. Adrian dropped in his seat. Elmer stopped for a moment and watched Adrian. The gleam in his eyes. Smile on his face. Redness streaking across his cheeks. Been a long time since he saw a pep in the kid's step. Then it hit him. Adrian was happy about hearing about a pending fight.

"He turned off the ignition and struggled as he slid off the seat."

A big smile. Rapid nodding. "Now it's on."

Elmer stood, holding his back with a hand, "He looks at the guy as he starts bobbing and weaving and throwing punches at the air and says—"

"What'd he say?" Adrian exploded from his seat, clobbered the air with a fist, "What a moron." Gritted out with clenched fists, "Fucking guy needs an ass-whooping," he said as his face crinkled.

Elmer shuffled around the porch, with the hand on his back, "He sputtered out . . . you know acting like he was scared, hurting."

"Yeah."

"Sputtered out," he chuckled again, "said I have a bad back. Can you help me stretch before we fight?"

Adrian kicked at the chair and stood silently with a drooped face and swelled lip. Elmer leaned against the rail and smacked his lips as he waited. Then, Adrian spoke, "Why didn't he kick his ass?"

"Who says he didn't?"

"Did he?"

"You tell me."

Hands on hips. A glare, "He didn't."

"Why not?"

Adrian knew but didn't want to say, instead said, "It's your story," and turned around and faced his house. Saw Russ lurking at the window. Adrian flipped him off, spoke to Elmer, "Should have beaten that ass."

"Why didn't he?" Elmer asked in a boisterous tone.

A quick turn. He flicked his hand and said, "The guy was acting like an idiot . . . standing in the road . . . picking a damn fight for nothing." Both stood silent for a moment, Adrian said, "The sensei made him look foolish."

"Like an idiot."

"Yeah . . . he made him look like an idiot."

"Exactly," Elmer said and jabbed a finger at Adrian. "That was worse than an ass-beating . . ." Another jab. "Which he could have given him."

Adrian sat, crossed his legs, and released a long exhale. "I get it."

Elmer moved to the front of him, studied him through squinted eyes. "Do you?"

"Yep."

Elmer preached, "It takes more of a man not to fight . . . to walk away. Nobody wins a fight."

*I've won all of mine.* "I guess you're right."

"Fighting doesn't get you anywhere, but . . . trouble." Elmer sat, hand on Adrian's knee. Adrian's gaze dwelled on Elmer's hand as it maintained a grip. When he looked up, he saw a tenderness in Elmer. He was in no mood for a lecture today. The strange girl had a grip on him. Elmer spoke softly, "Nuttin' was ever accomplished by fighting." More sternly, "Nothing was accomplished by fighting last night."

*Met the girl of my dreams.* He rubbed his hands, "Cuts and bruises."

"A welfare-looking yard."

A chuckle. Slow and long. "Yeah, a damn mess."

"Ay huh."

"Well," Adrian said and stood up. "Good talk . . . good talk, Elmer. But, I—"

"What?"

"I better get the yard cleaned up."

"Wait a minute," Elmer said and flashed a hand before Adrian got by him. When Adrian stopped, he patted the seat, "Sit for a second."

"Elmer."

Slower, "I'm—not—finished. Sit down."

"Elmer!"

"Don't sass me, boy."

A whiny, "Fine."

"So . . ." He changed directions and scooted his seat over and put his arm around the kid. "So do you remember when it started?"

"When what started?"

"The anger."

"Oh God," Adrian said and searched for the answer in the clouds, "for as long as I can remember."

"I don't want to blow smoke up your ass," Elmer said and when Adrian glanced over, he laughed, "but you seem to be a pretty good fighter."

Adrian smirked, massaged his nose, "Yeah, like I said . . ." He held the finish.

"Yeah . . ." Elmer gave him a weak shot to the shoulder, "where did you learn to fight."

"My dad," he murmured as he picked at a nail.

"Dads will do that sometimes."

"Yeah."

Elmer shuffled in his seat, heard the scratching at the door and let Rocky out. When Rocky went over to Adrian, he naturally scurried his head under his hand. Adrian's mind was off in some long-forgotten place. He snapped out when he heard, "Do you remember the first one?"

Adrian jumped up, spit over the rail, "Think my kid brother was nine, ten . . ." He shook his head, "We were living in this hideous trailer in Illinois, up by Chicago. We had to move there when my dad lost his job at a tractor-trailer factory . . . tough times . . . tough times." He crossed his arms, his air sputtered. Elmer could tell he was struggling with the memory. He never heard Adrian or Cindy speak about a brother. "Before, we lived good." His eyes took in the neighborhood, flipped a can off the rail into his yard, "Better than this place."

"Most places are."

A mile-wide smile led to, "I had a green machine, Elmer." He smacked his hands together, "poof, it was all gone." He put eyes on Elmer, who was attentive, silent. "It was like we were hit with one of those damn Star Trek guns. One minute we are living in a neighborhood, like the one with E.T., then we were in some dump."

"Your dad?"

"He was cool as fuck before we moved, coached Alex and me in baseball, football. Took us places . . ." he got lost in the clouds again. He shivered his head, "Um . . . sorry . . ."

"No, no, take your time. I appreciate you opening to me."

"Yeah," Adrian softly said, rubbed the back of his neck, "after, he was just—uh—uh, angry all the time." He massaged both eyes and inhaled deeply. "Only man I've ever been afraid of." He went silent for a moment, "Only person." He pulled the seat over to the rail and sat and faced Elmer. "There were some older kids who lived in the park. Fifteen, think one was sixteen, think I remember seeing him drive." Clenched fists. Grinding teeth. "I hated them."

They exchanged glances.

"They always picked on Alex and me, new kids, younger, easy targets." His eyes drooped toward the deck, softer. "One day, Alex came home with a black eye, and my dad," he gasped. "Fucking asshole." He swiped at his nose, "My dad blew a gasket." He made a demonstrative growl, "Bam," he said, "did you kick their asses?" Adrian flailed back, gestured with his hands, "What was I supposed to do, Elmer?"

"Adrian?"

"What, Elmer? What was I to do?" Before Elmer could respond, "I had one choice." Elmer pulled at a lip as he conjured up a response. Adrian held up four fingers. "Four," he jabbed the four fingers at Elmer, "four of them." He stood again, arms crossed. "Bam," he barked and pointed at the window, "if you come home tomorrow without your knuckles bloody," he held a fist in the window at his reflection and dog-faced the window. Lighter, just above a whisper, "if you come home tomorrow . . ." He lowered his fist, just his reflection, and himself, in a whisper, "beat my ass."

He heard Elmer exhale and light up, "I'm . . ."

A stoic face. He murmured, "The next day, I walked up to the biggest one and I hit him as hard as I could." He touched his right fist and looked at Elmer. A defeated look. "The others jumped on me." He faced his house, spoke louder, "I never ran out of gas. I kept swinging. Swung until they gave up and ran off." He turned and pointed at Elmer, "That is when I knew."

Elmer cleared his throat, shuffled over to the door, and let Rocky in, "Go on." Then, to Adrian, "What did your dad say?"

"Fuck," he said loud and long. Hand to his ear. Nose. Turned his arm around and showed Elmer the scar, "I looked like Rocky . . . the first fight with Apollo."

"And?"

Adrian slapped his hands together and broke out in a manic laugh and twirled around, stopped, "He said I better have won."

"That's it?"

"Yep."

# CHAPTER 14

**B**am asked Russ about the girl, and Russ told him he thought she came with Chloe. She had been etched in his mind since the moment she touched him. Monday could not come soon enough. They abandoned their customary seats in the back row in second period typing class and slid into two behind Chloe, who was in the front. Bam didn't waste any time. He smacked Russ and whispered, "Ask her."

Russ's eyes tailed Mr. Watson from behind as he passed, "I will later," he said.

"Now."

"Later."

A kick to her seat. Nothing. He crumpled a sheet of paper and tossed it over her shoulder. Struck a nerve. She fumed and turned her head like in *The Exorcist* and growled out a "What?"

Bam flipped his thumb, "It was him," he said innocently.

"Ah," Russ said. She steamed. *Bitch.* He didn't want to incense her. He smiled, fake as hell. Hoped she bought it. "I'm sorry," he said. Such a gentleman. "I was wanting to ask you about the girl you brought to the party the other night."

"What party?"

*Stupid bitch. The fucking party where you got so drunk you pissed in the yard.* Russ reached under the table and finger-tipped Bam's thigh. Long and pointy. This conversation was worth a pound of flesh. "Oh," he smiled again, "I'm sorry for the confusion, the party at Bam's on Friday."

Chloe veered away, front and center. Watson was still spewing his bull-shit. He didn't come up for air. Bam whispered, "After class," out of the side of his mouth and drilled his thumb in Russ's thigh, who let out a pained whimper from way down.

Bam's patience wore thin. He approached Chloe after class. "Hey," he said. She held a glare like she just stepped in shit, "Oh, it's you."

*Yeah, my house was good enough for your ass.* "The girl the other night." "Susan?"

Sounded good to him. He's never seen Chloe hang out with anybody else. She was the school snob. "Yeah."

"She's my cousin." If her face froze, she'd be the ugliest girl in school, win the Halloween contest as a witch and wouldn't even have to wear black.

"Um."

Chloe was hip to his game. She figured out his play. She lurched her upper body back and squawked out, "She wouldn't be interested in you." She continued with a laugh.

He imagined shoving his fist down her mouth and pulling her tongue out. Wanted to call her a bitch but stayed focused. "Chloe, please," he said in a beggar's tone. It was more than he intended.

She stepped back, thinking things were about to get awkward, and looked him up and down, like the time he did it to her and said he would rather beat off. She held her hands out before he begged and said, "Bam, my Uncle Mitchell would not approve of you." A laugh. An eye roll. In this rare moment, for today, she had the upper hand on Bam. She was vivacious and boisterous. Made sure she was loud enough for everybody to hear. She crossed her arms and said, "I don't approve." She pushed through Bam and Russ, leaving Bam with his mouth open.

He called out to her, "Chloe." As she continued to ignore him, he hollered, "just give me her number."

Chloe didn't try to conceal her distaste for him. She snapped around and said, "I would never . . . never, Bam." She spun around so fast she could have drilled herself into the floor and marched off.

"Fucking bitch," Russ seethed. He glanced over at Bam after hearing him release a defeated breath. He put his arm around him, fingered his trap, and gritted out, "Don't worry about her, dude."

Bam nodded.

Russ cheesed, "That chick is a dime a dozen."

"Yeah."

Russ released him and gently shoved him and pointed, "Catch up after class?"

"Yeah," Bam said and stared at the far wall at the end of the hall. Russ's head passed in and out of his line of sight as he threaded his way through students.

Bam stood in the hallway, rejected, as the other kids funneled into their classrooms. Dejected, he decided to skip the rest of the day. He started toward the exit but heard the voice from behind, "Mr. Franklin?" He ignored the voice and continued walking. When his hand reached the door, the voice called out louder and closer, "Mr. Franklin."

Bam's defense mechanism against turmoil, stress, and disappointment was to act out. After the fight and the disappointment in Elmer, he wasn't looking to cause himself any more trouble. He released the door, and sighed. "Yes, Mr. Stump." Tried to fake it the best he could under the circumstances. He turned, "Sir."

High school principal Jack Stump questioned him with a condescending tone, "Not feeling well today?" Stump wasn't the avuncular type, wasn't one the students remembered fondly or wrote down as the teacher who had the most positive influence on them.

"Nah," he said and touched his throat, "Sore, think I might have the flu."

Chin in hand. Questioning eyes. A hum between his lips. He twirled around him, bird-dogging him with a curious interest. On his first pass, Bam kept his focus on the doorknob directly ahead. *Mind over matter, and Mr. Stump doesn't matter.* On the second pass, Mr. Stump stopped at Bam's nine o'clock and stepped back with one hand on a hip, the other on the chin. "Interesting," he said in a bombastic tone. He continued circling Bam until he was in front. "That is not the news I heard this morning in the lounge."

"Never been, so I don't know what you are talking about."

"In fact," he looked left and right and stepped forward. He was a house dog who barked behind the door. Pampered and coddled. Bam imagined he was bullied in his youth, wet willies, caged in lockers, a virgin until—well, possibly a virgin today. Bam was angry but felt sorrier for Mr. Stump than anything else. "The rumor is you're quite the fighter. I sure hope you can make a living fighting."

Bam arched a Saturday night wrestling eyebrow and rose on his tips, and looked down at Mr. Stump, who took a step back, then another before he dislodged a neck muscle looking up at his student. "I can hold my own." Mr. Stump grinned and touched his dappled beard.

Bam couldn't resist, "Another go at being a man?" Mr. Stump returned a questioning look. "The beard," Bam gestured with his chin, "looks like you can't grow one . . . yet."

Mr. Stump continued, "By looking at your attendance record and grades, let's say . . . I'm sure you're a big disappointment to your parents. Mr. Franklin, pugilism is no way to make a living. I'm more of a pacifist myself. I like to use my mind to get ahead in life."

Bam dropped his head to stymie a comment that would get him expelled. "Sounds good, Jack. I had no doubts you were a pacifist. Have a quality day, Jack," he beamed and walked away.

"Mr. Franklin. Adrian, am I using words too big for you to understand?" he gibed.

Bam stopped and turned around. Exchanged hateful smiles with Mr. Stump. Bam stared until Mr. Stump became uncomfortable and looked away. Bam stood and soaked in the win. After turning to walk out, Mr. Stump scoffed, "You'll be in prison one day."

# CHAPTER 15

**B**am was in a sullen mood the following days. For the first time, he was thinking about his direction in life. Desires and goals. The night he met her and stood on the porch and peered out into the darkness of despair, he told himself he was going to die in the slums. Now, he was sure of it. Cindy figured he was sick. Elmer assumed he was mad for being hijacked in the mouth. He was heartbroken. Didn't eat or drink much the past three days. Russ was disquieted by his behavior, his friend distraught over an unknown girl. Bam was letting her prissy cousin get the best of him. By the fifth day, Cindy had enough and forced him to the grocery store with her. When they got home, she was going to escort his stinky ass to the shower. He was a slow-moving blob. At the store, by the third aisle, he felt like curling up in the corner and using a loaf of bread as a pillow. Struggled to reach aisle four.

He had just stepped forward when he saw her, froze. A jolt of life. She and her mom were in a conversation. Strolling toward him. He was wallpaper. An item on the bottom shelf nobody purchased. Nine feet away. His eyes caught hers, held them for a fleeting second. She stopped. *Oh my God, she remembers.* He did his best acting job, kneeling at the bottom shelf and examining the available sugars. *Sugars?* He felt her pass and stole a look. Insignificant. Strolled by without a care in the world. Laughing and giggling with Mom. Was she talking about him? Telling Mom about the foolish boy she met at a party? The kid with the bad haircut and worst temper. He watched her walk away. "Hey," he called out and immediately regretted it. It surprised him. *Good, she didn't hear me.* She did and turned around as her mom continued talking. Too late to back out now. "Do I know you?" he said and played it cool. Stuffed his fidgety hands into his pockets. Stood like he didn't care. He did. Met her in the middle and tried not to overdo it, "Susan?"

Her face opened to a smile. *She's only being nice.* "Yeah," she said and started to say something else but stopped with her mouth open.

He stepped in. "Bam," he said. "We met . . . we met the other night." He waited a moment to see if she remembered. "The other night at a party."

Beautiful and funny. "Oh yeah," she said and giggled. "You're the one . . ." She held it and tossed an air punch. He grabbed his nap. She cocked her head to the side until she saw his eyes, "You were pretty mad."

He could feel his hands shaking and jacket quaking. An epic failure. "Ay huh," was the only thing he could think to say.

She could tell he was displeased or embarrassed or both. He caught her eye once again and turned to walk away. Assured he would never see her again. She surprised him, "My cousin mentioned you asked about me." *That fucking Chloe.* He stopped but didn't turn around. She pressed on, spoke up, "What were you wanting to ask?"

He hesitated before turning around slowly. He took a slow tour of the aisle, should have packed a bag lunch, stopped on her and dove in, "I was wanting to say thank you for stopping me from doing something stupid the other night."

"No problem," she replied.

A pause.

"And I was wondering if you would . . ."

She didn't blink or look away. Waited for him to finish.

"Wondering if maybe you would go on a date with me . . . some time . . . if you didn't have a boyfriend or girlfriend."

A giggle.

"No," he said and reached out to touch her. He caught himself and stepped back, "not saying you look gay or anything, but—"

Another giggle.

He cursed himself under his breath and turned red.

She saved him. "I'm not gay . . . not saying there is anything wrong with that."

"Absolutely not."

"And I don't have a boyfriend."

"Good . . . I mean, okay."

Another giggle.

"I think you should talk."

She chuckled. Snorted. Covered her mouth. Cleared her throat and took a deep breath, "Okay," she said. "Okay." She sniffled and giggled again. After she got her composure, she said, "What is your name?"

He sent her a quizzical look.

She studied him, said, "Your real name?"

"Adrian."

"Adrian," she said and smiled. Both were more relaxed. She grabbed his hand, "Adrian is a good name."

*Heard that before.* Now, he was feeling cool and somewhat confident. "Nobody calls me that."

"Not a fan."

Buzzkill. He shot her a chagrined look.

"Well, Adrian," she said much louder than needed. Point taken. "Be at the library at seven on Friday."

"Library?"

"Yep, you are welcome to come if you want."

*Don't say it too quick. Be cool.* "Sure."

"Okay," she smiled and nudged her head, "I better catch up with my mom."

"Okay."

"Friday?"

"Friday."

Bam held his air as he watched her push the cart. When she was out of sight, he gritted his teeth and released the pent-up emotion. All was not lost.

# CHAPTER 16

Bam heard the door screech open on its rusted hinges. Slam shut, and feet stomped around the house. A wrestling of bottles. A cabinet opened and closed. A heavy step at the stairs. "You up there?"

A weak, "Yes."

"Dude?"

He stepped back, neck out the door. "Yeah," he said sharply as Russ poured one down his throat.

Russ pounced up the stairs. "Hey," he said and stepped back with his hand over his mouth. Extended a searching eye and let out a "Whoo." Added a snarky, "What have you done with my friend."

"Funny," Bam said slowly like he was defusing a bomb as he pulled another wild hair hanging from his nose. Blinked and added, "Damn, those hurt."

Nose high. Jowls hanging. Squinty eyes. "That's why I don't mess with mine," Russ said as he examined his in the mirror.

"Moron." He ran his hand over his head and adjusted his tie, "What you think?" Bam said, prepped out in a purple shirt.

"I think it looks like you are going somewhere, but . . ." He joined the two bottles in his hands together, "We were supposed to drink."

"We drink every night."

That searching eye again, a pause, then. "Yeah," he said louder, "that is what I said."

Face to mirror. Hand to tie. A glamour pose. "I'm meeting her in the library."

Russ eased the beers on the corner of the sink and did a once-over on his friend, "Little overdressed?"

"You think?"

"Nah," his face froze, "maybe a .... lose the tie."

"Seriously?"

"Just go without it . . . first impressions are . . ." He grabbed a beer, finished it. "Go with the purple, no tie."

"That is what I've been telling myself," Bam said. He exhaled and eyed himself one more time in the mirror. "Best I can do," he said this less confidently and hung the tie over the shower curtain.

Russ snickered, "Damn."

"What?"

"You really seem to like this chick." Lower with his lips closed, "A girl you have spoken with like one and a quarter times. A time and a half."

"Spoken to her twice." He had felt inadequate since the night she agreed to meet him. Unworthy. Not good enough for a girl living on the other side of town in Yaples Orchard. Cobbled streets. Brick mansions. Even the mailboxes were brick. It sounded rich. A garage on Ewing was rich. She had the four-car variety. He tried to think rationally to calm his jangled nerves. "Probably wasting my time. She might not even show up."

Russ tried to ease him before Bam broke out in a full-fledged sweat. "You're the best friend I have." Most times, Bam would have punched him, nettled him back for a comment like that. Not today. He needed a pick-me-up. "She would be crazy not to see the greatness in you."

Bam let his air out slowly, "Okay," he said and pushed him away, "that's enough."

Russ gestured with his hand down the steps, "I'm going to go find my own peace tonight."

"Good luck."

After he heard the door slam, he leaned over the sink and stared at the man in the mirror. *You can do this. You can do this.* "Russ," he yelled, "my ride." He long-jumped down the stairs and crashed onto the porch. Saw the one taillight turn left on Main. He mumbled, "What the fuck," at his stupidity. He told Russ, right? He meant to tell him. He was sure he told him he needed a ride. The library was five miles from his house, and he was supposed to be there at seven. He crouched and peered inside, "Six fifty-two," he screamed and kicked the rail. He interlocked his fingers on his head and paced around momentarily. Looked over at Elmer's. Lights on. Could see the television from the window. Elmer in the recliner. He shook his arms out like he was back in junior high and did the only thing he could.

"Elmer!"

"Hellfire."

"Elmer?" he repeated and lingered at the door.

"Scare an old man to death, coming in here hollering like a damn wild man."

"Elmer."

"Old man trying to watch his shows and—"

Stern and sharp Adrian said, "Elmer." That got his attention. "Can I use your car?"

"Oh," Elmer said and gave him a long look, "why you dressed like . . ." He didn't finish. Tried to prompt Adrian with a nudge of the nose.

"The library."

Elmer said nothing.

"The girl."

Elmer said nothing.

Exasperated, Adrian said, "I'm meeting the girl tonight."

Nothing.

"At the library."

"Oh," Elmer said, the corner of his lip rose. He spoke to Adrian as he shuffled into the kitchen, "Be yourself." He grabbed the keys off the hanger next to the refrigerator. "Be the man I know you are." Adrian stared. Elmer grabbed Adrian's hand and slapped the keys into the palm, and cupped his over Adrian's. "Leave the boy at home."

"Thanks, Elmer."

"Careful," he hollered as he sat.

Adrian hustled to the car and jumped behind the wheel and flipped the ignition. Revved the engine and shifted into drive. At the edge of the driveway, he braked and shifted into park. Laid his head on the steering wheel and waited. *Don't do it. Don't do it.* Forehead met the steering wheel. Harder. A third time. He turned off the ignition and opened the door like an old man and gingerly walked up the steps and peered in through the front door. Stood lanky and defeated.

Elmer saw his reflection over Alex Trebek on the television. "Back so soon?" Adrian dropped the keys into Elmer's lap. "Change your mind?"

"I flunked my driver's test."

Elmer rocked himself off the chair and gathered his coat off the kitchen chair. "I know," he said as he zipped.

"Wait," Adrian stepped around the chair, "you knew?" He stopped Elmer as he tried to walk by, "Why did . . . the car . . . why did you let me—"

"You want to sit and talk about it," Elmer said and began to unzip, "or do you want to go see this girl?" He waited for Adrian to respond. When he didn't, "We can talk about it in the car."

Adrian stood with his mouth ajar, thumbed toward the door, "We'll talk about it in the car."

"Can we go now?"

"Just get in the car, Elmer."

"Hellfire," Elmer said as he followed Adrian out the door.

They pulled out of the drive and turned right out of the driveway. A left on Main. Adrian relaxed a little when they made the first two lights. When they caught the third, he caught the time on the Huntington Bank sign, "Oh fuck," he said, "it's seven ten."

"Relax," Elmer said confidently, "she'll be there." Adrian adjusted in his seat and chewed on a nail. "We will make it."

"The car?"

"Your mother told me."

""Elmer, why did you let me take the car?"

"The boy I knew," a quick glance at Adrian, "would have taken that car without any care in the world." He punched it on a yellow, winked at Adrian, "We will make it." He looked in the mirror. "Would have taken the car," he shifted lanes and blew past the fifth light. "Most in your situation would have taken the chance tonight." He turned left on Paint Street. Adrian glared down at the library on the right. "Why didn't you?"

"Here it is, Elmer."

"I know where the damn library is," Elmer said and pulled into the parking lot and shifted into park. "So . . ."

"Because I didn't want to disappoint you." Adrian adjusted himself, "You're my Mr. Miyagi." Elmer felt his eyes well up. Adrian got out of the car and held the door open, peered in at Elmer, "I don't want to disappoint you anymore."

"I don't bust grapes. I bust ass." He flicked his hand. "Now get your ass in there." Adrian smiled and slammed the door. When he got a few feet away,

Elmer honked. Adrian trotted back and opened the door and before he could say anything, Elmer said, "Remember Mickey loves ya."

"Rock loves you."

# CHAPTER 17

Adrian power-stepped into the library. Skidded to a halt and considered the structure. This was his first visit to any library. The large, modern-designed building was intimidating, white columns, two stories, and miles of books. He opened the outer door. Felt the sweat take its natural course. He opened the second door. The reception desk was ten feet in front of him. "Can I help you?" Mildred said, dressed in her best June Cleaver outfit. "We have a new selection of bestsellers." She smiled.

"Eh," he said and ran a hand over his hawk and slid back on his heels, "I," he began to say as he saw her above. He inhaled deeply, kept his eyes on her as he spoke to Mildred, "What I want is upstairs," he said and toed the first step and stopped. *Get a grip. Be yourself. She is just another girl.* Another step. Mildred cocked her head to the side and looked at him suspiciously. *Wait, she isn't just another girl.* He looked again. She was crouched down, gently moving her finger along the spines of books as she scanned titles. He slowly continued up the stairway. When he reached the landing, he ran his hands down the front of his shirt, collected himself, and searched for her. He found her in the Gs.

She was talking to herself out loud, "A is for Alibi, B is for Burglar . . . oh," she said, jumped back and turned when he touched her on the shoulder.

"I'm . . . I didn't mean to—"

She hit him on the shoulder. "Don't be silly," she said and turned away. When she didn't feel him behind her, she turned on her toes, smiled and waved him forward, "Are you coming?"

"Oh. Oh . . . yeah, I'm right behind you."

"Do you read?"

Adrian lied. "Yeah, a little."

Her eyes gazed at titles. Fingers slid across spines, "Who is your favorite?"

"Stephen King. Yeah, I like Stephen King."

"Steven King, huh?"

"I really enjoyed *Cujo*." *I do love* Cujo. *Elmer and I watched it like six times. It was only a little white lie. Oh my God, she has read* Cujo. *Don't say you have read* Cujo. *She's read* Cujo. *She's read every Stephen King book. I'm dead.*

She scrunched her nose, tapered her lips, and clattered her teeth, "Ugh," she said, "I'm not a fan of horror."

*Thank God.*

"Like horror movies less." She leaned down and continued scanning, "I lean toward the classics, *The Catcher in the Rye, The Grapes of Wrath, Where the Red Fern Grows*," she got vertical, "Books like that."

*Dumb ass. Should have read* Where the Red Fern Grows *when it was assigned in English.* "I've not had the pleasure of reading any of those."

She picked a book and showed him, "This sounds interesting."

"*A Time to Kill?*"

She hit the cover with a palm and looked at the author, "John Grisham," she said.

"Never heard of him." *Must not be good. Elmer and I have never seen it.*

"I think he is new," she said and pushed past Adrian and headed toward a table. She sat down at a table as big as a wagon wheel. He sat across from her. Alone, beautiful silence filled the room. Only sounds were the electric current humming from the lights and the wings of a moth banging against the window.

He wondered if she could hear his heart thumping. He could. He sat upright, straight as a pencil, as his hands twiddled in his lap below. He felt a pool of sweat on his waistline. He untucked his shirt, hoping the air would help. "Thanks for agreeing to meet me."

"Everybody needs a new friend . . . right?"

"Friends," he mumbled, face melted into sadness. Then, he cleared his throat, "Susan," he said, "what do you like to do?"

"Well," the smile pulled him in. "I read a ton. I enjoy writing in my journal." She pursed her lips and looked at the ceiling out the top of her lids, "Hang out with my family and friends." His soul drowned in the pools of her eyes, suffocating in a tsunami wave. Two teeth showed themselves in the corner, out of the left side of her lip, "And you?"

She sounded like Charlie Brown's teacher as she spoke. He was focused on her. The overhead light ricocheted off the whites as she was frozen with her mouth open. He rubbed his thighs, up to the groin, down to the knees. "Oh . . . did you say something?"

A giggle. A hand to the mouth. "I asked what you like to do for fun."

His finger found a gap between a coat of polyurethane and wood, fingernail pit perfect. He scratched up and down, creating his own indentation. "The usual stuff, I guess."

"The usual?"

*Get it together. You are losing it.*

She smiled, leaned in, and whispered, "What is your favorite book . . . ever?"

He was wound drum-tight; anxiety beat its sticks on his psyche. He was wondering if he was beginning to look as ruffled as he felt. *Does this purple show my sweat? Holy fuck balls!* "Yes," he blurted out.

"I asked what your favorite book was?"

Her simpering smile flustered him. He mused about the lie he was about to tell. Listened to the fan spin above, pounding its sound into a headache, praying she couldn't see him bleed sweat. She waited patiently with her mouth ajar, hatch to her soul open. His feelings, raw and primitive, scraped against his mind and heart, squealing to get out. Incandescent bright as it moved to the front of his mind. He decided to dive in. Abruptly, he said, "I lied before," raw and vulnerable.

"Lied?"

"I've read one book my entire life. My mom is an alcoholic. I think . . . no . . . I know. I'm on the brink of becoming one." He inhaled, "Most people at my school are afraid of me. My best friend is a retired prison worker who walks with a cane. My other best friend is a dog." He licked his lips, continued, "His name is Rocky. Today, I'm not a great person. But," he pointed at her, "One day I will be better than I am. It might not be tomorrow, but I will get better." He lowered his finger, gripped his head as he stared at the table, "I've been with other girls." He swallowed, "But the moment I saw you," he lifted his head and stared at her, "I have not stopped thinking about you." A shake, a wry smile, then he lowered his voice, "I don't get it. Can't explain it. I wish I could. But I know," he raised his voice, now stern and confident. "It might sound crazy to you. Give me a chance to be in your life." He wilted and dropped his head under the table like a turtle in a shell. He vice-gripped his knee with both hands to stop the earthquake shaking. *Say something. Say anything. Say it's okay.*

Her eyes lingered on him as he spoke passionately. Watched his lips part. Saw the strength in his face. Felt the heat from the spark in his eye. He thought it was over when she didn't say anything for a moment. Felt eternal for him. She was taken by his brusqueness. She shifted in her seat, smitten. She said, "Adrian," in a soothing tone. He felt his heart tumble off a cliff, tongue stiffened and laid flat in his mouth, he remained mute. Then she smiled and reached over to touch his arm. His face softened. She immediately noticed his breathing change. Color came back to his hands.

His desire winched his face up from below. He gave her a vulnerable look, "Yeah?" he said, unsteady. He gathered himself and sat up, worked a stress pang out of his neck and waited for his heart to slow its beat, then added, "Elmer told me to be honest."

She sat primly, an eloquent appearance with a humble tongue. Plummy voice. Eyes the sapphire blue craved by jewelers. His face wore the struggle. She gave nothing away. She tousled her hair, long and blonde. Flowed over her shoulders like a waterfall. The scent penetrated him. "Elmer sounds like a wise man," she said and sent a sultry stare his way.

His desire crept up the back of his neck like a feather. Cataracts of emotions flooded his mind. Several responses whirled around, and he pulled out, "He's old." *Old? Very subtle, moron.*

"Hmmm . . . old?"

"He means a lot to me."

Susan changed the subject with, "What was the book?" and cupped her chin and tilted her head to the right.

Felt like ants were walking up his spine, "A few years ago, my mom and I were at the grocery, and I spotted this paperback."

"What was it?"

He spoke with his hands, "Had this cover of a face, sideways." He searched for his words, "Looked like the guy from *Goonies*."

"Sloth?"

He smiled, "Yeah, Sloth."

"I love that movie."

"Elmer loves that movie." He shrugged, "I love it too, but Elmer recites line after line. A quick shake, "The book. I brought it home and read it cover to cover."

"What was it?"

"*Forrest Gump.*"

She sucked in her lower lip, "Interesting, I've never heard of it."

"You would like it. It is so damn funny. Sorry, darn."

"So, Elmer, huh?"

"Yeah, he's pretty much my . . . he's the closest thing I have to a father."

She strummed her fingernails on the desk. "Does he read?"

*I know this one. Western. John Wayne? No, I got it.* "He's a big western guy." Adrian nodded, added, "Louis L'Amour."

"Western."

"Yeah, *The Daybreakers* is his favorite book. About a guy named . . ." He struggled to find him, "Heck, what was his name? Satchell . . . no . . . Sacke tt. About a gunslinger named Sackett. Can't remember his first name. Elmer tells me all the time I need to read it."

"Maybe you should read it, read it for him. Surprise him with a book report or something."

"Book report?"

"A verbal book report?"

*Probably cause a heart attack.* "Hmmm. That's not a bad idea."

"How long have you lived here?"

"My mom and I moved to Ohio a few years back . . . it's just her and I." Being honest felt liberating to him. "My mom has a boyfriend." He is tone changed when he said, "Scott. He's a drunk like her. She says she loves him. I call her his punching bag." He caught himself, *don't say it to her.* "But, if you can't tell, I'm not a big fan. They been dating a few years now." He sighed. A slight chuckle led to, "Pretty much stuck with each other. Nobody else would be willing to put up with their shit." Adrian kept some to himself: failed to mention the previous half a dozen before Scott.

"Oh, I'm sorry." Then when after Adrian waves it off like it wasn't a big deal, she said, "Elmer?"

He returned a smile. The fear and anxiety abated in him, "Yeah, and Rocky." He added, "Our dog."

A smile, "You love dogs?"

"Excuse me."

"Nothing," she gulped. "Your dad? Any siblings?"

The smile retreated, "Just my mom and I."

"Oh," she wanted to question him more, but didn't want to pry. Saw the lost boy return momentarily. She continued with, "Chloe told me you asked about me."

He massaged his neck, "How about this weather?" he blurted out.

"Nice save. Nice save." She leaned back in her seat, crossed her arms, "so Mr. Franklin."

"Mr. Franklin?"

Her brows narrowed until they touched, "Yes, Mr. Franklin. What do you do for fun?" She leaned up, made a noise with her mouth as she sent an air punch his way. "When you aren't out fighting and carrying on like a raging mad man," she leaned back and waited for a response.

His shade turned from red to white, "I was wondering when that subject would come up." Her posture remained uninviting. He put down his guard and elbowed the table with head in hand, "I was hoping we could forget that night ever happened."

"If it didn't, we wouldn't be here right now."

He retreated, shrunk in his seat and slouched. Pulled on his bottom lip repeatedly, stopped before he pulled it off the bone and waited for the numbing to ease and said, "I really didn't want that night to be your first impression of me."

Susan unfolded her arms, leaned in until her stomach touched the table, stared, and said, "Adrian." When he looked at her, she added, "This is my first impression of you." He tried to hide his large smile. It hurt his face. "By the way, I wanted to mention the other day . . ." she held her tongue.

"What?"

"It's just . . ."

"Come on," his voice shifted gears. "What is it?"

A smile led to, "Adrian sounds so much better than Bam." She showed teeth, a full set, "Yeah, I think I'll call you Adrian."

He sighed, laid back in his seat, "You sound like Elmer." He drew a circle on the table with a finger. "He refuses to call me Bam."

She forcefully batted her eyes at him and shrugged, "Like I said, wise man."

Both giggled.

Shyly Susan asked, "You plan on seeing me again?"

Surprised, his mouth opened with a zombie stare. He searched for the right response. He chose his words carefully as though they hovered over a minefield. "There is nothing I would enjoy more, Susan." His heart quick-sanded down to his stomach as he waited for a response.

"Nobody has ever been that honest, so vulnerable with me," she said. "It was shocking and adorable at the same time. I think I would enjoy seeing you again."

His cheeks were ablaze. Palms sweaty. Words bounced around in his mouth like pop rockets. He managed to sneak out, "Okay."

They sat and talked for two hours—life, dreams, goals, everything under the sun. Susan noticed the time, "Mr. Franklin." His eyes followed hers and he caught the clock. He heard her say, "I need to go soon."

He flipped his head around, "I understand."

She changed the subject, "What do you think about Chloe?"

He hated her. "She's okay."

"Okay?"

"Yeah," he said and continued the lie. "We don't hang out with the same people."

"She's been to your parties."

*Everybody comes to my parties.* "Sometimes . . . on special occasions."

"What was the special occasion last time?"

*It was a Friday.* "It was Russ's birthday." *Good save.*

"She hates you."

*No shit.* "Really?"

"Oh yes."

"Huh."

"If I'm being honest, she is the reason why I agreed to meet."

"Do tell."

"Chloe is my cousin and I do love her. But . . ." She bit her lip in embarrassment.

"Tell."

She rambled on, "She's a little stuck up. I didn't see her for a couple years. We just moved back to Sherman. I was surprised by the way she acted."

*Damn, I do love you.* "I never noticed."

"Yeah," she said, unconvinced. "So," she leaned over and smacked his hand, "You might want to thank her."

He sucked in his lip. "Interesting." *I won't.* "And now?" She already told him, but he wanted to hear it again.

"Time will tell."

They walked down the stairs together, side by side. Before Susan got too far away, Adrian grabbed her by the hand. When she turned, he said, "This is the best day I had in a long, long time," and placed a copy of *Forrest Gump* in her hand. Added, "You won't be disappointed." He released her hand. Before that night, before her, he was in thrall to his emotions. Now, he belonged to her.

She clenched her jaws, looked at him sternly, and began to lean in. Quickly, she turned and walked away, hollered back, "Me too."

Adrian stood momentarily until she was out of sight, felt light on his feet, yelled, "Yes."

An exasperated "Shush," he heard from behind. Fingers to the lip, a vulture eye. He imagined she was tapping her foot behind the desk.

He raised a hand, showed both sets of teeth, and returned a poignant "Sorry," and did his best moonwalk out the door. He burst out the library doors invigorated and howled at the moon. Sucked in the cool air and tried to tamper expectations; he wasn't one to believe in his good luck and had experienced little. High on life, he decided to walk the five miles home. As he sauntered down broken sidewalks, smoke pushed itself high in the sky, marooning the wishes and excitement the stars had to offer. A brooding night would accompany Adrian home. Cats meowed, dogs growled, engines roared, lights flickered; nothing pulled his mind from her. He saw the stars, the dreams through the darkness of the night. He strode past all with a click in his step. Anticipation of telling Elmer about his night tugged him forward. He sped his pace and loped back to the house with a strum in his voice. Whistled as he stepped.

Adrian crashed through the front door. Elmer sprung out of the seat, "What the hell?" he said, "You trying to give me a heart attack?"

Adrian stopped, whirled a digit, "You never moved so fast." He broke out in a dance, "I'm in love, I'm in love . . ." he belted out in a singsong cadence.

"Don't get ahead of yourself," Elmer said as he sat. "And stop that damn dancing. You look like you're trying to shake a rat off your damn leg."

Adrian jumped on the couch, "Elmer . . ."

"Take it slow. Treat her right. Make her feel special, and she'll never leave you." He nudged his nose at him, "Good men are hard to find these days, my boy."

"Elmer, you act like you are some Casanova or something."

"Hellfire," he abruptly said, "this pickle has been more places than ol' Bessie."

Adrian slapped his head, "Stop," he held out a hand, "I'm getting a visual."

"Hey, just saying, it's bigger than a baby's arm." He started laughing, "I kill me," he said and slapped his knee. I should have been a damn comedian."

"Funny-looking."

"I can give you a few pointers. Let Elmer help you."

Reluctantly, Adrian said, "Sure."

Elmer hunched forward, elbows on knees, smoothly looked at Adrian, and baseball-gripped his cane.

"What . . . what are you doing?"

He firmed his grip and said, "Tell her." He let out a whooping Motown, "Baby! Baby . . . you are the bubbles in my bath."

"Bubbles?"

Elmer flatlined, "Don't interrupt me." Motown, "Baby, you are the cherry in my pie."

"What if I don't like cherries?"

"Who the hell doesn't like cherry pie?"

"Can't remember the last time I ate pie."

"Ay-huh, well, I guess you could use apple." He snapped his head back and belted a Motown tune. "Baby, you are the hair on my head that keeps me warm." Suddenly, he stopped and held a smile, "So . . ."

Fat lips. A slow exhale, "I think that if I listened to your advice, I'd be single the rest of my life." He smacked the couch, "Live on this couch for the rest of my life."

Elmer laughed, "Well, kid," and hopped up, "it's past this Casanova's bedtime." Adrian popped up and heard, "Get some sleep." Elmer hobbled toward the bedroom door, he stopped, flipped his head, "I'm happy for you, son."

"Thanks, Elmer."

"Goodnight . . . make sure you take our dog out in the morning, so I don't have to drag my tired bones out." Elmer inched his way around to face Adrian, "Oh, by the way, I'm having a Casanova camp next weekend down at the school. Two-day camp—teaching all you young kids how to pick up and keep girls." He sent Adrian a suspicious look, "What color t-shirt you want?" He began to count his fingers, "We got white—"

"Such a comedian," Adrian said and snickered.

Elmer blew Adrian a kiss. "Don't forget to take your buddy out before you leave."

"Yes, sir." As the door closed, he hollered, "I'm going to make everybody call me Adrian now."

Silence.

Adrian pivoted and headed toward home, stopped when he heard the bedroom door open, "You have always been Adrian," he heard. "You just needed someone other than an old man to tell you."

"I know."

"Goodnight, son."

Adrian walked home after taking Rocky out, hung his shirt in the closet, and placed his pants on the dresser. Eased his way onto the edge of the bed and pulled off each sock. He grabbed a t-shirt and shorts out of the drawer and dressed. He walked into the bathroom and looked at the stranger in the mirror. *Who are you?* Crazy eyes looked back at him without a twitch. He did a mental inventory of his life. *They are wrong about you. You are better than this.* He looked down at the wastebasket and then eyed the stranger once more. *Show them all.* He tilted his head toward the right shoulder and reached up, and took out the earring. *That isn't you. I can't be you anymore.* He ran his hand over the surface of the ring and the tip and tossed it in the basket. He gritted and ground his teeth as he watched his jaws move like they were breathing. *The shock will probably kill the old man.* He laughed inside and pulled his t-shirt over his head, and placed it on the toilet. Opened the cabinet and grabbed the shaving cream. Lathered up his head and shaved the hawk off. *No more. Your story will not end on Ewing Street.* He turned on the faucet and ran water over his head and face and neck. He closed his eyes and raised his head. Took three breaths and opened his eyes, "Hi, Adrian," he said to the man in the mirror.

He went into his bedroom, skyed above his bed, and landed in the middle. It broke down on the corners. He let out a loud, maddening laugh and did snow angels on the mattress.

# CHAPTER 18

# Conner Wallace
# 2009

onner had goals. One was not to catch a nickel in a Nevada prison. He was chuffed to watch Colt bellyache about the beatdown he received as his posse and girlfriend leaned against the cruiser. He could not hide the tears, the pain, and the embarrassment. Conner was a vagrant who lived by a creed, and it was uncompromising. Once in prison, Conner tried to stay on the straight and narrow; values and goals don't always travel the same roads. He hit a man so hard that the blood leaked profusely out of his pores, looked like he suffered from a disease birthed in an African jungle. The inmate walked behind a female officer as she was making a round in a housing unit, and he grabbed a full loaf of her cheek. Conner was lying on his bed, two beds in front of her, saw the entire scene. He heard the officer yell and snap around. The inmate ran past her toward Conner. The officer made a demonstrative gesture and chased after him. Conner stood up, split two standing in the aisle, and raised his hammer hand. Nailed the face of Mr. Grabby like wet, rotted sheetrock. The punch broke the orbital bone. After an emergency trip to the hospital, the assailant was immediately transferred out. Conner should have been awarded a medal, but instead, he received thirty days in isolation. He went the entire time without uttering a single word except to one person.

For his five-year sentence, his routine didn't change much. He was a creature who lived in his own mind. The outside world couldn't penetrate or interrupt his thoughts or actions. The incident at the Sand Pie, the sentence, the act of protecting the female officer was not part of his plan. It was slowing down his return to the woman of his dreams. He focused on his physical health, push-ups, sit-ups, body squats. Did hundreds to thousands a day for five years.

Five years later, NEMESIS stretched across his upper back in big, black lettering. Everton F.C., a Liverpool professional football team, ran down the back of his left triceps. Conner preferred Everton over the other Liverpool team, coincidentally named Liverpool. His left shoulder displayed the Union Jack and the United States flags. Down the back of the right triceps, Liverpudlians and Scouse were scribed. Residents of Liverpool are called Liverpudlians, and Scouse represented the Liverpool accent and dialect. Conner was a prideful man, and none were more prideful of his home than Conner. From the bottom of his jawline to the top of his chest plate, Unicorn was scribed in majuscule letters. By his appearance, he didn't look like an individual a person would challenge or anger. He was lean Angus beef, mesomorph body type, elastic long-sweeping muscles, more Appalachian-looking than Colorado Rockies. The tip of the triangle started at his waistline and ended at the base of his shoulders. As broad as a man could be. Shaved head, long dark beard with sprinkles of gray, piercing brown eyes, looked like a descendant of a viking. The scowl on his face was a permanent tattoo. An enigma, his appearance didn't match his quick wit and humorous banter. Conner walked out of the Nevada Prison a free man.

He acquired a rat bike in Las Vegas and traveled northwest through Reno and Lake Tahoe. Took the scenic route: Yosemite to San Francisco, down the Pacific Coast Highway to meet Damon Gill in Anaheim, California.

Gill and Conner housed together in J Block at Hoover. Conner intervened and saved Damon's ass when five illegals got the jump on him during an attempted assault. It was like a pack of wolves jumping on an unsuspecting doe. Damon educated Conner about the growing and lucrative underground fight scene out west. The uncanny foreigner was always ready to tangle for money.

Damon was released five months before Conner and set up shop in Anaheim. He was going to house Conner and manage him in the illegal fight game. Conner jumped on CA 91W, cruised to exit 28 for Lemon Street/ Anaheim toward Harbor Boulevard. He turned on N. Anaheim and arrived at the Sinking Ship.

He walked through the bar onto the patio and saw Damon waiting at a table. Damon saw him and jumped up out of his seat, beer in his left hand. "Welcome to So Cal," he said and shared a fist. They took their seats and Damon ran through the ins and outs of the game. "Every week we will get a text with the location of the fight. Could be out in the desert, an old warehouse . . . hell, it might be down at city hall." He finished his beer and slammed it on the table and smiled, "Damn, bruh, it is good to see you."

"Nah, shit, ay friend. Id like some beat'n de 'ell crap out of a few guys."

"Good, good," Damon said. "Point is, we have to be ready at a moment's notice." He hovered in his chair, peered over Conner's shoulder, and snapped his fingers, "Where the hell is the damn waitress? Need another." Dropped in his seat and said, "We have to be ready. Can't be surprised when we get notified." He studied Conner, trying to get a read on him, "This is big business, and some of these dudes are scary, bruh." Conner remained silent, face granite tight. "Are you ready for this?"

Conner crinkled his nose, narrowed his brows, and leaned forward in his seat. "Juss point me in de direction." He needed the money and wasn't cut out for conventional work. His best job skill was fighting. He traveled the western states for two years before getting himself locked up over the incident in Reno. From eating barbeque in Kansas City to visiting the Needle in Seattle, dropping down to Portland, and visiting every bar and nightlife along the way. He trekked the backbone of California, hung out in the desert city in Arizona, drove in the isolation of West Texas, and rode bulls in Dallas. Never crossed east of the mighty Mississippi. The hobo on a bike dipped his toes in the Great Salt Lake, detoured to the Mile-High City, and ended up at the Sand Pie. His two-year journey of self-discovery and reflection was over. Now, the coffers were dry, and it was time to fill up and head east and find his girl. The fight game fit him just fine. He walked with a purpose and focused. Quick-witted and slightly crazy.

Damon slapped the table, "That is what I wanted to hear."

Conner heard the waitress behind him say, "Hey, I'll be helping you for the rest of your visit. Tabitha's shift is over."

"Hey, you," Damon said, smiled with lust in his eyes.

"Can I get you two boys a drink?"

Damon said, "Do you have two nipples for a dime?" He offered another smile. He was five-ten, two hundred and twenty pounds. Looked more like an overgrown pitbull. He sloshed around, wobbled when he walked. He could throw a punch but was nowhere close to the fighter Conner was. He was a stationary target, relied on one big haymaker to land. After seeing Conner in action, he knew he had a meal ticket. He might have thought he was King Kong, but Conner was something different. He was Godzilla on Viagra, the world his whorehouse.

The waitress returned an ungrateful and forced grin.

Damon continued, "You know I used to be a doctor, I focused on beef injections," paused and smiled at Conner, spoke to the waitress, "I took care of moles, colds, and every unopen hole."

She put her back to Damon, "Sure, you do," she said as she looked at Conner, "Drink?"

"Canna get a Guinness?"

"For you?" she said to Damon.

"Another Coors."

"Ta, love," Conner said as she walked away.

Damon was kickstand hard between his knees. He flexed his neck muscles, shook his head and let out a Wile E. Coyote, "Damn," long and loud.

Conner didn't flinch, sat still like he was on a job interview and listened to his friend ramble.

"I haven't had any pussy since I got out of the damn joint," Damon said and clenched his jaws. "Did you see the tits on that babe?"

The waitress returned, dropped the beers on the table, heard Damon say, "How about you and I work up an appetite later?"

"I'm on a diet," she said and walked away.

Damon ogled her ass. "I got your diet hanging," he shouted and laughed, offered a fist to Conner, who obliged. He clawed his beer and took a long swig and said, "You ready to make some dead presidents?" Before Conner could answer, the waitress walked by. Damon cupped his jewels, hollered, "If you change your mind." Twisted his head back to Conner, "Sure you're ready?"

Conner cornered a lip and picked up his beer and slurped it empty. "Point me in de direction," he snapped back and slammed the bottle.

The waitress returned and moved her hand like a flyswatter at Damon and gave him a buzzkill when he began to speak. She took in Conner as she extended over the table to reach for his bottle.

Eyes on eyes.

Her tit knocked over Damon's drink. The liquid high coursed across the table and waterfalled on his lap. He jumped back, yelled, "Fuck."

Conner laughed from his teeth, face red, veins throbbing from his neck. He said, "yous a show Damon."

The waitress adjusted herself, "Sorry," she said to Damon and placed a brick of napkins on the table. Turned to Conner and said, "You have a name?"

Conner waggled a finger at her, "Juss anuvver virgin's piddle ma'am." She sent questioning eyes. He extended two fingers and gestured toward the bottle. He looked at Damon, spoke to her, "Not intiested." He spoke to Damon, "Meff."

Her face contorted in surprise.

When she was out of sight, Damon said, "Bro, what the fuck?" He scooted up in his seat and placed his elbows on the table, "You can take the ole girl back to my place."

"Not intiested." Conner started to tell Damon what his intentions were, his destination, tell him about his girl. Then he thought about it. The Devil had him, had him for a long time now. No reason to get Damon involved, and he figured he wouldn't understand. She lived in his head. Damon was a means to an end, and when he was no longer needed, Conner would cut bait and leave.

"Fuck it then," Damon said and crossed his arms. "I'll give it another shot."

She returned with two more and heard Damon say, "I really think you and I would have a lot of fun."

"Young man," she said, a laugh began in the pit of her stomach, "You couldn't handle me. Plus," she eyed Conner, "I'm interested in tall, dark, and foreign over here." She cupped her tits, "What is your name, stranger?" When Conner didn't respond, she said, "I love the accent." She crossed her arms under the breast, inviting Conner in, and offered a flirtatious grin.

"Conner."

"Well, Conner," she said and put her tits on the table, "I get off in a few hours . . . I'll buy you a drink."

"Nah," he replied and stared at a crease in the top of the table.

She sent a devilish smile. "I'll make it worth your while." She moved closer, lips near his ear, "Why don't you tell me what you like?"

Conner leaned away and licked his lips, showed her his eyes, "Like fe yous ter shit inna bag and beat me wi'it," he replied with an unassuming look.

She stepped back, "Oh, I never," she gasped, turned away, and stomped off.

Damon's face turned three shades. He headbutted the table and cackled like a mental patient with his head between his knees. He came up to catch his air, back of his head smacked the table, "Bruh," he said, rubbing the back of his head, "that was the funniest shit I've heard in a long time." He watched her Guinness Book badonkadonk sway and sideswipe a table, causing a patron to spill his beer. "She was all over you . . . why don't you get on that?" Finished with a mumble out of the side of his mouth: "If she had yellow pants on, someone would climb in her ass thinking it was a taxi."

Conner listened, square jaw chiseled out of granite and stern eyes.

Damon cooled, "Just you haven't had a piece in over five years and your first outing out, you have one throw herself at you."

Conner massaged his beard, sat back in his chair, "Am not out e'yer socialize and ay' I gut a girl." He scanned the room, hoping she wasn't coming back for round three. "Ay didn't need anymore." Conner picked up his empty and put it on the table next to them, "This is business."

Damon lipped his bottle. "Your loss, pal, your loss." Swigged, "Maybe she'll give me a shot now that you shot her down."

The waitress replaced herself with another. Both drank the rest of the day. They formulated a game plan and returned to the hole-in-the-wall Damon rented. Only good thing about it was it was on the Pacific Ocean.

Nightly, Conner stood in the ocean surf and looked out at the sky. It had a salubrious effect on his fragile state. Waves of purple, orange, and yellow streaked against the drowsy sun. Needles of sand pulsated against his toes with fragrances of salt in the air. He reflected on the only woman who captured the monster's heart. He ached to return to her. His journey of discovery was soon to be over, and he would be reunited with her. So, he had hoped.

Over the next year, Conner fought monthly, sometimes weekly. He won hundreds of dollars on some and thousands on others. He developed a reputation and cult following. Damon had been of use; he guided Conner to the best and most profitable fights. Slowly, rumors of a potential super fight between the new sensation, Conner, and reigning champ, Chevy Maddox, began to swell in the underground community. After months of negotiations between Damon and Chevy's handlers, the fight was set. Damon walked on the surf and stood behind Conner, "We got the fight with Maddox."

Conner didn't turn around, kept his eyes on the surf. "Sound as a pound," he said.

"Good?" Damon said and moved up on Conner's shoulder. "If you win . . . when you win, you will pocket at least fifty grand."

Conner grunted.

"Would have thought you would have been more excited."

"Regardless," Conner spoke in a whisper, eyes full of the portrait, "This wul be de last one." He was ready to go home; the money would fund his trip home. He had been gone long enough.

Damon swallowed the shock. "Bruh," he said and moved in front of Conner, "we have a good thing."

Conner looked through him.

"You win this, you and . . ." he paused, moved his head side to side until Conner eyed him, "we write our own ticket."

Conner shot a harsh look back, the first for Damon, then looked over him. Damon stepped back out of his personal space. "Nah," Conner said, calmer than he looked, "this is it ay, then I'm going to see a friend then ay goin' back ter me gril."

Damon kicked at the water, grunted, and clenched his fists, "I don't get you," he barked. "We came all this way and now you want to jump ship?" He stomped toward the surf and returned with his hands on his hips, "You're going to walk away?"

Conner inhaled.

Damon grabbed two hands of hair and bent down and screamed. Took a few deep breaths and calmed himself, "Who is this girl you keep talking about?" Conner didn't blink. Granite face. Eyes searching for something in the distance. Damon scooped a palm full of sand and massaged it in his hands and spread his fingers, and watched as each grain funneled through his fingers like Conner and his relationship. A year of success washed away in an instant. He tried once more. "You must really love her, man."

*The Devil won't keep us apart.*

"All the women out here." Damon was growing agitated he couldn't get through to Conner. "I see them throw themselves at you every night." Third time a charm, he playfully hit Conner on the shoulder, "Just go with one. One time, you will stop thinking about this mystery girl." In their year together, Damon had never seen Conner speak on the phone, receive a piece of mail. The more he thought about it, he'd never seen Conner have a conversation with anybody, including him. Not a real conversation. One of substance.

Conner kept his head down and kicked the sand.

Damon gasped, "I don't get it . . . I do not understand you," he said and jabbed his finger at him.

Conner finally spoke, "Thus is nah it for me." Stepped toward the water, moving past Damon, "Am done afti this and we go us separate ways." He wasn't in any mood to explain himself, spoke serious and stern. He was desperate to get home. It had been a long ten years. When he started this journey, he had planned and anticipated it would take no more than five years to execute his plan. The Sand Pie incident and Colt threw a wrench in his plan.

*The Devil won't keep us apart.*

# CHAPTER 19

# Conner Wallace
# 2011

The fight with Chevy Maddox was prescheduled. A fight of this magnitude had to be. There would be no text, no rushing to the event, or fighting without notice. The fight would get the build-up, like the promotion of a championship fight or a big movie premier. Conner had fought twenty-one times over the past twelve months, with only two lasting more than ten minutes. The undefeated wrecking ball from Liverpool would go into the match as a big underdog. Conner was big, ferocious, and unforgiving. He was a great white shark.

Chevy Maddox? He was something different. A megalodon. He stood six-eight and weighed over three hundred pounds. He had never been beaten.

The day before the fight, Conner stood in the surf enjoying his view. Tranquil, mind free of the noise of life. *The Devil won't keep us apart.* "You ready for tomorrow?" he heard Damon say from behind.

"Dun worry about, Damon. It's me fate," he said, maintaining his gaze on the neverending blue and beyond.

Damon gasped, placed his hands on his hips and moved up next to Conner. "Have you seen this fucking guy?"

Conner lowered his head and pushed his toes into the sand.

"He eats nails, Conner. This guy is a killer. A killer, Conner." Damon moved to the front and stood in front of Conner until he looked up. When he did, Damon added, "And you're out here working on a damn tan like it's a vacation."

"Iddle be sound as a pound, kidda. Don't worry."

"I'd be a little more optimistic if you were focused."

"Ye nah why nobody 'as evun seun de Loch Ness Munsti?"

Damon sucked in his bottom lip and stood silent.

"Because ay killed 'im."

Damon hunched his shoulders and put his head down, and started his walk back to the house, but he stopped. "Hey," he yelled back, "I thought the Lock Ness Monster was in France."

"Read a bewk, Damon."

Damon shrugged, "An honest mistake."

The morning of the fight, Conner rose out of bed as morning light winked at him through the blinds. He pulled up his britches and picked up a pair of socks off the floor, whiffed them, and put them on. Then he bent and slipped on his shoes and double-tied them. He stood and touched his toes. Again, and held the pose. He got vertical and stomped through the house and out the door. Smiled and soaked in the rays and the ocean salt.

He jogged off and quickly picked up the pace. Steadied himself when he felt his cadence was enough, and muscles flared with pain. Three miles in, he fired a snot rocket and blew past the pier with strings of phlegm skiing from his mouth. *The Devil won't keep us apart.* Then his mind went canvas black with absent thought as he uncoupled visions of her with each stride. Today, like each day before, his focus needed to be on someone or something else. Before, he failed. Today he could not. Three miles later, sunburnt orange and spent and soaked in sweat, he slowed to a walk, then stopped. He angled his head high, eyes closed, and listened as his air funneled out of his nose.

He stood with his hands on his head and glanced around as his heart returned to a normal beat. At his eight o'clock, an outdoor gym surrounded by a chain link fence. Conner glared with a curious look as one stood in front of a bench press, howling and barking. One man, then another, slapped him across the face with frying-pan-sized hands. Conner cringed and gritted his teeth. Directly ahead, a middle-aged man trotted toward him shirtless, wearing spandex pants with a turtle popping out and pink sunglasses. Conner's eyes followed him as he passed. His lip twitched as he held a laugh. On his right, on the beach before the blue and beyond, the wonders of the world, half a dozen tourists strolled on the beach as they enjoyed the surf. One gawked at the foreigner like they just found evidence of aliens. He smiled and broke out in a full-face grin like a circus clown in the middle of a show. He was ready and focused. Manacles of his past locked away, at least for the day. Fear of failure buried miles back in the surf.

Conner napped on the way to the fight. Damon was concerned; Conner was either crazy or stupid. What kind of crazy was what was important? Did Conner care if he won? Did he even think he could? He must have asked himself those questions. Damon sure did. Was he napping because he knew he was going to get an epic ass-whooping? Or was the crazy son of a bitch that confident? The matchup on this hot, humid Sunday was at the Puente Hills Landfill. The largest garbage dump in the world. Home to over seven hundred acres of Los Angeles waste. Closed on Sundays, the home of rodents and other varmints would host thousands of spectators, from the filthy rich of Hollywood to the corrupt of the underclass.

Damon and Conner arrived at the landfill to the roar of spectators and black fowl circling above. Conner watched as a cavalcade of limousines and six-figure cars inched their way toward the arena. He wondered who they loved. Nobody loved Conner except two. Who drives out to a rat-infested, maggot-breeding, nasal-damaging place to watch grown men spill blood and break bones? The world had failed him, failed itself, failed all of them. He knew he was making the right decision by leaving.

The pit was an acre wide and long. A perfect square excavated to dirt, formerly under tons of disregarded trash. In the wee hours of the night, dozens of dozers excavated the area for the pugilist spectacle. The only thing more obnoxious than the grandiose design was the parade of luxury limos and wannabe dignitaries in their suits and hiding behind their sunglasses. Inside the pit, a taut, two-inch nylon rope attached to five-foot metal rods protruded from the ground, creating nine hundred square feet for the ring.

As Conner entered the circle, Chevy Maddox arrived from the other side, parting pillars of men, dressed in a full robe big enough to cover a Tahoe. He turned around in a circle with his hands above his head to acknowledge the crowd. He was confident and showed a gratuitous amount of gasconade to the crowd. Conner saw G.O.A.T. scribed on his back big as a billboard. "Goat?" he questioned Damon and pointed at the robe.

Damon leaned up on his toes. "It means the greatest of all time," he hollered.

Conner rocked back and forth on his tips, "Oh, ay see," he said and did a lazy uppercut swing with his right hand.

Chevy disrobed and flexed his upper body in the direction of Conner and let out a scream. A bestial man. Communicated with blunt force trauma. "Oh, it's over, Damon," Conner said. Then, "Ay can't fight this guy." He stood across from the giant with a pair of black swim trunks; no elaborate robe, nothing. He hid his eyes from his opponent, from his friend, from all the noise and chaos.

Damon gulped, hesitated, then said, "You can't fight this guy?" He grabbed Conner by the elbow, "Why not?"

Conner pulled away, raised his head like a triumphant gladiator, and pointed across at Chevy, "'Is legs ay ter small," he said and laughed out the back of his throat. "Skinny 'e lewks like a roadrunner."

Damon said, "Oh, his legs are like the roadrunner." He chuckled and pushed Conner, "Don't scare me like that."

"This coyote is go'n ter eat these legs," he said and chomped his lips and snapped his jaws at Damon.

Damon slapped Conner on both his shoulders. "That is what I'm talking about."

Chevy took a few minutes walking around the circle, eyeballing Conner and slapping hands with his fans. Strutting around with his hands flailing at his sides. He took three pictures: two with suits and one with a little lady and a baby. Yeah, everybody assumed this was going to be like all of Chevy's other fights, smooth and easy. Both men took the center of the circle in a ceremonial start. No reason, really. There were no rules. Eye-gouging, biting, nothing was off limits. Only way to win was with a knockout or a tap out—meaning one man gives up.

"Did yous eat de guy am suppose ter be fight 'n?" Conner asked the bigger man.

Chevy looked down at his adversary, then Damon, "What did he say?"

Damon glanced at Conner, then Chevy. He took a step forward, cupped his mouth with his hands, and yelled, "He asked if you ate the guy he is supposed to be fighting."

Chevy smiled and shrugged his shoulders at Damon and Conner. He grunted and flexed in front of his opponent. The crowd went wild. Chevy spun around with his arms high like he was already celebrating. Conner stepped forward and leaned his neck out, "Do yous fuck goats?" When Chevy stopped in bewilderment, Conner asked again, "Do yous fuck goats?"

Damon stepped forward to join Conner, put his hand on his arm, and said to Chevy, "He asked if you fucked goats."

"I understood what he said!" Chevy screamed at Damon.

"Sorry," Damon said and retreated to the corner.

Conner stood flat-footed where he was with his hands clasped behind his back and showed a sheepish grin.

Chevy faked a punch toward Conner's head. Conner didn't flinch. Chevy yelled, "I'm going to kill you, little man."

Conner hit his fists together in front of his chest, turned around, and walked back to Damon. He turned around to face the ring. *Devil will not keep us apart.* He squatted down and jumped up, "Wa' do yous think 'e sees whun 'e normally fights?"

"Huh?"

Conner repeated the question.

Damon blinked his eyes, "What do he sees when he normally fights? Conner, bruh, you must get focused," Damon said and grabbed his friend by the triceps.

"Fear . . . 'e normally sees fear, Damon." Damon stared at Conner, "Am nah afraid," Conner grinned and then said, "and 'e thinks am crazy," he jabbed a finger at his temple.

"You are crazy. You're the craziest son of a bitch I ever met."

Conner jostled his head. "Yis ay am," he said and looked across at Chevy momentarily, then faced Damon and screamed, "E's brick'n it. This fight is already over."

Damon whispered, "This fight is already over."

The fight began and Chevy quickly took the center of the ring. Conner walked slowly toward him. *The Devil will not keep us apart.* Chevy threw a left jab. He moved stiff but quick, a mannequin in the wind. Conner slid to his right like an ice skater, smooth and graceful. He could feel the friction against his beard as the massive hand passed by him, hitting only whiskers. As he slid to the right, Conner did a one-hundred-and-eighty-degree turn and connected to the back of Chevy's head with the palm of his left hand. Chevy went to a knee and quickly looked back, expecting a rush from his opponent. "Ay don't deck a fellar whun 'e isn't lewk'n," Conner yelled out and bounced on his feet. Focused, he only heard the rapid thump of the beat of his heart. Screams moved the ground under his feet. Echoes spun the fowl in the air.

Conner stepped back, giving Chevy a wide berth to get up. He got up shakily, like a newborn born in the wild.

Chevy heard high-pitched screams in his ears. His vision tunneled to the sky above. He focused on the flocks, wishing he was one of them, free without fear. He gathered himself, kept his eyes on Conner as he got back up, peered at the crowd, and then Conner, wiped the dirt off his chest with the palms of his hands and showed frightened eyes. He hesitated, then rushed and released a right cross. Conner ducked underneath and hit the chin of the bigger man with his right palm, and walked away. The giant staggered back four steps and grabbed his chin with his right hand. Conner waited, moved his head side to side, his nose wrinkled as he inhaled, and he gestured for Chevy to come toward him.

Chevy stumbled forward through the dust and thunderous roars, mean-mugged Conner, and pushed the toes of his right foot into the wasteland to gain his footing, waited for the start gun to go off in his head. He had never been in a real fight. He didn't know how to control his emotions or bottle the fear inside. It fizzled and bubbled, fighting to explode out. He failed to learn how to react in stressful situations. He was unable to fight the urge to succumb to the fear building inside. It wrapped itself around his heart and squeezed his lungs. His pulse beat ignorance in his mind. His eyes darted around as spectators clapped and offered encouragement. The hunter was now the prey. He looked across at Conner. The dead eyes sucked him in.

The soulless eyes, dark as a black hole swallowing a sun, peered back at him, eager to peel the skin off his bones. Conner heard Damon bark out, "Put your damn hands up!" Conner cocked his head to the side, eyes on the bull, and clasped his hands behind his back. Conner saw the devoid of fight, smiled at Chevy, and crooned his head out high. "What the hell are you doing?" Damon screamed and jumped in place. "Hands up."

Chevy's mug turned sour when Conner angled his chin out. Chevy never fought the brave or crazy. Conner was crazy brave and hospital crazy. He was attuned to what Chevy had planned. He saw the movements before his opponent thought about doing them. He didn't need any preamble to know what was to come. He saw a gleam of hope on Chevy. He almost felt bad about what he was going to do to him.

Chevy saw his opening when Conner closed his eyes. The start gun echoed in his head. He pushed off his right toes and barreled toward the chin like a rhino. The glide, fluid movements replaced with stiffness and tensed muscles. Fear lanced through his body, took away his ability to breathe. A locomotive train without fuel to burn rushed Conner. The punch was slow and clumsy. The act caused a hullaballoo in the crowd. Most hollered in appreciation, thinking they were going to make a mint after Chevy landed the punch. Conner swayed his head back and forth like he was listening to cool jazz. He opened his eyes and watched the fist come. He slid his head away with the punch. His jaw cracked, fist forging steel. Oh's and ah's from the crowd rang his eardrums. Chevy watched Conner stumble and drop to his right knee. Conner shook the wobble out and got to his feet. He sucked on his gums and spit a tooth at his feet and cracked his neck and bounced. Chevy put his hands on his knees, bent over, and panted in the failure. Conner rubbed his chin, "Yous hit hard," he said and slid to his left, "but not hard e-blewdy-nuff."

Chevy let out a scream and balled his fist. "Come on."

Conner glanced at Damon and sent a reassuring grin and stared down Chevy with the darkness in his eyes. Chevy stepped cautiously, agitation set in, and he threw caution to the wind and ran toward him. Whites of his eyes expanded, and his mouth opened, he hurled a right hook. Conner stepped in toward his body and greeted him with a knee to the chin.

Chevy lay defeated, and Conner stood over him, snarled, "Ay we go'n to be friends?" Chevy rubbed his face. Conner didn't relish too long in his pending victory. He grabbed the leg of the giant, who didn't fight the inevitability of his defeat and let out a scream. Evil swept across his face, "Ay dun need er 'uv any friends," he growled and dropped an elbow on the knee. Chevy flopped around on the ground as Conner walked toward Damon. "Beep, beep," he said and walked by his friend and through the crowd.

"Oh my God," Damon screamed and grabbed his face.

## CHAPTER 20

# Adrian Franklin
# 1992

Adrian stumbled across the broken sidewalk as familiarity took him toward Elmer's. He looked like a drunken wino trying to dance in the wind when he crashed on the porch, splintering two wood spindles. His glassy eyes bulged, "Did I do that?"

Elmer heard the banging, the crack of wood and peered out and saw the boy lying on the porch. He'd seen Adrian drunk before, but this was something different. Elmer walked out the front door, under-hooked the arms and tried to drag him in, "Adrian," he struggled, "I can't lift you by myself. I need you to help."

A moan. A chuckle. Then he caught his footing and pushed himself up, "El-mer."

"It's okay, kid." He dropped Adrian on the couch.

Adrian opened his eyes and saw the ceiling. He spun like he was mounted on a plastic horse going around on the carousel. "El-mer . . . Elmer, you need to get away from me."

Elmer limped into the kitchen, opened the cabinet, and pulled a glass, spoke as he filled it at the sink, "Why is that, kid?"

"Because," words got stuck in his throat, he forced them out, "Because I'm a loser." He raised his voice, "I'm nothing . . . I'll be nothing." Slurred his speech as he said, "I'm no-thu-ng."

"What's wrong, Adrian?"

Adrian pushed his left hand against the couch and maneuvered himself into a sitting position. His right hand caught the edge of the couch before he crashed headfirst onto the carpet. His head swayed, and back on the carousel he went, round and round. His head bobbed and weaved like a heavyweight, his eyes closed. He pecked his lips to wet them and sneaked out, "El-m-er," a head bob, then, "she left me."

Elmer huffed, "Oh, Adrian, I'm sorry."

The couch reached out and grabbed him and wrapped him tight as his shade-drawn eyes flickered. His hand inched up from below like he was a puppet on a string, and he waved a finger across the room, "And-you're-going-to," a laugh, a whimper, then, "leave me . . ."

Elmer said, "I'm not going anywhere, Adrian." He reached the couch, palmed Adrian's shoulder, and rubbed. "I promise."

Adrian sloshed around the couch like a fish out of water, flipped his back to Elmer, and said, "This is so much more comfortable than that damn bed I have." His lids opened, and he mumbled, "You will leave." A fist to a cushion, then, "You will see." He stopped moving. Elmer stepped away and heard, "You all leave or die on me."

Elmer picked up the glass off the table, sat it back down and said, "Adrian?"

"It's okay, Elmer," he said and flipped back toward the room, "It's my lot in life, my destiny. I've learned to expect it." He closed his eyes and exhaled.

Elmer sat and waited. Minutes went by, then Adrian sprung to life and got vertical. He sleeved mucus from his face and hung his head. Elmer joined him on the couch and crooned, "I'm not going anywhere," he said and rubbed his neck.

Adrian rose and weaved his way into the kitchen. Elmer followed. He waited for Adrian to say something, fall, cry, anything. Adrian stepped forward, then back, his head spun. Elmer placed a hand on his arm to steady him, "Why don't you sit back down?" He steered Adrian back to the couch, and after he dropped, Elmer walked into the kitchen. He hoped Adrian was out for the night. He reached into the cabinet and pulled down the coffee. Filled the pot with water. He sensed he was going to be awake all night watching over Adrian.

"I killed my dad and brother."

Stunned. Shaken. Elmer dropped the coffee and stared at the boy.

He mumbled on. "Bet you didn't know that . . . did you . . . Mister."

Elmer put a filter in. Thought about the words spoken and finished with coffee grounds. "Adrian."

"I think my life would have been different if they were alive." He inhaled deeply. Chin on his chest. Eyes closed. "Dad could have taught me about girls . . . maybe . . . maybe football. Alex and I could have played outside." Eyes opened. He fought to get up. "He would have liked Rocky." He sat up. His head swayed from side to side. A wide smile. A laugh. "Rocky," he whispered. He frowned. Sniffled. His voice cracked, "My mom would be around more . . . she wouldn't drink as much." He collapsed into the couch. Moments went by, and Adrian raised an arm. Fought gravity and lifted a finger. Pointed in the kitchen. Blind man with a gun, he said, "You will leave next."

Elmer ignored that. Stayed silent as he thought about what to say. Heard Adrian cough and mumble. He listened to him inhale and exhale. Watched with intensity until Adrian settled and then refocused on what to do about him. Adrian had unspooled in hours. Susan was the reason he steadied himself and dropped his juvenile behavior. Set goals. Elmer tried and failed. He wondered if he would be enough to keep him on the right track.

Then he heard a grunt. A whimper from the couch. Uttered words dripped out, incoherent and weak. *He killed his father and brother?* He sat at the kitchen and sipped. Looked over at Adrian intently. Visible peaceful. Mentally torn. *No, that boy wouldn't harm anybody he cared about.*

"Scott." He stood up and began to laugh.

"Adrian?"

He killed the laugh, light switch quick. Snorted. Wobbled. His arm stretched out and caught the couch. He blinked until his vision was clear. One step. He caught his balance. Another step. He reached forward with his left arm and touched the back of the recliner. "Scott," withered out. A rumble came out as he cleared the phlegm. Rocky hunkered down under the table next to the recliner. Eyes down. Tail snaking. Nose in the carpet. He tried again, "Scott!" he screamed. A third step, his momentum pushed him into the kitchen chair. Elmer took a quick glance as the chair tilted and then fell when Adrian pushed by and leaned against the sink. He put his head in the sink bowl and coughed and spit. He sleeved his mouth and turned on the water. Splashed hands full of water on his face and stood up. "Better," he said.

Elmer stood in front of the fridge and waited.

"Scott," he said again. Laughed louder and pointed at Elmer, "he wouldn't be around if my dad was here." He flicked his finger in the air, searched for

Elmer's eyes, then, "I . . . I . . . do you like Scott?" Before Elmer could answer, Adrian added, "Do you know he beats on my mom?"

Elmer knew. He had seen the damage on her face; bloody, bruised, scratches down her neck and arms. He also knew Adrian was always gone when he beat her. After, Scott would stay away for a few days. Elmer always knew he would only see Adrian sporadically. When Scott returned, Cindy pleaded for him to stay out of it and not start trouble. Adrian would retreat to Elmer's.

Elmer didn't bring it up with Adrian. Felt Adrian would when he was ready. Didn't think it would be under these circumstances. "I know," Elmer said softly and stepped toward him.

"No," Adrian said and held out a hand.

Elmer stopped, "Adrian?"

An aggressive hand toward him. A firm, "No." He pulled his hand back, massaged the back of his neck, and said, "I'm bad luck. I'm garbage, Elmer." He held a smile, wide and bright, "You need to throw me out with the trash." A flat stare like he was looking through him into a portal of darkness, reduced to a whisper, "Maybe I'll get a nice cushy spot at the landfill."

Elmer frowned. Eyes welled up.

"Come on, Elmer," Adrian said and slapped the counter, "That was a little funny."

"No," Elmer said firmly and reached out as he stepped.

"No," eyes wide and hand out. "Stay over there, Elmer."

A step.

"Please."

Elmer stopped and retreated to the fridge door. He spoke softly, "I know you are hurting."

As a buoy on the ocean sways with the tide, Adrian rocked side to side. Shades closed. He licked his lips and smacked them together. "Have I ever told you about my Aunt Martha?"

"Martha?"

A sliver of an eyeball, then, "Yeah, the one who got pregnant."

"No."

"You remember the day we met?"

"You and I?"

"I remember like it was yesterday." That laugh returned. Laughed so hard his eyes teared up. Mouth open. Eyes wide. He pointed at Elmer, "I hated you, old man. You made fun of my name."

Elmer cracked a slight smile as he remembered that fateful day. "You were . . ."

Adrian twirled around, "I went running into the house to tell my mom about Rocky and you." He stopped, caught himself against the counter, "I love that damn dog." He leaned forward with narrow eyes, "Elmer," he swallowed, licked his lips, "Do you . . ." blinked and moved his stiff neck, "Does Rocky love me?"

"Loves you more than me."

The buoy sways as the wind picks up inside him, "Right after I tell her about Rocky, the phone rings." He braces himself with his left hand, the right leads an orchestra, "My mom's carrying on . . . blah, blah, blah." He looked at Elmer with an anger he hadn't shown.

"Adrian?"

"She comes out and says it was Aunt Martha, and she is pregnant." Big smile, "Isn't that exciting?"

He held the smile as Elmer said, "Adrian, I don't under—"

His face went neutral. Eyes closed. Then, his shades exploded open, "Yeah, Mother," he yelled, "that is great fucking news!" He slammed his fist on the counter. The rattle shook the cups in the cabinet, startled Elmer. Rocky retreated to the couch. Nose pushed under. "Wrong answer, Mom."

He lumbered toward Elmer. Emotions a yo-yo on a string. A smile came and went. Rage filled his mouth, his fist clenched. "How could she let her do that to me?" Speaking turned to screaming, "How could she let her do that to me?" He bumped the corner of the fridge as he crossed by Elmer and headed toward the couch, "How did she not know?" he said quietly.

Elmer watched with tears. Tears not seen since the day Bessie died. "What did she do Adrian?" The boy collapsed onto the couch. Elmer followed, "Tell me. Tell me, son."

Adrian ripped at the cushion with his hands, "Her fucking stubble face against my skin." He tossed the cushion on the floor, sat up and glared at Elmer with tears in his eyes, "Who the fuck she thinks she is?" He jumped up, his head's toward the ceiling, fists clenched, "I'll kill that fucking bitch."

Heavy breathing. He leaned forward, hands on knees. Back to vertical as Elmer slowly stepped through the living room. He stopped at his chair when he heard, "Stay back." Shades closed. Adrian licked his lips. Shades flickered. He laughed again. He floated back to the couch and as his back hit, he asked, "Are you proud of me, Elmer?"

Elmer gingerly sat in his chair with his eyes on the boy.

Adrian looked at Elmer, one eye closed, finger out. Like a sniper through a scope. Whispered, "You should be." Finger snapped back, laughter again, "Ha, ha, I lost my virginity at eight years old."

Elmer felt like his soul had been pulled out of his open mouth. He finally realized the extent of the pain. He said nothing.

"Yes, Elmer." He rolled over and faced the back of the couch. "My aunt was a piece of shit rapist." Then, "Bet you didn't see that coming." He jumped off the couch. Elmer followed. As Adrian made his way to the door, he said, "Forget about me." He opened the door and spoke without looking, "You don't need this bullshit, Elmer."

"Adrian, wait."

"Susan left me. She left me, Elmer," he cried and slammed the door.

"Son?"

He retreated to the couch and sat.

"She left."

"I know, son."

Vertical he went, with a questioning tone, he said, "How did you know?" a long nooooo and a smile. "Did she tell you she was going to leave me?"

Elmer wiped a tear away, "No," he swallowed and batted his eyes, "you told me."

He slumped back into the couch, shades closed, "I did?" Face toward the ceiling, elongated neck. His head spun on the carousel. He murmured, "Oh, Elmer, I'm so drunk." Then went mute.

Elmer waited minutes. When he thought Adrian was out for the night, he stepped into the kitchen and poured a cup of coffee. He returned to his seat and watched Adrian sleep as he sipped.

"Susan . . . Susan . . . don't leave me." His head and body slid toward the edge of the couch like slowly fallen timber. "I'll get better." His eyes returned. Groggy and half-opened. "Susan?"

"She isn't here, Adrian," Elmer said and leaned toward him. "Go to sleep."

Shades closed. A deep, slow inhale. He slurred, "Her dad made her do it."

"Mitchell?"

A burst of laughter. A cough. Upper body vertical, hands on head, eyes below. He showed his eyes and said, "I'm pretty sure he doesn't like me anymore, Elmer." A crack of the neck. A winch. His lips vibrated as he blew all his air out. "Pussy."

"What happened?"

Flat features, serious tone. "Can you believe it?" A long lick of the lips, then, "He said I was a violent person, Elmer."

"What?"

"He read it in the paper." Nothing. "Elmer . . . geez, old man." Louder, "He read about the domestic violence in the paper."

"Oh," expressionless. Then, "but you were just protecting your mother."

Wide eyes. He licked his lips. Blinked twice. Smiled and extended his hands out, "No matter to the fucking yuppie in Yaples." One slap of the hands. He pressed his palms together like he was smashing rocks. As he grinded his teeth, he said, "Should have let him kill that bitch." Two fists, a dog face growl, "Fuck."

"You don't mean that, Adrian."

His head weaved back and forth, "Why not, Elmer?" Gestured with his hands, "Then," his eyes scanned the room. "I move in with Rocky and you." He continued to scan, "Where is my dog?"

Elmer gestured back over his head, "Under the table."

A smile. He leaned forward, kneed the floor, eyes on Rocky, and cooed, "Come on, boy."

Rocky stared. Elmer said, "Think the yelling scared him."

A sigh. He pushed off, and dropped on the couch. "Great." He sent a suffering gaze toward the dog, "Now he hates me."

"Scared."

Slow and light, "Other than you, he's my best friend." Elmer and Adrian met eyes, "I'd die for that dog."

"Adrian?"

"Did I tell you what Scott said the night he called the cops on me?"

Elmer inhaled.

"He said he had been waiting for me to turn eighteen." A laugh. A prolonged smile. "He did say it as my hands were wrapped around his neck, and he turned a new shade of red." Adrian demonstrated with the couch pillow.

Elmer remembered. He thought Adrian was going to kill Scott. It was the first time Elmer appreciated Russ. The rage got him and took over. If it wasn't for the friend, Elmer had no doubt Scott has going to die. Russ pulled and pleaded until Adrian released Scott from his grasp.

Adrian continued, "He had been waiting to call the cops on me. Waited until I was an adult. Fucking piece of shit tricked me." Wide eyes, crouched nose. Shrugged and said, "I don't care." Shook his head side to side, "Don't care, Elmer." Then, "Stop beating my mom, and I'll stop whooping your ass." Louder, more forceful, "I warned him, Elmer. I warned everybody not to mess with me."

"Adrian?"

Shades flickered, back on the horse. Around and around his mind went. He fell back onto the couch and spoke fast, "Did I tell you about the first time we had sex?"

"Who?"

A sigh. A gasp. "Stay with me, Elmer. Susan . . . Susan, the girl I dated."

"Oh."

As he held his head in his hand, he smiled, and a tear raced down his face. "I cried, Elmer. Cried like a baby." He licked his lips and looked for understanding in Elmer. When he got it, "I wanted to wait until we were married."

An open mouth, a silent, "Oh."

Adrian jumped up, legs spread. He grabbed his crotch and bellowed out, "She wanted this. Wanted the hammer." He laughed. Fell on the floor. Cried and screamed, "Why won't she love me? Why can't I be loved?"

Elmer leaned forward and rubbed his back with a palm, "You are loved, kid. I love you."

He swiped him off. Stood up and continued to cry. Hand on Elmer, "I know, I know you do." He gently patted him on the back, then again. "But why won't she love me?" The gates broke open, no more laughter, just tears, rivers of them.

Elmer collected Adrian and steered him toward the couch. "Sit."

"I just want to be normal. Normal people get loved," he whispered and embraced Elmer. Held him tight.

"I love you, kid."

"No," he said and slid away from Elmer, and stumbled toward the door. "You don't need me in your life. I'm bad news." He jarred open the door. Glanced back at Elmer, "Who's been bamboozled now? Yeah," he stepped outside, "I know what it means."

# CHAPTER 21

Adrian hated his bed the most when he woke up from a hangover. Other times it was bearable. It swallowed him whole. He felt like a hot dog in a bun, constricted his movement and air. Before Susan, it became a habit; he and Russ drank nightly. After Susan, he slowed way down. He was as dry as the Sahara Desert. Like Biblical times, his life before Susan and after Susan. BS and AS. His eyes rolled back into his head as he realized he would never be the same. He crawled out of bed. Old habits die hard. His head hits first. Throbbed and new aches pulsated from new places. He went into the bathroom and scavenged through the cabinets. *Where is the aspirin?* He stepped into the hall, yelled, "Mom," grabbed his head, "do you know where the aspirin is?"

"Check the cabinet."

"I did."

"It isn't there?"

Head down. He massaged his temples and hollered back, "I wouldn't be asking if I found it." He slammed the bathroom door shut, walked into his room, and slid into bed.

Heard from the door, "If you wouldn't drink so much."

*If you were a better mom, maybe I wouldn't.* He covered his face with the pillow.

She continued, "Bring your laundry down. I want to get it started before we leave for the weekend."

*Wait, what?* He tossed the pillow to the side, "What?"

His mom appeared at the door. "Scott and I are going away."

He wished she would stay. He never needed her more. Began to ask and stopped. He remembered the last time he had asked her. Thirteen, busted lip, black eye. Hungry and lonely. Too embarrassed to walk over and talk to Elmer. Cried and cried, begged her to stay. I will only be gone a few hours, she said. Few hours? Returned four days later and Scott in hand. First time he met him. Hated him the moment he laid eyes on him.

"Stop," she smiled, "he is really sorry about what happened."

"Sure, he is," he tossed the pillow at the door. "Just get out."

As his mom continued to rant, Adrian ignored her and thought about the night before. *I have not done that in a long time. I don't think I've ever been that drunk.* Then it hit him. *What the hell did I tell Elmer? Oh, shit, I told him.*

He snapped out of it when he heard, "What is that smell?"

"Mom," he said when she walked toward the closet and grabbed his shirt from the night before. "I wouldn't have grabbed that if I was you."

"Yuck," she said and tossed it at him. Headache didn't stop the chuckle. She deserved to get a little vomit on her.

"What the fuck, Cindy?" He caught the shirt and threw it toward the door.

"Adrian Franklin!"

"Just get out."

Calm and slow, "We will be back Sunday night."

As she walked out, he said, "No rush."

Elmer thought about Adrian all day. Wondered how long before he saw him again. Never peeked out those blinds more than that day. When he heard the steps stretched under the weight, he almost jumped up to meet him at the door. He stayed calm. When Adrian knocked on the door, he said, "Why the hell are you knocking?"

"Um, I figured—"

Elmer turned around and hollered over his shoulder, "Get your ass in here." Adrian looked left toward the Red Bone. Right toward the street formerly belonging to Leo and heard, "What the hell are you waiting for?"

"Yeah," he said, entered, and sat small and slumped like a stranger on the couch. Watched Elmer go into the kitchen, fill a cup of coffee, and return.

"Here," he said and handed the cup to Adrian, "think you probably need this after last night."

"Thanks."

Adrian sipped and looked up to see Elmer sitting in his chair staring at him as he drank his coffee. Both drank in silence for a moment. Felt like an eternity to Adrian. He spoke first, "Elmer, I just want . . . no, I need," he cleared his throat, "I need to apologize for last night." Adrian waited for a reply.

A sip. Cup on the end table. "Ay huh."

They met eyes. Quickly, Adrian turned away and said in a quiet voice, "I don't want you to think bad of me."

Elmer skimmed his tongue over his teeth as he glared at Adrian. "Kid," he said and picked up his mug. "The only thing that pisses me off right now," he drank.

"Elmer," Adrian said, exasperated, as he waited for Elmer to drink.

He drank and pointed his finger at Adrian. "After all this time together, you think there is anything you can do to make me not want to be in your life."

"Well, I—"

"You might be two foot taller than me, but I'll shove this cane up your ass." He smiled and jabbed the cane at Adrian.

Adrian nodded. "Stupid old man." Smiled back, added, "I should have dropped you years ago."

Both laughed.

Elmer spoke, "I love you like a son." He got up and sat next to Adrian on the couch and put his arm around him. "You can tell me anything."

Adrian felt his body relax. He blew and sipped.

"Stop being a pussy," Elmer said as he struggled to get up. He slid into his chair, "Couch is uncomfortable for the old man."

"Probably because of me."

"Probably. You've slept on that couch a hundred times or more."

"Yeah," Adrian said as he rubbed his hand over the cough cushion. "It's where I feel the most home."

A raised cup. A wink. "Maybe we can get you a new one, son." He drank and looked at Adrian.

At that moment, Adrian went from guitar string tight to relaxed as night-club blues. He drank and sat his cup on the end table. "So about last night."

"Susan's dad is an idiot. Scott is a piece of shit."

"Um . . ."

"Aunt Martha?"

"Elmer," he said, "I don't . . . I." Adrian couldn't finish. Last night was the first time he spoke about Aunt Martha. And it wasn't with a clear mind. He figured he would tell Susan one day.

One day, when they were both older than Elmer. Years after they had been together. Never crossed his mind Elmer would be the first to find out his secret.

Elmer studied him, saw the pain in his face, the struggling in the tone, and he jumped in, "Adrian, she is not different than any man who rapes a child."

Adrian pursed his lips in embarrassment. Felt a headache coming on. Different than a hangover.

He had ample experience with those types. "I told myself it was normal." Shrugged. "No big deal." Elmer continued to stare. "You know," shrugged again, "Get over it. Move on." He spoke faster, "It was a long time ago, so get over it. But," he faked a smile, frowned, "I never could . . . did." Muttered, "I've never spoke of it . . . til . . ."

"Until last night."

"Yeah."

"Why?"

"My dad and brother died. Mom and I moved here. Things never got better. Figured . . ."

His eyes went to the ceiling, and he released air from the pit of his stomach, "Telling my mom wouldn't have helped anybody."

"You could have told me."

He narrowed his eyes and spoke sternly, "How do you tell someone? How do I tell you?" He said "you" with emphasis.

"Me?"

"Elmer?"

"What?"

"I'll just say you're not the soothing type."

"Well." Elmer shuffled in his chair as he thought about his next words. He couldn't argue with his point. "I'm glad you told me. I can't imagine how you have felt all these years."

Adrian smiled when he saw Rocky come through the kitchen, "Come here, boy." Rocky planted himself under the kitchen table. "I know, boy." Adrian moved to the kitchen, forehead on the table, and palmed Rocky's head. "I'm sorry, pal." Then to Elmer, "When my mom told me she was pregnant."

Adrian stopped and waited as Elmer joined him at the table. When he sat, he let out a short laugh, "Let me try and explain it."

"Take your time."

"At that age, you know how women get pregnant, but you don't know it is a nine-month thing . . ." He let the sentence hang for a moment. "So . . . when she told me, I honestly was worried that . . ." He let that hang because he was too embarrassed to finish.

Elmer picked up on it, "Ay huh, I get it, kid," he said. He wanted to be terse with his words and listen.

Hands on head. Deep breath. A murmur. "Sounds so stupid now."

"It's not stupid, Adrian."

"It's embarrassing. Men don't get abused. I've never heard of a boy getting sexually abused by a woman." He glanced at Elmer, and when he saw his eyes, he lowered his, "Heck, you hear stories about female teachers touching boys, and all I hear is guys saying they wished it was them."

"You have nothing to be embarrassed about. Yeah, you're right. We don't hear about boys being abused, but trust me, it happens." He thumbed over his shoulder and leaned in, "She is just as bad as those bastards sitting out in the pen." Elmer wanted to ask what happened to her but chose otherwise.

Elmer had numerous experiences with abusers, men usually. When he thought about it, only men. Men who abused their children, grandchildren, nieces, nephews, neighbors, and strangers.

Adrian was his first experience with a victim, first boy. But he knew it wasn't as usual as most thought. And the pain Adrian was experiencing was no different.

Adrian snatched memories from the depths of his soul, opening the memories and pain of the past. His mind hitched a ride on the merry-go-round.

# CHAPTER 22

# Adrian Franklin
# 1983

Bam and his family lived in the new Sacred Heartland subdivision, located in Kankakee, Illinois, a stone's throw from Chicago. A hundred and ninety homes were built. Split-level with three color choices. Cindy visualized vomit when she looked at the green. Jack saw white as dingy. Blue it was. Jack recently started his ninth year at the tractor factory.

Cindy was a stay-at-home mom. Jack grossed over sixty thousand dollars a year, three times the average income for a family of four in America. Life was good. Their four-bedroom sat at the end of the cul-de-sac on Washington Street, named after the state, not the person or the city. Maybe it was named after the man if the state was named after him. Adrian argued with his younger brother, Alex, about the origin of the street name. No matter. Parallel to Washington was the Oregon Pass, followed by Grand Canyon Street.

The Cleavers or the Bradys would have been pleased to live in Sacred Heartland. After the first year, the asphalt roads still had the chalkboard appeal. Lawns were properly manicured, and the roofs sparkled like gems against the summer heat. Smells of backyard barbeques and laughter filled the summer nights. Yes, good living indeed. In the winter, from the sky above, Washington Street lit up like an airport runway with welcome signals for Ole Saint Nick.

Bam was happy. The family was happy. Cindy bowled in a league on Wednesdays. Jack on Thursdays. All bowled in a family league on Saturday mornings. All had custom balls, bowling shoes, and gloves. Adrian bowled a two twenty-five at the age of ten. Averaged much less.

The boys played football. The Bourbonnais Bears. Fit perfectly. Adrian's favorite team was the Chicago Bears. He played running back, number thirty-four, after his favorite player: Walter Payton. Jack told anybody and everybody, "My boy has the talent to make it all the way." Wishful thinking. Prideful father.

Martha, Cindy's younger sister by six years, started sitting for the boys on weekends. The boys didn't particularly like Martha; she was scary looking: Top heavy with stork legs. Straw hair. Spring rains slipped off like running water off a gutter. It looked like she combed her hair in a mixer. Mr. Potato Head eyes, big and bold. Dijon yellow teeth. Meager-minded. Spoke in a raspy voice. Started climbing in bed with Bam after a few months. He felt her girth collapse the side of the mattress; he'd roll toward her side. She moved closer, a python slithering after a doe. He trembled and flinched. Heart throbbed in place. He was in the python's lair. She'd slither her right hand over his body. Boobs pressed against his back. A gentle pull of his hand. His hand between her legs. He felt the warmth. Mucus engulfed his hand. The rest is left unsaid.

# CHAPTER 23

# Adrian Franklin
# 1985

Bam could never get used to the move from the burbs to what he called the turds. The summer of '85 in Kankakee was hotter than a coal miner's ass after a sixteen-hour shift. The Franklins lived in a trailer as small as a shoebox after the job moved to Mexico. Jack pumped gas a mile down the road. Cindy waited tables at the local diner. More times than not, Bam and Alex were left to fend for themselves. The park was unmerciful. Haggard men and wandering eyes. Pot-bellied and shirtless, they lumbered around the park with a can attached to a hand. Lollygagging day and night. It would be a hellacious task for them to break free. The only drive into the park was gravel, the axel-breaking kind. Cindy told the boys there was no need to go to the sea; the drive up the road was seasick crazy. Dust bloomed and busted and stuck on the trailers, stucco thick. A dripping sink hummed them to sleep at night. Wretched coughs of the wild woke them in the mornings. Angry and agitated beasts, chained to every tree in sight, howled and plowed circles in the earth as they fought to break the chains of life. Often, Jack saw himself in those dogs. Felt sorry for the beasts. Grew angry. He wasn't born poor, didn't live without until now. He wondered why the poor tied themselves to animals they could not feed. He hated hearing those dogs in the mornings. Trapped like him. Tarps were as valuable as money in these parts; tarps were used as window and porch covers. Patched holes in the roofs. Covered cars, the broken kind. Trees twisted and curled high. Patches of leaves as the trees slowly died. Even the dirt was cursed. Smog mushroomed over the park, clouds of despair. A graveyard for the living. Allowing only ambient light to shine on their desperation.

The night before, Bam snuck out of the trailer and went into the car. Fumbled around under the seats, in the seats, and on the dash. Coins were his prize. An arcade four roads over was the best thing, the only thing going for the park. Secondhand, thirdhand, last week six operated. This week it was five. Dig Dug was his game. The owner, Bryant Baker, an old carny by trade, received them as a gift last summer. Twenty in all. He boasted about those machines, claimed he owned the only trailer park with an arcade. Increased the rent sixty dollars. Cindy picked up another shift to cover it. Bam pulled out eighty-four cents, enough for eight games. He was on his own tomorrow; Alex had been sick for a week. If tomorrow was anything like the day before, Alex would sleep the day away after Cindy administered his medicine.

Bam woke to the persistent coughs, weeded the sleep out of his eyes, and stumbled into the kitchen. Found the note Mom left and the coins. He hefted up four big, beautiful, shiny quarters and grinned ear to ear. Eighteen games would be played. Keep him occupied half a day. He dressed quick and checked on Alex. Asleep. Normally, he would have been saddened, but today he got to play eighteen instead of nine. He busted out the door and sprinted for the field. He reached the edge of the field and panted and searched. He would have to step gingerly and hop and skip across the field to dodge dog shit like guerrilla mines. After the last hop, he sprinted the two roads over and into the arcade. Played three hours. Best day of the summer. He returned itchy and dusty, mosquitoes doing a dance on his neck, and checked on his brother. Bent over and plugged in the floor fan and angled at Alex's feet. He inched the door shut and went into the living area.

He jumped into the chair and stared at his reflection in the television. Three channels and boredom. His eyes shifted around the room; the ceiling with mold growing in the corner, the kitchen table with empty cans holding it down. He dropped to a crouch and looked under the chair and found a magazine. Pulled it and flipped. Saucer-size eyes. His first flesh of boobies. Out of his left eye, he saw it—a half-smoked cigarette Jack had left the night before, before he passed out in another drunken stupor. Flipped again. He felt the smoke stare at him. Begging him to taste. Flipped. Eyes shuffled between the page and the cigarette. "Stop looking at me," he seethed. Another flip. He could feel it in his bones. It continued to tempt him. He mean-mugged the stick and picked it up with two fingers and flicked it across the room. Then, he relaxed and pulled the magazine closer. The smoke stick gazed up at him from between the legs. He moved his knees to block its sight and flipped the page. Then, he closed the magazine and tossed it to the side. Eyed his new friend and picked it up and placed it near his nostrils and whiffed. He placed it on the end table and walked into the kitchen, and opened a cabinet. Empty, once there was cereal in that cabinet. He pulled a drawer, mouse droppings and utensils. He pulled the next drawer, and there he saw it. He picked up the lighter and sat in his spot, and picked up the stick. He struck the flint and lit the stick like he had seen his father do many times. At first, he just wanted to hold it, feel like a man. The bond between the boy and his stick was too much to overcome. He looked cross-eyed as he held it above his head and slowly maneuvered it to its destination, its home. A new relationship cemented between the lips.

He inhaled and coughed. Heard the scream of an engine. His car. His dad. He never forgot that sound. It was unique. Only belonged to him. He peered out the window and saw the car sway up the driveway like a boat in rough seas. He scurried around and waved his hand in the air like he was swatting flies. He tossed the cigarette under the chair, jumped on the couch, and sprawled out on his side. Smiled when Jack entered. "Hey, Dad." Jack eyed him, grunted, and corkscrewed his way through the house and into the bedroom and collapsed next to Alex. Bam followed. "I'm going out to play." Jack growled from his throat and tore into a pillow. Bam scurried outside, hot and nervous. Skipped in the yard, out of sight. The stick bonded with the pages of Hefner and smoldered under the dry couch. Jack smelled the smoke and stumbled out to check and tripped and hit his head. Hours later, after the flames were extinguished, Alex was found in the bed, Jack between the couch and chair.

# CHAPTER 24

# Adrian Franklin
# 1993

I t took Elmer a long time before he decided to broach the subject of the father and brother's death with Cindy. She could tell him to go away. He figured he had built enough capital with her over the years. On a Tuesday, Cindy came over to borrow a cup of laundry detergent. "Mr. Ray," she said, "appreciate it." As she turned to leave, "Payday Friday I'll get you back."

"I'm not worried about the detergent." He jumped in the deep end, "Was wanting to ask you about something Adrian mentioned to me one day." He hesitated before asking, added, "Been awhile ago. But, it's something I can't get out of my head."

"Okay," she said, and when he opened the door, she went in, and Elmer followed. Stood and took a seat when Elmer did. "What is it?"

"Adrian mentioned," he paused and swallowed, "said something about him killing his father and . . ." He held on to the rest as he watched Cindy's face. Dread appeared in her eyes. Energy rushed out of her body. Spirit sunk in quicksand. Room closed off around her, suffocating her in the moment. "Cindy?"

Softly, in an earthquake tone, she said, "When did he say that?"

Her face told him something bad happened. Elmer offered up his own question, "Can you tell me what happened?"

Her shoulders slumped. She melted. Eyes turned from desert dry to lake wet. She screeched, "They died in a fire a few months before Adrian and I moved here from Illinois." It was true. The boy killed his family. Elmer slumped into his chair. Cindy jumped up, lit a cigarette, and paced the floor in a frantic state. Ashes trailed behind. She fidgeted and said, "We were having a rough time." Elmer swept the image of his boy killing his family from his mind and did his best to listen. A quivering lip. A stutter. "The trailer was rundown, a far cry from what we were used to, before . . ."

Elmer leaned up in his seat with his hands over his face, tried to help her, "Before Jack lost his job?"

She stopped and puffed as she saw Elmer melt and exhale, "He's told you a lot."

Not enough. "He's told me some things." He held her eyes as he wondered about Martha. Wondered if his mother knew her sister raped the boy when he was younger. Prayed she had no prior knowledge of the incident. How could he continue interacting with someone who let her child get sexually abused? That story was for another day; he had enough on his plate for today. Elmer added, "Just hard for me to believe that boy . . ." His eyes misted over, "Did he kill his dad and brother?"

The nicotine calmed her, her feet stopped moving, she hugged herself, "Jack and I were forced to leave our boys alone," a head bop, "while we worked," she said like she was asking permission. She squeezed her face, whites shaded over her hands, she muttered, "I know it was wrong, but . . ." She squeezed and pressed harder. When she released herself, her skin had a patchy redness. Quivering turned to sobbing, "Those boys were too young." Like finding dynamite in a mine, "Oh my God!" she screamed. Elmer imagined she was back to the day it happened. Driving home from a long and unfulfilling day at work and finding two souls she loved more than herself extinguished in a fire. "Oh my God, we left our kids home alone."

"Cindy?"

"They . . . they weren't even teenagers." Her knees crashed against the floor, the sound echoing in the room. Her head met floor. She extended her bony hands, grasping the ankles of Elmer. Her breathing slowed, then she said, "He didn't kill them."

He reached down and tried to lift her dead weight, "What?"

She began to shake and hyperventilate.

He held her like a doll. "Cindy," he said, "stay with me." When she returned from the distant memory, he took a steady hand and guided her to the couch. "Sit a minute," he said and went into the kitchen and fetched a glass of water.

"Thank you," she said and looked at him with trusting eyes.

After she drank half the glass, Elmer said, "I'm sorry I brought up these, old . . ." hand to the face again, "I shouldn't have dug up old wounds."

"It was a fire," she said, glass on cheek.

"Did Adrian—"

She stared over his head at the picture of Elmer and Bessie, wondering what her life would have been like if Jack had lived. What life could have been if the tractor factory stayed in Kankakee. Did it help people in Mexico as much as it hurt her? For her, there was life before the closing and life after. Two sides of the same coin. Heads you win. Tails you die. For Adrian, the day his father and brother died was his tractor company day.

Elmer reached and gathered her pack from the floor and pulled one and held it out. Cindy reached for it and lit and puffed. Puffed like a train. Then, she rocked on the couch in silence. Elmer waited and watched. Every few seconds, she looked at him. Turned away in embarrassment, in guilt. Turn away to hide her failure. She felt as guilty as Adrian. Skin and bones and alcohol.

Chin high. Smoke teasing the side of her mouth, she said, "When I got to the trailer," she sniffled and started to cry again, "he was sitting on a tree stump." He sat still as a painting. Face locked, jaw shut. An absence in his eyes. Void of life. Skin a polished white shell. A ghost boy in a gray world. "He was just sitting there." She whispered, "I always wanted to know what he was thinking at that moment. I never asked. We never talked about it." She leaned up, eyes on the floor, "When I got there, I asked where Jack and Alex were." Elmer jutted his chin out as he listened, hand on jaw, a piercing look. She surged, "He wouldn't say anything . . ." She met eyes with Elmer, lower, "It was like he didn't even hear me." Elmer figured he was in shock like when he found the dog. He shivered at the trauma Adrian had experienced. She launched herself out of the seat, caught Elmer off guard, she pounced around the floor, flailing her arms. "Nobody would tell me where they were." She nested her hands in her hair and paced.

Elmer jumped in, "What happened to them?" He knew what Adrian told him but needed to hear the truth from Cindy.

She snickered, bit at her lip. Elmer thought she was losing it. Reminded him of the insane back at the pen. "A neighbor," she said, face twisted into a sour look, hoisted her voice to a diabolical level, "Where the Leaves Fall . . . Where the Leaves Fall . . . Where the Leaves Fall!" Elmer went expressionless and white. Cindy stood in front of him, whispered, "They were ash in the ground." Then, "It took me way too long . . . took me years to figure out what the crazy fuck was saying." She tittered unexpectedly and snapped her mouth shut. Elmer was convinced she had lost it. She was starting to think the same. "Oh, Mr. Ray."

Elmer felt like he should say something but couldn't find the words. He sighed and stuttered audibly.

Cindy sat cross-legged on the floor directly in front of Elmer and looked at him with a quizzical look. "Adrian just stared at the ash. Firemen and cops running around. I couldn't get him to move. He just sat there. Wouldn't say a word. Just staring at the fire." She cocked her head sideways and stared at Elmer. "Why did he do that?"

"Um."

"Why did he just sit on that stump and stare?"

"Shock maybe."

Cindy played with the laces in her shoes as she spoke. "Afterward, I had to get far away, Mr. Ray." She raised her arm and made a rainbow motion in the air. "Far away from there. I still smell the smoke sometimes . . . sometimes. Sometimes." She whined, "We just needed a fresh start." She leaned up and grabbed Elmer's hand, "Doesn't everybody need a fresh start sometimes?"

"Yes."

She smiled, lost it immediately, "My sister, Emily . . . my sister, Emily was living in Columbus at the time." She threw her hands in the air, "So we drove right over." A wry smile. "Sometimes people need fresh starts."

"Yes. Yes. New places can be new beginnings for people." Elmer rose and took Cindy by the hand, led her toward the couch, "I'm always here for Adrian and you, always."

She sat small and frail on the couch and whispered, "Sure you can tell I've been having issues."

He had seen her deteriorate but said nothing.

"When it gets worse for me, it gets worse for Adrian."

"Hem."

She vice-gripped her hands between her legs to try and stop the shaking. Her teeth rattled, "I'm having serious problems, Mr. Ray."

Silence sucked the air out of the room as she rocked side to side, and Elmer stared, discombobulated without words.

# CHAPTER 25

# Conner Wallace
# 2011

Conner was double-fisted as he waited for Damon, who was en route with the winner's share. He waltzed in the place like he owned it. Clicked his tongue like he just didn't care. Yes, they had a successful day. By the time Damon arrived, Conner had gulped six. They were quiet for a while, drinking and laughing, neither mentioning the fight nor the money. Damon finished his third, then placed an envelope in the middle of the table. "There is seventy-five thousand in there." He snapped his fingers at the waitress, "Give us another round." Damon pulled another envelope and placed it next to the other, "Thirty in that one."

"Thirty?"

Damon Cheshire-cat grinned at Conner, "I placed a wager on you." He let out an animalistic whoop and stood up, "This man right here," he pointed at Conner and yelled, "is the greatest fighter in the world." Damon jumped in his place, eyes busting out of their sockets, he looked like an addict on a week bender. "God damn . . ." He stopped and caught his air, lower now, "You are some kind of beautiful." His eyes glistened at Conner like he was a lost treasure found in some barn.

Everybody stared, including Conner.

"Okay," he moaned and sat down. "Thank you," he said to the waitress when she put two down. To Conner, "Bruh, I honestly never met anybody like you." He eyed the envelopes and spun one across the table, "You earned every penny." Conner thumbed it and pulled it toward him, heard, "Open it."

"Am juss a regular guy, friend." He picked it up and slid it in his front pocket. "Yer a good friend, Damon." He grew glum and wasn't accustomed to having feelings for another person. His focus had been dialed in on one goal, one person for so long.

Damon raised his bottle, "Yes, Conner, we are friends." He swigged, "and thank the lord," his tone raised. "You're a dangerous man," he said and spun the second envelope toward Conner. "This one also belongs to you."

He squeezed his fists tight until white.

"What now?"

Conner raised his head and unclenched his fists.

"Are you sticking with that being your last fight?"

Damon was used to Conner speaking in a matter-of-fact, stern way. Now, he looked pained. He reluctantly mumbled, "Yis." He looked away, "Am leav'n in de morn'n." She flashed in his mind. *The Devil won't keep us apart.*

"Tomorrow? You're going back to Liverpool in the morning? When did you book a flight?"

"Nah, Am rid'n ter Ohio."

"You . . . you . . . you are going to Ohio?" Damon moved his beer to the side and leaned forward in his seat, "You never mentioned Ohio."

"Ay, I'm going to finish up some business, and dun am go'n ter be wi' me girl."

"Business in Ohio?" He swiped at the beer with his hand and waterfalled it down his throat, "Hell," he said, "let me ride with you. We can take our time, visit some clubs, find us......find me some hotties on the way." He sledgehammered a fist on the table, "Count me in."

Conner slowly drank his beer. As he waited for Damon to finish his pitch, he thought of the irony, luck, maybe fate of the news telecast four days prior. First, if he had never turned down the waitress a year ago, she would have never given Damon another look. Damon wasn't proud; he didn't suffer some masculine complex for being second choice. Shocked, hurt, or bored after Conner shot her down, the waitress chose to tangle with his little buddy. Now, a year later, both were back, this time for a third chance. Conner leaned back in his chair and slammed water, and observed Damon bob and weave his way back to her heart. Most entertainment Conner had the entire year. Behind the bar, beyond Damon and his girl, an old face popped up on the television. The ugly type, skin-crawling, teeth-clattering, nightmare-giving kind. He inched his way toward the television, eyes on the face, and listened to the story. Then, he chuckled at his unforeseen luck. The last puzzle piece dropped in his lap from thousands of miles away and a lifetime ago. Fate had a way of showing itself. Paved the roads for Conner to travel. The television was a big blinking light for Conner.

Damon sensed Conner wasn't thrilled. But he pressed on. He didn't even have a haphazard plan on how to survive without Conner. "There isn't anything out here for me anymore." He wasn't good enough to make money fighting on his own and lacked job skills. His prospects after Conner left were few and far between. "I'll ride with you, and after you fly out, I'll," he drank, "well, I'll figure it out."

"Why dun yous find a girl and settle down out here." He reached for the envelope and pushed it toward Damon, "Take it, start yous a business er firkin." The meal ticket became a friend. Conner knew what he was when he first met Damon, when Damon offered to house him in California. Damon had more going for him than he realized. He was an adept negotiator. He could sell a pig farm to a Middle Easterner. And Conner appreciated what he did for him over the past twelve months. Made him feel human again.

Damon laughed out his teeth, "What the hell do I know about being a businessman?" He waved the envelope at Conner. "This is your money," he said and tossed it at Conner's chest.

Conner swigged.

"You know I was married once?"

Inquisitively, Conner said, "Nah shit, yous found a girl to marry you?" He showed his beer to Damon, "That's a knee-knocker, ay tell yous."

"Yeah, bro, a Filipino girl."

Conner covered his heart with a hand, "Damn, Damon, ay thought ay wuz de first foreigner yous loved."

Damon laughed, "I do love you in a platonic kind of way. But, if I ever had to sleep with a dude, I—"

"Yer ter much," Conner said and held his hand out.

Damon looked at Conner blankly, "I'm dead serious."

Conner ate his bottom lip, "It breaks me heart."

Both laughed.

"She was much prettier than your ass." He swallowed the last of his fifth. Looked at his friend in a new light. This was the first time he had seen Conner let down his guard.

"De say love is blind," Conner said. "Bright your girl wuz deaf and dumb lay'n wi' yes ass," he quipped.

"Yeah, yeah, I know. My dad told me that before. Love is blind. She must be deaf and dumb. Ha, ha."

Conner winked, drank and before he could say anything, Damon said, "She was something else."

"Wa' 'appened? She get deported?"

Damon flipped a cap at him, "No, man, she was born and raised in Los Angeles. Had the smoothest skin. Not a hair on her body."

"Didn't yous bring e-blewdy-nuff goats ter keep 'er?"

"Hey now," Damon tipped the top of the bottle at Conner, "I've never paid for a piece in my life. That girl loved me." Then, "Well, if we don't count the time I picked up the hooker and got the blowjob, then found out she was he, if you know what I mean." He crinkled his nose, "No shit, bruh. I was depressed for weeks."

Conner covered his ears, "Damon, Damon," he shook his head in disgust, "Yous don't 'uv ter tell me everyth'n." He cringed at the slimy thought.

Damon continued, "You should have seen my dad when I told him about her."

"Wa did he da say?"

"He looked at me all serous and said, Damon be careful."

"Wa?"

"Be careful. That girl might be your sister."

"Sister?"

Damon turned solemn, "He said in Vietnam all he did was shoot Charlies, drink, and fuck Philippine girls in Tokyo or something."

"Think yous mean Manila."

"Yeah," Damon eyed his friend, "you're smarter than you let on." He had surmised in their time together, Conner was smart, smarter than he was, smart enough to have a formal education. He figured he was hiding from his past. Damon trod lightly and chose not to poke the bear. He didn't want to risk the chance of running off his cash cow. Now, he was afraid of losing his best friend if he pried too much.

"Not me, juss a dumb feller oo only knows 'ow ter fight," Conner said and showed a fist.

"Uh-huh," Damon said thought about his next words for a second, thought twice about letting Conner keep his con, "I'm calling bullshit."

Conner changed the subject, "Did yous tell de story ter yer girl?"

"Yeah," Damon said and glanced around, "Where the hell is our waitress? I need another." Pointed at Conner, "You?"

"Nah."

"My girl didn't find it funny. Hey, hey," he called out, "Can I get another?" Then to Conner, "Nice with the change of subject."

"Yer a good friend, Damon. Yous make me laugh. Ay wul miss yous." Conner extended his hand over the table, "now I've 'ad tree real friends in this lifetime." In his decade of roaming, Conner never allowed anybody or himself to grow close.

Damon showed his hand and pulled Conner closer, "Then stay, bruh."

"Maybe inna different life, but in this one, me path wuz chosum."

The illusion Conner built over the years quickly faded away over the past minutes. "If you ever need anything," Damon said, his voice cracking, "you call me, and I'll be there for you." He released his grip and sat.

Neither spoke a word for minutes, Conner stifled his newfound emotion and spoke first, "If ay ever need anybody, I'll call yous."

Damon reached over to the next table, and grabbed the pen, "I'll give it right back," he said. He wrote a number on a hundred-dollar bill and folded it up, and handed it to Conner. "Don't give that number out to hookers and telemarketers. Wait, you can give it out to some tramps. Just make sure they look good."

Conner placed the folded bill in his pocket, "Yous might regret giv'n me yer number, friend."

Then, Damon spoke in the sincerest tone Conner had heard from him, "Anything . . . you need anything, I'll be there."

He longed to return home, be with her, but an ancient feeling which laid dormant inside rose from its deep slumber and fought to survive. Love had stricken him sick before and almost killed him. He vowed to never care for another again. Damon had impacted Conner more than he could have known, softening the chisel of his façade. Small changes lit the corners of his soul, bringing air and life to the dormant feeling. Smoothed the edges of his face, changes only art dealers saw in phony paintings. Words clawed at the lining of his throat, fighting to escape and be spoken. Conner chewed them and swallowed. *Stick to the plan. The Devil won't keep us apart.*

Conner rose early the next morning and packed and quietly exited before Damon woke. He gave the house one long look. Felt apprehension and excitement at the same time. If it wasn't for her, he would stay and build a happy life. He was smitten by a pernicious man but shackled to the past. He roamed the earth like a blind man with pain and revenge as his eyes. He couldn't turn back now. The voice in his head spoke and gave him a jolt of life. He jumped on his bike and headed east on Route 66. He pushed it, stopped only to fuel up before laying his neck down for a few hours in Albuquerque. The wheels rolled over the asphalt without mercy. Twenty hours later, he hit the pillow in Memphis. The following day, he swung through Columbus, Ohio, and jumped on I-71, northbound out of Columbus. Three hours later, he was in Cleveland and searching for an old friend.

# CHAPTER 26

Conner roamed the neighborhood where his old friend lived for weeks before he finally caught up with him. He got a break when Lyle crawled out of the basement of his momma's house as Conner was riding through. Mothers were the last to disown their own. He followed him to the local park and watched from a distance as Lyle Perkins stalked the Shady Ridge playground outside the suburbs of Cleveland. He was on the hunt for his next victim. He moved along the walkway. A father pushed his three children on the swings to his right; oldest looked about eleven, youngest in a stroller. *I bet the middle child would be a lot of fun.* Lyle let out a cartoon giggle, touched his stomach with a palm and kept walking. The father looked back when he heard the giggle, "What the fuck are you looking at?" Lyle said. The father pulled the stroller toward him and quickly got his middle child off the swings and walked away. Lyle blew a kiss, bowed, pivoted around, and skipped. Clouds hovered above, racing in from the south, pushing a thunderstorm. The crowd was thinning out quickly. Lyle strolled around for hours, swung himself, climbed the monkey bars, and ate an ice cream cone. The moon came out and showed itself with a nibble out the top. Lyle peered up and studied her. All he saw was the aftermath of a gunshot wound to the head. Death, terror, and destruction were the only things on his mind. The temperature dropped, darkness exploded in the night, and Lyle kept stalking. Lyle had become a national sensation; his picture and his story were plastered on every newspaper and network from Bangor, Maine, to Los Angeles, California. He was recently released from the Ohio Rehabilitation Systems. Lyle was doing a life sentence for two counts of rape and murder.

Emily Michael was nine, enjoyed playing softball and had recently received her first phone. Charcoal skin, jet black, her skin glistened in the sun, natural chubby cheeks, she looked like her face got stuck as she blew out with her lips wrapped around her thumb. Owl-shaped eyes, gumdrop lips and a button nose completed a thing of beauty. Lyle grabbed her as she walked home from school on the third Monday in October of 2009. Her body was found a half mile from Lyle's home.

Tara Bullock was sixty-one and recently retired. She had pale skin, torpedo breasts, and varicose veins road-mapped up her thighs. She had eight children, five grandchildren, and one bingo habit. Tara played four days a week, ten boards at a time, and always wore the same shirt—a white t-shirt with "WHAT HAS 75 BALLS AND KEEPS THE LADIES SMILING? BINGO!" embroidered in purple letters over the chest. She won six hundred dollars on Thursday. She had planned to celebrate with a five-star dinner and a trip to the casino. Lyle jumped out of the alley one block from her house. Lyle didn't discriminate. A true sociopath who acted impulsively and violently in the blink of an eye. After he was done with Tara, he dropped the body and used her cash to drink himself stupid at the bar.

Lyle was released from prison on a technicality. He won an appeal over an overzealous rookie entering his premises without a proper search warrant. All the evidence used to convict him was found in his residence. Nobody blamed the rookie. The whole city walked on eggshells when Emily and Tara came up missing within days of each other. The day he was released, Lyle considered the news camera in front of his face, smiled, and waved with both hands, said, "Hide your women and children," and screamed into the camera. The entire nation saw his act.

The raindrops splattered on the sidewalks. Lyle continued to stalk in the roar of the night. The scraping, banging against the sidewalk startled him. It grew louder and closer. Lyle stopped and snapped around, "Who's there?" No one responded. The noise drew closer. Lyle squinted and waited. Then he saw a man walk out from behind a tree and stop and look at him. "Do I know you?"

The man dropped the ax onto the sidewalk and leaned against it.

"This isn't funny, man."

"Lyle Perkins?"

"Yeah," Lyle said and glanced around. The park was empty. The last car drove by as Lyle was swinging.

The man didn't move. He continued to lean on his axe, "Lyle Perkins, yous and ay have a date wi' destiny."

"Destiny?" The sky began to sound its horns. Lyle gestured toward the man, "I don't know what the fuck you are talking about," he said and started to walk away.

"Thuz is nah place fe yous ter 'ide."

Lyle stopped, turned around, and faced him, "Do I know you, friend? I'd think I'd remember someone with an accent."

"Ay we friends?" Conner asked, he picked up the axe and swung it over his shoulder and walked toward Lyle.

"Don't come any closer, man. I'll waste you."

Conner kept his pace.

"I don't think I know you," Lyle said and slowly retreated. "Go away. Get away from me." He hesitated. Conner kept his pace. Lyle continued, "You better piss off, man, before you get hurt."

Conner stopped.

"That's what I thought," Lyle said, his tone more confident than before. "Get out of here before I hurt you."

"I'm not scared it, Lyle. I'm norra little girl er an owd woman." Conner started toward Lyle. "Oh ay dun need nah friends, Lyle." He grabbed the axe off his shoulder and carried it in his right hand, showing a sinister smile, "Am go' ter make an exception fe yous."

He approached Lyle; the lightning opened Lyle's eyes to the body of the man holding an axe at his side. "What do you want?" Lyle said.

"Ay want yer hands," Conner growled. "I'm go'n ter stop yous from be'n saddy."

"You're a real fucking tough guy with an axe," Lyle screamed back. The skies opened above.

Conner grasped the weapon between his hands and let it fly. It ripped the air above and stuck in a tree. "Ay dun see nah axe." Conner stood in the rain, seven feet in front of Perkins, "Do yous remember me?" Five feet. "We met once."

Lyle shook his head and stepped back. "I don't know you," he said and stuck both hands out in front of him, "Stay back." Six feet. "I'd remember someone like you." Seven feet, he stopped, "Who are you?"

"Oh," Conner said with a jingle in his voice, "sorry 'bout dat." He cracked his fingers, "'Ow rude o' me. Am Conner Wallace."

"I don't know any Conner Wallace."

Conner moved closer, "Lyle, when yew was born, they slung the kid and kept the afterbirth." He snapped his jaws at Lyle, "Yer days o' terror end tonight."

Lyle turned to bolt the scene, tripped over a root, and face-planted in the soggy earth. He raised his head and gripped the dirt to get traction, heard, "Take de weapon," from behind. He got to his feet and saw the axe on the right. He picked it up and held it like a baseball bat, in a stance and flexed.

Conner folded his arms across his chest and leaned against a tree, "I'm going ter graft yous de chance yous na guv all o' doz girls and women."

Lyle flexed, jostled the weapon in his hand, spoke with confidence, "What do you want?"

Conner took off his drenched shirt, flung it over a limb, "Ay," he said loudly in a screech, "ay want yer balls Lyle, doz hands," he wiggled both hands and touched between his legs, "Yous did yer dirty work wi."

"Whatever I did to you, I'm sorry."

Conner laughed.

"Just let me go, and I won't hurt you."

Conner raised his head to the sky with his arms out, ready to be sacrificed, "Take yer shot, Lyle. De weather is gett'n werse, and I'm los'n me patience."

Lyle raised the axe to his side, the blade reached to seven o'clock.

Conner pointed, "Move yer rite fork up de shaft, Lyle," he demonstrated, "toward de blade." He showed a swing, "Yous wul 'uv better control."

Lyle moved his right hand up and swung the blade with more control. Felt stronger.

"See," Conner said, pleased, "better control."

"Who are you?"

"It's time, Lyle," Conner stepped toward his prey.

Lyle waited for Conner to get closer and swung the axe at the shoulder. Conner caught the wood barrel with his left palm, Lyle's throat with his right, and touched forehead to forehead. He snapped, "Such a disappointment," and pushed Lyle down on his back.

Lyle looked up with his mouth open as the monster stood over top of him. The screams of pain washed out by the sky above. The blood splattered on the sidewalks as the pain released the cries of agony. As the onslaught continued, the shrills were the trumpets to the thunderous drums from the violent skies. In unison, the sounds echoed in the darkness above the arena.

Hours later, Conner strolled into the Fourth Precinct with a bag over his shoulder. Sgt. Bass stood behind the desk and watched the stranger place the bag on the counter. "Forget your umbrella, pal."

Conner grinned, "Nah wack, it's juss a little rain." He opened the bag and stepped back, "Not like we get in England."

"What you got in the bag?"

Conner took a seat, and crossed his legs, "Oh," he said and massaged his beard, "a little gift ter de wirld from Conner Wallace." He gestured with his head for the sergeant to look in the bag. The sergeant peered in; he couldn't see anything. "Don't worry, nowt wul bite yous."

The sergeant opened the bag and reached his hand in, felt around. His eyes exploded when his hand held another hand. He dropped the hand on the counter and pulled his weapon, "Freeze," he yelled.

A smile stretched across Conner's face, he dropped to the ground and laid face down with his hands out. Cops surrounded him, processed him, and placed him in an interrogation room. Shortly after, a detective entered the room and heard Conner say, "Me balls ay gett'n a little squishy sitt'n e'yer."

The detective sat across from Conner and pulled out a notepad, "I understand you are wet and would like some more comfortable clothes." He pulled a pen, opened the notepad, "Maybe you should have thought about your possible discomfort before all the commotion you caused tonight."

Conner placed both hands flat on the table, "Ay yous 'ere ter intimidate me?"

The detective dropped the pen, "No, sir," he said and glanced at Conner's mangled hands. Both looked like they had been fed to a starving dog. Abrasions born from the flesh and bone of men heeled ugly on his hands. He flipped his over and, for the first time, realized how smooth they were. He imagined his suspects looked like they were dragged over sandpaper. He cleared his mind and said, "I'm here to get the reasons for the heinous act you committed in the park."

"Good, because am hungry as an Egyptian sluv."

The detective started, "How do you know Lyle Perkins?"

"'E chased like go-forbids," Conner said and leaned up at the confused face across from him. "'E wuz a schewl bus chaser." He slammed his fist into the table, "He should 'uv ben swallowed by 'is ma." He grabbed between his legs, moved his hand up to his mouth, and swallowed. Smiled and showed his pearl whites at the detective and chuckled. "Gulp."

The detective fidgeted, picked up the pen, "How did you do it?"

Conner wiggled his cuffed hands and wept, "Didn't you see de fuck'n hands, lah?" Conner turned stone-faced, "Afti ay ripped 'is throat out."

The detective shivered in his seat. He had never met someone like Conner, so matter-of-fact, with a complete lack of remorse and any fear for the outcome of his act. "Um," he said and mumbled. Then, "I mean, how did it start?"

"Oh," Conner said and relaxed in his seat, "yous should 'uv seun it." He sighed, "He wuz like oh please blah, blah." His hand went all puppet sock. He spat to his left, eyeballed the detective, "Fuck'n pussy." Conner was disappointed, angry about his encounter with Lyle. He assumed, hoped, Lyle would have put up more of a fight. He walked around parading in front of the cameras, talked tough, and he didn't even put up a proper fight. "If I wuz a woman or a child, 'e would 'uv been a big tough guy." He yawned, "You're boring me." Detective sat silently. "I'll confess to yous, take yous to the body. Ay splattied 'is ass all over de park. 'E cried like a damn girl. It wuz pathetic."

The detective scratched his scalp and searched for his next words.

"Come 'ead. Ay don't want nah kid er ma' find'n de remains," he barked and touched his head with a finger. "Dat would fuck up a kid." During the encounter, Conner wasn't thinking about Lyle or his feelings. His thoughts were with the little girls, mothers, the best friends who were unable to sleep at night, having nightmares about a big bad man coming into their windows. Lyle caused pending divorces due to stress and loss, depression, increased drinking habits, and self-destruction. Lyle was the catalyst for prescription drug problems and increased anxiety across thousands of homes. To Conner, he prevented any future problems by ridding the world of Lyle Perkins and sending him to the deep below, to the dark, hot place. He wouldn't repent. He committed a laudable act for all mankind. Conner Wallace effaced Lyle Perkins once before and now, forever. He signed the confession, crumbled it up tight into a ball, and flipped it into the chest of the detective.

# CHAPTER 27

# Adrian Franklin
# 1994

drian heard a shout of pain coming from downstairs. Before that, some banging. Figured it was Scott rummaging through a cabinet after hours, maybe days of drinking. Before today, Adrian wasn't upstairs in that bed, his former bed. He moved in with Elmer shortly after Susan dumped him. Only visited his mom when Scott was out of town. Things like that happen when throwing fists was the only way the two communicated. They tried to communicate in silence: knuckled brows, grunts, and sighs. If they had to, two or three-letter words. Before today, after Susan broke up, Scott stayed somber and sober around Adrian. The boy was now a man. He'd outgrown and outmuscled her ole man.

After the shout of pain, Adrian stood at the door and listened. Begging some god above it wasn't what he thought: Scott taking shots at his mom. He knew the cabinets were empty: he had searched a few hours prior. Hours after he had locked himself out of his house, Elmer's house. The one and only weekend Elmer skipped town.

"Never no damn food," he heard. Then, flesh against flesh. He pulled the door open and switched on the hallway light. Cindy was backside in the closet, at the bottom of the steps. Closet door on top. Scott pushing to get her.

Gun-barrel black eyes stared at him when the light hit. Liquor ignited Scott. Before he could spew anger, Adrian leaped from the top, landed on the sixth step, and jumped again. Hammer fisted the Cro-Magnon forehead. They spilled into the living room. Adrian on his stomach. Scott on top of him, at the knees. Underneath, on, and above, pieces of the glass coffee table. A shard stuck Adrian above the belt line. Adrenaline pumped blood on the carpet, on Scott's fist as he delivered three blows to the side.

A ruckus in the closet took Scott's eyes. Two feet kicking at the air. Cindy got to her butt, and after she saw her boy covered in blood, she hissed, "I told you I'd kill you if you ever touched him again."

Scott got to a knee, pressed against Adrian's head to get to his feet. Swiped both palms against his chest, spit a mucus bomb to the side, and said, "Had enough of your shit." Looked down at Adrian, unconscious with the meat of his arm over his head, and spoke to Cindy, "And I told you I was never going to let him touch me again." He kicked Adrian in the chest, in the head, but stopped when he heard a click.

Cindy meowed, "I'm tired of this life. Tired of you." Scott swallowed. Face went quiet. Limbs scarecrow still. Cindy watched. Held the gun with limp wrists.

Deaf, dumb, and mute went all dumb: "You don't want to shoot me . . . babe." Limp went steady. Clint Eastwood strong. Scott pushed out, "You love me," through clenched teeth. Not even he believed it. A sickness had him long before he met Cindy. It had her now. Scott introduced the long-lost friends. Soaked her nerves. Caged bad memories. Drowned new memories. Liquor was more important than air to her now.

She repeated herself, "I'm tired of this life." By this time, she was frail, eyes sinkhole deep. She spoke with an ache.

Both heard a faint, dull sound come from Adrian. Cindy couldn't make out the mumble. Scott heard, "Mom."

Scott slid over a foot when Cindy screamed, "Get away from him."

That stirred Adrian. He got to an elbow and collapsed again. He saw the gun, her pointing it at Scott. He glanced up at Scott. His eyes frozen on Cindy. Adrian caught hers, "Mom," he said as his mind wrestled with his words. Then, "Put . . . put the gun down."

Third, last time, "I'm tired of this life," she said with an edge in her voice, the fingernail-holding kind. She looked at her boy with a suffering gaze and said, "I'm sorry. I'm sorry, Adrian, you deserved better." She shuffled to her right, gun firm in hand. Near the bottom of the steps. Straight across from Scott. Wall sconce burned bright behind her. Stretched her shadow long and thin. Her stomach dropped. Then, conviction and courage rushed over her body and touched her trigger finger.

Adrian flinched when he heard the first shot. Curled into a fetal. Clenched his teeth. Closed his eyes, tightest than ever before. Then, he heard the second. His ears hummed. Heard a faint thud.

# CHAPTER 28

# Adrian Franklin

The broken spirit lay peacefully in the hospital bed with an IV in his left arm, monitors attached to his chest. Elmer sat in the recliner with his cane across his lap. This was their third week Adena Regional Medical Center. He remained either dreaming or in a nightmare. Elmer asked himself that question a million times over the past two weeks. Recovery was probable, but had his spirit finally been broken? How does one overcome all the death and destruction in his family? The turmoil and pain experienced over the years.

Elmer was startled by the clatter of footsteps at the door; he was the only visitor over these sixteen days. Russ was off saving the world on a boat in the Navy. Elmer let him have that one, was proud the wimp signed up. "Mr. Ray," she whispered and tip-toed in.

He blinked and got upright, "Susan," he said and grabbed her by the arm, "come over and sit down." Then, "I'm glad . . . he will be excited to know you came."

"Thank you," she said. Elmer slid a desk chair over next to her and laid his hand over hers as she looked at Adrian. Her eyes welled up, and she clasped her fingers around Elmer's. "Has he been awake?"

"No," he said, "been like this since he was brought in."

"I would have come soomer."

"Oh, it's . . ."

"I just found out what happened from my cousin."

"Cousin?"

"Chloe called me this morning." By the look of Elmer, she sensed something was off. "Mr. Ray?"

Elmer got to his feet and stepped toward the window and looked out, "Susan, you and I have gotten to know each other well . . . during your time with Adrian."

"Yes," she said. And they did. She and Adrian spent more time at Elmer's than anyplace else. Mitchell wasn't a fan of the local kid from the east end. Bad end of town. He heard the rumors about the kid, and after the newspaper clipping, his opinion became fact. Adrian wasn't too keen on letting her hang out at his house. Cindy was obnoxious when she was drinking. Even he thought his house was beneath her. Same bed, same house, new bricks, and new books to hold up the ends of the frame. Bed sloped to the left corner now: book side.

After Adrian, after graduation, Susan chose to stay close to home. Not for Mitchell or her mom. But for Adrian. She still had hope. She attended the branch on the hill: Ohio University-Sherman. Each day, after class, she took a slow drive on Ewing. She almost felt like a stalker.

"I wouldn't want you to think I didn't tell you . . . I called your house that night and spoke with your father." Elmer heard her sigh. He turned and smiled, "I'm sure he got busy and forgot." He saw the anger build in her, her body tense up. He returned to the seat. "You're here now." He wrapped his arm around her shoulder, "Relax."

She swallowed tears and composed herself, "How is he doing?"

Adrian had multiple surgeries. One to remove blood in his chest cavity, which led to a collapsed lung. The kick to the head caused a minor brain bleed. The puncture wound was eight inches deep. Elmer knew the outcome could have been fatal. Adrian experienced some luck for once.

Elmer calmed and remained positive, "Oh, honey," he said and gestured with his head at the bed. "That kid is a tough son of a gun." He leaned in toward her ear and whispered, "And old Elmer here has met some of the meanest bastards you or I will ever see."

She forced a smile.

"Yep," he continued, "my boy ain't going to go away that easily." His eyes misted over, he sniffled and licked his lips, "He's going to be fine in no time."

Adrian had made tremendous progress since he had met Susan. Elmer recently assisted him in getting a job as a corrections officer. A more difficult endeavor than he even thought. Getting hired at the prison required a background check and a clean criminal record. Prospective employees needed a valid driver's license and a GED or a high school diploma. Adrian had a driver's license and a high school diploma. The criminal record was the mountain he had to climb. Adrian was convicted of domestic violence. A domestic violation conviction precluded an individual from the right to carry a firearm. This minor detail was an automatic rejection on a job application for an officer. This was the second time Elmer sought assistance from Angelo Gallo.

Elmer knew Angelo's pockets were deep and influence broad. After receiving the call from Elmer, Angelo notified a judge under his thumb, August Bench. Judge Bench changed Adrian's original plea to not guilty and scheduled a trial. Day of the trial, Scott failed to show, and the case was dismissed. It went easier than Elmer anticipated.

The grand theft auto charge Adrian forgot to tell Elmer about required Elmer to kiss ass, a lot of it. He later told Adrian he owed him a lifetime supply of Chapstick. Chapped lips led to a job, a career for Adrian to build on. Elmer's biggest concern was how Adrian was going to control his temper and deal with the numerous child molesters he was going to encounter. Adrian promised to behave and be professional.

By the time Gallo and Judge Bench were done with Adrian's file: police reports, witness statements, charges, and fingerprints wiped clean. Physical copies and computer files were deleted and burned. Adrian Franklin was as clean as a nun coming off a ten-year sabbatical in Nepal.

"Last night, I had a feeling that was so intense," Susan said softly. "It consumed me. Made me unable to sleep, eat. I had trouble breathing." Her hand went to the chest. "A feeling that can only be experienced when two souls are connected, and one is in pain. The other," her mouth got stuck as she processed. She looked at Elmer, "The other can't find peace." She cupped Elmer's hand, "I can feel him in the very core of my soul." She wept, dropped her eyes, nasal, she continued, "I had to know he was okay," her air sputtered, "and he's not."

Elmer fought the urge to cry and cleared his throat, "He missed you," he said and pulled his hand out and covered hers, "Rocky and I were getting tired of hearing him moan and cry." He gave her a pat, "He never lost hope." He looked at Adrian and spoke to her as he squeezed her hand. "Russ wanted them to get matching tattoos before he shipped off." Another pat. "Adrian refused to do it." He met eyes with her, "Hounded the boy to get one. Adrian told him you wouldn't approve."

Susan pressed her fingers into her forehead. Stress, thought Elmer. Guilt gnawed at her. *If I never left him, I . . .* She laid her head back. Elmer could see the veins running up her long neck. A long sigh. *If I was there, I should have been with him.* Pursed lips. Locked eyes. A slight shake of the head. She exhaled. *I promise, I.*

Elmer stood up, "Going to need a coffee," he said. Then, at the door, he glanced back, "Get you one?"

"No, thank you, Mr. Ray." She stood up and pulled the chair closer to the bed, and slumped into it. Rolled her head over her left shoulder when she heard muffled voices at the door. When the sounds drifted off, she picked up his hand and held it against her cheek. She imagined life without him—med school, a few years overseas, a condo in Columbus, another at the beach. She shivered at the thought and erased it from her mind. *This is my life, not theirs.* She swayed from side to side as she held his hand. "In all the chaos of this world," she whispered to the walls, "and all the different paths and people we could have chosen," she opened her eyes and spoke to him, "you and I met, and I choose you." She leaned up, gently kissed his cheek, and spoke into his ear, "I choose you." Another look, a sniffle, "It was our destiny. You are the only person I never doubted and felt safe with." She kissed his hand and spoke softly and intimately, "Have you ever heard about the legend of the invisible thread?" A slight smile. "Our souls are connected. The legend said there is a string of fate that holds two souls together. Am I yours? Are you mine?" A gasp. "My soul craves your company." She grasped his hand tighter, hopeful of a reaction, "Please come back to me. I will not leave you again. I promise."

# CHAPTER 29

drian recovered after the incident. He was itching to get back on his feet and spend time with one of his only friends in the world. The one who never questioned him. Would never leave his side. He did what the doctors asked and laid around on the couch for two weeks. On the fifteenth day, he took that friend on a walk. On the way back, he saw her pull in across the street. "Come on, Rocky," he said and hustled onto the porch.

He heard the car door close and then, "Adrian." He opened the door, unleashed Rocky, and closed the door with Susan and him on the outside. He faced the door, and slid his head forward until his forehead touched the door. Felt her presence behind him, "Adrian," she said, stepped closer, "why haven't you taken any of my calls?"

He ignored her question and asked his own, "Why are you here?"

She moved next to him and rested her left shoulder on the house. Pulled his chin toward her with two fingers. Holy balls, he missed that touch. He didn't fight. Agitated, she said, "Why won't you look at me?"

He looked to his right. Lowered his head and stared at the porch. Silence between them. He spoke, "Susan," he paused and forced himself to say, "just go."

She pulled at his wrist. He snapped his arm back to his side. She gasped. Hands on hips. Pecked the deck with her foot. Sighed. Stared.

He put his hands in his pockets and stood defiantly, his back to her.

She gently placed her hand on the back of the shoulder, spoke softly, "Adrian, look at me." A hand full of his shirt. A tug toward her. Slowly, he turned to face her. She stepped forward, whispered, "I miss you."

Adrian stood strong, looked at his lost girl and asked, "Why?"

She pressed on, "I called, like, every single day since I heard about the accident."

He tensed up and stepped back and laughed. "Accident?" Arms crossed over his chest. Stern eyes. "Is that what people are calling it?" He rolled his eyes. Smirked. "An accident?" He exhaled deeply and ran his hands over his bald head, "Yeah," he said in a loud voice, "my mom blew her head off in the downstairs closet."

"I know."

He pointed over her shoulder.

"Adrian?"

Jabbed his hand, "Right over there, Susan."

She stepped forward and began to wrap her arms around him.

Palms out. A step back. "Don't . . ."

Susan stopped, arms frozen in the air, "I'm sorry," she whimpered. "I," she dropped her arms and retreated, "if you don't want me here, I'll go." She stopped and waited for him to respond. He remained silent. Her tone changed to desperation, "I'm sorry. I messed up." His eyes returned, focused and sad. "I realized it, but," she raised her voice, "I'm here now, Adrian. I won't leave again. I thought about you every day, and when I saw you . . ." Her voice faded. She sniffled. Pushed a tear out of her eye. She whined, "When I saw you in that bed . . . I felt like," she swallowed and wrapped herself in her arms, "I felt like I was dying."

Adrian opened his mouth to speak but closed it and remained silent.

"I love you, Adrian," she said passionately. He almost caved.

He ran his tongue over his upper lip. Itched his temple and stared at her. He flatly said, "We don't belong together." He sounded so cold and distant to her. Acrimonious words he had never said to her before. She felt her lungs fill with air. "You have so much to look forward to," he said and grabbed her by the shoulders. "I'm not going anyplace. I'm stuck here." He moved inches from her, eyes peering down at her. "We had our fun, but we were just kids." He released her and stepped back, leaning against the rail. Cool and confident. She narrowed her eyes at this new Adrian. A person she had yet to see. He continued, "We had our fun, but it's not in the cards. We are from different words." His hand spanned out from his side, "This is my world."

"I see."

"Yep. You will find someone your parents approve of, and you won't even remember my name."

She pivoted and stood more defiant than he did. Her eyes stalked him as he rocked on his feet to ignore her glare. A faint smirk. Then she spoke, "So," she said long and drawn out. He returned a quick glance and turned away. "That is what this is about."

He covered his mouth with a hand, muttered, "What?"

She nodded vigorously to convince herself, "My parents." Convinced, she spoke louder, "This is about my parents."

He shrugged in affirmation.

Annoyed. Mad at herself. Her eyes stopped on him like a predator on a prey. The loudest yet, "I don't care what my parents think." She ground her teeth together, rock on rock, continued to throw words at him like punches, "I don't fucking care what they think." She cursed for the first time in years. The first time around Adrian for effect. It didn't work.

He countered and punched back, "You cared before."

A gut punch. She lost her air. Felt her heart drop and skip a beat.

"I needed you." Now vulnerable, he lowered his guard and spoke from the heart, "You didn't even stick up for me. You knew Scott was abusing my mom."

Her face melted. Eyes drooped. Air shuffled in and out like somebody was playing the accordion.

Adrian was unrelenting, "You didn't fight for me. You didn't fight for us, Susan."

Her shoulders dropped. Eyes fell. She shivered. Trembled when he said, "I moved on." Her neck went hot. She attempted to soothe it with a hand. Direct. Firm. He added, "You should move on." He lied. He didn't move on. Never dated. Never reached out to another girl.

Battered and shocked, tears took over and raced down her face. She opened her mouth to speak, stopped, and opted to think about what to say. The proper words to light the fire in his eyes. Fear of losing him forever ate at her. He sounded adamant about moving on. Her features changed from distraught to utter defeat. Her legs weakened. Vision blurred. Pixels of defeat shined brightest in the darkness of her sight. She stooped and chased after tears with both hands. Adrian froze and studied her with a baffling eye.

She gagged. Heaved air from deep inside. He watched her head jostle. Back quaked.

"Adrian," she shrieked. Raving blood rushed in her ears. She begged with her eyes. Tried to light his spark with her voice.

Silence.

She gazed up, innocent and heartbroken, and questioned him, "What was I supposed to do, leave?"

Silence.

His heart skipped a beat. Hers sped as she waited for an answer. The wind scooped a cup of leaves and rolled it between them, cueing Adrian. "Yes!" he screamed, looking down as she knelt. He pointed and scolded her, "If you believed in us, you would have left." He held a finger up, lowered his voice, "All you had to do was believe in us, one percent." She rose. He repeated himself, "One percent."

"I . . . I."

"You didn't believe in me," he balled a fist, held it between them. His shield. His protector. He hit his chest. Then again. She blinked and flailed back.

"Adrian."

"You can't imagine how that made me feel."

She lowered her head.

"You threw me away because your daddy." That caught her attention. "Had an issue with me kicking the shit out of Scott. If he had an issue before." He chuckled, "He sure isn't going to allow you to be with me now."

"Adrian," she wailed and collapsed again. This wasn't the plan. Once maybe, but failing at his feet twice? No. She expected Adrian to break quickly. She knew, as all others did, he worshipped her. Put her on a pedestal so high the clouds were under. She gasped for air, for words like a pending death sentence. She began to wrap her hands around his legs and never let go. She stopped herself and gazed up with the saddest eyes and said, "O-okay."

Her sound, the pain cleaved through his body and gripped sliced his heart. He trembled momentarily and then said, "I'm sorry."

She got up and sniffled. He swiped at her nose with a finger. The first for both. He wiped it on his pants and said, "He probably blames both their deaths on me." He stared at his lost girl. Pivoted around her and opened the door, "Go home. Your parents are probably worried about you."

He stepped in before she could respond. Her foot stopped the screen door from closing. He felt her behind. He snapped around and grabbed her by the shoulders. Pushed her against the door. Flipped her around, his eyes on her back. His left arm ran from her waist to her breasts. Right hand shivered up her thigh. He leaned up, his words tingled her ear. He whispered, "Is this what you want?"

Skin on her neck prickled, "Yes," fell out of her mouth.

She was in the grasp of his soul. He wrapped around her like a fabric. In this moment, she never felt safer. She trembled under his clutches. Suffocating. The tingle buckled her knees. He felt her weight drop in his hands. He picked her up, gently placing her on the couch. His right hand ripped her shorts off. He slid the fingers of his left under the panties and snapped them off with one pull. Raised her legs vertical, lying flat on the couch. He lunged forward, running his lips down her inner thigh. The kiss sent needles down her spine. She flinched. He grasped the back of her neck. "Don't move a muscle," he commanded. He ran his nails over her bottom, gripping it tight with his hands. A soft bite. Followed by the sensation of his fingers in her. She wiggled forward, and he forcefully said, "Don't move." As the throbbing entered her, she heard, "I'd die for you," and then a tear collapsed on her back.

# CHAPTER 30

# Conner Wallace
# 2012

**E**ven after confessing to murdering Lyle Perkins, Conner spent six months in the county jail before a trial and sentencing, pushing his timeline back further. He was sent to Hamilton County Complex, the Supermax of the Ohio system, due to the violent nature of his crime. A security level four center. Home of the most violent, reckless, and uncaring men institutionalized.

Conner was placed in G-Block. Single-man cells, eight to a side. He spent twenty-three hours a day isolated from the world, with only his thoughts and books to keep his mind occupied and sharp. Bare, white block walls, a tomb for the living. The sufferable realness of his existence was only surpassed by his nightmare of waiting to rejoin his love. He ate three meals a day, defecated, slept, did everything in his tiny house. Each day the same, eat, read, write in his journal, sleep, push-ups, sit-ups, body squats, anything to keep his mind and body occupied. From morning to night, he did calisthenics in his cell. Pulling and pushing, sweat dripping, and rage building inside. *The Devil will not keep us apart.* Push and pulled. *The Devil will not keep us apart.*

Eight single-man cells were on his side. Occupied with seven whites and one lonely black kid. Mike Byers was convicted of murdering a Cincinnati police officer as he ran from his first burglary. As he ran, being chased by the men in blue, anxiety and fear built inside, and he shot back without looking like he was in a B-rated action movie. Being the unluckiest kid in the world, a bullet hit one directly between the eyes.

Conner and his compatriots were allowed one hour of outside recreation per day. A thirty-by-thirty fenced-in yard. A basketball hoop was the only recreational equipment. Some played, most sat quietly talking and enjoying fresh air and the sun. Twenty minutes in, Conner finished a set of push-ups and observed the Byers kid gazing off to the horizon. Three men approached him from behind, "Hey, nig," one called out. He was albino, had a Nazi symbol tattooed on his forehead. On his left stood another, small with the same tattoo on his right shoulder. The third flanked the right side. He had a similar haircut but lacked the symbol. Conner figured he was a probate or something. Byers attempted to slide down the fenceline and go back to the safe confines of his cell. The probate blocked his path. Now the kid was surrounded by a pack of hyenas. He faced the fence, heard one rattle off in a deep voice, "Does it bother you I called you a nigger . . . nigger?" The albino was the leader, the *unteroffizier*, or a sergeant, in the Nazi Party recently created in the joint. Gang activity was the norm; Aryan Brotherhood, Bloods, Crips, and Latin Kings shared power and space and influence in the inmate culture.

Conner was heedful of their plan. Seen it before, would see it again. It was as natural as bad food in the joint. He slapped the dirt off his knees, sidestepped between two, and crashed against the fence next to Byers. Pushed off and flipped around and leaned against the fence. The three stared at him. Byers flinched and stepped away. Conner's eyes volleyed between the three, stopped on the leader. He pointed, "Ey," he said, agitated, "Why wasn't ay invited ter de party?" he asked nonchalantly.

"Private party," Albino said.

"Oh," Conner shaded his eyes with a hand, "think I'll stand e'yer get a tan." He wrapped his fingers around the links of the fence, "Don't wanna get sickly white like yous."

"You friends with the monkey?"

The probate said, "You're our kind, friend."

"Ay dun see nah monkey," Conner said and clasped his hands behind his head and leaned deep into the fence, "and I don't have nah friends yous racist fuck'n pigs." He closed the hatch of his left eye to the sun and turned the slightest from the glare. Thought for a second one was going to try and steal one to his head, none did.

The third guy finally spoke and said, "This has nothing to do with you." Squinted and scowled. Half-ass attempt. Needed more practice.

Conner considered him and then the other two, "Ay yous trying to compensate for your tiny dicks?" He let the words dangle in the air, like bait on the hook, waiting, begging for them to nibble. Scared the fish: Thought they were going to be cut. The probate felt a tingling sensation in his rectum. Twitched like a virgin on prom night.

The albino had a brutish appearance. Voice to match. He probably won several fights before he swung a punch. He hardened and growled and barked out, "This is none of your business," and opened his arms. "What you going to do, fight us all?" Conner was mildly impressed with him.

Conner heard him, eyes bird-dogging the guy on the right, the probate, as his left hand slithered down his leg to pull a shank. Conner knew he wasn't game for this type of fight. His hand slithered, started to flail like a fish out of water before it reached its destination.

Conner winked at him, "Ay wuddun do that if ay wuz yous." He stopped moving, hand plunged into the sock. He heard, "Yous might lose dat hand of yous." After Conner saw him get vertical with his hands empty, he spoke to the leader, "I'm mak'n it me business." He threw a stiff arm in front of Byers when he tried to scoot away. Conner gritted, "Need ter learn ter fight some time." He pushed him against the fence with the thickness of his arm and stepped in front of him. Kid felt safe, fence behind him and a breathing brick wall in front. Conner snarled, hollered at three, "Yous want de monkey?" He stepped forward, arms out, "Yous have to through de zewkeeper. And me de zewkeeper."

Two glared. One turned his head away.

"Yous go'n ter pay if yous want de monkey," he said and gave them an indulgent smile. Nerved the Albino. Gave his two partners the willies like they saw their pending deaths in a nightmare.

Conner knew he had them when the leader said, "How much?"

He absorbed the words, stopped himself from laughing, and spat them to the side. His dialect was intimidating, tone was bone-chilling. The next words would crush their bones. He snarled back, "Blewd . . . buckets o' it." Added, "I'm go'n ter stop yous from be'n saddy."

They stood in bewilderment. Never seen a guy with such confidence. Looked at him wide-eyed, like he was dropped from an alien ship. Moments went by without a sound or a movement. The leader's face contorted to show anger. He looked like he was in pain and fidgeted in his place like a child seconds away from relieving himself. His voice lacked conviction when he said, "We'll stomp both your asses out."

Conner let the words unreel in his mind, and eyes danced between the three. He jabbed and stepped toward them. All flinched. Conner giggled like a schoolgirl, sputtered out, "Pussies."

The third guy flanked on the other side of the leader slouched with a vacant face and pitted eyes. He made a furtive movement with his hand, down his side and into his back pocket. His eyes betrayed him, showed weakness. Conner waited until his hand was submerged in the pocket and yelled, "Boo!" He flinched and swayed on his feet and turned away. The leader slung a look and gestured for him to remain in his place. He complied, twitched like a first-time offender readying himself to steal his candy bar. The probate, first to try and get the drop on Conner, showed hardness and steeled himself in anticipation. Showed a wandering eye. Conner appreciated it. He had been itching for a fight. He looked at him and said, "Good for you." He stepped toward the leader and stopped, grinned, a devilish grin birthed from hate, not meant to be a pleasantry. He stood tall over them. They sensed he was confident of the outcome. The leader stone-faced Conner silently. Conner returned the favor and ground his molars. He saw the apprehension in him. Conner tensed up. Tendons in his arms breathed as he tightened his fists.

The silence grew more uncomfortable for them as Conner continued staring. He heard Byers's breathing pick up. He eyed the two on the ends. One was sweating like he was in a sauna, the other pale and jumpy. Conner slowed his breathing, thought about palming the nose of the leader, watching it shatter like a porcelain doll. The picture in his mind pleased him. He smiled. He figured the other two would scat. If not, he'd backhand one like a bitch and do a three-sixty and back-fist pale face. He spoke first, hoarse and angry, "Yous go'n ter bore me to death er ay we go'n ter fight?" Veins in his arms neon-blued out of his skin, like nightcrawlers to the rain in the dead of night. Voice bloomed as the anger bubbled over, "Come on!"

The leader scrolled through the ways out of the pending fight. They came to spread their wings. Build clout in the joint. Now, they were in a dire situation. If they backed down under the pressure of one, they would be crushed by the forces of many. His eyes shrunk in his head. Conner beamed of light. They acted like a cackle of hyenas, but they were a clowder of kittens. The other two felt every tick of time hammer in their minds as the leader contemplated what to do. Their legs stuck in concrete, fettered to the ground by fear and unable to move. Reluctantly, the leader stepped forward like a child on his first pair of ice skates with a fist, and the others followed. Their eyes looked like a china doll dog in heat running from a Cane Corso. A speck of guilt wallowed in the corner of Conner's mind. *This is like playing poker with the blind.* But, no matter, as soon as the leader crossed the threshold on his tiny skates, Conner was going to take his money, mushroom his nose and hump those little china dolls. They called Conner's bluff. Now the foreigner was going all in. Then, the horn sounded to signal the end of recreation. Conner horse-laughed, pointed his finger at them, "Nah wonder Germany lost de war," he hollered loud enough for a guard to trot over. All three slouched, melted like wax under the hot sun, and moved wearily away without a rebuttal.

Byers's body warped under the anxiety; he had never been in a fight. He soiled his pants as he waited. Conner noticed but chose to remain quiet. He watched the kid walk away embarrassed with his head down.

Conner didn't want a fight. He had enough of it and didn't need any more setbacks. But he had a code. He didn't like bullies or fights with the odds stacked against the underdog. plus, had the repertoire to deal with people like them.

## CHAPTER 31

# Adrian Franklin
# 1997

Adrian peeked out the bathroom door and hollered down the stairs, "Elmer, are you ready?" He checked the time on the clock, "We need to be going. It's two o'clock." He tightened his tie, tucked in his shirt and hustled down the steps. It was a big day for both. Elmer had yet to formally meet Adrian's future in-laws. In-laws. The term made Elmer tear up every time he thought about it. He was going to miss having the kid around twenty-four hours a day. And if he was being honest, he didn't think he would ever find anyone to marry the boy off to. Adrian had his concerns: Elmer was losing steam. Struggled to get around. Sixty-two caught up to him quickly. Rocky was thirteen. He struggled more than the old man. Adrian and Susan had talked about getting a new pup. Help the transition after Rocky passed. Even had a name picked out: Brutus. They found a black Labrador Retriever pup in Circleville. Been throwing hints at Elmer. Knew the dog had to be the same breed and color as his beloved Rocky. They planned on bringing up the subject after today's events. Last week, at the veterinarian, the doctor didn't have many encouraging words about Rocky.

Adrian had come a long way. Susan had practically lived with them and Rocky. Adrian visited her house frequently; however, the environment and atmosphere made him feel uneasy. Old wounds didn't heal that easily. Today, Elmer and Adrian were headed over to the Platts' for the "Granddaddy of

Them All": the 1997 Rose Bowl. Their Ohio State Buckeyes were playing the Arizona State Sun Devils. It was the first opportunity for Adrian to show off his surrogate father to Susan's parents.

"Elmer," Adrian called out as he descended the steps.

He heard, "I'm coming," from the bedroom. "You can't rush perfection, boy."

Adrian leashed Rocky, "Going to take him out really quick."

"Okay."

Adrian opened the door, looked back, and shouted, "You better be ready when we come back." Minutes later, Adrian and Rocky entered as Elmer was strutting out his door, "What the—"

"I did it again, Adrian."

"Did what?"

Elmer slicked the edges of his hair, smiled, "I somehow got better looking today." He nodded, "It's a damn curse, I tell you." Adrian blankly looked at him. Elmer grabbed his jacket and cane off the chair and walked by Adrian. "Tired of waiting. Let's go."

Adrian curled his lip, waited for Elmer to reach the steps of the porch, and yelled, "You're a pain in my ass, old man."

Elmer raised a hand.

Adrian locked the front door and jumped off the porch and got behind the wheel. Turned on the ignition, Elmer started his rant, "Biggest game of the year, Adrian."

Adrian pulled out, "I know."

"We have a perfectly fine television right here," Elmer said and thumbed out the window. "My recliner is here," he nosed the window, "and you're dragging an old man out in this weather, across town."

"Elmer."

"To some yuppie house to watch the Rose Bowl."

"We talked about this."

Elmer snapped his head around at Adrian, "Who is the pain in the ass?"

Adrian turned left on Main and laughed, "Oh," he said, "you're the pain in the house."

"This weather makes my bones hurt."

"Susan will hurt your bones if we don't show up."

The Platts were as different from the people Elmer dealt with on a regular basis as night was from day. He wore overalls while they dressed in suits and formal dresses. Five-bathroom house compared to one and a half. Coffee versus a fine wine. Elmer rejoiced when Bill Clinton was elected president. Mitchell Platt played eighteen holes of golf at a rate of one hundred and fifty dollars a round and drowned his sorrows with three other rich yuppies in Orlando.

"What kind of name is Mitchell Platt anyway?"

"Just a name."

"Sounds ridiculous, kind of girly." Elmer looked over at Adrian like he ate chalk, "Don't you just want to go all Bam on him."

"Hey," Adrian said and kept his eyes on the road, "don't you mention that name to them."

Elmer shooed him with a hand and looked out the window, "Sounds like a little prick."

"He is a normal man, just like you or me."

"Bet his hands are as smooth as a baby's ass." Adrian didn't respond. "Bet he hadn't worked a hard day in his damn life."

"Regular Joe, Elmer."

"Regular as the dump I took this morning."

Adrian gripped the wheel and swallowed a pending laugh, "Behave yourself tonight."

"Yes, sir."

"I'm serious. No outlandish outbursts during the game." Adrian honked the horn, "Get the hell out the way," he yelled.

"You tell me that then you yell at a car that can't hear you."

"Mr. Platt is different. I'll give you that."

Elmer pursed his lips at Adrian. "What outbursts are you referring to?"

Adrian shifted his eyes between Elmer and the road, "You're joking," he said and turned the wheel. "You go batshit crazy over a damn first down, Elmer," he eyed him again.

Elmer lowered his brows, "That is how I watch the game."

Adrian gestured with his arm and raised his voice, "You cuss."

"So, do you . . . so does Susan."

"You carry on . . . yell all game long."

"So."

Adrian slammed on the brakes at the stoplight and put the car in park, facing Elmer, "I don't throw things at the television."

"That was one time."

"Elmer—"

"The light is green."

He put the car in drive and gassed the pedal, "Elmer," he said. "I'm going," he said when the car honked behind him. Then to Elmer, "You can't throw stuff at their television."

"I did that—"

Adrian cut him off, "You can't do it. Their television cost more than our house probably."

"Well, Sus—"

"No, Elmer," Adrian snapped back. "Susan isn't going to pay for it." He gasped, tightened his grip, and leaned up against the wheel. "Just don't throw anything." He paused for a moment, glanced at Elmer, "You hear me?" When Elmer acknowledged him, "Nothing."

Elmer's tone changed, voice low and steady, "I wasn't going to say Susan would pay for any damage I may or may not cause to their household goods. Until you interrupted, I was going to say Susan told me to be myself." He looked through the front window and smiled.

"No, Elmer," Adrian replied, "You can't go crazy during the game. They don't even like football."

Elmer slapped the dash, "Then why the hell are we watching the game over there?"

"We have spoken about this."

"We," he pointed at Adrian and himself, "the three of us, we watch the game at our house."

"Elmer."

"It's a damn tradition, Adrian. If we lose . . ."

"We're not going to lose."

"If we lose, I'm," he scooted closer to Adrian, spoke lightly in his ear, "I'm going to blame you."

Adrian knocked him with his shoulder, "Get back over there, you damn creep."

Both laughed.

They drove for minutes in silence, Adrian said, "Just relax. We're not going to lose this game."

They pulled into the driveway, Adrian turned off the engine and grabbed Elmer at his knee, "Be good."

"Get your damn hand off me," Elmer gripped and slapped his wrist, "you little freak."

Adrian hit his head against the wheel. "This is going to be so bad," he said as Elmer gingerly stepped out.

"What the hell are you doing?" Elmer leaned in and said, "Why are you still sitting in the car?" Elmer hugged himself as Adrian eyed him, "I'm old. This cold weather doesn't do my body any good." As he shut the door, he added, "Let's go."

Adrian got out and met Elmer in front of the car, "Holy shit," Elmer said. "Think they have enough damn lights?"

"This way, Elmer," Adrian said and walked up the sidewalk. "Be careful."

"Damn yuppies," Elmer mumbled. "Couldn't they put some damn salt out for an old man? I fall I'm going to sue his yuppie ass."

"Be good, please."

"I'll try, but I'm not promising anything. I'm too old to change."

"Great," Adrian said, ringing the doorbell. "I'm dead."

"Do I have to take my shoes off?"

"Elmer."

"Hey . . . oh, never mind."

"What?"

"Nothing."

"What is it, Elmer?"

He waved him off, "Nothing."

"Spit it out."

"Why the hell are you ringing the doorbell?"

Adrian whispered, "It's the right thing to do."

"You don't ring the doorbell at my house."

Adrian spoke out the side of his mouth as he looked forward, "Because I live there."

"Oh," Elmer paused and then looked over, "I mean before you moved in."

Adrian widened his eyes at the sky and spoke a little prayer and turned toward Elmer, "I was twelve," he said flatly and turned toward the front.

Elmer tapped the cane against the porch, "Oh," he swallowed, mouthed "I forgot."

Adrian ran both hands over his head, "Just be good." The door opened. "Happy new year, Mrs. Platt," he said and hugged her.

"Happy New Year, Adrian." She turned her attention to Elmer, and smiled, "You must be the famous Elmer Ray my daughter always talks about." Gesturing at both, "Don't stand out here in the cold. Come in, come in."

Elmer caught Adrian's attention, said, "It is cold out here."

Elmer and Adrian walked in. Mr. Platt met them at the door, "Adrian," he said and sent him a hand.

"Sir."

"Mr. Ray," he said and ran his hand down his tie, "I wore this for you, sir." The tie was a combination of scarlet and gray with an Ohio State emblem.

"It is a very nice tie, sir," Elmer said and politely shook his hand like an aristocrat. "A very nice tie indeed."

Adrian cast harsh eyes at Elmer and mouthed, "Stop."

Elmer shrugged his shoulders.

Judy showed a small smile and stuck her arms out, "It's finally here," she said with a screech. "We finally get to meet the legendary Elmer."

Elmer showed his biggest and brightest smile and jumped into her hands.

"Oh," Judy chuckled at Mitchell and Adrian.

Elmer hugged her, mouthed, "She loves me," over his shoulder at Adrian, who covered his mouth to hide a laugh. Elmer released her and stepped back and eyed her up and down, "Mrs. Platt," he said, "you look real pretty Tonight. Forty years ago, I would have taken you home."

She covered her mouth, "Thank you." Smacked his shoulder, "you better be good."

"Made an honest woman out of you."

His facetious remark tickled her pink. She giggled and waved him off, "Oh, Mr. Ray . . . you're terrible."

Adrian smacked his head, heard Susan say, "Hey, babe," after she embraced him from behind. Whispered in his ear, "Is he behaving?"

He turned around, whispered in her ear, "He made a pass at your mom."

She hit him on the shoulder, "No way."

"Yes way."

"Oh shit."

"'Oh shit' is right." He got Elmer's attention with a wave. "Sit at the table with us."

The five of them took seats at the table. Dinner before the game started at five. Judy served turkey, dressing, potatoes—baked and mashed—rolls, casserole, and apple pie. Adrian and Elmer never ate so good.

Mitchell extended his plate out for Judy to fill and spoke to Elmer, "Mr. Ray, I hear you retired from the penitentiary?"

"Yep," Elmer said, "Adrian, pass me those potatoes."

Mitchell bit at a piece of turkey, gestured with his fork, "They should shoot all those damn monsters."

Elmer chomped and glared at Mitchell. Adrian kicked him under the table. He knew Elmer didn't appreciate the comment. Elmer always prided himself and taught Adrian to respect and have empathy for those incarcerated. Rehabilitation was in the title for a reason. He swallowed and smiled at Mitchell.

Mitchell started to speak, "I don't under—"

Elmer cut him off, "They really aren't that bad," Elmer said, turned to fork some turkey. Continued with, "Some leave and some return. Most just want to do their time and go home." Elmer knew where Mitchell was going. Had heard his hackneyed opinion from people he respected more than he did the yuppie from Yaples.

Mitchell jabbed the fork in Elmer's direction, vehemently said, "Son of bitches need to get off their lazy asses."

Judy tried to get him off the subject, mumbled, "I can think of better dinner conversation, as she carried the turkey toward the kitchen.

"What did you say, honey?"

"Dad," Susan said with her mouth closed, "enough."

Mitchell cackled at her, looked at Mr. Ray but spoke to his daughter, "I'm sure Mr. Ray would agree too many people lay around on welfare and choose not to work."

Elmer glowered over as he continued to eat. Chewed slowly. Even more slowly as Mitchell stared with a fork full of turkey hovering below his mouth, waiting for a response. Elmer swallowed and dramatically dropped his fork for effect. It worked. Adrian and Susan snapped their heads around like they heard a car crash. Elmer pointed a nub across the table, "Mitchell?"

Adrian tensed up. He didn't like the tone he heard. A familiar tone, one he was on the other end of numerous times over the past decade. The preaching kind. "Elmer—"

Elmer swatted at him, pushed on at Mitchell, "Jobs don't fall out of trees for most folks. They don't get handed jobs from their parents . . ." He bit. Chewed. Spoke with his mouth full, "Like some." Oh, that hurt. Elmer knew

Mitchell's story: worked one job his whole life. For his daddy's business. Now his own. Inherited.

Susan grabbed Adrian at the elbow and squeezed until he looked at her. Her facial expression told him to say something, "Elmer," he said and grabbed the plate of casserole, "you should try this." He scooped.

Susan chimed in, "Broccoli casserole."

Adrian filled his plate, smiled at Elmer, and hummed, "Eat up. It is so good."

Susan added, "Maybe I'll make some at the house next week."

Adrian returned to his seat. Elmer chewed and continued to glare at Mitchell. Adrian kicked Elmer under the seat and gave him a stern look. Elmer shrugged and then smiled down at the end of the table at Mitchell, who scooped as he spoke, "If we cut off welfare—"

"Dad?"

"Wait," he silenced Susan with a hand and looked at Elmer as he spoke, "if we got rid of welfare, it would force people to get jobs, maybe stay away from the criminal elements in society." He finished and searched for a response in Elmer. Elmer maintained his composure, and choked down as much food as his belly could handle. "Mr. Ray?"

Elmer shot a dour look across the table as he chewed. Chewed and swallowed. Adrian and Susan watched cautiously. Both were as unsure of his pending words as a gambling addict was of lottery numbers. Elmer kept his eyes on Mitchell and lowered his fork onto the plate and cupped his chin in a hand.

Mitchell said, "Don't know why we continue to coddle people."

Elmer said, "Can I ask you a question?"

Adrian lowered his head. Susan cocked her head to the side and hid her eyes on his shoulder when she heard her dad say, "By all means."

Elmer went on, "Have you ever had to question how you would pay your bills? Electric? Phone?" He pushed his plate toward the center of the table, "Some people, most families, can't afford big ole fat turkeys like this on Thanksgiving. Many children don't get to experience lavish Christmas decorations or trees. I just have one question. What would you do to feed your family?"

Mitchell eyed the ceiling, mouthed the question as he pondered an answer. Then he gave a terse, "Get a job," and dismissed Elmer with an eye roll.

Elmer was tired of the inane comments. He said, "Most don't have the advantages you or I have. What are you willing to do to feed your family?" Flatly, he said, "Would you kill for her?"

The words hit Mitchell like a sledgehammer. His mouth gaped open under wounded eyes, and mumbled, "I get it."

Elmer pecked at the last of his food, smiled ruefully, and said, "I hope so."

Mitchell released a dull thrum as he listened.

"Mr. Ray," Judy said and smiled, "ready for dessert?"

Elmer checked his watch and stood up, "Hold that thought," he said, then to Adrian, "Let's go kid," he knocked him on the shoulder. "It's game time."

Adrian got up and joined Elmer on the sectional in front of the seventy-two-inch television. Susan sat on the other side of Elmer. Mitchell took his spot on the recliner and opened the paper. He put his glasses on the edge of his nose and flipped to the business section of the *Columbus Dispatch*.

*What grown-ass man in this state doesn't enjoy watching Ohio State?* Elmer thought to himself. His face shot contempt across the room at him. "Turn it up," he said to Adrian. "I can't hear the damn thing over the paper."

Adrian said, "The paper isn't making any noise."

"Turn it up," Elmer repeated, "when he flips the damn page, it does."

"I'll turn it up, Elmer," Susan said and took the remote out of Adrian's hand.

He glared at Adrian, "Thank you, Susan."

Elmer fidgeted in his seat. The Rose Bowl was the most popular college football game of the season. This year, his beloved Buckeyes were playing. Both he and Susan had been anticipating this game since the regular season ended with a loss against their archrival, the University of Michigan. The team up north, Elmer would say. Adrian had grown to love the Buckeyes as much as Elmer over the years and brought Susan into their little group.

Over the first two quarters, in a close game, Elmer performed admirably. There were no angry outbursts, just a few moans and claps as the game progressed. Adrian glanced over and smiled numerous times, to show his appreciation for the effort the old man was giving. Elmer rolled up his nose and bulldogged him back.

In the middle of the fourth quarter, Arizona State led 17–14 and was driving to extend their lead. Elmer grew antsy and felt victory was slipping out of the hands of the Buckeyes. He hollered out, "What the hell is he doing?" His pale skin immediately turned reddish. "How the hell you jump offsides with the ball right in front of you?" He stood up. Adrian steadied him with a hand before he fell back into the couch. Elmer gestured at the television. "Coop," he called out, "get that son of a bitch out of the game!" He said with his hand extended.

Mitchell folded the paper over his lap and looked at Elmer, "Who is Coop?"

Susan interrupted, "John Cooper, head coach of Ohio State."

Elmer reached over to try and hit Adrian, who ducked away, "Adrian," he said, "why is sixty-two even in the damn game?"

Adrian flicked saliva off his face, "Elmer—"

"I wouldn't let him," Elmer licked his lips, "I wouldn't let that kid mow my damn yard."

Susan pushed Adrian up. He put his arm around Elmer and spoke in his ear, "You're embarrassing me." He took a gander at Mitchell, who was studying them both, "Let's sit down," he said calmly, "It's only one play." After they both returned to their seats, Adrian pointed at the screen, "Look," he said, "see sixty-two is leaving the field." Then, "Are you happy now?"

Judy leaned forward, hands on her knees and spoke to Elmer, "He must have heard you." She moved away and turned and smiled, "I'm sure he is a nice boy."

Elmer continued, "Maybe he would make a fine neighbor one day. Bring me my damn mail. But he can't play football." The camera zoomed in on the face, "Too short, fat like me, slow and ugly. Look at that face, Adrian," when Adrian sourly looked at him, "Seen better heads on beers. Looks like ten pounds of assholes smashed into a beer bottle." He ramped it up, "Fell out of the ugly tree and hit every single branch. Looks like a bastard alligator." Adrian gave him a blistering eye. Elmer mellowed, a little, "He couldn't play football for the Mount Union Purple Raiders."

Mitchell jumped in, "Mount Union?" He leaned up to see Elmer. "My business partner went to Mount Union."

An eye for Mitchell, then Adrian. Elmer heard Mitchell snicker and say, "Don't know what the big deal is . . . only a stupid game."

Elmer tried to surge out of the couch. Adrian caught him across the chest, "Look, Elmer."

"What . . ." He furrowed his brows at the tube.

"Come on, guys," Adrian said to the television. To Elmer, "Pay attention. It's our last chance."

The Buckeyes pulled it out on a last second pass. Elmer relaxed. Adrian and Susan hugged it up on the corner of the couch. Mitchell kept reading his newspaper. Then, Adrian stood up and motioned for Elmer at the door. Both went outside and returned minutes later. Elmer moved away as Adrian gently walked into the living room and stood a few feet in front of Susan. He felt cowardly and small. Same feeling he had in the library. Words twisted in his mind like leaves in a tornado. Elmer caught on, cued him up with, "Didn't you forget a package?"

"Package?" Susan questioned. Mitchell held Judy in the chair. Elmer stood proudly in the threshold between the kitchen and the living room. Adrian fumbled the package and almost dropped it. Susan nervously giggled, "What is going on?" and looked at Elmer. He shrugged. Then Mom smiled like the day her daughter was born.

Mitchell said, "Don't look at me. I have no idea." That response got an elbow from his wife.

She looked at Adrian, but could only see the top of his bald head. Noticed he missed a spot. Then, his eyes ascended from his feet to her eyes and slowly extended the package, "You forgot one of your gifts."

Surprised, Susan eked out, "Oh."

"Open it . . . open it," Judy clapped. Mitchell shushed her.

"Okay," she said and opened it as she kept her eyes on Adrian. She dropped the wrapping paper and felt the cover with her fingers as she watched Adrian turn white. "Oh," she said again as she looked and held up the book. Book to chin. "It's *Forrest Gump*."

"First edition." That was Elmer.

"What the hell is a Forrest Gump?" Mitchell couldn't resist. Judy gave him another elbow.

Doubt swelled in his eyes, Adrian reluctantly said, "Open it."

She did. Adrian dropped to both knees, a beggar's stance. The book had a cut-out like in a spy movie—a black ring box nestled in the pages. Susan didn't need to open the box to know what it was. "Oh my God."

He shakily grabbed her hand with his. Started tearing up before her. "From the moment I met you," he said, his other hand joined the two, "I wanted to be better, better for you, for me."

When he hesitated to catch his breath, she mouthed through tears, "Yes."

Elmer mumbled, "He didn't even get to ask."

Susan giggled at his comment and peered over with a harsh eye. Pursed her lips and cracked a smile. Elmer smiled back. Judy jumped up and hugged

Adrian. Susan joined to make it three. Mitchell said, "Hell, I didn't know anything."

Elmer smiled when Judy said, "Horseshit."

Mitchell got up and stepped over and extended his hand, "Welcome to the family . . . son."

"Thank you, sir," Adrian said and returned his handshake.

Susan looked at Adrian, mouthed, "He called you, son." Adrian shrugged and massaged his neck and grinned.

# CHAPTER 32

# Conner Wallace
# 2019

onner was transferred after some long years at Hamilton, five more than he thought he would have to do. Out-of-cell time was increased by four hours at the Montgomery Center, a security-level-three center. A welcome change for Conner. The miles of fences suffocated the energy and joy out of the rabble of men as they wandered the grounds of the penitentiary. The one-man gang sashayed down the main walk separating the housing units on the left and recreation area to his right. As he scanned his surroundings, a group of Rainbow Coalition members lounged on the bleachers overlooking the softball fields, scoping out potential playdates for the night.

Peaches, born Shane Simon, named after the classic western movie, was doing a five-year bit for a hit-and-run. He worked the night shift on Livingston Avenue in Columbus and picked up a john. As the two of them were tongue wrestling, the john maneuvered his fingers between the slit of a skirt and two smooth legs, only to find a set of family jewels. His order of a taco replaced with beans and franks. After the shock and awe, he beat Shane black-and-blue and skedaddled out of there. Shane gathered himself and slinked away and got behind the wheel and plowed his ass over. The john ended up with two broken legs and a bleeding spleen. Now, Shane sat idling by with his long blond hair in a bun, blush and eye shadow conjured up from colored pencils purchased in the commissary. His pants were two sizes too small and rolled up above the ankles, displaying those smooth legs. He weak-wristed a gesture toward the second baseman.

Jeremy Wilkes, the second baseman, married and the father of two, sent a wink and smile back. Jeremy claimed Peaches as his own three days prior. Tomorrow, Jeremy will visit with his wife and kids and eat frozen pizza, chips, and sodas from the vending machine. He'll proclaim his love for his wife and thank her for sticking by him. She'll put a fifty on his account so he can shop for Little Debbies and soda. Tomorrow night, Jeremy will pitch, and Peaches will catch. After, both will watch a movie and snack on those Debbies, and wash them down with soda.

The crow's nest, more like a stationary turret, was located outside the main fence and provided guards a way to police the activities of the wards of the state from a distance. The gray uniform, the shiny silver badge, and the visible stock of the shotgun provided an intimidation factor over any potential unruly behavior or tomfoolery. Even the innocent act of holding hands would bring down the wrath of one of the watchers. The officers were perceived as soldiers, menacing the exiled souls from their immobilized turrets built to keep the reckless caged from existence. Montgomery had four turrets, each placed to cover all vantage points along the front fence and recreation yard. If they failed, two patrol vehicles roamed the outer fence to stymie any last daring attempt to escape the confines of the institution.

Jay Scott manned the turret closest to Peaches and the softball fields. Yelled, "Fag and Peter Puffer." A complete schlub, he lived in his parents' basement, played video games, and was addicted to porn. He was ten hours removed from being dumped by his internet girlfriend, Sasha. She was a Russian girl living in California. She immediately fell in love with the obese Jay and his charming personality. She planned to move to the Dayton area and live in the basement with Jay and sleep on the twin bed with him. Jay stayed off the sweets for six days and began a walking program to impress Sasha. He sent the thousand dollars she needed to move with Western Union and drove to the airport in a rented limo and tux. Waited six hours with his homemade sign at his chest and rode home alone. Good thing? He lost eight pounds. Bad thing? He lost a thousand dollars to three guys in California and eighteen spots in the rankings of his favorite video game. Peaches and the others would pay for his heartache.

Conner continued his stroll; inmates thronged the recreation yard. Looked like a chessboard; inmates self-segregated into masses based on race.

This game had hundreds of squares and maneuvers, not the usual sixty-four. Thousands of pieces roamed the board, fighting for a slice of the pie. The basketball court was behind the bleachers, past the softball field. Pieces played round ball. Black Rook dunked over two White Pawns. The crowd roared. The pieces took their sports seriously, best way to demonstrate their masculinity. Idle hands are the Devil's workshop was never truer than in the big house.

A mixture of Black and White Pawns cycled through a calisthenics workout near the track located at the south end of the complex. White Pawn did push-ups, Black Pawn sit-ups, Black Knight body squats. Muscles throbbed where they stood. Endorphins leaked from their pores. The Devil didn't have any work here.

As Conner approached the edge of the track, a White King dispatched his Bishop to scold three Pawns in a contraband transaction gone sideways. Bobby Fischer, they were not. Conner returned north; the solemn walk is a moment of clarification for what he must do. A moment soon to be over. A Black Knight maneuvered to the far right. Bishop jaunted to the front and to the left. Three Pawns collapsed from the front; the King hovered in approval from a distance. Checkmate. The White Queen was surrounded. As the tuckets blew to signal the cease of movement, Conner turned to see the fight. Mayhem was their game, and they were pros at it.

"Everybody down," rung out from the speakers attached to the buildings, as the games came to a sudden end. A long blast of the siren led to correctional officers wading their way through the crowds of inmates as they gawked from the rails of the board. Soon after, the surrounding area was filled with officers, multiplied like cockroaches as the siren continued to blare.

Conner knew the routine, he dropped to his chest and placed both hands behind his back to show he wasn't itching to join the struggle. Dirt met eyes. He waited and popped up when he heard four being dragged by him and the siren silenced.

The next morning, Conner strolled into a building at the end of the compound. "Howdie," a young female said in an American-apple-pie greeting. Rookie. Yet to succumb to the stresses and pressures of corrections. Months from her first marriage. Years before an affair. Thoughts of divorce yet to be seeded and watered by the company of misery. Then, "Can I help you with something?"

"Me mom's recently passed away, and I wanted tell me brother. Us mamma passed suddenly and ay loss track," Conner politely said.

She sucked in her lower lip at the side. Her forehead wrinkled up, "Sir," she said, "do you have an interpreter?" She turned away from the desk and faced Conner, leaned up, "I'm having a difficult time understanding what you are asking," she replied in a tiny voice.

Conner gestured at the pen on the desk. She smiled and handed him a pen and piece of paper. He wrote, "Can you tell me where my brother is living? Our mother died suddenly, and I'm trying to locate him." He handed the paper to her, sucked in his lower lip like a toddler asking for ice cream.

She read the letter and looked up at Conner, mouthed a small "Oh." She returned the lower lip gesture to show affirmation and sympathy for his loss. "What is your brother's number?" she asked as her head dove in the computer screen, and she started pounding keys.

Conner wrote A23496-7 on a piece of paper and slid it across the desk. After punching his number in the computer, she looked up, "Oh, that sucks," she said. "He just left Montgomery two weeks ago."

Conner frowned.

She returned to the screen and read over his report, "He transferred to Sherman. It's south of Columbus." Then, she smiled, "Good things, looks like your brother has done well for himself over the past few years." In a jovial tone, she said, "His security level was reduced from a level three to two. His good behavior has resulted in him dropping security levels two years in a row." After Conner asked about how he could get reduced to level two, she said, "Well, like your brother, you will have to stay out of trouble. No fighting, no disrespect to staff, basically a model incarcerated adult." She smiled, "I'm sure you could do it." Then, "Our department tries to drop as many incarcerated persons to level two as possible." That tone again, "Our mission statement is to touch as many people as we can and reduce recidivism rates." She had an aha moment, "Get your education, participate in programs. Security Level reviews are based on a few factors." She rattled them off, "Education level, number of violent offenses committed while living in a center, over forty years of age, and family involvement." Conner thought about his record as she spoke: he immediately passed two of the four criteria. He knew he could pass a GED test. He was over forty. His lack of family involvement and his violence record concerned him. He couldn't fix the family involvement issue. But he had stayed violence-free for a year.

Conner gave a thumbs up, "'Ow long do yous think 'e wul be at Sherman?"

"I understood you that time." Glanced at the monitored and offered, "I'd say for years . . . if he stays out of trouble. Sherman is a level one and two center." She motioned with her hand, "Can't get any lower than one." She chuckled at her words. Stood up and sat on the edge of the desk, "Sherman is one of the easier places to do time. When someone gets transferred there, they usually try and stay out of trouble."

Conner gave her a cowboy greeting, two fingers to his forehead, and said, "Thanks, miss," and returned to the board.

"You're welcome. I'm glad I could help."

Conner turned to continue a morning stroll down the main walkway. A time for calm reflection. The Kings were out dispatching the Knights and other pieces to do their dirty work. Conner stopped in the middle of the road and scanned around, looking for meddling eyes and anyone threatening his existence. He dropped to a knee and tied his shoe, giving all comers a chance to break a fever of apprehension and grow brave.

None did.

He strutted with dervish movements with the sun at his back, baking his skin dark and native. Pawns, Knights, Bishops, Kings and Queens invisible to him and his purpose. When the calisthenics equipment came in sight, he jogged over and jumped down. Dirt ate his face. He pushed and pulled for hours. Thoughts of him, of her, seeped out of his mind. He stopped when his mind was empty of thought.

He entered the main walkway, slowed his roll, and parted the board like Moses. "Hey, Wallace?"

He kept walking.

"Wallace?" the voice called out from the distance. The young black male picked up his pace and jogged up when Conner stopped and looked back. He tapped Conner on the shoulder, "You remember me?"

Conner glared at him, "De monkey?" he said uncertain.

The male gasped, "No man." He stood with his hands on the hips aggravated, he had hoped to find an ally at his new institution. After seeing Conner's work, he knew he wouldn't find a better one. "My name is Mike Byers." Then, "We were together at Hamilton." Conner stood expressionless. "Remember," he added, "you saved my ass from those Nazi guys."

"Aha, de monkey." Conner turned and walked away.

Mike waited for Conner to get twenty yards in front of him and called out, "Can I walk with you?"

"Why?" Conner hollered over his shoulder. Byers didn't respond. Conner turned around. For a moment, he regretted helping Byers with the Nazis. He cursed himself. "Nah, monkey," he said and walked away.

"Because you need a friend," he yelled back trying not to sound like he was begging.

"Ay dun need any friends."

"Maybe I do."

Conner stopped, lowered his head, stepped back, and looked at the kid. He was small compared to others. Small, young, and innocent. A small guppy swimming with the sharks. He stood and fidgeted in place. Mike didn't even try to look tough. He sulked in his posture, wore his sullen disposition as a badge of honor.

Conner waved him forward. Mike smiled and ran up and joined his new friend in the stroll. Conner quipped, "I'm not go'n ter pull me pocket out fe yous ter 'old ed ter."

"What you say?"

"Na mind, juss keep up."

They walked in silence for a few moments. Conner strutted, moved like a wild animal, graceful, tall, and strong. He steepled above most literally and above all metaphorically, then Conner asked, "Why you banged up, Mike?"

Mike blew a tire with his lips, "Some cops set me up," he said and rolled his eyes.

"Ay see."

Mike stopped and reached up and grabbed Conner's shoulder, "You don't believe me?"

Conner glanced at him, then his shoulder, inhaled deeply at his nostrils and gritted his teeth.

"Oh," Mike said and watched intently. He tensed up and slowly removed his hand, "I'm sorry."

"Everybody says de ay innocent," Conner said and walked toward his housing unit.

Mike watched him walk off, "Are you?"

"Nah, am guilty as charged."

"Same time tomorrow? Wallace, same time tomorrow?"

Conner raised a hand and continued through the door. He waffled back to his cell, showered and gorged himself full and napped.

# CHAPTER 33

# Conner Wallace
# 2020

onner thought about dialing the number numerous times over the past decade. He imagined every direction and move and could not come up with a way to do this on his own. After all the years, he was going to make his first phone call.

"You have a collect call from the Ohio Rehabilitation Systems." the automated voice said, "Will you accept the charges?"

*Ohio? I don't know anybody in Ohio.* "Wait, yeah . . . yeah, I'll accept the charges." It had been years since Damon Gill heard a peep out of his old friend. He knew he was going to Ohio for a visit, but after all this time, he figured he was back home in England. It had been years since they took control of the fight scene in So Cal. After Conner left, Damon capitalized on the fame Conner brought to him. Fighter after fighter approached him to manage them and help book their fights, and Damon was given more credit than he deserved. He knew it, but he figured anybody would have done what he did. The fabled monster from across the pond was spoken about daily. He had eleven fighters under his thumb. He raised his cut to sixty percent; most were willing to pay to fight in the biggest fights on the circuit. He scheduled, motivated, and promoted. A win–win for everybody. He even shocked himself by how good he was at it; all his fighters appreciated and respected him.

"Go ahead, caller."

"Conner?"

"Damon."

He raised his voice, "Conner? Holy shit, I can't believe it is you." He had long hoped to hear from his friend. He told stories about Conner. Was happy to talk about him when people asked. He missed the fighting but missed their conversations more, the humor and unforeseen intelligence, and the loyalty and passion he brought to Damon's life.

"Ariite, friend, yous married?"

"Hell no, bruh. I'm too busy out here making that mon-ney." Conner's words caught up to his mind, his face went blank, and his tone shifted, "Ohio Rehabilitation Systems," he said, "Conner, are you doing another number?"

Conner breathed in the phone.

"Bruh?" Damon waited, "Bruh, talk to me."

"Need yous ter come ter Ohio."

"Ohio?"

"Montgomery, Ohio."

Damon listened. He wasn't upset about Conner taking him up on his pledge. He was sad of the circumstances. As he continued listening to Conner, he grew mad at himself for not pressing the issue and making Conner take him years prior. He smiled thinking about the last statement. Make him. When Conner finished, he said, "Let me get my guys situated and I'll be down." He squinted over at the calendar hanging on the fridge, "Let's say within the next three weeks."

Twenty days later, Damon was processed through the visiting area and was placed at a metal table and chair. Two guards escorted Conner and sat him across from Damon. When the guards walked away, Damon said, "Well, you got me back in prison."

"Sorry 'bout dat, me friend . . . but ay need yer help."

"What did you do, kill somebody?" Conner shrugged. Damon whispered, "Who the fuck you kill?"

"Why are you whisper'n? Ay 'uv already been convicted, Damon."

"Good point," Damon said, smacked the table, "you hungry?"

"Nah."

"I remember what prison food tastes like," he said and stood up. He pulled his wallet, fingered through his cash, "What you want?"

"Ay didn't br'n yous e'yer ter feed me."

Damon pursed his lips crooked, tilted his head, "Every penny I have is because I met you." He slapped one on the table, "This one."

Conner eyed the bill.

Damon pointed, "A hundi." Then, another, "Two."

"What's going on over there?"

Damon quickly grabbed the bills, put his hands up, "Sorry, officer."

"Yous forget about 'ow ter act d'n visits?"

Damon plopped down, ran his hands over his hair, "Shit," he blew out, "nobody visited me." He wiped gel on his pants, "Serious," he continued, "let's get some snacks."

"Coke, Snickers, and bag o' Doritos."

Damon stood, bowed, "Coming right up, sir."

Both munched and stared in silence. Damon spoke first, "You want to talk about it?"

"Affi anuvver Snicker."

"Looks like you could use one," Damon said and gestured with his eyes at Conner's midsection, "Skin and bones, bruh." He went to the machine, returned, and tossed the bar at him, "This about the girl," he said and made air quotation marks, "One you need to see?"

Conner ripped open the bar, stopped, and dropped it on the table. Looked at Damon, then the room, heard, "Bruh?" Looked at Damon again, averted his eyes and shuffled in his seat.

Damon plopped down across from him and cupped his hands together on the table. This was a different Conner, a side he never seen before, "Conner," he said.

Conner scratched his chin, teethed his lip, and said, "Okay." After Conner told the full story, his story, the plan conjured up over a decade ago, he half-expected Damon to walk out and never come back. A small part of him, in the depths of his soul, hoped Damon would jump on the first plane out of Dayton and fly home and get his shit together, settle down, never to think of Conner Wallace again. Who was he to ask someone to jump to ride this roller coaster with him? Damon listened intently. His mind churned with each detail of Conner's life. He'd nod, sigh and gasp as he listened. Reality was stranger than fiction. Conner dropped his eyes, "Can't get 'im without yous," paused, murmured, "Need yer 'elp gett'n ter Clouser."

When he was finished, Damon creased his brow and stared at the ceiling. Conner nursed on the candy bar as he watched Damon's face contort and body fidgeted as he thought about what he just heard. He lowered his gaze, sniffled, "You asking me for help?"

A smile.

He glanced around, leaned forward until his ass was off the metal seat. "You know," he said sternly, "if you would have told me all of this years ago." He sat down, drummed his fingers, "I would have helped you."

"I know."

Damon showed that mischievous grin and raised both brows. "Damn," he said, "this is going to be a lot of fun." He leaped like a dog jumping for a meaty treat and smacked the table on his way down and winced, "Isn't it?"

"And yous say I'm de crazy one." He looked at Damon and realized he felt like his old self. Life had a purpose. "Ay do appreciate yous do'n this, I—"

"Hey," Damon waved him off, "what else do I have to do?" He rubbed his hands together, "This is going to be so fucking epic." He gritted his teeth, "We are going to be legends. This guy is going to shit his pants."

Conner stone-faced him, "'E's go'n ter do more than dat."

Damon eyes shined when he thought of the mission. He rubbed his hands together like an Eastern healer and dropped them. Face melted; he didn't want to damper the excitement of the conversation.

"What?"

Damon leaned up and whispered, "How the hell is this going to work? Bruh, remember . . . I have a number." He flailed his arms back when Conner blankly stared back. "We did years together in Nevada . . ."

"Oh."

"He says oh." To the other visitors and inmates, at the tables, louder now, "He said oh." Both looked around and saw some side-mouth whispers. The visitors and inmates returned to their conversations. Angry outbursts were common occurrences in prison visiting rooms. Monthly, often weekly, an inmate would burst in rage, often after his wife, girlfriend, or mistress said, "It's not you. It's me." Of course, it's him. Hard to keep up with the Joneses and bills when your man is supplying eighteen dollars a month. Other times, visits were abruptly cut short when one stole a kiss from a loved one, either for affection or to pass drugs. Later, after the visit was terminated, Casanova would hover over the toilet, grunting and sweating like he was birthing twins. The birth was very profitable.

Conner leaned forward, gestured for Damon to join him, put his hand over his to ease him. It worked. Hell, yes, it worked. Conner wasn't the type.

But he needed to assure his friend the plan was solid and the risk was worth it. "It's called rehabilitation systems." And when Damon lowered his brows, "Rehabilitation be'n de key wor'dz." He retreated in his seat, cracked his neck, and showed a speck of a tooth, "Don't worry. Tell de truth, yous wul be sound, dee ay always lewk'n ter suv a soul. Yous wul custy in perfectly."

Damon hung on the words with his mouth ajar, "I can't—no way it will—"

Conner nodded.

Damon contorted his face, "Perfectly huh?" He asked, "Is there another way?"

No response.

"I really have to go join the dark side?"

"It's not as bad as yous think."

"I guess . . . man, I always said you were cooler than it is hot outside." Damon looked at Conner sideways. He raised his octane, "And it's hot as fuck outside today. Damn," he sleeved the sweat from his brow and shuffled his eyes around the room, "Sure the fuck gets hot in Ohio." Barely audible, he added, "Always thought Ohio had snow on the ground or something."

Conner remained placid.

"You know," he shrugged his shoulders, "part of the snow belt."

Flatly, Conner said, "We sound as a pound?"

Damon stood and sent a fist Conner's way, after knuckle met knuckle, he said, "We good."

# CHAPTER 34

# Adrian Franklin
# 2001

Adrian felt like a new man with Susan by his side and Elmer's guidance. He quickly rose through the ranks at Sherman Correctional Institution. Correctional officer led to sergeant then to lieutenant. Susan settled in at Adena Regional Medical Center after graduating with a nursing degree from OU-S. They set the summer of 2003 as a wedding date and chose to live in sin, purchasing a house in a middle-class neighborhood on the south end of town. Better than the east end. Worse than Yaples. Few miles from Elmer. Opposite side of Mead paper mill. Cindy was buried up on the hill near their house. Adrian jogged up their daily. Spoke to her. Forgave her. Thanked her for moving him to Sherman.

Adrian did his best to live by the company motto, protect the public, the staff, and the inmates. Tried, most times successfully, to treat everybody (staff and inmates) as he wanted to be treated. Greeted all with a "please" and "thank you." He was well-respected. Fair and firm and consistent in his attitude and behavior. He had long ago caged his demon, built a tomb deep in his mind and dropped a skyscraper on it to keep it away. It did its best to escape.

Splatter was the nickname given to inmate number A2-128746, and spitting on the staff was his way to cause chaos in his world. He spit on fourteen staff members over a nine-day period. On the face, arm, chest, even spit in the eye of a female nurse. He knew the policies. When confronted, after the act, he cooperated and completed his time in isolation. He didn't give staff any chance to dish out their retribution. Staff walked around on eggshells around him. It was a game Lt. Franklin had yet to play. He heard about the inmate and the act and felt the impact on staff morale. After the fifteenth staff member felt the wrath of Splatter, Lt. Franklin had heard enough of the complaining. He walked into the major's office and felt him out.

"People are talking about the incidents in segregation with the Splatter guy."

Major Phillips dropped his glasses and studied him. "What you think we should do about it?"

Franklin crackled his knuckles and stretched his neck high. "Think you should let me take care of him tomorrow."

Major said nothing.

"I'll have a little talk with him . . . one on one . . . see if I can get him to stop the bullshit."

Major said nothing.

"He's not going to stop unless we do something about it. I'll write the report. I was making a routine round on range and saw him trying to hurt himself."

"Okay."

"I'll have one of the officers make a noose."

A smile.

"If he has any bruising . . ." He held the rest as he watched the major's expression. He felt in the clear, " . . . the injuries can be contributed to him trying to fight back, falling into the rail as he attempted to escape his cell."

"And everybody else?"

"I'll take a write-up for taking their keys down range." He figured this was the only way to keep others away from the incident. Violating policy and making a security round by his lonesome. This was the best opportunity to press the issue with Splatter. Cameras had yet to be installed in the isolation unit. He felt confident in success. Everybody wanted something done about his nonsense. Nobody would do anything. The officers in the unit would play Franklin's game and write reports to fit his narrative. Nurses the same.

"You don't want any help?"

"Nah," Franklin tried to hide the smile. The demon beat against the walls of his soul like a moth searching for the light in the window. "I'm good."

"Okay," major said calmly, "do it as soon as you come in."

"Thank you."

The next day, Franklin walked into the entrance building and clocked in. Went through the four sally port gates between the entrance and his office. He entered his office and put his lunch in the refrigerator and strolled back to the segregation unit like he would on any other day. Once in, he bantered back and forth with the regular officers and asked for the keys.

"I'll go with you," Meyers said.

Franklin stuck his hand out and wiggled his hand, "I go alone today."

Meyers looked at him with a curious look and said, "Okay."

Franklin took a step up and glanced back, said, "When I give you the signal, open Splatter's cell door." To the other guy, "Make a noose."

Both smiled and bumped fists.

Franklin started on the third floor and walked E and F range. Descended and eased his way around the second floor, C and D range. Saluted the officers and opened B range. Covered B range and flipped to A range. Stepped slowly and stood at the door of A-10. Splatter had his pants down at his ankles, reading a book as he relieved himself. Franklin glared as he waited. Splatter finished and dropped the book on the bed and cleaned his ass. Flushed and peered out at the lieutenant, "What the fuck you want?" he said.

"You know what today is?" Franklin said.

"Day I fucked your mommy?"

"Your day of reckoning." The cell door slid open on its hinges. When Splatter heard the clank, clank, clank, his eyes hung open. Arms went out in a defensive motion as Franklin rushed in and dropped an elbow against the side of the face. Splatter fell on his bed. Franklin jumped on him.

"This . . . is . . . against . . . policy," Splatter said as his arms covered his face as he tried to dodge punches.

"Piece of shit," Franklin said and landed a blow against the temple.

Splatter croaked out, "Ah," and baby babbled and spit bubbles off his lips. Franklin cocked his arm back in a shovel hand and fired another shot across his face. A sledgehammer echo ran the range. Someone rung out, "Damn." Splatter's eye drooped into a runny breakfast egg. Nose hung to the side like Laffy Taffy. Eyes spun like a turd in a toilet. Franklin raised his hammer hand forged in the shovel shape, soaked in mucus. He spaded Splatter's hair like a mop and rung his hand dry. "Sick fuck."

"You . . . can't . . . do . . . this," Splatter sputtered out.

Another smack. The egg ran red. A red blotch tattooed on the face. Franklin thought about what Susan might think of his actions. An angry vein burst in his neck. He knew she would not approve. He blamed Splatter. He wrapped his hands around his neck. Closed the distance and got face to face and exchanged spit. "How do you like it?" he barked and sucked until his mouth ran dry, and the luge cut off his airway and launched an elephant shot. He watched it roll like a pinball down the face, curling around the nose and into the clown's mouth. Not satisfied, he fired a meat-hanging Balboa left into the ribs. Got a little scared when he heard a crack. He leaned away and examined the face, "You alright," he said, sounding serene. It wasn't. Splatter gutted out a moan. "Good," Franklin said and loosened up the rib meat with two more shots from a fist as big as a cinder block. Hurricane strong. Beat it into sinewy meat. The second punch punched holes in the dam. The third collapsed it. His bladder failed, leaked piss down his leg. Shit his britches. Urine, shit, and sweat commingled to spread a goat-puking sensation.

Franklin eyes flared wildly. Spit as he hissed, "You ever spit on anybody ever again, I'll fucking kill you." Splatter bellyached something inaudible. Franklin fryer-panned his face and said, "You hear me?" That got a reaction; Splatter went limp like a wet noodle. Franklin kneed his chest as he got off him and studied him from the cell door. Ran his hands down his pants and sleeved the sweat from his face, and backed out of the cell. Gave a thumbs up down range and waited for the cell door to lock. "I better never have to see you again."

# CHAPTER 35

# Conner Wallace
# 2021

onner hated the new corrections officer; all the young ones got stuck on second shift—prime hours for the condemned. Most, if not all, used their new perceived power to act like men. Walking around with chests puffed out, shoulders high, and fly off the handle at the drop of a hat. He figured most were left at the altar, or earlier in life sucked at sports, or had to fuck the fatty because no other girl would give them the time of day. They came to work to feel some sense of masculinity. To spread their wings. To gather a story to tell a local as he sipped on a beer. War stories. They were warriors now. Made time harder for Conner. He watched his back, his words, and his actions more during the hours of two to ten.

The one-hundred-and-eleventh graduation class of the Ohio Rehabilitation System graduated after five weeks of training—mental health, interpersonal communication, firearms, and other mind-numbing subject matter. Subjects and lessons which make a person question their job choices and jab an eye with a pen. After the academy, new officers held the pocket of senior officers for two weeks before being thrown into the den with the wolves. The new officer took his seat with the trainer, "How do I look up the location of an offender?" he asked.

The veteran snickered, "Relax, son." He patted him on the back, "We're state workers. We pace ourselves." Gestured with a finger at the screen, "We do our security rounds every half hour, make sure the natives are breathing and no sign of blood. Come back here to this seat and log in this computer and get up a half hour later and make another round." He nodded, "We count these prisoners seven times per day. Six in the morning, ten forty-five, four, nine at night." Slapped the knee of his new friend, "You'll be on third shift. You will count at eleven, one, three, and five in the morning right before you get relieved by the morning shift. Unless you get mandated to first.

"Mandated?"

He chuckled, "Yeah, get called and asked if you're cold. Then, the captain says you're frozen for the next shift because some asshole bangs in."

"Bangs in?"

Another chuckle, "You have to learn the lingo kid. Bang in means an officer called in sick." He leaned back in his chair, thumbs in his belt. "Make your rounds every half hour to make sure someone isn't dead or fighting. We count to make sure someone hasn't escaped. Eight hours and thirty years later, you'll get you some mailbox money."

"Huh?"

"A check in the mail when you retire."

"Oh." He peered out over the screen, onto the range. "It's just," he said and swiveled in his chair, "I think a guy I went to high school is here, and I'm . . . I'm not so sure I want to . . ." he shrugged, "I . . ."

"I get it." He scooted up toward the computer, collected the mouse, and flicked the screen, "What's his name?"

"Hold on," the new officer pulled a piece of paper out of his front pocket and unfolded it, "23496-7," he said.

"Clouser?"

"Yeah, that's him."

He pushed himself away from the desk, "He's one of ours. Lives down in A-1. Life sentence for aggravated murder."

"Ay-huh."

"If you want him transferred, you need to speak with a shift supervisor and complete some paperwork."

"Thanks," he said, "I'll be sure to do that."

Vet leaned up and stuck out his hand, "I'm sorry. I'm Bill Wilkes, twenty-nine years."

He returned a hand, "Damon Gill, day one."

# CHAPTER 36

# Adrian Franklin
# 2002

Adrian relaxed in his swivel chair. Eyes on his fish tank, on the orange fish. Big Orange. The aquatic bulldozer: his lot in life was to move the red rocks on the bottom. Back and forth. Day after day. Mundane but beautiful. It eased Adrian. Calmed his anger. Soothed him. Relaxing moments in his day. New day, new job: promoted to Unit Counselor. Focused more on the rehabilitation side of the department. Help incarcerated adults become restored citizens. Elmer said, "Adrian, this is where you can make a real difference in the life of one individual. Keep him from re-offending." Elmer had never been prouder.

He heard the knock at the door and waved him in.

"Sorry to bother you," a voice said.

*Why did you then?* "What can I do for you?"

He followed Adrian's gaze and said, "Nice fish."

He ignored that and asked again, "What's up?"

Frightened eyes. Small and mute.

Adrian tried to tug the issue out of him, "Can't help if I don't know."

His eyes darted around the room, stopped on the door window, he muttered, "People are threatening me." He drifted toward the opposite of the desk, closer to Adrian, a safe zone.

"Who?"

He didn't respond.

Adrian keyed up his computer, "What's your number?" He punched keys with his left and took a drink with his right as the inmate rattled off his number. He dropped his glass and read over Inmate Zimmerman's file. Eyed Zimmerman, who waited nervously with a finger in his mouth. Adrian finished and broke his cardinal rule. A rule he and Elmer discussed many times: don't ever look at their charges or read their charging documents. Adrian said, "Names?"

Zimmerman let out a valley girl, "Uh," squealed "you know I can't tell you."

Adrian spoke in a concerned tone, "They scare you?"

"Yes," Zimmerman said as his lids drooped over his whites. Chin nosedived.

"Feel like you are being cornered?"

A keening welp. *Good, somebody cares about his situation.* "Yes, very much so, Mr. Franklin."

Adrian stood and sat on the corner of his desk with a somber face, "They threatened you with physical violence?"

A sniffle. Bat of his eyes.

Adrian kept poking, "They touch you . . ." He searched for the proper words as Zimmerman backed up against the wall. "They touch the one-eyed swamp monster?"

Zimmerman tried not to glare.

A flat tone, "Did they?"

"No," Zimmerman snapped back. Saw Franklin's hand coil up into a fist. He crouched against the wall. Franklin filled his eyesight. It couldn't be. He was the one who was going to help him.

The tone returned, "You feel like you have no way out?"

Zimmerman felt better. The stress scrambled his mind. He frowned and said, "Yes, yes."

Franklin grew in Zimmerman's eyes as the demon pressed from inside. He yelled back, "How do you think your victim felt?" A megaphone in the ear. Mist against the side of the face.

Zimmerman bounced in his catcher's stance and wept.

The demon was out. Franklin threw haymakers, "You like touching little kids?"

"No," he yelped.

"You sit up at night thinking about what you did?"

"Please."

Adrian wanted to laugh. He didn't. He tapped Zimmerman on the head, a high school bully move. "Zimmerman." He hoisted his eyes up, red with fear. A condescending tone, ripe with sarcasm, "Shouldn't you just go back to your bed and . . ." Adrian crouched down, "and fucking kill yourself?" Adrian stood up and stepped back. Zimmerman ran out of the office.

Adrian retreated to his desk and swiveled around and faced the wall. He immediately felt bad for what he had done. Susan had been a positive influence on him. He tried. Zimmerman's file lit the fuse. Elmer warned him. Zimmerman was a card-carrying member of the North American Man/Boy Love Association (NAMBLA). He advocated for the advancement and approval of pedophiliac love. Adrian inhaled deeply and blocked out the images in his mind, then the phone rang. He listened for twenty seconds and exploded out of his seat. Phone met wall. Fist met fish tank. He screamed. Hordes of eyes gathered like flies in his window. A one-man war raged inside the tiny office. Fate had a way of showing itself.

# CHAPTER 37

# Conner Wallace
# 2022

onner finished his last journal entry and shipped it out to Damon before his transfer went through. The plan was coming together, and he didn't want this minor detail to ruin his entire plan. Plan he had set up almost two decades ago. When the last notebook arrived in the mail, Damon placed it in the trunk of his car with the others and stopped by an Office Max on Bridge Street and purchased three bankers boxes, and loaded all the notebooks. He pulled into the Law Offices of Overmeyer and Stanley, located at 162 Ewing Street. He got out of the car and took in the neighborhood. He had a particular interest in it now. He walked to the trunk and carried the three boxes to the front door of the law office. He dropped the boxes and stepped in. "Can I help you?" he heard.

"Yeah," he said as he approached. "Have three boxes I need delivered."

"Boxes?"

"Yes, ma'am."

"Sir, we aren't a delivery service."

"My boss . . . your client, requested I bring them here." He jabbed his finger into her counter.

Bewildered, she spoke out the side of her mouth as she searched for a pen and piece of paper, "Doesn't make any sense, but . . ." Then, "Name?"

"Excuse me?"

"Name of your boss."

"Conner Wallace."

Her eyes scrolled through the client list, then, "The packages?" Damon gestured with his neck. She followed and saw the boxes sitting outside. "Can you get the boxes, please?" He returned with the boxes and dropped them from waist-high to the ground. When she shuddered, he smiled. She ignored him and looked down at her paper. "Address?"

"145 Ewing Street"

"145 Ew . . ." She dropped the pen and jabbed her finger over his shoulder, "That is literally right across the street."

"I know," he said and pivoted on his toes and walked out, not before saying, "Have a nice day."

The same night at work, Officer Gill sent the following email to the block sergeant requesting the following move.

*Sgt. Smith,*

*I'm requesting the following move due to the need for porters on third shift. Our two regular porters were recently fired for engaging in a physical altercation. The showers are getting extremely filthy and need to be cleaned on a nightly basis. The warden came through yesterday and complained. I don't want her or the residents bothering you about this problem. Third shift can fix the situation. We have an inmate moving into Cell 224B tomorrow from Montgomery. If you look on the move sheet, his name is Wallace 36621-9. Currently, the other bed is vacant. I request Clouser 23496-7 be moved from A1 to E2 Cell 224A. Clouser was my regular 3rd shift shower porter in A1, and he has agreed to assist me with our problem.*

*Thanks for the consideration,*
*Officer Damon Gill*

# CHAPTER 38

# Adrian Franklin
# 2022

A drian remembered the day he met Susan; it was day one of A.S. He didn't broach the subject with her. Hoped she was preoccupied with getting their house in order. They had been busy over the past two weeks, moving and decorating. "Babe," he said, and kissed her on the earlobe. "You want to run over to the library with me?" She snapped around and smiled. "What?" He stepped back, "Why you looking at me that way?" She held her suspicious eyes and blinked. "Susan?"

A short rattle of the head. A wry smile. "Just surprised," she said, "that came from left field."

He lied. "Yeah, I know, a new book by King came out, and it sounded interesting to me." *Don't ask the title of the book.* "I can't remember the title . . . some of the guys at work were talking about it."

Her eyes locked in on him, coldly said, "Guys you work with?"

He wasn't taking the bait, "Just get your shoes on, babe." They pulled into the Ross County Library. Adrian led the way and headed upstairs and entered at the G's. He stole a look at her and skimmed over the titles with his fingertips, and said, "I remember standing at the bottom of the steps and watching you do what I'm doing now?" He stopped and pulled a book and pivoted around, and faced her. Chest to chest. She could smell the toothpaste from the morning. He clasped her hand, never taking his eyes off hers, "You took this book home," he said and gently placed it in her hand. He heard her breathing, her chest froze up. She swallowed and softly said, "You remember the book I took home?"

A slow nod of the head, a mouthed, "Yes." Her cheeks collapsed as she exhaled. He pivoted around and continued through the G's.

She saw him pull another. "Which one is that?"

He turned around with his hands and book behind his back, he was already crying when he dropped to a knee. She exhaled. Hands to the face. Fingertips stopped below the eyes as she watched him intently. "Susan," he whispered and showed her the book: *Forrest Gump.* "When I saw you the first time, you were like an angel saving me from making a huge mistake." She wiped an eye. "Every moment since that crazy night . . ." He let that linger in the air as she giggled. "You remember?"

Another giggle. A flip of the hair. A sniff of the nose. She bent down and whispered, "How could I forget . . ." she held it, then, "Bam."

A suffering, "Oh God."

She got vertical and extended a hand, "My Adrian," she said. He melted three inches.

He continued, "Ever since that night, I have never been the same." He clasped the ring with two fingers and studied her as he said, "Will you be mine?" as tears chased each word.

She swiped at both eyes and shook out her hands, "I'd never be prouder," she said and melted into his hands.

Susan, their life, bounced around his mind. Then, he woke into a nightmare. The dream a blur. A fog burrowed in his mind; it started in the occipital lobe. The doctors stood at the end of his bed and slowly floated above his sight. Hospital room blue appeared gray to Adrian. Everything in sight moved like it was encased in jelly, slow and methodical with no direction. "Mr. Franklin," the voice said from the end of the bed. Adrian glanced around the room and then stopped on the two, "Adrian," she continued, "I'm Dr. Jenni Kennedy." She slid a hand on her colleague to her left, "This is Dr. Jerome Brown." His eyes rolled high and then back to them, "Do you know where you are?"

The fog seeped into the cerebellum. He sat slumped on the edge of his bed like a question mark. Drool leaked from the corner of his lip, slowly pooling on the floor below. Silent movements. Drifting in a swing. Adrian didn't respond.

Fog guided into the temporal lobe. The doctor tried again, "Mr. Franklin," she met eyes with her colleague, who gestured for her to push again. "Adrian, do you know your current location?" Her voice bellowed loud and stretchy. His head jolted back and rested chin on his chest.

The fog rose to the parietal lobe. "Mr. Franklin?" she said a third time and moved to the front of him. His eyes caught her toes and moved up her body until he saw a face. She held the pose and said, "Mr. Fr . . . a. .n."

"Susan."

"Mr. Franklin?"

"I need . . . need to get home for dinner."

The frontal lobe soaked in the last of the fog. His tongue was dry and leathery. "I-need-to-go-home." He raised his head and raised his right lid; a sliver of white saw her. "Home."

"Adrian, do you know where you are?"

"Work." He raised on the tips of his fingers, struggling to get up. Dr. Kennedy frowned at Dr. Brown as she moved closer and gently pressed on Adrian's shoulder. "I . . . I need to be getting home to Susan." He fell back to his butt. Tried to shake the cobwebs out of his head.

Dr. Kennedy said, "No, Adrian, you are not at work. You are at Adena Regional, you—"

Then the call came back to him, and he began to tremble, and shook his head at her, "No." His limbs tensed, sweat poured, he spoke louder, "It can't be true." He violently flailed from side to side and screamed, "Susan!" The nightmare was true.

Dr. Kennedy shrilled, "Adrian," and turned to Dr. Brown, said, "get the orderlies." She stepped away toward the wall and watched as Adrian raged on the bed like a bat trapped in a room.

Seven days after the episode, Adrian woke with the fog lifted. As his dosage of medication regulated, he was more aware of his surroundings and circumstances. Morning to night, a cavalcade of knocks, screams rushed over him like an avalanche. Peace was not existent in this hospital. He laid silently when Dr. Kennedy entered.

"Mr. Franklin."

His eyes met hers.

"Do you know why you are here?" she asked and pulled a chair closer to him. He eyed her with the clipboard wrapped between her arms. She smiled. Pulled the board from her chest and studied the chart, "Adrian?"

He turned over and faced the wall. His back to her and whispered, "I threatened to kill everybody and myself at work." He heard the click of the pen. The turn of a page. Firm now, "I'm not crazy, Doc."

"Do you still have—"

He aggressively flipped over to face her. Head on pillow. Eyes on her. Spoke with hostility. "Doesn't really matter anymore, Doc."

She cleared her throat. Dropped the pen in the white jacket pocket. Placed the clipboard on the stand next to the bed. Sat up in her chair and crossed her leg, asked, "Do you have anybody you would like to call?"

"No."

She continued, "The hospital is not allowed to give your personal information or status out to family."

"I don't have any family anymore."

"Or . . . friends."

A blank stare.

"We can't even acknowledge you are a patient here if someone asked or called . . ."

He blinked.

"Not even if a Mr. Ray called and asked us about you."

He flipped to his back and put his arms behind his head.

"Someone has to have a four-digit pin . . . pin assigned to you," she paused. Then, "They need you to give them your four-digit pin to contact the floor or set up a visit."

She snapped around toward the door when the scream exploded from outside. He closed his eyes again and inhaled deeply from the nose.

"Okay," she said and pulled a piece of paper and wrote a number, "I'll leave your pin here on the stand, if you would like to give it to Mr. Ray." At the door, she stopped and turned, "Elmer has called so many times. He is worried about you."

Adrian pulled a pillow from behind and covered his face.

The next day, the eighth since her death, sledgehammering on the wall nearest to him woke the demons inside. He jumped off the bed and bodied the door. Listened, then telescoped an eye to the tiny window. The banging continued. Adrian fisted the door. Looked again. Nothing. More banging. Fisted the door and looked again. He stepped back and kicked it. Nothing. He started banging like a wild animal and screamed, "Fucking knock it off before I come out and kill all you motherfuckers!" He stepped back, blood red and exhausted. Stepped back and geared down his breathing. His fists ratcheted tight. He grunted when prying eyes looked in on him from the other side of the door.

For the next two hours, he paced the floor of his room in a sedated limp. Six steps from one side to the other and returned. On the first pass, he counted sixteen tiles on the floor. His eyes swung around the room as he paced. A spider weaving a web caught his eye on the fifty-ninth pass. It hung out at his two o'clock, in the corner, above the door frame. He stopped and stepped closer. The spider was statuesque. A ninja stalking its victim. Adrian whispered, "Spider, spider on the wall. Get down from there." He leaned against the door, neck exposed and apple out, eyes under the web. "Can't you see that wall is plastered? Get down from there, you stupid bastard." A snort. A lick of the lip. He paced. His mind spun like a tornado.

He spoke fast, "Favorite movie? *Ghost*. Favorite book?" He stopped and gestured with his hands at the wall, "Of course, *Forrest Gump*." He gripped his face and tried to peel off the skin as his pace quickened, "She wanted a honeymoon in Taiwan; get one of those bungalows, lay in the hammock all day." He stopped and jabbed a finger in the air, "Yes," he said, "babe, we can go horseback riding, do anything you want." Started pacing, eyes on the tile; *one, two, three, four*. He stopped counting the tiles and eyed the spider once again, spoke to him, "She wanted to join the mile-high club." He cocked his head to the side and closed one eye to the ceiling light, "You think she knows what I did to Splatter?" He pointed at the spider, "Do you feel bad for what you are about to do?" He asked as the spider inched toward a fly it had in his web.

Adrian jumped back at the sound of the locking mechanism in the door, arms cocked and loaded. He relaxed when Dr. Kennedy opened the door. His eyes tracked her across the room. He noticed the thin file cradled in her hand. Thinks they must not think he is too fucked up. At the prison, he had dealt with the criminally insane, the mentally disturbed. He cradled files thick as bricks. She laid the file on the table and pulled a chair toward the bed. Gestured for him to join her. He put on his game face and sat on the edge of the bed. Dr. Kennedy spoke. Adrian sat quietly, attentive. She assumed he was listening. He was not.

His mind was as clear as it had been since her death. Glassy eyes masked a new focus, camouflaged a fierce eye with purpose. A new goal. Her death corroded his dreams of a future. The spider launched a new path. For the first time since he arrived, he could smell the urine deep in his senses as the odor wafted into his room. He touched his nose, sniffled. Heard her say, "Hello."

He flashed his eyes at her. Waited a fleeting second and said, "Hey."

His eyes shuffled around the room, bland and cold. Listened to the groans and moans echoing from the hall. A new smell, not urine or cleaning supplies. Waste, human waste, was being painted on the walls in the next room by the mentally disturbed as he used his hands to create his picture.

"Can we talk about how you are feeling today?"

His air stuttered at the revelation. Skin shaded over. His blood ran hot. He stood up and walked over to the wall. Stretched high on his tips, whispered, "How am I going to catch my prey?"

"Excuse me?"

Adrian stood motionless, statuesque.

"Adrian, did you say something?"

He exhaled and deflated. Went flat on his feet. He lowered his head and turned toward her with his hands clasped behind his back and smiled.

"Mr. Franklin?"

A flat stare. A short breath. Then, he spoke, "Her death was tragic." His voice cracked. Lip quivered. His eye twitched. He fingered his eye and continued, "She was taken too soon."

Dr. Kennedy frowned.

"But," he continued and returned to the bed. He looked at her and said, "I have a lot to live for, and I need to go home and make her proud of me."

She peered back with apprehension and silently wrote a note in the chart.

He spoke sternly, "I'm going home."

She said nothing, her eyes spoke for her.

"I'm an adult. I have the right to check out of here."

She scribed and dropped the pen inside the chart and snapped it closed. "Yes, Mr. Franklin, but—"

He cut her off, "No, Doc." He waved a finger, dropped it when he saw the fear in her, "I . . . I . . ." he pointed at the wall, "all the banging and screaming," he said and rapidly nodded. "I can't handle all the . . . noise." He saw her features tighten. She held a dubious glare. He continued, "I'll be better off at my own house."

She saw the vulnerability. She forced a smile. "I understand," she pointed at him, "But I expect to see you here for outpatient services." She continued,

"Can I get your word?" Firmer, "I believe the outpatient services will help you will the coping issues, the grieving process."

Hand on his chest. A smile to try and hide his detachment. Then, "I promise."

"Okay," she said reluctantly and keep her sight on him as she gathered the file. He sat silently as she exited the door.

After hearing the locking mechanism, he slipped off the bed and walked toward the door, and looked up, "There you are." He rocked back and forth on his heels and cocked his head, and watched the scene above. "Get him. Get him." Louder, "Trap him," he said as the spider spun his web around the fly and crept forward. "Yes. Yes."

Graceful. Stealthy. The spider balanced on his way toward the fly. Adrian hummed to his new friend. Moved closer. Smiled wide. Sent him his hymn, "Oh spider, spider on the wall. Don't you see that wall is plastered? Get down from there, you stupid bastard." Another step. Hands gripped tight. He held the words, "Get 'em," like it was a grenade.

# CHAPTER 39

# Conner Wallace
# 2022

Conner passed his time at Montgomery with Mike Byers at his side. He grew to be his Damon in prison, his friend and confidant. The physical confrontations and trouble were behind him. His goal of being dropped security levels and transferring were within his reach. He entered the system as a level four inmate and dropped to a three. He was perceived as being of sound body and mind, had a spotless disciplinary record over the past two years, tested out of the GED, and was considered a low-risk offender for his age. He was set to have a security level review in the next two weeks.

Conner and Mike passed the endless days and nights working out. Mike had gained thirty pounds of muscle. Conner worked in recreation, passing out equipment: basketballs, softball gear, and jump ropes. Mike was a tutor in the library. Conner had learned Mike was beyond smart and particularly skilled in computers. He taught the kid how to survive the rest of his game on the chessboard.

Institutional life was snowglobe living. Each day, the globe was shaken up, and new Kings and Queens emerged. Hyenas and vultures rose as the old decomposed on the side. Every square on the board had perilous conditions to navigate. To survive, one eye needed to be scanning the board and the other on the concrete jungle. Conner taught his young protégé the survival skills necessary. This wasn't grandma's snowglobe on the mantel above hanging stockings.

As Conner approached his level review scheduled for March eighth, he aimed to have one last lesson with the now twenty-three-year-old. He climbed up the bleachers, stood, and surveyed his surroundings like a troubled mongoose waiting for the slithering predators to make a move. The quiver of cobras had bedded down for the evening. He slowly hunched down and sat. A quorum of transvestites and gays glared with disgust at his intrusion. He ignored them and gazed off in a tranquil state and waiting for his friend.

"Conner?"

He took a deep breath.

"Conner?"

He waved Mike up.

Mike climbed up and dropped down next to him and waved his hand in front, "Why we up here?" His eyes flashed at the group of men, "With these guys?"

"Yous see all deez cockroaches?" He pointed out toward the yard, "You dun get ter close ter dam." Surreptitiously, he watched his surroundings with a sniper stare. Mike opened his mouth to speak, Conner added, "Dun let dem smell de fear." He had guided Mike on the rules and regulations of institutional life, like don't tell on others. "Snitches get stitches." At Montgomery, snitches got shanked. Never borrow anything from anybody, not even a pen. The penalty would be harsh; one soda equaled two back, or more. Always walk tall with your eyes forward and never eyeball anybody or let someone stare you down. If someone threatens or presses you (sex), hit them first and hard. Institutional love? Don't mess with boys—AIDS, Hepatitis B, or C. He taught him how to eat well without visits to the chow hall, inmate meals known as "breaks." Conner gave him two of his favorites—two summer sausages, two bags of rice, one cheddar block, one pack of tortilla wraps mixed. Add two slices of Velveeta cheese, one pickle and some seasoning. For dessert, one bag of sugar, one jar of peanut butter and one large chocolate fudge. All ingredients were available in the commissary.

"I won't. You taught me how to handle myself."

Conner studied his face and wrapped his arm around him, he said, "Listun ter me, am not go'n ter be e'yer ter watch over yous."

Mike stayed confident, "I know," he said and patted his friend's leg, "When you think you'll leave?"

His faced scowled over, "'Opefully next week."

"Damn."

"Dun worry am gett'n yous outi e'yer."

"I'm going to die in this fucking place," he said in jest. "Those dirty cops won."

The night Mike was arrested, he ran into a dark alley, into the closed end of a paper bag. The light raced away from him, he heard, "Stop," from behind and when he did, "I just want to ask you a few questions."

He responded, "Excuse me?" As the officer approached, he said, "Are you talking to me, sir?" He walked slowly toward the cop standing in front of the light. As he came into view, the officer realized Mike didn't fit the description of the suspect who robbed the liquor store a block down. Mike was six feet tall and black. The suspect was about the same height, but the weight was a hundred pounds off and the suspect had a full head of gray hair.

"I'm sorry," the officer said, "But have you seen a large African-American male," he gestured with his hand at the jaw line, "with a full beard run through here?"

"No, sir," Mike said and pointed over the officer's shoulder, "I came from Orange Avenue." When the officer followed the finger, "I was at my girl-friend's house."

The officer smiled, said "Okay." Then as he walked away, he added, "Be careful walking home."

"Yes, sir," Mike said and turned. The shot came from behind his ears. He jumped, felt the pee against his groin. "Stop," he heard. "He just shot Rollins," a cop called out on the radio.

Mike eyes swung on the pendulum left, right, left, right. "Who . . . me?" Whites of his eyes popped out of his sockets. He saw the flash first. The bang of the gun reached his drums at the same time as the pain reached his brain. He fell to the ground. Cold steel was pressed against his head with a boot in the middle of his back.

"Trust Conner. Yer days ay not go'n ter end in dis place. Before ay met yous, ay 'ad one friend in de wirld. Now ay 'uv two and ay dun forget friends."

"Hope not," Mike said, "I consider you a friend also." After a moment, Mike worked up the courage to ask, "So, since we are friends . . . I . . . I just curious. I don't know much about your past except for the girl you mention."

Bruised by the stories of life, wounded by the memories of his past, unloved in his existence, Conner was now riddled by his feelings. That ancient feeling excavated a hole in his head, cocooned itself, and hatched. First Damon, now Mike had him questioning his chosen path and purpose. He spoke softly, "Ay wuz a da' once."

Shocked, Mike leaned away and tilted his head, "You," he said, "you were a dad?" He caught the sadness in Conner. The first-time vulnerability cracked his shtick. "You said were."

"'Is name wuz Tyrell."

Mike considered the name and began to ask what happened to him, instead said, "Tyrell?" He had known a Tyrone once. Never a Tyrell and never heard the name used for a white boy. "Family name?"

Conner's lips anchored down, "Bewk. Tyrell wuz de main feller in me father's fuv bewk."

Mike squeezed his face between his hands and leaned forward, "This is the most you have spoken about your life. I beginning to think you were a damn alien or something."

Conner nudged him. "Oo yous 'uv out there?"

"Just my sister." Their eyes met. "Her name is Oprah-Jackson-Byers," he said and smiled when Conner gave him a strange look.

"And yous questioned Tyrell."

Both laughed.

"She goes by OJ," he showed his hands, "If the gloves don't fit—"

"Yous 'uv ter aquit." Conner high-fived Mike. Mike hesitated before he dropped his hand when he realized Conner put his hand up first. Conner watched Mike yawn, and a new thought crossed his mind. For a thousand days, he had slept little. The nightmares woke him, tugged on his heart. Last night, he slept eight hours. The night before, seven. For the past two weeks, he has slept like a newborn. The end of his days had lost its meaning, changed by that ancient feeling. "Ironic."

"What?"

"Tell me about yer sister."

Mike blew air, "Oh," he said, "she is something smart . . . could hack into the CIA probably."

"Computers?"

"Oh yeah."

Conner's eyes moonwalked back and blew air out the corner of his mouth.

Mike continued, "She's the only one who believes in me. She got arrested for harassing one of the witnesses."

"Cop?"

"Yeah."

"Wa' about yer parents?"

"Mom died when we were young." He stared blankly, "Some days, I forget what she looked like." He gripped his fists tight and pressed his eyes shut until he saw her. When he did, "Our dad raised us right." His tone changed as he grew angry, "He taught us how to act right." Conner swallowed and started to ask the question when Mike added, "He died last year of a heart attack." He stood up and clasped his hands behind his head, "It was from a broken heart." A slight shake of the head led to, "This killed him."

He felt Mike looking down at him. Conner said, "Juss 'ang in and gizza me some time." After a long minute of silence, Conner added, "Yer me monkey."

Mike dropped a playful elbow on his shoulder, "I hate you damn foreigners."

The following week, Conner had his security review and was granted a drop in security. He was scheduled to be transferred to Sherman Rehabilitation Center.

# CHAPTER 40

# Adrian Franklin
# 2002

drian and Elmer didn't speak as they drove to the cemetery. Adrian exited the vehicle. The pain started deep inside. His soul was the first to cry. He drudgingly took a step, descried the dirt surrounding the grass ahead. He knew it was her. The headstone was yet to be there. Clenched jaws. Shallowed breathing. Glossy eyes carried the lost boy to her gravesite. As he reached her, his knees gave out, and tears overwhelmed the boy. He lay in a fetal position over her. Broken with no answers for what had occurred. No understanding of why she was gone.

"Susan," he wept, "I miss you so much already. Please don't go. I don't . . ." his words faded as his lungs worked in overdrive. An inhale. A shifting exhale, "I can't do this without you," he whispered.

Morning birds chirped in the distance. Leaves wrestled on the branches and the lost boy continued to cry.

He laughed. "I remember," he began to say and laughed louder. Birds leaped from their stoops, "I remember the first time I met you. I had that stupid haircut." He yelled back at Elmer, "You hated that damn haircut."

Elmer continued leaning against his car and remained silent.

He took a deep breath and let it fumble out between his lips, "Russ and everybody else said I didn't have a chance . . ." His voice reduced to a whisper, "I knew I had to have you. You were born for me." Forehead met dirt.

Elmer watched from afar and saw the boy shivering, "Adrian?"

The spring air stirred him. He mumbled in the dirt, "Do you remember when you broke up with me?" He flipped over and fisted the dirt with the meat of his hands, screamed, "Because of that fucking Scott."

Elmer stepped forward and stopped at the first row of stones.

He wept, cried out, "I never gave up." Sat up, chewed on his lip, eyed Elmer, and turned away. "I . . . I . . . I . . ." Hand to mouth, a bite at a hand. "I stayed out of trouble because I wanted you to be proud." Her soul pulled him toward the sky, "I wanted you to be proud of me," he screamed to the clouds and collapsed to his side.

Elmer saw the shivering. He stepped forward and called out, "Adrian?" After he didn't respond, "Son, you need a jacket."

Adrian raised an arm with his palm out, "Elmer," he said, "let me sit here awhile." He lowered his arm, "Come back to get me later."

He heard the car door open and close, and footsteps, and after, he felt the jacket draped over his shoulders, "I'll be in the car waiting for you." A moment of silence, the car door opened, "I'll be sitting right here. You take all the time you need."

Silent as the night. Deep in his mind. "Come back to me." Winds picked up and danced across the land. "Do you remember when I asked you to marry me?" A smile. Deep inhale. Exhale. "You should have seen the work Elmer and I put in to find a book with the original cover."

He pictured Susan, the crooked smile; then he opened, Elmer racing away in his vision. He tried to walk; the grass stuck to his shoes. The only thing in sight to move was Elmer, small and smaller he appeared. Brambles wrapped themselves over his ankles, up his thighs, squeezing him at the waist. He sways in a windless wind. Sodden features engulfed his face. He attempted to form words, call out to Elmer; his tongue knotted and collapsed in his mouth. Slowly, he sunk to the ground like peeling paint. After he buckled, he lay wasted on the ground, frozen in time.

# CHAPTER 41

# Conner Wallace
# 2022

Conner and the window were one as the bus rambled toward Sherman. A glue wall of fog shrouded the ninety-minute bus trip from Dayton. The transportation bus arrived at the rear sally port of the institution at two-thirty in the afternoon. As the bus entered through the second gate, Conner scanned the campus-like atmosphere. Sherman, the largest center in Ohio, was vastly different than Hamilton or Montgomery. Residents of Sherman roamed the jungle free. Checkers was the game.

Albert Clouser was moved to E-Unit at eleven thirty the same morning. "Who the hell got me moved here?" He bitched to the officer behind the desk.

The officer ignored his tone, glanced at his move sheet and said, "You're in cell 224A. It's upstairs to the right."

Clouser stood in place. "Seriously," he said. "Rockwell, why am I here?"

"Upstairs." His words nudged him away. "Last cell."

He continued to plead. "Come on, man." Then, "You know I'm a level one now. I'm not supposed to be in an orientation unit." He glared at the range above. "I did my time in this shithole."

Rockwell sucked on a tooth, took his glasses off and stood up. "I don't care where you think you should live," he said calmly.

"This is—"

In two steps, the officer was on the other side of the desk, face to face with Clouser. "This is what?" He drew closer. "This is what, Clouser?"

Clouser slouched, dropped his eyes, and lolled his head on the chest. "Nothing," he said, small.

Rockwell cooled. "All I know is your name is on my move sheet." He gathered it off the desk and showed Clouser.

"I know. I saw it."

"Just get up there and speak with unit staff when they get in."

As he walked slowly up the stairs, he continued griping. "This is some bullshit, man." Another step. "I've worked my ass off to get to A-Unit."

"Now, Clouser!"

Two more steps, then he swiveled around. "What time does unit staff get in?"

"Eight-thirty, nine."

Another step, he pivoted and looked down. "Can't you call someone?"

A glare behind the desk. Keys rattle above. "Clouser."

He heard the bark from above.

"Get your ass up here, now!"

"Damn, Young," Clouser said, then he spoke out of his teeth. "Thought your ass transferred out."

"What you say, prisoner?"

"I said it was nice to see you."

"Ay-huh."

"I'm not supposed to be here."

"I don't know shit, convict," Young said and slid over to let Clouser pass. He did and stopped in front of the cell door. Young approached, unlocked the door, opened it, and smiled, "Welcome home."

Clenched jaws. Dagger eyes. Small mouth.

"You have something you want to say to me?"

"Nah," Clouser said and stepped in. Then, after it was locked, "You're lucky I'm a level one." He tossed his things on the bed and yelled, "Fuck!" Heel met metal. Fist to glass. He got jailhouse courage. "Lucky I'm behind this door . . . Young . . . if I ever see you on the streets."

A voice rang out from the side, a singsong cadence. "He going to fuck you up if he gets the chance. He going to fuck you up if he gets the . . ." It faded as Clouser retreated to the back of the cell and peered out the window.

From the angle and direction offered, he could see the street five down from his house. He imagined what might have been.

Hours later, Conner was escorted to E-Unit, "Welcome," he heard, "you are in cell 224B." The officer stood, handed Conner an orientation book with the unit rules and regulations. "The officer will let you in."

"Get your ass up here, inmate," Young hollered out, "I don't have all day." Conner took the slow walk up, hands cuffed behind his back, holding the little property. His eyes checked his new home. An anemic pulse radiated throughout the cell block. Faint whispers. Low moans. Only life was the commanding voices of the two officers, who barked orders and bounced cell to cell with a constant rattle of cuffs and keys. A cockroach trotted under a cell door. Conner swore he saw it carrying a potato chip. Dirt as thick as flour led him up. A musky odor showed him the rest of the way. Inmates peeked out of the nail file windows, eager to get a glimpse. This was no Shawshank or Oz; the voices were muted, and the eyes stared scared. At night the tongues of the condemned howled prayers to the farthest corners where only dust and mites heard.

Conner followed the officer to his cell. Stopped and waited and when the officer opened the door, he stepped in. He dropped his duffel. Clouser was standing at the end of the bed with his back to him, folding his clothes and putting them in his footlocker. The door slammed. The officer said, "Back up," and opened the cuff port. Conner leaned his body forward, pushed his arms back, and wrists out the port. The officer unlocked the cuffs, said, "Arms in."

After the port closed, Conner heard, "Welcome to hell."

He winched as he twisted his wrist and said, "I've seen worse." Picked up his duffel, "This is Candyland."

Albert put the last of his belongings in his box and locked it shut. Stood up and scanned his new mate. "Yeah, you will be fine," he said after noticing Connor's girth. He knelt and slid into the bottom bunk. "I just got here today." Smacked the bed and said, "I got bottom." Conner walked over to the window and looked out. Albert kept shooting words at him. "Maybe you can get moved to a bottom bunk soon." He laughed, "Your big ass is going to be uncomfortable up there."

Conner cracked his neck and turned around, pointed, "That one mine?"

Albert crossed his legs and put his arms behind his head and eyed the locker, "Yep."

Conner was now secured in a six-by-eight, two-man cell more suited for a gnome. Bricks encased a bunk bed. A wall-mounted table the size of a notebook and an open-air toilet lined the other wall. No solitude in taking a dump. In summer, conditions were as hot as Africa without the wild safari. Winter as cold as the East Antarctic Plateau. The constant clatter of a broken radiator overwhelmed all sounds, even the groans, moans, and cries from other cells. These sounds, with the tit and tat of scavenging rodents, ruled the night. The intrusion of cockroaches hindered sleep. The building hummed like a spitfire flying at a hundred feet.

Albert popped up, dropped his drawers, and sat on the toilet. Hands over his eyes. Head down. Conner emptied his duffel on the bottom bunk. Pulled the first item and folded it. Placed it in his locker. He sat on the bed and picked up a pair of socks, eyes on the floor, folded and dropped it in the locker box. Albert glanced up, released a guttural growl to get Conner's attention. When it didn't generate a look or a reply, he said, "Bottom one is mine."

Conner picked at a tooth and eyed Albert. Picked up a shirt and folded it. Heard, "I said you were on top."

"Yeah," Conner said, "I heard you."

Albert wiped and stood up. Pulled his pants up and knocked the flush with his foot. He walked to the door and leaned against it, eyes on the window. "What's your name?"

Conner continued to fold his clothes.

Albert knelt when he heard the cuff port open and the officer call out, "Clouser."

"Yeah," he said, mouth hanging in the opening.

"You asked for unit staff?"

"Yeah," he hollered, "send one of them up."

"Not here yet."

He elbowed the door. "When they get in?"

Cuff port slammed shut.

"What the fuck?" Albert said and stood up. He nestled his nose up to the sliver of Plexiglas in the door as the officer was walking off. "Come back," he yelled.

"You're not moving today," the officer hollered back over his shoulder.

"This is bullshit." He listened to the sound of keys grow distant, slammed his palm against the door. "Send one of them up." Agitated, he foreheaded the door and pivoted around, and glared at Conner, who had dropped down and pushed out a set of a hundred push-ups. "You don't sound like you're from the States."

Conner hesitated at the top, with his arms extended, then kept pushing.

"You from Australia or something?"

"Nah." He sniffled through his nose and flexed his pecs. "Here to take care o' some unfinished business," he said and grabbed Albert's towel from the rail and wiped down his chest. He turned and showed Albert the flags on his arm. Shot eyes at Albert's arm.

"Norma Jean, he said and dropped down again. "She wuddun be ter proud o' dat one."

Albert squibbed, "I like it," and giggled at the shoulders. He felt his body flush when Conner glared from below. He covered his Marilyn with a palm. Conner pushed. Pushed and rolled over. Kept his glare on Albert with each sit-up. Albert grew uncomfortable, felt his stomach turn over. He said, "Who is Norma Jean?"

He icily said, "Norma Jean…Marilyn Monroe's real name. Lewks more like Marilyn Manson."

"Lewks more like Marilyn Manson."

Albert bent down and pulled a t-shirt from his locker box. As he put it on, he heard, "De Yankee rock star."

"Yeah," Albert said and pulled the shirt over the tattoo. "I know who he is." Albert cradled himself with his arms and settled down at the end of the bed with Conner on his right doing sit-ups and the door on his left. He was abnormally uncomfortable with his new bunkmate. He had had many before, but none made him feel so unsteady and small. He has torn between remaining silent or having a conversation. He chose more small talk, "England . . . How did you end up here?"

Conner sped up his set like a demon.

Albert fidgeted and said, "What's a guy from overseas doing up in this shithole?" He gathered himself and stood up and kicked the door. Flipped around and leaned against it, arms over his chest.

Conner finished, jumped up and grabbed Clouser's towel as he watched but didn't say anything. Towel down the left arm. Eyes on Clouser, who glanced away. Down the right. Over the chest, "Fate," he said and dropped the towel on the bed. "Am exactly whuz wanna be. E'yer with you."

A quizzical glance.

"E'yer with you."

Albert thought he understood what he said but wasn't positive. He moved toward his bed and picked up the towel with two fingers and placed it on the edge of the sink. "You can keep it," he said and rubbed his hands over his thighs. He slid gently into his bed and laid sideways, eyes on Conner as he moved toward the window.

He lingered at the window, Conner said, "Have ever beun in love?"

Albert sat up, knees to his chest, arms over his knees. "Love?"

Conner flipped around, moved toward the bed, looking down on Albert, he spoke softer, "Someone uo ay immediately knew I'd slay do Loch Ness Musti fe. Id die fe her at a moment's notice."

"I've been locked up too long," Albert said and pulled his knees closer.

"Oh, am go'n ter see'n her real soon." He pushed away from the bed rail and dropped down, "Beun wait'n years to see her." Clouser watched in silence as Conner did another hundred push-ups and sit-ups. After he counted three sets of a hundred, Clouser flipped over and faced the brick wall and closed his eyes. Conner pushed out another two hundred and stood up. He kicked the bed and said, "'Ow long yous beun down?"

Clouser mumbled, "Twenty years," and flipped over. "You?"

"Ay did a few years at 'amilton and Montgomery," he said and opened the sink and splashed water on his face. "Real shit'oles compared ter this place."

"Oh yeah, I did some time over at Hamilton a decade ago." He sat upright, "First bit?"

"Nah, did six years am Nevada," Conner snarled out as he grabbed the rail and stretched his pec out.

"No shit? Damn, you get around, friend." He hesitated before he asked, "What you get locked up for?" He squeezed his eyes shut, thinking he made the cardinal mistake of asking about the offense. "Nevermind, I—"

He didn't finish before Conner turned around and smiled, "W's de reason a fellar does anyth'n?"

A shrug.

"De ladies get me up ther trouble." Arms spread, knees bent, "Can't help myself because o' de ladies," Conner finished and cupped his jewels.

A snort. A cough. Albert pointed and said, "I know exactly what you mean."

Conner abruptly stopped smiling and turned away before he went too far. He walked to the window; the radiator thrummed in his face as Albert continued to squawk behind him. He felt like he was losing control. He hummed, *the Devil won't keep us apart. The Devil won't keep us apart.*

"Hey."

*The Devil won't keep us apart.* Conner had anticipated this day for so long, at times, he did not believe this dream, his only goal in life, would come true. No matter the sacrifices he made, the destruction caused, the institutions he lived in, the number of fights, it all was in his reach, if he didn't blow it.

From the first night he met her, Conner got a feeling that was difficult for him to describe. Like being underwater, unable to breathe, seeing rays of sunlight projecting through the darkness of water as your lungs slowly kill you. As you speed to the surface, lungs collapsing and death approaching, you breach the water, and the inevitability of death is gone. A feeling, a joy, was what Conner felt each day he was with her. Euphoria? A feeling similar to what an addict gets when he gets a hit? A first climax, over and over.

She was born for him. Two bodies sharing one soul. She was the place his demons could hide, escape the corruption and evil which occupied his mind, his world for so long. An escape from evil that hindered sleep and caused his nightmares. From the first moment he spoke to her, his direction in life, his thoughts, and feelings about his future changes. She was his compass.

"Hey."

The buzzer rang. An officer called out, "Count time."

"It's going to have to wait," Clouser said and stood up next to his bed. He gestured toward Conner, who was pacing back and forth. "Hey, it's four o'clock here. We do a standing count at four. Must stand next to your bed, can't be up walking around."

Conner stopped at the foot of the bed until the officer passed by and counted their room. After the officer passed, Clouser said, "I'm not feeling well," and rubbed his throat.

Conner cleared his mind, put his game face on, and jumped into Clouser's bed and spread out. He received a pair of darted eyes for the act. He said, "Yer throat hur'?"

Clouser went to the sink and spit. "Yeah." Then, he turned around, hand on his throat, "Must be coming down with something." Spit again. "Or all this damn stress of moving to this shithole."

"Yous 'eard wa' yous do whun yous get cut it de wild?"

A blank stare.

Conner repeated himself.

He saw Albert's mouth move like he was repeating the phrase to himself. "Cut it de wild?"

"No."

A laugh from deep in the belly. Hand on the stomach. "Yous piss on de cut."

"Piss on the cut?" Albert turned, put his head in the sink, and spit again.

"Want me ter piss down yer throat?"

Clouser listened to the words cross his mind with a look of dismay, like he was hit with a phantom punch by the invisible man. Unexpected and confusing. He wanted to be mad, should have been. He feared his new bunkmate. His body went hot, then cold. Scared. His face slacked. Fingers numbed. A frightened look as if his thumb was in a grenade pin. He shot a hapless grin and snapped his mouth shut. Then, after a minute of silence, Conner laughed. Put Clouser at ease. Conner held a mysterious smile like he knew something Clouser didn't. Clouser said nothing. Fear pulled at him again. When he saw Conner drop his pants and show his junk and do a long pull to admire himself, his eyes hit the floor. Then, he turned and peered out the window, mumbled, "That shit must have been funny in jolly ole England."

Conner slid over to the toilet and relieved himself.

Clouser kept his eyes in the window until he heard Conner flush. Heard the bed moan when Conner jumped in his bed, again and changed the subject. "We will be getting called for chow soon."

"Sound as a pound. It's gewing ter be a long night."

"We don't get rec until tomorrow."

"Ay knuw."

# CHAPTER 42

# Adrian Franklin
# 2022

Elmer never thought he would be visiting Adrian in the hospital, especially not a second time. He was a lost boy now. Suffered a stroke at the gravesite. Elmer gingerly stepped off the elevator on the fourth floor and approached the nurses' station and stuck the vase of flowers out, "These are for you," he said. "I heard it was someone's birthday." He had taken up partial residence at Adena Medical Center. Nurse Michelle, Adrian's nurse, had taken to Elmer like Adrian did to him all those years ago. She knew they only had each other.

"Thank you for the flowers," she said and as she put them down. "I'm not sure if he is in the room. I just arrived on shift." She stepped around Elmer and as she went by, she said, "Give me a minute and I'll go check." She returned with a horrified expression on her face and grabbed Elmer by the elbows. "Mr. Ray?"

"What is it? Is he okay?"

"He left sometime in the middle of the night."

# CHAPTER 43

Conner and Albert and a hundred and forty-two inmates were escorted in military formation to the chow hall. Being an orientation unit, they didn't have the luxuries of meandering around the yard like the other inmates. Movements and recreation time were closely monitored for their first thirty days at Sherman. This was one of the main reasons Clouser was pissed about his move. An officer stood in front, one in back, with the inmates in between and escorted by the resident units and library and recreation hall. Walked between the designated yellow lines throughout their journey and into the chow hall. After receiving their trays, inmates sat in the next available seat. Whites forced to sit with blacks. Bloods with Crips. Straights with gays. Nobody was discriminated against.

They were allowed fifteen minutes to consume their meal in silence and then escorted back to their cells. Food trays were made like any local school; one inmate loaded the main course, another the vegetable, the last the dessert. Prison did its best with the aesthetics, large and open, indigo blue. Four seats to each table. Clean. Free abundant labor. Workers assigned to clean tables. Floor sweepers. Mops. Trash dumpers. The appearance was unable to camouflage the wretched smell. Like meeting the person of your dreams, clean and beautiful. They get two feet from you and open their mouth to speak, and the smell smacks you in the face. Smell wasn't like a five-day-old, spoiled milk smell. More like a dog's fart. The generic smell.

E-unit was escorted back to the unit. Clouser slept. Conner was full of adrenaline as the seconds ticked away. He sat on his locker box at the end of the bed, sandwiched between the bed and wall. The long, rectangular window was at his three o'clock. The natural light was dimming as the night howled to wake, and the sun floated down on the other side of the building. He reached up and pulled a string of light. It teased. Flickered . . . flickered . . . hissed, then turned bright. His focus was lost on the bare concrete wall with no paint for these saints. Clouser stirred and flipped in his peripheral. Conner dreamed upright, forearms on knees, eyes closed.

His mind wandered back to the I-40 out of Amarillo. Angry winds released by Mother Nature beat against the bike. Tumbleweeds owned the lands. It was 2002, the beginning of his journey. Meteor Crater two days later. As he stood outside of the crater, the insignificance of the world humbled him. No one would remember her, or him, or what happened to her. He would make all of them remember. One day.

Pipes behind the wall ached and moaned as heat sped into the radiator. Ticked. Tacked. Rattled with each release of heat. Shuddered and cried an insufferable noise. Walls moistened over. Sweat pooled beneath him. He opened his eyes and caught a bead of moisture twisting down the concrete wall. He watched it tumble down three blocks in a frozen stare. He didn't hear the music of the pipes. The shuffling in bed. Only the beat of his heart. Then, Conner heard the guy next door scream hysterically. "They come at night and rape me." Banging, fists flying against the door. "They come through the windows and fuck my ass. Do you hear me?" A sudden scream, then he yelled, "Come in. I'll show you." Boots hit the stairs and sounded like a crash of rhinos ascending.

Conner walked over to the door and crouched down, ear to the steel door and heard the guards unlock the cuff port. He knew a lack of cooperation would lead to the use of less lethal chemicals; it wouldn't kill him but would incapacitate him. Seep over to Conner's cell and lead to moving him and Clouser. He gulped fear and pressed his ear tighter against the door. Minutes went by as two officers tried to talk sense to the guy.

"Get your ass up here and cuff up," one said as he fidgeted with the cuffs in his hand.

The other guy said, "We'll move you downstairs so we can watch you. We won't let anybody come through the window and hurt you."

Conner thought this guy had some sense. The other guy wasn't helping the situation, "What did they look like?" He shouldered his partner and laughed, "Did he have a big ole cock?"

The guy with sense tried, "Come on, man. Let's move downstairs." He lowered his voice as he spoke through the cuff port. "You know what is going to happen. You don't come out, the black suits are going to come up and blast you." He stood up and shrugged at his partner, said, "Call a supervisor." Turned his attention back to the inmate, "I won't let anybody get you."

The situation had reached the others on the range. One hollered out, "Don't be a pussy. Fight those motherfuckers."

Another said, "He's a chomo anyway. Hope they gut you."

Laughter rumbled through the building.

One said, "Cut yourself."

Others picked up the chant like at a local basketball game, "Cut yourself! Cut yourself!"

Albert stirred and let out a puppy whimper like he was experiencing a bad dream. Conner's mind shifted from confidence to fear. *The numerous hours of planning this and some dumb fuck suffering from a psychotic break is going to ruin it.* He sighed and considered his options; he could do the deed now, quick, and easy. It would be like a virgin blowing his wad seconds later, unsatisfying and regrettable. He jumped up and cupped his hands on his head and walked to the window and paced. A quick look and back to the window. On the return, he grabbed his new towel off the sink and turned on the water. He mashed the towel as water soaked it. He turned off the water and twisted the towel. Twisted until it wouldn't turn. He kneed the floor and stuffed the towel between the door and the concrete. Went into his locker and grabbed another and swung it over his shoulder. If needed, if they used less lethal chemicals on Adams, he planned to wrap the towel around his neck and face and use it as a shawl. Desperate times indeed. Then he turned and sat with his back toward the door, eyes on the lump in the bed and waited. Waited with eyes and an open mouth on Clouser who rustled and moaned as he slept.

The guard with sense unsnapped his pepper spray holder and turned sideways as he spoke to the inmate. As he quietly pulled the spray from the holder, he said, "Adams, don't listen to them. You don't want to hurt yourself."

They came up the metal stairs onto the second-floor landing. Military-style boots with thick soles. Dressed head to toe in black.

*Good*, thought Conner, *he is speaking to him like he's a human being.* If the inmate started to harm himself, the guard had no choice but to spray him and attempt to protect the inmate from self-harm. If that happened, Conner's plan could possibly be derailed for the night.

He stood up, filled the window with his head, as the gang in black suits and helmets, a supervisor joined the officer in formation in front of the door.

The black suits were a combination of a football uniform and roller derby: amateurish helmet, weak shoulder pads, elbow and knee pads.

Conner closed his eyes and exhaled. Moved to the door and watched as two in black spoke outside of his door. One was laughing as he spoke, "Motherfucker bent over and spread his ass cheeks to the captain."

The other guy said, "What the fuck? What did he say?"

"Crazy son of a bitch says they shave his asshole before they fuck him."

Then, all heard, "Look at it, Captain," from the hysterical. "Look, Cap."

Conner watched the first guy lean over and look over the captain's shoulder. He returned and whispered in his partner's ear and giggled. Conner imagined the guy bent over with his butt cheeks apart, showing his hole to the captain.

Captain Jenkins looked the part. Tall, fit, pressed white shirt. He had been here before. He spoke calmly, "Dad," he said. He always said," Dad," when he spoke to anybody, an officer or an inmate. "I see it. Let's go ahead and get you moved closer to the officer's desk."

The hysterical inmate ignored him and jumped in bed, sat toward the back, near the wall, upright, holding himself. He glanced at the captain and hid his eyes.

"Come on up, Dad."

Nothing.

The captain spoke loud enough for the inmate to hear, hoping sense would reach him, "Okay," he pointed, "Jennings, start the camera." After he did, "You five line up and say your name and the part you will be playing." As they lined up, he finished with, "And no bullshit. Let's get this done without a clusterfuck." Jenkins pulled a pair of black gloves out of his back pocket, slid them on, and stood out of sight.

"I'm Officer Bradley, helmet A, and I'm the shield." Bradley was a moose in a suit. Brought lunch every day and ate at least three inmate trays daily. He wheezed taking a dump. A perfect character for the shield man. First in, shield led the moose to the target. Target being Adams. Knock the wind out, bring the bitch out of him as the others grab the limbs and secure him. "Officer McGuire, helmet B, and I'm right arm." McGuire was Rambo in training, Army Reserve, high and tight cut, looked smooth and fit in the suit.

"Officer Perry, helmet C, and I'm left arm." Chewed-up bubble gum in a bottle. Sloppy. Wore his uniform to the grocery store on his day off. *Chicks*

THE DEVIL WON'T KEEP US APART

*dig a man in a uniform.* Maybe not at the store he frequents. One-bedroom apartment, PlayStation is his recreation.

"Officer Downing, helmet D, and I'm left leg." Stuttered and sweating. His first time. A cherry pop. Graduated high school ten months ago.

"Officer Fleming, helmet E, and I'm right leg." The prodigal son. Father was the warden. Bright future. Respectful.

After they shuffled through, Captain Jenkins addressed the camera, "I'm Captain Jenkins, here at the Sherman Rehabilitation Center, in E Unit, Inmate Adams 2-453895 has threatened self-harm and refused to cooperate with security staff. I have authorized a cell extraction. The team will enter the cell and secure the inmate and escort him to the bottom range and place him in a safe cell to prevent self-harm."

"Kill yourself."

"You fucking pussy. Don't give up."

Jenkins spoke over them, "After he is secured in the safe cell, medical will provide Inmate Adams with a shot to—"

"Let the school bus chaser kill himself."

"Jenkins, you are a cocksucker."

"Medical will administer a shot to calm the inmate."

The five-man team got in formation. Jenkins placed the key in the lock and before he unlocked the door, Inmate Adams called out, "I'm coming up," and placed his hands through the cuff port.

"Good choice, Dad."

More laughter rumbled out, then, "You pussy."

After Adams was secured, they escorted him by Conner. He nodded when the last in black exchanged eyes as he passed. A thank-you nod of appreciation for saving his night. The squad carried Adams down the stairs and placed him in a suicide cell, a dry cell, a steel slab with a thin mattress, no sink or toilet, and four barren white walls. Stripped his clothes off and dressed him in a Velcro robe, and shot him in the ass with a drug just a step down from an elephant tranquilizer.

Conner turned his attention to Clouser when he cackled like a hyena on laughing gas and said, "Sounds like you hate that stuff as much as me." He calmed when Conner didn't look amused. He shot up and took his turn at the window. To Conner, "It will bring the bitch right out of you." He palmed the door and yelled, "Stay strong, Adams."

Conner untied the towel around his neck and tossed it on the floor and jumped in the top bunk and laid down. "What's yer story?"

Clouser sat on his bed and said, "Not much to tell really."

"Whuz yous from?"

"Would you believe it?" he said and collapsed on his bed. "From right here in Sherman." He lifted his feet and curled a toe in a spiral, "Grew up five miles from this place. Two stop lights and turn right. Three signs and a left. Go down two streets and take a right. I can see my old man sitting on the porch right now." Took Clouser almost two decades to get back home. Figured he would be happier; Sherman had a reputation for being soft. He didn't expect the place to pull on his heart. He spoke softer, "I could be home in ten fucking minutes."

Clouser had grown up in a middle-class neighborhood in the heart of town. His father was an accountant. Mother worked as the librarian at the main library. Albert was their only child and always a disappointment. If you asked him, Albert would have said his decline started after high school. Ask his parents, and they would say when he got a mush fake tattoo on his right shoulder at fifteen, 740. Area code of Sherman. He wasn't dumb, but he also wasn't asked to join the high school debate team. Graduated in the bottom third of his class. His parents pushed for the military. Albert was soft, weak, and clumsy. He had no desire to sweat it out for a minute of any day. Lazy more than dumb. After high school, he lived on a diet of Old Milwaukee and McDonalds. Smoked two packs of non-filter cigarettes a day. Jobless, other than the three months after high school, when he worked on a fork truck at the paper mill as summer help.

Conner eased into it. "Why yous banged up?" He hesitated. He didn't want to spook him or cause an incident so early in the night. Chomos, school bus chasers, rapists were vile, even by the ugliest of inmates. Back in Nevada, Conner had encountered a child rapist driven to suicide by hazing, blanket parties with soap, comments, and theft of property. He heard Clouser gasp. Conner stayed calm, smirked, "Oo did yous kill?"

Clouser said nothing.

Conner tried to prompt him with, "Ay killed this bitch."

He relaxed and placed both feet on the bed above and hands behind his back, "I was young." Louder, "A drunk." Softer, "Did a ton of drugs." He lied. "My girlfriend just left me." Clouser was not sexually active. Judy, his perceived girlfriend, was given the nickname Dirty Judy. Her feet: she didn't wear shoes. Nobody really knew why. Comfort maybe. She had a motto— bring her a pizza and a six-pack, and she would sleep with anybody. When Clouser finally pulled the trigger and knocked and flashed the pizza and the six-pack, she woke the next day and told him not to tell people about their encounter.

"Can we keep this between us?"

A gut punch. Clouser hollered back, "I have the reputation to keep." He pulled on his shoes and heard her laughing, "What are you laughing about?"

Judy bit into the cold pizza and chewed and mouthed, "I'm the one who went hogging." Swallowed and licked a lip, "I was probably your first."

Clouser tied his shoes and didn't respond.

Judy pushed harder, "I busted your cherry."

"Shut up, bitch."

As he opened her door, he heard, "Next time, it will cost you a twelve-pack."

"I left her house early in the morning and was driving home." He still lived with his parents on Allen Avenue. He was running ragged; the night before, his parents sat him down and told him it was time to get out. They didn't say it very nicely or ask; he was given three days to move his shit out. "I was so fucking stupid," Clouser said, allowing himself a small frown. A feel-sorry-for-me moment. His voice reflected it. His eyes began to redden. He had tried to erase the indelible stain from his soul a thousand times over the past two decades. His past stirred to the surface. It didn't impact Conner. He didn't respond, didn't offer a hint of care. The bed didn't even offer a squeak. Clouser pleaded, "Who the fuck runs at the crack of dawn anyway?"

Then Conner spoke, "Tell me."

The rumble in the voice caused Albert to cringe, he moussed out an indolent, "Okay."

# CHAPTER 44

# 2002

She didn't wake up to the alarm. She woke to her fiancé smashing at it with the palm of his hand. It took two swats to silence, the third put a scheduled trip to store to buy a new one on the to-do list. She curled up and softly kissed him on the back of the shoulder and said, "Time to get up."

"I'm up."

As always, she snapped out of bed and gathered her clothes and dressed and brushed her teeth. Opened the closet door and grabbed her running shoes and glanced at the bed. He was flipped over on his side, pillow over his head. "Up?"

A muffled, "Yes."

"Ay huh," she said and tied her hair up and slammed the closet door.

He rose and flung the pillow at her and said, "Told you."

She turned to walk out and hollered over her shoulder, "You're going to be late for work."

He collapsed and covered his head, yelling back, "They'll wait for me."

"I'll make coffee."

"Good," he mumbled.

Five minutes later, he stretched in the door frame and yawned. "Running today?"

She handed him a mug, kissed his cheek, and ducked under. "Seen my watch?"

To himself, "Guess that is a yes." To her, "Probably in your nightstand." He heard the drawer open and slam and her stomp toward the bathroom. He cheesed a smile as the location crossed his mind and hollered out, "Check under the bed."

"The bed?"

He mutters to himself, "I'm chopped liver." To her, he said, "I ripped your clothes off last night . . . remember . . . I—"

Straight-faced. Flat voice. "Oh, sorry, babe."

"Chopped liver."

He didn't hear her come up behind him. She kissed his back, whispered, "You were wonderful," and ducked under and went into the kitchen.

"Yeah," he cheesed again as she went to the fridge.

She popped her head out and smiled, "You're such a dork."

"Your dork," he said and raised his brows. She closed the fridge and packed her lunch.

"You can have the last one."

"Sure?" she said and held the banana between them.

"Yeah, I'm good."

After she zipped her lunch bag, she went to the sink and filled the water bottle and took a long swig, heard him say, "Stay on the main road today."

She swallowed and put on the cap. "I always do when I run without you."

He saluted her with his mug. "Love you," and turned toward the bedroom, "I'll call you after."

"Hope it goes well . . . love you most," she said and hit the door. Outside, she lowered her toboggan and toed her right foot, then left. Pulled her left foot, right foot, behind her butt. Her eyes drifted up the hill. It was one of the reasons they bought the house; the first time they saw the house, they walked up the hill, and she knew it was the perfect hill to run. It shocked him, a hill being a check in the positive column. She astounded him on many levels. She set her watch for forty minutes and mentally went over her route in her head. *Five eight-minute miles, girl.* The first time she ran, their first day in the house, she made it two hundred yards, marked at the entrance of the cemetery. Dead tired, felt like she belonged under one of those graves.

Today, she busted out of her shoes as she started, sure of herself that this was her moment. After the two hundred yards, she ran with a rhythmic lilt. The cool air tingled her throat. She closed her mouth and found her stride, and eased air out of her nose as she pumped her arms, eyes down, a foot in front of her. *Get it, get it.* A car honked, but she kept pumping and moving. She felt like the top was near and shifted to another gear. Her mouth hung open, cheeks blew streams of cold air, her legs grew wobbly as a burn swelled in them. Finally, she looked up and smiled under the pain. The top, yards away. She pushed and stumbled off-balance and screamed to finish the hill in a run. At the top, she bent over and elbowed her knees and peered down at her house, a fleck of a picture. Smiled and waved as she saw him back out of the garage and head the other way. *Did he see me? Gosh, he isn't going to believe I finished on the fourth try.* Then, she twisted around and gazed at the route, which seemed so far away. Eyed the time. *Oh crap, I have over four miles to go.*

She stretched for a few seconds and pushed on. After the climb, the route flattened out for roughly a mile. The straight shot gave her time to gather herself. She felt good, confident, and knew once she made the turn, a steady decline was upon her and a short jaunt to the floodwall and home. Shower and dress in sixty minutes flat and off to work. Glass half-full is what she always told her fiancé.

She adjusted her cap and pulled it down over her ears as the air teased them with a prick. Glanced at her watch. *Pick it up.* Swiped at her brow and the pending sweat and squinted at the community college directly ahead. The summit before the drop. She sped up. Heavy breathing. Heart drumming. Lips cracked like asphalt weathered over the winter. She licked and sprinted. Before the fall in the round, she adjusted her stride and heeled her way down the lane, long as her first climb. At the bottom, she caught her air and ran with effortlessness down Western Avenue, turned left on Woodbridge, and galloped down the slight decline like she was on a pogo stick. At the bottom, with the country club on her left, she strode onto Fairway Avenue. Sleepyheads still in their beds, and school buses an hour away. A mundane neighborhood yet to wake. She turned right on Allen Avenue. Five houses from Piatt, she didn't hear the car slow or his first honk. Her sixth sense jarred her around. Her hearing was captured by the headphones, missed the second honk. Her eyes showed her a lustful smile. He hung out the window and panted like a collie. Licked his lips and blew her a kiss. She didn't give him the satisfaction. She kept to herself and didn't respond. She flipped a tendril of hair off her brow and pushed on. He saw something much different and punched the gas. A manic laugh the companion to his irrational thoughts. She veered left on Piatt Avenue. He blew past and accelerated toward High Street. She glanced back and exhaled when she saw him speed away and eased her way to Orange Street. At the end of Orange, she hopped on the floodwall and hung a right, back toward High Street.

He hit High Street, pulled into the BP gas station, jumped out, and went in. Pulled a Dew out of the cooler and asked for a pack of smokes. He flipped her a ten and told her to keep the change. Smiled and stretched his lids high, and asked her for her digits. Maybe if she hesitated, the day might have been different. She didn't. Not a laugh or blush of a cheek. Pupils calm as an isolated lake. The rejection and humiliation, the third in twelve hours crushed his manhood. He ripped the smokes off the counter and tore open the pack, and lit one as he stood outside his car. Sucked and puffed like an addict, then he saw her. Top side, on the bridge, as it spanned High Street. A majestic trot. She was headed east toward the park, making her way home. He dropped the cigarette at his feet and tore at it with the heel of his shoe, then looked around, flung his door open, and spun out south on High Street.

She passed the dog park, then the school, pushed it by the city park and over Bridge Street. She was feeling strong and light. Commanded her air. She pressed onto the most isolated part of the path. An area she had never ventured into without her fiancé. She felt so damn good. Her anthem, their anthem, came on, "Living on a Prayer."

Her heart filled with blood. She took three short bursts of air and sprinted. Her cadence flowed with the music. Caught herself mouthing the words. She ignored the pain in her legs. The burn in her lungs. She sprinted. Dust kicked up from behind her feet. *Sprint! Sprint!*

Boom!

The predator jumped out of the brush on her right. She didn't see him. He shouldered her. She flew with the leaves. Landed ten feet away. The left side of her body on asphalt. Head on a stump. He slithered toward her. She was disoriented. Struggled to get to her knees; her left arm hung. Saved her life from the impact with the stump. An accretionary pain, a fog in her head, she didn't comprehend as he said, "How do you like me now?" He circled in front of her, shoed her hand, and tore into it like it was the cigarette, "Teach you to flip me off," he said as he circled around.

He saddled her flat, leaned forward, and chewed on her ear. Spat dirt and wrapped his left hand in her mane. Pretended to bronco up as he laughed. Heeled her thighs and clucked from his tongue, "Giddy up, bitch." He eased back, right hand high and proud, and he moved his body in a wave. Then he dismounted and splayed his legs with her in between. Eyes shuffled left: the river drifted in a murk. Right, a hillside of brambles. Beyond, a street and homes. Straight ahead and behind, the path was the emptiest it would be all day. His eyes plunged as she ripped at the dirt with her right hand and nails as she tried to crawl. He stomped on the headphones as a new song rolled through, chittering. He backhanded them toward the river and heeled her back, "Where are you going?" He circled to her front and crouched down. The stump cleaved her at the eye and down the face. "Yuck," he said, "You don't look so hot, tits." He stood and glared around dubiously; he had never been on the running path. Then he handed her by her spandex and pulled her over the asphalt, cheese-grating her face. He stopped under a tree, in the brush, the poorest lit area his eyes could see.

# CHAPTER 45

Weeks after Adrian suffered his stroke, a young man entered the Huntington Bank on Huckabee Avenue on the south side of Cleveland and stood in line for the next available teller. Quiet and still. Ignoring the little girl in front of him, tugging on her mother's sleeve as she asked for a sucker. The mother pulled away and shushed her. He didn't even lower his eyes when she plopped down and fussed. Loud and angry. He stepped forward as the woman drug her away by the arm and out of the bank door. He heard, "I can help who's next," and stepped up. He pulled a note out of his front pocket and unfolded it, and read the note. He slid it across the counter with a finger. He gulped and touched his throat with a hand. A warm look. Vulnerable eyes. She returned a faint smile. "You want to close the account?"

He dug in his front pocket and fetched his driver's license, and slowly let it hang in front of him by his tips. She examined it and wrote down his name. He stuffed it down his pocket.

She scanned through her computer and wrote the account number. Slid over a piece of paper and said, "Sign here, please."

He signed his name and slid the paper back.

She kicked her chair back and got up with the paper. "It will just be a minute." She walked back to an office. He stood still; eyes moved with her. She spoke to a man in a suit and pointed at the young man. The manager glanced at him and punched at his computer, and glared at the screen as he chewed on a fingernail. He pulled a pen from his shirt pocket and scribed on the same paper. He held it up without acknowledging the woman.

She grabbed the paper out of his hand and walked back to her station, and flashed the paper in front, "Just one more minute," she said and went into the vault. He stepped back, interlocked his fingers at his waist, and scanned the lobby. Garish images rolodexed across his mind. His respiratory system sputtered. He tightened and gasped. Lungs stretched and recoiled. He blinked and squeezed his eyes tight. Exhaled out of his nose and snapped back.

She returned with a bank bag and dropped it on her counter, "Okay," she said and sat and scooted up her chair. "Forty-eight thousand dollars." She scanned the lobby and leaned forward, whispered, "Don't you have anything to put this in?"

His face went long. Eyes wide, he raised a lip and shook his head.

She tapped a pen on the counter and looked over her shoulder to the left. One colleague was attending to a customer. Two in the drive-thru window. The manager was neck-deep in the computer with the phone attached to his neck. Then, she said to the man, "You can take this."

The man reached over and picked a cherry pop from a cup and unwrapped it. Grinned and plopped it in his mouth. Sucked and licked. Pulled the sucker out of his mouth and pulled the bag over and secured it in his hand, and said, "Nah need ter count it."

The lady snapped up and placed her hands on her hips, and returned a quizzical look. "Is that British I hear." She yammered on, "My husband and I went overseas last summer. Ireland, Scotland . . . he played golf at St. Andrews." She rolled her eyes. "London . . . sounds like you are British."

He sucked on a tooth and waggled the pop, and winked, "Nah, ma'am," he said and dropped the pop in his mouth and spoke out the side, "I'm from southern Ohio."

"Ay huh," she said with her mouth half opened.

He flipped the bag over his shoulder and walked away. At the door, he flipped the stick in the can and went into his front pocket and pulled his driver's license out, and stared at it for a moment. As his hand began to shake, he dunked it in the trash can and walked away.

# CHAPTER 46

"Roll call," the captain called out from behind the desk. Forty-three officers gathered around the desk to receive intel from the past sixteen hours and receive their work assignments.

"Gill," the officer said as he approached the desk.

The captain kept his eyes on the roster as he spoke, "Where you want to go?"

Gill leaned in, finger on the schedule, and scrolled down with his finger and eyes, "Hell, Cap. I feel like a million dollars tonight."

"Bet you do."

"I'll take E-2."

"Your funeral, Gill," the captain said as he wrote Gill's name.

Gill stepped back and stood in front of the soda machine and waited until all the other assignments were full. Listened to the captain give his speech about an attempted assault on staff earlier in the day and the situation in E-Unit with Inmate Adams. "Go to work," he said as he stood. And as they filed out, "Be safe."

"Who I got tonight?"

The captain looked at the schedule and said, "Tyler."

A wink. A thumbs up. "See you in a few hours."

Gill hustled through the hall and caught up with Tyler, and slapped him on the shoulder. "You and me tonight, kid." Tyler had three months in the system and was using the job as a stop-gap while he was attending nursing school. Gill pointed at his lunch bag and said, "You bring schoolwork?"

"Notecards like always."

Gill jumped in front of him, "So good to see kids these days try and better themselves."

"Funny guy."

"I'm feeling good tonight. You take care of the computer work and I'll do every round tonight."

"Awesome," Tyler said and bumped his fist.

"No problem."

# CHAPTER 47

onner sprung from the bed like he needed to vomit and grasped the sink with both hands and cast his eyes down. Inspected the door when he heard the lock on the cuff port unlatched. A mouth peeked in through the cuff port and said, "Third shift is here. Keep it down," and closed the cuff port and locked it. A bang, then, "See you in morning, Conner."

Conner pivoted around to the mirror and tilted his head, and slanted an eye at Albert. He drew him into focus and eased his grip. Clouser was still on his back with his legs high. A couch stain confessing to his therapist. He said, "When she flipped me off, I just snapped." Conner lathered up his face and head and slowly shaved all his hair off. *I can't be you anymore.* Gripped the edge of the sink with both hands and eyed himself, then Clouser in the mirror. He bent down, head in the sink, and splashed water on his head until the shaving cream washed away.

Two cups of water on his face, then he turned around and addressed Clouser with, "Wa' wuz 'er name?" The time had come. He felt invigorated. Asked again. His eyes dilated, hot around the edges. A wave of emotions hit him. Stopped him momentarily. He scowled, "Wa' wuz 'er name?"

"Huh," Clouser said and cupped his chin. "What was her name?" He snapped up and stood. He snapped his fingers and said, "Savannah."

"Savannah?" His face cloaked the rage inside. Conner dropped the hammer again, "'Er name?"

"Yep, Savannah, the girl with the fine ass."

Conner's eyes turned cold. He looked down at the concrete and mumbled, "Savannah?" He crinkled his nose, stepped forward, and barked, "You

263

think 'er name wuz Savannah?" Another step. Clouser pushed himself against the rail. "Yous don't evun remember 'er name?"

Clouser squirmed toward the other end of the bed. A rat caged. He put his hands out. An easy, "Yeah, yeah. Maybe it was Sarah." A forceful stop with a hand as Conner stepped closer. "Wait." Hand on head. "Samantha . . . yeah, it was Samantha."

Conner stopped and glared as he cocked his head to one side, then the other. Lit the fuse one last time. "'Er name?"

An audible sigh, in a lighter voice, Clouser said, "Samantha." He swallowed a scream and stood with his mouth agape.

The reality of the situation eluded the predator. Conner was close enough to smell the chili from the dinner meal on Clouser. "Samantha?" he said. Repeated it, "Samantha," He released an exploding chuckle like the start of a Fourth of July celebration.

"Yeah."

Conner's mind exploded. Eyes moistened over. He ground his teeth and struck. Left arm to the mouth of Clouser like a cobra; caught the meat of his thumb between the teeth. His right arm grabbed Clouser's left. He pulled him away from the bed and pushed him toward the window. He pressed his hand against the mouth and slammed the left arm into the radiator over and over until he heard the snap.

As Clouser went to the ground, Conner pulled a sock from his pants and placed it in his mouth. A deep inhale, an exhale, then he crouched down eye to eye with Clouser. He spoke softly, "Do yous think is 'ow Savannah felt?"

His cry was as Conner had expected, whiny as a newborn. Tears washed warm over Conner's hand; snot bubbled out of Albert's face. Eyes bulged, bloodshot and scared. The first blow to his chest cracked a rib, sputtered his air. The sounds from his lips muted like the calm of the wind before a mighty storm. He didn't know it then, but now, he knew he was in a quarrel he could not win, locked in a chamber with the force of nature and the blood of hate.

"Ay yous still with wi' me?" He gently kicked Clouser for affirmation. Knew he wasn't dead by another moan. Conner reached under the tabletop and pulled and pulled into a snap, picked up the broken leg, and sat on the edge of the bed. Reached under, grabbed his laundry detergent out of his locker box, and started a hum. Pulled the case off the pillow and ripped it into long and thin shreds. He took his time and covered the leg with shreds and tied them off. He laid the leg on the bed and poured detergent on it until it was soaked. He stood over Albert and whistled.

Nothing.

He whistled again and kicked him.

Albert looked up. Conner smiled as he beat his new stick against his hand. Albert's eyes widened.

Conner grabbed his leg. Albert tried to flail away. Conner dropped his toy and punched Albert in the jaw. When Albert came around, his arms were tied to the radiator. Left leg tied to the bottom post of the bed. Right leg was free. He swept his leg around the sticky concrete. Felt cold tingles under his ass. Balls stuck to the floor. Then he knew he was naked below the waist. He heard, "I'm go'n ter graft yous a chance ter take this like a feller." Conner popped out from the other side of the bed and beat his toy against his thigh. "I'm go'n ter graft yous an option. Yous can either insert this," he showed it again, "er fight, 'n ay break yer legs and force it."

Albert laid still. Legs crossed over. Ankles locked tight.

Then, Albert thought he heard the strangest thing. "But first, do you know why I am doing this to you?" It was perfect English. Coming from the mouth of the maniac standing over him. "Do you know who I am?" he said and pulled the sock out of his mouth.

Albert licked his lips and swallowed, spoke above a whisper, "No."

Conner spoke calmly, too calmly, scared Albert even more. "What was the name of your victim?"

Albert remained silent.

Conner grew agitated and hopped off the bed and grabbed the free leg, and cocked his head at Albert. "Her name?"

He violently shook his head, began to cry, and said, "I don't remember."

He tore at Albert's flesh as he stared at him with a growl. Eased up and dropped the leg, and returned to the edge of the bed. Stared at Albert for a long while. Finally, he said in a calm voice, "Her name was Susan." Expressionless and flat, "She was everything to me." Then Conner shivered at his shoulders and stood up. "I'm Adrian Franklin," he said and forced the sock back into the mouth. He grabbed the toy and Albert's leg, "I've been waiting for this moment," he said and forced the toy into the rectum. Stopped when he couldn't get any more in.

Albert spirit fell and ebbed toward the edge of his existence. He grew still and flinched as he shivered on the cold floor.

Adrian swayed over top of him. His mind whirled. Breathed heavily as the wrath was finally released. He looked at Albert. Small and broken. His eyes pulsed back with each flair of pain. Adrian's breathing hit another gear, a bear running in a grove of trees. He eyed Albert once more, grabbed a finger, then the arm. Snapped it like a twig above the elbow. Albert released a piercing sound. Head fished from side to side. He relieved himself. The dank scent of urine and blood itched the senses. Uncaged, unhinged, Adrian hovered over him, then when Albert stopped moving, he toed Albert's index and middle finger and pressed until they squelched against the concrete floor. Then he said, "Won't be picking your nose anymore."

Adrian sat on the edge of the bed and stared at the fissure above Albert's elbow. Blood leaked out slowly like satisfied lava from a crater. Slow and beautiful. Congealed over the cold concrete. Albert panted, then gurgled on his own blood. He cleared his airway and touched his elbow. Shuddered when he felt the inside of his meat. He looked up to see a grisly smile under pitted eyes. Painted by Death himself with a sickle from hell dipped in her blood. He could hear the death rattle coming for him. Searing the pain in his body. All his senses focused on the pending arrival of his last breath. It was coming, but not soon enough.

"Why did you have to take her?" Adrian cried as he looked up at the ceiling. He lowered his head and took his sixteen-inch shoe, and sledgehammered the side of Albert's face. Once. Twice. Blood flooded the room; touched each of the four corners.

Adrian geared down his breathing and caught the moonlight out the window as anger and grief tussled on his face. Moved toward the window and looked placidly beyond the fence, through the trees, into the heart of the land. Panic in his heart dropped and eased the beat. He curled up in the bed. His eyes jostled between Albert and the window. He was covered in sweat. The cool stale air overtook his body, shivered his skin, and rattled his teeth. He closed his eyes, "Albert," he whispered. He flopped over and faced the wall. "You brought this on yourself. You and I would have never met if you didn't take her." He flipped again when Albert released a dead man's moan. "It will be over soon," Adrian said as Albert's skin slowly changed from red to pale. Pale to deathly pallid. Clouser stole his life in the time it took him to smoke a cigarette. Five minutes burned a picture of hope. A future of mind-numbing excitement. He stole his life, and now his was quickly becoming extinguished.

Malice bubbled out of his black pupils like tar in a baking sun. His eyes held the frozen shape of Albert on the floor. There would be no more bloodshed. The flow of tears dried. Now his wrath was complete. Death released its grip on him. Fatigue set in; his bleary eyes were ready for eternal sleep. He released the tension in his body. He had roamed the lands with death as his companion. A glutton for the wrath of his sadness. He saw his path without seeing. His lungs weakened as blood slowly dripped from his heart.

# CHAPTER 48

# Present Day

**E**lmer says, "Adrian wrote me a letter." Stories of Adrian Franklin caused momentary paralysis in Murphy. He sat in a tonic state as he came to grips with today's events. He lay his head back on the chair and swiveled around. Spun and spun like a child as he tried to make sense of what he was told. Elmer adds, "I was as shocked as you."

Murphy stops, "What about . . ." he stammers and scratches an eyelid, "fingerprints?" He still isn't convinced Franklin was Wallace. Couldn't believe a man would disappear for twenty years just to come back and seek revenge. Movies are not reality. Elmer looks at him quizzically. Murphy keys up, "You said Adrian had been arrested, and Wallace did time in Nevada before he came to Ohio." Elmer's facial expression remained the same. Murphy slammed a palm and yammered, "We . . . law enforcement . . . We would have found out Franklin and Wallace were the same person years prior." He flailed his arm, "When Wallace got convicted and locked up for first-degree murder. When he killed Perkins."

Elmer remains silent.

"Fingerprints, Mr. Ray."

Elmer looks back with disgust, "Small town." Louder, "Smaller twenty years ago. Back then, police reports and fingerprints weren't put on some damn computer." Murphy knows all too well about small towns being sporadic about passing on information to national databases. They were overworked, understaffed, and underpaid. "Plus," Elmer says, "everybody assumed

Adrian was dead." Elmer didn't mention Angelo Gallo. Gallo was dead. Before he died, years before, he tried to go somewhat legit. Created a company: The Gallo Group. Nothing good will come of telling Murphy about the favor for Adrian, the things he did for Elmer to keep the kid clean.

Murphy flails, "What about the parents?"

"His parents were dead."

"No," Murphy catches himself before he explodes. Calmly he says, "Did her parents ever look for him? Look into the bank accounts?"

They searched for a few weeks. Elmer resented them for not trying harder. Hated himself more for giving up hope. "Not long enough," he says. His eyes go scarce.

"Twenty years," Murphy mumbles. Flips a pen and picks up another.

Elmer perks up with a hint of a smirk. Prideful, thinks Murphy. "Perkins."

"What about him?"

Murphy sees the mouth move and hears the words, "Perkins was Splatter," but can't wrap his head around it. He twirls a pen between his thumb and forefinger. He whispers now, speaking to himself, not Elmer, "Crazy son of a bitch."

Elmer fumbles the roll, picks it up and flips to another letter, "Let me read you this letter."

Murphy doesn't respond. He just stares.

*Dear Elmer,*

*I don't take solace in writing you this letter. I've thought about the words to say to you after all these years and the belief I perished. I did die. A version of me died the day he took her from me. After her death, I just couldn't go on under the same circumstances. Just think it was my fate since birth for it to end like this. By the time you read this letter, he will be gone. Dead. The only goal I've had since the last day in the hospital. Me? I'll be gone. Heaven? That isn't for me to decide.*

*Over the last twenty years, I've thought about you more than you know. Our talks on the porch, your advice and lectures. Funny, I missed the lectures the most. You were the father I never had. My mentor, the person I respected more than anybody. I know this must be a disappointment to you. I hope one day you can understand why I had to take this path. I couldn't walk away from this fight.*

*Love you always,*
*Adrian*

Elmer folds the letter in half and sticks it in his shirt pocket, "The boxes were delivered to my house a few days after the murder."

"Why do you think he sent them?"

"Closure," Elmer says, stonefaced, sadness painted in his eyes, "Think he didn't want me to feel ill of him."

"He only killed two people."

Elmer stares him down, says, "Maybe Adrian was right."

They look at each other for a minute. Murphy slides the photo of Albert Clouser toward the other end of the desk, "You can keep this as a memento."

Elmer explodes out of his seat like a frog in a hot pot, "You self-righteous son of a bitch." He snaps the photo off the desk and looks at Clouser for the first time. Cools and says, "What would you have done?"

Eyes on Elmer, then a picture of his daughter dressed in her issued whites at her Columbus Police Department Graduation, Murphy says unemotionally, "This isn't a movie, Mr. Ray. We can't have people roaming the streets carrying out a form of vigilante justice." He looks at his daughter's photo again.

Elmer gingerly sits, eyes on the photo. He rasps out, "I don't know what I believe anymore." Then after seeing Murphy's eyes, he firmly says, "All I know is Adrian was a good boy . . ." He glances at the photo and holds it up, "This doesn't happen if Albert Clouser drives straight home that morning." Shakes it and extends it out toward Murphy. "What would you have done," he barks louder. Lighter, he says, "If he would have taken her?"

Murphy's eyes shuffle between the photo and Elmer, says slowly, "We are a law and order society, and—"

"Bullshit," Elmer interrupts, "you pulled that horseshit from the damn manual." He flips his hand toward the shelf behind the desk. "Probably read that shit before you go to bed."

Murphy isn't deterred. He smirks and says, "You trying to convince me or yourself?"

He pulls his roll from his shirt pocket, "Let me—"

Murphy puts up a hand, "Mr. Ray?"

"He wrote—"

Murphy stands and scoots to the other side of the desk. As he reaches for the papers, Elmer pivots around. "Mr. Ray?"

"Let me read you . . ." Elmer's crying, shaking, "Let me read you something else he wrote."

Murphy relaxes his arms, sighs, and shakes his head. "Okay," he says, "read me what he said."

Murphy helps Elmer sit and gives him a gentle slap on the shoulder, and sits on the edge of his desk.

*The day we visited Susan's grave for the first time, I was overcome with stress and emotion. In a flash, my life was changed. You know the rest. When I woke up from the stroke and heard the words come out of my mouth, I questioned my very own sanity. The voice that spoke the words was not my own. As I sat in front of the mirror and listened to the sound exit my mouth, I was taken aback. No matter what I did, my voice would not switch back to normal. I laid in that bed, thinking I was cursed. Thinking about Susan, missing the funeral, our dreams destroyed by him. How she must have felt on that morning. Thinking about her pain, what she had to go through, destroyed my reality. All my years working at the pen, I thought they had it easy. You know, we talked about this so many times. And after what my aunt did to me, the struggles I had in keeping it together. How was I expected to let him live? Watch his television? Eat commissary? Play basketball? No. No, Elmer, I couldn't let him do that. I had no way to get to him. I knew prison officials would have completed an interstate commerce as soon as he was sentenced if I worked in the department. Sipping tea in an Oklahoma prison. Watching the Giants in Upstate New York. He would have been any place but Ohio.*

*Elmer, it was destiny. When I heard my voice, the dialect, the plan jumped out. I ran through the scenarios, contemplated the plan of action and contingency plans. How could I get to him? How long would I need to wait? I needed it to be intimate. Wanted to hear him tell me what he did to her. Needed him to feel what she did. I had to get face-to-face with him. The new voice allowed me to be someone different. A new person. A new purpose. I walked out of the hospital before you arrived.*

*I emptied our bank account and bought a cheap bike and hauled ass west. I didn't come back to Ohio until I was locked up for the murder of Lyle Perkins. I know what you are thinking. Yes, I killed Perkins. I'm sorry, Elmer. I didn't feel bad. No regrets. Sometimes there are people who don't deserve to live. Live to continue to ruin lives. Perkins was one of those guys. He and I had history. Remember the story about the Splatter?*

*Well, I went west and roamed free for a while. Created distance and time between Adrian and this new person I'd become. Didn't have a name in mind. I found an old guy in a back alley in Kansas City. He was homeless. Some odd reason, he still carried around his wallet. I offered him a hundred dollars, and he gave me his identification, and I ran with it. After, I was Conner Wallace. From there, I developed my background and perfected my voice and persona. Took me a few years to figure out who Conner Wallace was about. He was me. I was him.*

*I know I'm rambling, but I've been wanting to tell you for so long. Okay, the voice. How to explain it . . . the stroke caused a neurological disorder. Rare medical condition. It's called foreign accent syndrome. There have been fewer than seventy confirmed cases in the last hundred years. Fate old man. Fate. Once, a Norwegian woke speaking with a German accent. An Arizona woman woke speaking British. Me? Took me a while to figure it out. I spoke with a Scouse dialect. I know it sounds crazy as hell.*

*Elmer, I never hurt anybody who didn't deserve it. I didn't do drugs or commit other crimes. I need you to know I didn't lose my way. You raised me right. I've always stood next to the underdog. Getting back to Ohio took much longer than I hoped. I ended up having to do some time in a Nevada prison. After, I used the skill I was best at; I kicked ass for money. When I saw the story about Lyle Perkins on the television, I knew my way back in, and I took it. I'm writing you this letter from Hamilton. Tomorrow, I'll be transferred home. Hopefully, with no interruptions, I'll be face-to-face with Albert Clouser. Finally, after all this time, I'll get the answers I need. I want you to hear this from me. I killed Albert Clouser for murdering Susan Platt. My only regret was taking twenty years to do it. When you tell my story, don't let anybody convince you I had multiple personality disorder or some bullshit like that.*

The letter slips between his fingers and feathers to the carpet. He grovels uncontrollably. Ruddy cheeks. The dough under his eyes has risen loaf size over the past hours of crying. He recoils in the seat. He had his day. Passed on the information. Now, it was his time to grieve. Grieve the second time for his lost boy. Murphy gazes over with bleary eyes and consoles Elmer with a hand. "Let it out. I know he meant a lot to you." Murphy notices the light off at his secretary's desk and figures it is well past three. He thinks about ending the day and walking Elmer to his car. But they will have to go over this again the next day. He needs all the information Elmer has on the whereabouts of Adrian before he can close the investigation. He strokes the shoulder, and when Elmer collects himself, he says, "I think we both can use a break," and steps back.

Elmer straightens up and tours the room and the hall with his eyes and then eyes Murphy, mumbles, "I should probably get going."

"Let's get a bite to eat." Then, "I know a diner downtown that serves some damn good comfort food."

Elmer looks at him with a surprised glare and says, "Carl's?"

Murphy gives him the first smile of the day. "Figured you knew as much." He gathers his jacket off the hanger, flips his hat on. "You have lived here all your life." At the door, he says, "It's on me."

"Damn right it is," Elmer says and shuffles by him.

"Foreign Accent Syndrome?"

"We'll talk about it after I eat."

CPSIA information can be obtained
at www.ICGtesting.com
Printed in the USA
JSHW082315150523
41720JS00003B/22